Midnight lowered his hand and said, "We are the one who waits in the darkest shadows."

Though he'd sobered up remarkably in the last few moments, Siyon was still *entirely* too drunk to make sense of that. "Well," he said, trying to keep up, "you can go back and keep waiting."

A frown creased down between Midnight's fine-drawn brows. "Keep waiting? For what? The awakening is upon us. Can you not feel the quickening? Can you not see the rising tide? Can you not hear her calling in your dreams? You may wait, but she will not. *We* will not!"

His voice was suddenly enormous, ringing from the alley walls, setting nearby dogs to barking.

It rattled Siyon's bones, but when he tried to clap his hands over his ears, suddenly Midnight was holding them, right in front of Siyon and staring into his face.

"You must come. It is your purpose and mine. We are but servants. Call, and I will come."

He pressed Siyon's hands together, with something small, and hard, and wickedly spiked between the palms.

Siyon winced, pulled against his grip—

And bounced off the alley wall, no one holding him.

No one here at all.

Praise for
Notorious Sorcerer

"Very rarely do I read a fantasy city so wondrously realized as Bezim. From the razor-sharp social climbing to the glimmering alchemist's library to the hidden realms beneath it all, I loved getting lost in this dazzling debut." —Shannon Chakraborty, author of *The City of Brass*

"A delightful and fast-paced ride full of flashy swordplay, high society, and thrilling magic. Reading *Notorious Sorcerer* made me feel like I was ten years old again and discovering adventure fantasy for the first time. Sheer glorious fun!"
—Freya Marske, author of *A Marvellous Light*

"A brilliant alchemical recipe! *Notorious Sorcerer* is a delicious mélange of my favorite things, remixing historical magic with class consciousness. I couldn't put it down."
—Olivia Atwater, author of *Half a Soul*

"[An] energetic epic fantasy debut.... The witty prose, endearing characters, and sense of playful whimsy throughout keep the pages turning. This is a charmer." —*Publishers Weekly*

"*Notorious Sorcerer* feels like a dream you don't want to wake from, with beautiful and broken people chasing elusive magic along a knife's edge in a beautiful and broken city. I devoured it and I want more!"
—Melissa Caruso, author of *The Tethered Mage*

"A real delight, with compelling characters and wonderful world-building that sucks the reader in and keeps them engaged from beginning to end." —Mike Brooks, author of *The Black Coast*

By Davinia Evans

THE BURNISHED CITY

Notorious Sorcerer
Shadow Baron

SHADOW BARON

The Burnished City: Book Two

DAVINIA EVANS

orbitbooks.net

Orbit
Hachette Book Group
1290 Avenue of the Americas
New York, NY 10104
orbitbooks.net

First Edition: November 2023
Simultaneously published in Great Britain by Orbit

Orbit is an imprint of Hachette Book Group.
The Orbit name and logo are trademarks of Little, Brown Book Group Limited.

The publisher is not responsible for websites (or their content) that are not owned by the publisher.

The Hachette Speakers Bureau provides a wide range of authors for speaking events. To find out more, go to hachettespeakersbureau.com or email HachetteSpeakers@hbgusa.com.

Orbit books may be purchased in bulk for business, educational, or promotional use. For information, please contact your local bookseller or the Hachette Book Group Special Markets Department at special.markets@hbgusa.com.

Library of Congress Cataloging-in-Publication Data
Names: Evans, Davinia, author.
Title: Shadow baron / Davinia Evans.
Description: First edition. | New York : Orbit, 2023. | Series: The Burnished City ; book 2
Identifiers: LCCN 2023013596 | ISBN 9780316398237 (trade paperback) |
    ISBN 9780316398336 (ebook)
Subjects: LCGFT: Fantasy fiction. | Novels.
Classification: LCC PR9619.4.E956 S53 2023 | DDC 823/.92—dc23/eng/20220310
LC record available at https://lccn.loc.gov/2023013596

ISBNs: 9780316398237 (trade paperback), 9780316398336 (ebook)

Printed in the United States of America

LSC-C

Printing 1, 2023

In memory of Catherine; we miss you so much

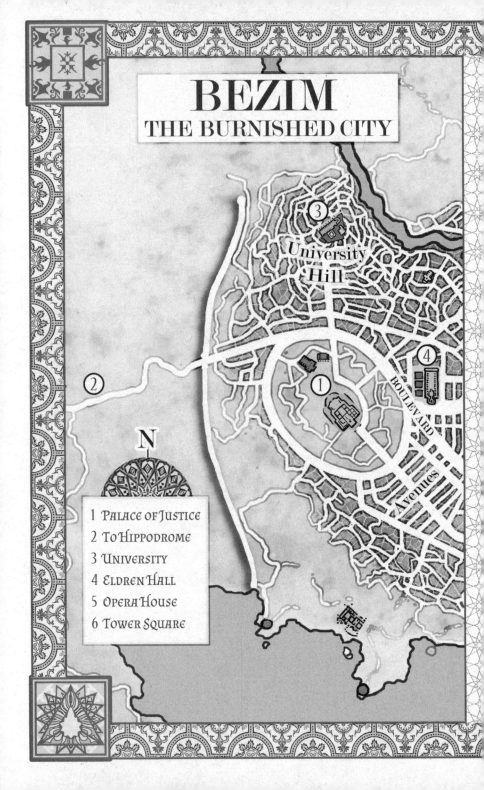

BEZIM
THE BURNISHED CITY

University Hill

BOULEVARD

Avenues

N

1 Palace of Justice
2 To Hippodrome
3 University
4 Eldren Hall
5 Opera House
6 Tower Square

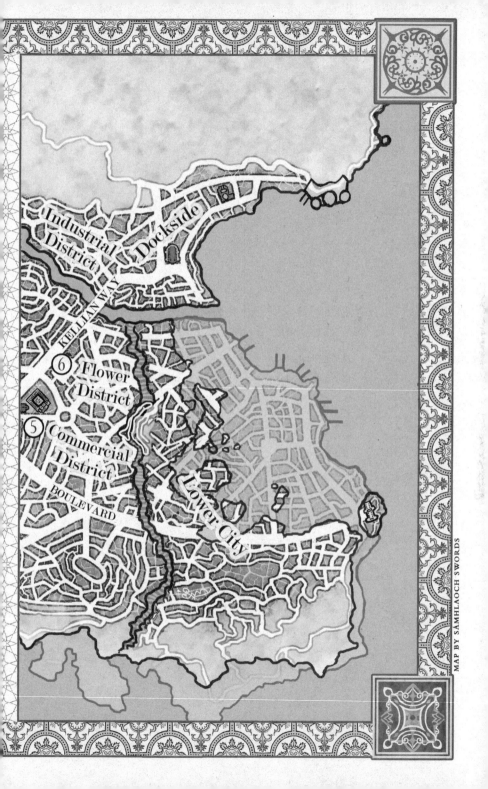

CHAPTER 1

The clerk at the front desk of the inquisitors' wing of the Palace of Justice eyed Siyon with a grumpy resignation that filled him with satisfaction about how he was living his life.

"We're not holding anyone on sorcery charges."

She was so sulky that Siyon couldn't resist propping an elbow on the counter and giving her a grin. "Yeah, but you'd say that even if you were." Her eyes widened in glorious outrage, but he was actually here for a reason, so Siyon snipped the line on her ire before she could reel it all the way in. "I'm here to see Olenka; is she about?"

The clerk sniffed. "Wait here, and I'll see if *Sergeant White* is available to speak with you."

The benches that lined the waiting area were still masterworks of discomfort, but at least no one else seemed to recognise him. Probably weren't expecting the Sorcerer Velo to have the freckles and reddish hair of a Dockside mongrel; everyone *knew* he was noble and grand and flamboyantly dressed.

Siyon had slung that old purple coat of Nihath's into a cupboard and happily forgotten which one.

Nearly two months had passed since the exciting events of the summer—when Enkin Danelani, son of the prefect, was saved from the ravages of a harpy (or so the story went) and Siyon Velo had...

Well, the stories never agreed on quite *what* Siyon Velo had done, but clearly it had been thrilling, and dashing, and entirely aboveboard because the Council now recognised him as the Sorcerer. Even if he'd apparently brought a demon into the Mundane, it was fine, because he had her bound to his every whim.

The first time Laxmi had heard that, she'd laughed so hard she melted into oily shadow.

Very little of the breathless gossip bore much of a resemblance to what Siyon remembered happening. He wished he'd merely snapped his fingers to summon the other Powers to parlay, instead of cutting a gate to the void between planes with a kitchen knife and his own desperation.

He wished he hadn't fallen through that gate holding Izmirlian Hisarani, his fatally wounded love, in his arms.

He wished...

It hardly mattered, did it? Wishes weren't worth much.

No one here looked twice at him, just an unshaven lout who slumped in a corner and stretched out his long legs, crossing scuffed boots at the ankle. Siyon rubbed at the headache that loitered behind his left eye like an alley cat waiting to pounce. Part lack of sleep, with his dreams dark and strange these days. Part too much reading, but he still had so much knowledge to catch up on, and no idea where the real answers might be when the wisdom of the vaunted Kolah Negedi had been proven...incomplete.

Mostly, though, the headache was the fault of the planar emanations.

They'd started the moment Siyon had stepped back out of the void—or rather, been hauled out by Zagiri. Energy skittering and skewing all around him, in bright swirls of Aethyreal mist, sharp and shooting Empyreal sparks, sinuous eddies and coiling smears of the Abyss. Every bloody movement echoed queasily in Siyon's vision.

At the time, he'd thought it the aftereffects of what had happened. Of what he'd done. Of becoming the Power of the Mundane.

But it hadn't gone away. Even here in the inquisitors' waiting room, Empyreal gold frosted the wall with stiff righteousness, and knots of Abyss and Aethyr tangled in the white-knuckled fingers of those waiting on news of their loved ones...or perhaps their partners in crime. Was that twist of purple and green worry, or guilt?

If Siyon knew that—if he knew even a little more about what he was seeing, or why—he'd feel a lot better about a great many things. What all this meant. What it was for. What he was supposed to be doing.

He was the Power of the Mundane...and he still didn't have a clue.

Someone kicked his ankle, and Siyon jerked upright. Had he nearly fallen asleep? When had his eyes closed?

He blinked up into a hawk-sharp face, haloed by a frizz of dirty blonde curls limned by lantern light. "I should let the desk clerk arrest you for slandering the inquisitors," Olenka said, looking down on him like an angel from on high. Apt, since she'd once been one, before she fell into the Mundane. "The harpy's a bad influence on you."

"I'm offended you think I need help," Siyon retorted. As he levered creakily up to his feet, he added, "Sergeant White?"

She snorted. "They wanted another name on the paperwork. I didn't think any of my others would really be suitable." Now Siyon was *extremely* curious about Empyreal naming conventions, but she just said "Come on" and strode away.

He needed her help, so he scurried along after her, which he regretted when she ushered him brusquely into an empty interview room. The furniture was stark and clean and tidy, but there were all sorts of unpleasant memories skittering around the bare, unsympathetic corners.

"I'd rather not—" Siyon tried to slide right back out again, but Olenka shut the door and stood against it with her arms crossed like she was barring the way to something she disapproved of. "Don't want your friends to see you with me?" Siyon quipped, perching on the corner of the interrogation table. He *wasn't* taking the victim's chair, no thanks. But then he realised—the name, this secrecy..."None of them know what you are, do they?"

Siyon supposed he couldn't blame her. Given that her colleagues worked in the branch of the inquisitors that policed the practice of alchemy, they might have thorny opinions about sharing a desk with a fallen denizen of another plane. And that whole branch had enough problems, with one of their star captains—and Olenka's former boss—now banished from their ranks in disgrace.

Sometimes Siyon wondered what had become of Vartan Xhanari... but he didn't wonder too hard. Especially not when he was sitting in a room much like the one where Xhanari had threatened him with the executioner's poison. Not when he still heard in his nightmares the rattle of Izmirlian's breath around the crossbow bolt Xhanari had put in his throat.

Xhanari had sent him a letter, soon after everything had happened. It might have contained an apology. Siyon hadn't read it. He'd set fire to it and let Laxmi make tea from the ashes.

Here and now, Olenka—now a sergeant in her own right—entirely ignored his questions. "Don't you have work you should be doing?"

Once upon a time, *work* for Siyon had meant carving a gate and throwing himself into another plane in search of the sort of bits and pieces an alchemist might pay him for, while dodging the attentions of the native monsters and beings...like Olenka. She'd once tried to sever the tether holding him to the Mundane with her broadsword.

Strange that he sort of missed it. At least his problems had been simple ones. Occasionally six feet long and on fire, but simple.

"That's actually why I'm here," he said. "You mentioned that the inqs might be less nervous—and less confrontational—if they weren't worried that I might turn them into frogs."

"Frogs did not come into it," Olenka corrected stonily.

Siyon ignored her; that hardly seemed an important detail. "So I've been trying to imbue a nullification into the silver of your badges—"

Her snort interrupted him. "How's that working out for you?"

Siyon was starting to think it might be impossible, actually. He'd even discussed it with Nihath Joddani, who had been known to trade Siyon imbued gemstones, and who would at least talk to Siyon instead of trying to harangue him about how Negedi *could* be interpreted to suit current events if you turned it upside down and squinted. (Ink and ashes, but Siyon missed Auntie Geryss fiercely some days.)

But none of that was the point right now. "But then I thought, your dowsing rods have a certain nullifying effect, right? That's what they're for. So could I take a quick squiz at one?"

Olenka sighed and rubbed at her face, like she had the twin sibling of Siyon's headache (which was still there, prowling around looking for an excuse to sink its claws in). The gust of her exhaled breath billowed a faint shimmer of Empyreal white. "If you're doing this to get the attention of the Working Group on Oblique Methods—"

"No," Siyon objected. But his voice sounded sulky and defensive even to his own ears. The Working Group on Oblique Methods was the typically circuitous name of the Council subcommittee responsible for overseeing the practice of alchemy in Bezim.

They'd sent Siyon a letter as well. It had been florid and beautifully ornamented and had thanked him for his service and assured him that they respected his very valuable time too much to ask him to do anything and would, in effect, be having nothing to do with him.

It was the politest and fanciest way Siyon had ever been banned from an establishment. Not that he *wanted* to spend his time sitting in a meeting of the sorts of azatani who thought squeaking their way through the labyrinthine processes of the Council of Bezim was a riotous good time.

But the governance of Bezim worked through those processes, and those committees. If anything was ever going to change about the parts of alchemy that were still illegal, it would have to start in the Working Group.

So yes, Siyon had sort of hoped that if he could present the inquisitors with an immunity against any untoward effects of stray alchemy, that might suggest that he should be more directly involved in things.

From the flat look Olenka was giving him, that little hope was both transparent and naive. But all she said was: "The dowsing rods are cold-forged star-iron. They're Mundane—entirely Mundane—which is part of why they react to material of other planes."

No, dammit, Siyon had been sure he was onto something here. "But couldn't I just—"

"I assumed," Olenka said over him, "that you were here for

something actually useful, like offering some help with the recent disturbances down in Dockside—"

Siyon's turn to interrupt right back. "Fuck that," he said, "you and Dockside are welcome to each other."

She rolled on without blinking. "—or bringing some insight about our spate of curse reports, or even trying to get involved with the trial of that poor bastard up in courtroom three, but instead—"

Siyon stood up from the edge of the table, a chill down his back like someone had frisked *him* with a dowsing rod. "What poor bastard? The clerk said you didn't have anyone on sorcery charges."

Olenka considered him with her flat grey eyes. "They're not straight sorcery charges."

Probably because every time the inqs had brought that charge in the last two months, Siyon had shown up in the courtroom—whether as a called witness or merely an unscheduled ruckus.

Three alchemists had been executed for sorcery during the chaos over the summer—chaos that Siyon had been instrumental in creating. The Margravine Othissa, Talyar the weaver, and a third whose name Siyon had never learned because his family had requested the records be sealed.

No one else was getting executed if he could help it. And he could. The definition of sorcery in the laws of Bezim stated that it was *endangering the city through the practice of alchemy.*

There *was* no danger to the city from alchemy, not anymore. Not since Siyon had become the Alchemist, filling a long-vacant gap in the planes and bringing the Mundane back into balance. There *couldn't* be another Sundering now. All the alchemists of the Summer Club—all the trusted and educated and *legal* alchemists—agreed.

The first time a judge had accepted that reasoning and thrown out the case, Siyon had smugly suggested that the law should be changed. Two months now, and it still hadn't happened. These things, he'd been told, took time. It was (you guessed it) the purview of the Working Group on Oblique Methods.

Meanwhile, the cog-toothed wheels of justice kept turning as they were.

Unless he stuck a wedge in them.

"Velo!" Olenka shouted after him, but Siyon wasn't waiting. Not when another life might hang in the balance.

Unlike the dutiful severity of the inquisitors' annex, the corridors of the Palace of Justice proper were elegantly adorned with gilt-framed paintings and niche-ensconced vases. Even the floor tiling was ornate, to reflect the stately dignity of the azatani government.

Siyon had no dignity. He sprinted down the halls, dodging around startled clerks, leaving objections and ruffled papers in his wake. He turned whichever way looked fancier, until he saw the gold-railed mezzanine overlooking the grand entrance hall.

The magnificently sweeping staircase, curving around the wall beneath the glorious copper dome, was crowded with gossiping groups. Siyon hoisted himself up on the banister and slid down with a merry shout of "Coming through!"

He stumbled upon landing, his breath coming short. A couple of months off running the tiles, and he was already an embarrassment to any bravi tribe. But Siyon pushed on, across the grand mosaic of the entrance hall and down the corridor to the courtrooms. The third set of doors was shut, guarded by a frowning white-sashed steward and a bronze sign reading COURT IN SESSION that sizzled with Empyreal energy.

"I need to get in," Siyon gasped. "I'm Siyon Velo."

The steward frowned more deeply. *Now* Siyon wished he'd brought the purple coat. Hard to summon up the majesty of the Sorcerer Velo when he was heaving for breath.

And then the steward's face hurriedly cleared, as he lurched into the stiffest pose of being at attention Siyon had ever seen.

A sharp voice behind him said, "What are *you* doing here? I sent a runner to tell you to stay out of this."

Siyon winced and turned to face Syrah Danelani, prefect of Bezim. Centre of an officious knot of clerks and helpers, she was a column of gleaming formal white, right down to the pearls braided into the crown of her ink-dark hair—the blindingly pure authority that the azatani of Bezim had grabbed for themselves and run with.

Resisting the urge to rub at his unshaven chin or further ruffle up his hair, Siyon said, "Ah. Must have missed me."

One of her eyebrows lifted slightly, as if she doubted his answer but wasn't surprised by the situation. She probably wasn't; likely they both knew that Siyon would have come running the moment he'd received the message anyway. "You can't keep doing this," she said. "There are processes. That's how stable government *works*." But she gestured sharply at the steward. "Well? Open the door."

The steward leapt to obey. Syrah gestured for Siyon to precede her.

The courtroom was brightly lit with lanterns and even more brightly lit—to Siyon's sight—with Empyreal zeal. Behind the bench, the magistrate's white sash gleamed, and there was a nimbus of energy around the grey-uniformed inquisitorial prosecutor, though he developed dark streaks of Abyssal red and green as he caught sight of Siyon and started protesting to the magistrate.

Easier to look at the accused, standing in a white-painted circle. Young, and from the tawny skin tone and high cheekbones probably from somewhere in the Khanate, though more than that was hard to pin down. Possibly this was a belligerent girl, dressed in a tight vest and hardy trousers, or maybe a pretty lad, with hair shaved down to the barest dark fuzz.

The magistrate hammered silence back into the courtroom, enough for Siyon to hear her sigh. "Welcome, Madame Prefect. And Master Velo. Again."

From behind Siyon, Syrah Danelani said, "Please carry on. I am merely here to observe."

Siyon wasn't. He blinked at the magistrate, and maybe he did recognise her through the lingering Empyreal haze. He tried a grin. "Your honour, you know what I'm going to say."

That there was no charge of sorcery to be answered. That there *could* be no charge of sorcery—which required not just unlicensed alchemical practice, but risk to the city—when Siyon had rebalanced the planes.

Allegedly. Especially when the world was a roiling soup of coiling planar energy like this, Siyon had his doubts, but it didn't seem to bother anyone else. As far as the other alchemists were concerned, everything was *fine*.

The prosecutor shot Siyon an unpleasant little smirk, tugging his grey tunic straight. "Your honour," he echoed, "as I was *saying* before this interruption, the accused stands charged with the sorcerous use of *foreign* magic."

The *what*? "That's impossible."

The magistrate glanced nervously over Siyon's shoulder, presumably at the prefect. Merely observing. "Do you know Mayar el-Kartou?"

"Just Mayar," the accused interjected. They were standing with arms tight-crossed over their leather vest—actually, was that a bravi vest? Siyon's gaze darted down—no sabre or belt, certainly no badge, but he wouldn't have wanted to drag his tribe into a courtroom either.

"Never seen 'em before in my life," Siyon declared, turning back to the magistrate. "But there is no magic; there is only alchemy. And alchemy only works *here*. So foreign magic isn't possible."

"Your honour," the prosecutor slid in silkily. "Given the tremendous upheavals this man has caused, who is to say any longer what is possible or not?"

Siyon hesitated, caught. He *had* done the impossible—or what had been considered impossible—more than once in the summer. He'd caught Zagiri, falling from the clock tower. He'd become the Power. And he'd sent Izmirlian Hisarani somewhere else entirely. Though only a handful of people knew about that, and just thinking of it caught the breath in Siyon's throat.

The magistrate narrowed her eyes. "It hardly matters what is possible outside Bezim when our laws and *your* remit"—she pointed her mallet at the inquisitor prosecutor—"apply only within the bounds of the city."

"And the offense occurred within the city," the prosecutor hurried to say, and flourished a fistful of documents. "I have sworn testimony from a number of accredited practitioners that the effects Mayar el-Kartou was witnessed producing are not alchemically possible without equipment that was nowhere in evidence. Therefore *something* untoward is afoot."

Siyon glanced sidelong at the accused again. What had Mayar el-Kartou—*just Mayar*—been up to?

"Something?" the magistrate repeated, with a little lip purse that might have been distaste. "Superstitions might be running rampant in the city's alleyways, but if you bring them into my courtroom—"

"Something verified!" The prosecutor brandished the testimony again.

"Something that isn't alchemy," Siyon chipped in. After intervening in this many court cases, after doing his reading, after having so many arguments, Siyon knew this particular part of the law as well as the magistrate did. "Not alchemically possible, he said so. Therefore not sorcery."

The prosecutor scowled like someone had taken away his favourite toy. "The intention of the statute is clearly to—"

"Doesn't matter," Siyon interrupted. If he'd learned anything from the past two months of wrangling with this, it was that *intention* didn't bail any water. The precise wording—the infinitely argued-over wording—did. "You want to start calling other things sorcery, you're going to have to change the laws."

He did grin then, wide and feral. *Please*, bring the laws up for discussion. Wherever they did it—the Working Group on Oblique Methods, or any other of the infinite labyrinthine committees that made up the working of the government like a school of myriad fish— Siyon would find a way to get at it. He'd find a way, and he'd worry the thing to shreds like a shark with a grudge.

"In the meantime," the magistrate declared, cheerful as a woman whose morning schedule had magically cleared itself, "I conclude there is no charge of sorcery to be answered by Mayar el-Kartou."

The courtroom erupted. Siyon hadn't realised the viewing gallery above—usually sparsely populated—was crowded today. There were a dozen black-clad bravi up there—so just-Mayar *was* a bravi— and a handful of shabbily dressed folk that he thought might be hedgewizards and other unlicensed alchemists, and there was even a knot of Khanate caravanners, in their vests and trousers and beaded braids.

All of them seemed pretty jubilant about the result.

Over the noise, the prosecutor was shouting, "—other charges can be brought!" And the magistrate was not quite shouting back about reliance on due process and the importance of thorough procedure.

When Siyon glanced back at the accused circle—brimful as a festival cup with questions for Mayar el-Kartou—it was already empty, a flash of black leathers disappearing toward the door.

And Syrah Danelani was in the way of Siyon's pursuit, with her attendant clerks fanned out behind her. She didn't precisely look unhappy with how things had turned out, but she also didn't look all that pleased with Siyon. "This isn't the best way to go about change," she told him, quiet beneath the noise of the crowd. "You're the Power of the Mundane, Velo. You have better things to do with your time."

"Like what?" Siyon demanded, hoping it sounded more like a challenge than it felt.

He was the Power of the Mundane, and he didn't know what that meant. He didn't know what he was *for*. He didn't know what he *should* be doing.

But he *could* do this. So he would. He'd hammer at the gates until they let him in, if he had to.

The prefect of the city sighed and turned to leave, tossing over her shoulder in parting: "At least get some sleep. You look like shit."

CHAPTER 2

Zagiri Savani had been at the hippodrome all afternoon, and she'd yet to see a horse, though apparently the Basilisk team had brought in a new driver from Lyraea, and despite some controversy with his paperwork, he'd been performing magnificently. Just magnificently.

She eased out of yet another conversation—the way Anahid had taught her, with a pleasant smile and a vague *do excuse me*—and slipped away, eyes scanning the room. It was long, and crowded, and swathed in sparkling little alchemical lanterns and even more sparkling society. Everyone who mattered—the highest tiers of the azatani and those lower with aspirations to rise—was here at the final formal social event of the year.

The hippodrome crowds were a faint and distant roar, and the racing itself unimportant beside the fiercer competitions underway here in the gallery. Refreshment tables ran the entire length of the inner wall, with the platters of delicate little nibbles and bottles of sparkling djinn-wine continually refreshed by the stewards. Along the outer wall, pairs of open doors framed with gauzy curtains let out onto a long balcony. The view was magnificent out there—not so much the nearby markets and bordellos and the Khanate caravanserai as the sight of the city wall rising over the rocky hills, with the domes and towers of Bezim glowing in the afternoon sun.

That autumn sun was still gloriously warm, but very few people were out on the balcony. All the opportunities were in here, and Zagiri was not the only person prowling in pursuit of them.

She slipped between all manner of conversations, keeping a careful ear out, the way Anahid had told her again and again she should. Most of the chatter had to do, one way or another, with the trade and discovery voyages that would soon be setting forth from the harbour, now that the storms of summer were abating. There were complaints about the usual delays and ructions in Dockside, from the workers outfitting the vessels. (Zagiri gathered it was the Laders' Guild this year that was getting particularly difficult.) More than a few guests were actually buying and selling last-minute shares in various ventures. Even the apparently idle gossip and discussions of Salt Festival plans weren't really all that frivolous, as families pried at one another's affairs, seeking any angle that might help them turn a greater profit in the year to come. There was even a knot of hushed debate about the ongoing turmoil in the Northern territories, and whether it might be dying down to the point that trade could be resumed.

Amid all this, there was also the ostensible reason for today's event. Up and down the gallery, the young azatani women who'd signed up to be sponsors at next year's Harbour Master's Ball were adorned by a pale yellow sash.

Zagiri was among them, her sash pinned so ruthlessly straight across her dress that she ran the risk of being stabbed if she turned around too fast. But while the other young ladies were considering the most useful debutantes to sponsor—and possibly even starting to flirt with the marriage offers they could consider after the Ball—Zagiri was stalking a very different prey.

She wanted a clerkship. She wanted a foothold in the Council, just a place to start. A chance to eventually become one of the people who could make—or change—the laws of the city.

A laughably modest ambition, almost flimsy in how small it was. What Zagiri *wanted* was to never again see the things she had over the summer, when alchemists and provisioners had cowered in the crypt of the Little Bracken safe house, fleeing a sudden crackdown on their illegal but previously tolerated occupations. She wanted the laws changed, the systems changed, the unfairness eradicated...

And she *could* do it. She was azatani after all. She was allowed in those halls and those decisions.

She'd left it far too late, of course. All of the entry positions for this winter had been assigned last autumn, in a rigorous and very competitive process.

All of the entry positions but one.

Or rather, it had been assigned, and it had been taken up a little early, but—or so Zagiri had heard—the young azatan had just been fired in disgrace.

There was a gap. If she was quick and keen, Zagiri could slide right into it. Otherwise, she'd have to wait another year to even get started.

This was far too important to leave anything to chance. So Zagiri had traded bravi favours to learn that the councillor now in need of a clerk was Azatan Palokani; she'd had to throw a duel to one of the Bleeding Dawn, losing flashily and making him look good, and she considered it worth the price. She'd asked her father and cousin for all the details on Palokani's history, interests, trading concerns. She'd spent *days* reading up on the jurisdiction of the Domestic Handling Committee, which Palokani was the undersecretary of. (Frankly it sounded unbelievably tedious, all paving and public works and festival planning, but Zagiri wasn't going to be picky right now.) And Anahid had nudged all her own contacts until she'd managed an introduction to Palokani's wife, which meant today Zagiri should be able to...

Ah, there she was. Anahid was standing in conversation with the Palokanis—the azata in a red headscarf as was her habit. Zagiri's sister was dressed far less flamboyantly, in a darker shade of the same blue Zagiri was wearing, but Anahid's ears glittered with elegantly set Northern turquoise baubles that Zagiri knew she'd won at a game of carrick in the Flower district.

She wasn't sure what she was most proud of Anahid for: playing so well or brazenly wearing her winnings among people who would be scandalised if they knew how she came by them.

Despite that little piece of outrage, Anahid looked utterly immaculate, her face serene and her grooming perfect. But as Zagiri caught her eye, her sister lifted a net-gloved hand to touch at one of her earrings.

That was the signal.

Zagiri moved quickly, grabbing a plate from the refreshments table and loading it briskly. She spotted a couple of young azatans in the crowd, heads close together as they watched the Palokanis closely, but Anahid had them so engaged in animated conversation—bless her—that it would be impolite to interrupt.

Unless you had a way in.

Zagiri detoured around a pair of startlingly blonde women in strange attire—from the North, she realised, and drawing their share of attention for it—and leapt into the fray before she could outthink herself. "Ana, look what—oh, I do beg your pardon."

She gave a very deferential nod, halfway to a bow, to Azatan Palokani, and one only slightly shallower to his wife (who wasn't a councillor, but *was* the family trader, and wealthy enough that her husband had taken her name upon marriage).

As she did, Anahid was saying, "Oh, do you know my sister, Zagiri? She'll be sponsoring next year, we're so very proud."

Which was Zagiri's cue to protest that she felt like she was lagging behind, having waited until nineteen to sponsor. Almost true—Zagiri certainly was one of the older sponsors in the room—but they'd decided to make a point of it because Azata Palokani had waited as well, and now she smiled genially and made all the right assurances. Everything was going according to Anahid's plan, and Zagiri gave thanks for such a surprisingly cunning sister.

"I'm so sorry to have interrupted," she continued, lifting her plate. "But *look*, Ana, they have Storm Coast pepper prawns."

Azatan Palokani's eyes lit up, just as they'd anticipated. Zagiri offered the plate around, and they fell into discussing the various trading routes of pepper—a dominant good in the Palokani portfolio. Anahid asked the azata a question about outfitting trade vessels for easterly voyaging (which Zagiri knew Anahid found largely boring, but no one else would guess from her avid attention).

Which left Zagiri and the azatan chatting politely. He seemed a little determined to stick to foodstuffs, but thankfully Zagiri only had to tug at her sash once before he said, "So you're sponsoring. What are your plans, then?"

He didn't mean for the sponsoring itself. There was very little Zagiri could actually plan about that; all the forms and activities of the Harbour Master's Ball were set down in stonelike tradition. Zagiri would choose a younger girl—one making her society debut—and accompany her to fittings, and teas, and rehearsals for the ceremonies and dancing of the Ball itself. And then, at the end of it all, she'd present the girl to the prefect at the Ball and, in so doing, be addressed as *azata* and join the ranks of the properly adult.

No, what Azatan Palokani was asking about were her plans for that adulthood. Zagiri had her speech all ready, hinting at all the reasons why she'd be *perfect* for Palokani's vacant clerkship.

But even as she drew breath to begin, a new voice sliced across their little group like an unexpected sabre strike. "All my apologies, Azata Palokani, but I must beg a word regarding—ah, the sisters Savani. How pleasant."

Zagiri turned on the interloper and took half a step back in shock, jostling into Anahid and scarcely noticing.

She'd last seen Izmirlian Hisarani with a crossbow bolt in his neck, blood on his lips, collapsing into nothing—literally, as he and Siyon had fallen through a gate beyond the planes. She'd hauled Siyon back—reaching into a wild nothingness that still added terror to her dreams—but Izmirlian had never returned.

This *wasn't* Izmirlian Hisarani. The hair was shorter and far tidier, and the face colder, and if the eyes were the same clear brown, they had none of Izmirlian's humour.

It was Avarair Hisarani, the elder brother, who gave each of them a shallow bow, calculated precisely for the heir to a first-tier family to the daughters of another. "Mother mentioned you would be here."

Anahid's hand tightened on Zagiri's shoulder, for some reason. Perhaps only the unpleasantness of running into him. Zagiri hadn't been old enough to meet Avarair properly, years ago, when their parents had been briefly considering the benefits of allying their families through Avarair and Anahid marrying. But Zagiri—and everyone else—knew exactly how that brief consideration had ended.

With Anahid slapping Avarair in public.

A nudge from Anahid reminded Zagiri of her manners; she gave her own acknowledging nod, but left the speaking to Anahid as the elder. "My compliments to your family, and especially to your mother for being so kind as to remember us. As I mentioned to her"—Zagiri blinked; when had Anahid been speaking with Azata Hisarani?—"I wish there was more I could do to repay her kind interest in my sister's forthcoming presentation."

A cold chill slipped down Zagiri's spine. Why was anyone of the family Hisarani paying attention to *her*? She couldn't think of any reason that made sense.

Save that she'd been there, in Anahid's parlour, when Izmirlian Hisarani had stepped out of the world. Not that they knew that. Not that anyone who hadn't been there knew that.

Zagiri looked up, into Avarair's cold and sharp and eerily familiar eyes.

"My mother is so generous." Avarair sounded on the verge of being furious about it. "She far outstrips me in that, and in patience also."

Behind Zagiri, Anahid sounded perfectly calm as she said, "And yet demanding cannot make the wind blow."

"Quite." Avarair turned away from them, to Azata Palokani. "There is a matter of some delay with the outfitting of the second ship, another disruption among the Dockside lading crews. My father has bid me bring you."

He cut straight across the group to speak with her, separating Zagiri from Azatan Palokani. Even as a tangled and brusque set of farewells was happening, another azatan sidled up to Palokani, turning him away into conversation with some bright-eyed young man.

Two moments later, she and Anahid were alone in the crowd, the Palokanis gone, and Zagiri's chance with it. Just like that.

Zagiri took a shaky breath and swallowed down the urge to smash the plate she was still holding, now as empty of prawns as her future was of a clerkship. "You said," she gritted out between her teeth, "that everyone believed Izmirlian had run off to the New Republic with an opera singer."

"Everyone except his family, it seems," Anahid replied quietly, and downed the rest of her djinn-wine in one swift draft. "I could murder him. I'm sorry, Giri. I should have realised we'd need to take that into account."

She should have *what*? The surprise of it knocked Zagiri free of her stiff and disappointed anger. She huffed a little laugh. "Oh yes, you only managed to think of *sixteen* details to make this go perfectly; I'm never going to forgive you for missing just one." She handed her empty plate to a passing steward. "It was a difficult leap, from a standing start, and I've only myself to blame for letting everything come down to this slender chance."

That line between her sister's eyebrows smoothed out a little. "What are you going to do now?" Anahid asked.

"Get drunk." Zagiri smiled to show she didn't mean it. She adjusted her net gloves and checked that her sash was still perfect. There were many other people here she should speak with. At the very least, she was committed to sponsoring at the Ball, and she needed to make the best of it. "Shall we start with Azata Malkasani?" The impeccable matriarch had overseen the Ball for many years now; Zagiri didn't need her sister's advice to know she was someone to stay in favour with.

"You do that," Anahid agreed. "I'm going to step out for some air."

She still sounded a little brittle. Had Avarair rattled her more than Zagiri realised? But in this crowd, all Zagiri could give her sister was a squeeze of the hand, a warm smile, and a quiet teasing: "Try not to kill anyone on the way out!"

Beyond the gallery, the hippodrome was another world entirely. Anahid stood a moment in the corridor and breathed in the dust rising from the track, twined with the scents of grilled meat and spilled wine. The sun fell hot on her skin, cut into stripes by the slatted roof overhead. Along the corridor that led toward the track came the thunder of hooves and of feet drumming in the stands, the roar of the crowd swelling and abating like surf on a beach.

There was nothing so very terrible about the party. Tahera Danelani wasn't even there; Anahid had seen her so rarely through the last half of the summer that she had to assume the avoidance was mutual. Which was something of a relief, even if they'd briefly been great friends. Anahid didn't regret using everything in her power to aid Siyon, but having used Tahera's secrets to blackmail her into that aid, she wasn't eager to face her in society. Or at all.

What Anahid really should have done, if she wanted air, was to step out onto the balcony. Linger in the shade, look out over the caravanserai and its stockyards. Even there, she'd be found. Chased after not for any great charm or merit of her own, but to be asked variations on the same sly questions.

Did she know Siyon Velo *very* well? (Was she sleeping with him?) Was it true he had summoned a being from another plane? (Could he bind the wind into the sails of a trading vessel?) Was he really from Dockside? (Could he be persuaded to intervene in the growing Laders' Guild difficulties?) Was her husband working with him? (Could she offer any insight on what he might do next?)

Perhaps that last one stung the most. It had been Anahid who took Siyon in, who handled the inquisitors, who ushered Siyon to his meeting with the prefect and faced down Captain Xhanari when he brought violence into her parlour.

But no, let's ask about *Nihath* instead.

It didn't matter. Azatani society had always seethed with speculation and gossip and bright-eyed avarice. This was a garment Anahid had worn all her life.

Did it suddenly not fit? Or had it always pinched and chafed like this, and she just hadn't realised?

That thought, more than anything, was what tipped her into motion, walking away from the gallery and toward the track. The hippodrome wasn't a world she was a part of. No one here expected a thing of her, and in that, there was a sweet freedom.

She stepped out onto the concourse, crowded and teeming beneath the striped awnings—people looking for seats, looking for friends, looking for refreshments, looking for a betting clerk. Anahid edged out to the sunny side that looked down over the tiered seating to the long, narrow course below. The sand nearly glowed under the afternoon sun. The chariots churned around the end of the spina, horses plumed in purple and white and orange and green, the drivers leaning their chariots into the bend. The white horses cut in below the purple horses, and a section of the crowd rose as one, waving white pennants and roaring their approbation.

It didn't give Anahid so much as a tickle of vicarious excitement. She was turning away again when something caught her attention. A flash on the track, another movement; was that—?

She could have sworn, just for a moment, from the corner of her eye, she'd seen a fifth chariot on the sands, out in front, shining golden in glory. But even thinking it seemed utterly fanciful.

From somewhere nearby, barely audible over the crowd's noise, a voice called, "Azata Joddani!" With a wince of regret—someone must have followed her after all—Anahid was about to slip away down the concourse when the voice added, "Ana *darling!*"

And instead Anahid turned with a smile tugging at her cheeks.

The Vidama Yilma-Torquera Selsan de Kith stood out in the crowd with her Republic-fashion wide froth of pale skirts and her sunlight-yellow hair twisted up on her head. She was tall—a little more than Anahid herself—and she waved merrily over the press as she nudged her way through. "My dear, *hello*, it's been positively an age."

It had been barely a couple of weeks. Three at the outside. There'd been a lot to do, preparing for today's event—and Zagiri had worked hard as well. Anahid had been so proud of her sister's efforts.

And then it had all been ruined by Avarair Hisarani's interference.

Anahid pressed down on the renewed flare of her temper and submitted to Selsan's extravagant air kisses. "I know, I missed you too," she said, or at least she'd missed the thrill of the carrick table. "I've been so busy, I haven't had a chance to come down to the District."

Selsan rolled her pale eyes with an overacted air of grievance. "You and *all* the other azatani players. I hate this time of year. The tables get so tedious. *Please* tell me it's over and the trade winds will whisk me up some play."

Anahid smiled. "No more formal events until the Salt Festival." The social season was done, and the trading seasons had commenced. Some ventures had already left the harbour, risking a late summer storm for the chance to be first into a foreign port.

"Six *weeks*." Sel clapped her hands with glee. "How splendid. You'll be coming out tonight, of course."

In all truth, Anahid had been yearning for it. In the last week of interminable social engagements, she'd caught her fingers tapping and her eyes straying to the tables where cards were being dealt out in far less interesting games. "I suppose I could," she said blandly.

Selsan wasn't fooled, laughing merrily and hooking a hand into Anahid's elbow. "Come and meet the others, and we'll see if we can't decide where we'll be playing."

She tugged Anahid into the arcade that ran beneath the upper level of seating. The air grew warmer, wisped with smoke and the scent of grilling meat. Stewards carried jugs of retzine and rakia between the crowded tables.

Each thick pillar of the arcade was encrusted with the boards and business of the betting clerks. They scrawled their odds in chalk on the pillar itself, erasing and adjusting them with every groan or cheer from the crowd. Gamblers loitered around them, exchanging coins for tokens with the clerks' young runners.

As they passed, Anahid craned to watch a clerk scrub out her number for the orange team and scrawl a new one. What calculations was she making? What considerations weighed against one another? Anahid ran her eyes up the column of numbers, wondering if there was a pattern. At the top, almost hidden in shadows, was another symbol: an S crossed by a stylised baling hook. It wasn't a bravi mark; thanks to Zagiri, Anahid was all too familiar with those. The baling hook suggested Dockside, but what was it doing *here*?

And then, as Selsan pulled her onward through the crowd,

Anahid's eyes fell on the hefty brawler standing beside the betting clerk's desk, discouraging anyone from arguing the result of the bets. He had a shaved head, and arms bared by his vest, and on his bulging bicep was tattooed that same S and hook.

Not the mark of bravi, Anahid realised with a faint thrill of fear, but of a baron—one of the four criminal organisers who oversaw the shadows of Bezim. Of course they'd have their thumb on the scales of gambling at the hippodrome.

Much as they did in the running of the Flower district, though Anahid had seen scant evidence of it at her quiet, private card tables. Nothing that spoke so clearly of a realm of violence as this tattooed thug.

Anahid was pleased to leave all that behind as Selsan pulled her in among the tables. Around one were gathered faces she knew: the Captain, looking as much the romantic pirate as ever, and a cluster of other players Anahid had met over hands of cards. She knew their playing habits better than their names—this one preferred to build runs, that one never called when she could raise, the other bluffed like a fiend.

The only stranger in the group was a stocky young man with the dark hair and eyes of the Avenues, wearing a longvest and a sulky expression. "And this is Stepan Zinedani," Selsan introduced him, with a muted emphasis Anahid couldn't quite decipher.

The name seemed familiar, though she hardly knew *every* azatani family, and in this setting Anahid could hardly use the angle or depth of Stepan's bow to judge his family situation relative to Anahid's own—you could barely call what he gave her a nod, more an acknowledging jerk of his chin.

Still, *she* didn't have to be rude. "My compliments to your family," Anahid offered. "Do you have significant endeavours planned for the season?" At least if she knew what sort of trade force they mustered, she'd have some idea of where his family stood.

Stepan Zinedani's mouth twisted, a little amused and a little... insulted? "Our endeavours are *always* significant," he spat back. "And we have no need of your fancy compliments."

That was when Anahid realised why the name sounded familiar. Zinedani *was* a lesser-tier azatani family, who took great pains to distance themselves from their fallen cousin. Because that cousin—Garabed Zinedani—was none other than one of the barons of Bezim.

Anahid had just offered her compliments to a crime baron's relation. Embarrassing, but she didn't know why Stepan was looking quite so put out with her.

Selsan passed the Captain back his now half-empty glass of djinnwine and flapped a hand to gain attention. *"Anyway,* where is the good gaming this evening? Stepan, are you open at Sable?"

He was still glowering like Anahid had spit in his eye. "Not to azatani," he said pointedly. "I'm not having drawing room boredom brought into my House."

That was quite enough of *that.* "I come to the District to leave the boredom behind," Anahid stated. "But I will not take my money or my play where it isn't appreciated."

Selsan leaned between them, shushing like they were barking dogs. "Step," she declared, "you're drunk and belligerent; if you don't like losing money, don't bet on the races. People who *aren't* being an ass—" She swept her pale hand around the rest of the circle. "I was thinking Gossamer."

The Captain pulled a face. "They don't open the back room until after midnight, and the general play is awful—with some exceptions, azata."

Anahid inclined her head to him; she had met Selsan—and the Captain again—at the general carrick tables at Gossamer House, on her first outing to the District over the summer.

She didn't pay too much attention to the bickering and bartering that followed. To her, one House was much the same as any other. The Flower district was a glittering and sumptuous banquet of evening entertainments, offering every kind of game, delight, and company that could be desired—but Anahid's interest was entirely specific. Carrick was far sharper and more intricate than the simple card games she'd learned to play in those azatani drawing rooms that Stepan Zinedani so derided. It had fascinated Anahid from the moment she'd first seen Tahera Danelani playing it. The friendship had been lost, but Anahid still had the game itself. And new friends, or at least acquaintances, with whom to play.

They finally meandered to something like a conclusion. "The back room at the Cypress Grove?" Anahid confirmed, eager to settle the matter. It was getting on; she should get back to the gallery before her absence caused too much comment. Or before Zagiri suffered another setback and renounced society to remain a bravi forever. Anahid might not have blamed her for it. "I'll see you all there at the Merry bell."

"*I* have more important things to be attending to," Stepan Zinedani declared to no one at all.

"Your loss," Anahid told him, catching Selsan's amused smirk as she turned away.

She almost hoped she *would* have the chance to play Zinedani, another night if not this one. Anahid would quite like to see that sneer crumble. At the table, she knew she could make it happen, sooner or later.

But for now, it was back to that room, those people, those conversations. That ill-fitting garment. Anahid sighed.

About one thing, Stepan Zinedani was absolutely correct: It was definitely boring, now that she knew what else the world could hold.

CHAPTER 3

This wasn't his first visit to the burial caves, so Siyon had come prepared. He had his little candle—green, which the chandler had told him was for promises in the funeral rites of the New Republic—that he lit with a snap of his fingers. The natural walls of the cave had been covered over with tiled stone, each marked with a little shelf below a bronze plaque. Siyon set his candle atop the puddle of prior green wax, beneath the plaque reading OTHISSA DE KORTAY.

He was sure she'd had a lot more names than that. Maybe in the New Republic you left some of them behind when you died. It wouldn't be the strangest part of their death rites.

Though Siyon supposed if you were going to hang on to mortal remains, rather than giving them cleanly to the sea, this wasn't unpleasant. Each shelf was crowded with merrily burning candles in all sorts of colours, among vases of flowers and little dishes of sweet-smelling oils. Not exactly what Siyon had been expecting, the first time he'd climbed up the crag overlooking the city to get to these caves.

In the New Republic, or so Siyon understood, they had underground crypts, not unlike the one beneath the Bracken chapel safe house. This was a make-do sort of burial, for those who died here in Bezim. Siyon wondered if Othissa would have preferred to be taken back across the Carmine Sea. He couldn't say. He hadn't really known her at all.

"I wondered who was leaving the green candles."

Siyon spun around, the cave a smear of shadowed Abyss and paler Aethyr around him, to find Jaleh Kurit standing in the entrance. She looked much as she ever had—her face too sharp to be beautiful, but too vehement not to be compelling. She was dressed in a muted orange, and at some point since summer she'd stopped wearing that kerchief over her hair, instead braiding her near-black curls around her head.

"You should have brought yellow for guilt," she said, the words a spiteful Abyssal spark on her lips, but she winced even as Siyon flinched. "No, I shouldn't have—"

"Why not?" Siyon interrupted. "It's true enough."

"Don't be ridiculous," Jaleh snapped, even sharper now. "*You* didn't execute her."

But if not for the part he'd played in the summer's various catastrophes, Othissa wouldn't have been arrested at all.

Jaleh eyed him, as though she could hear his thoughts, and they made her as furious as anything he'd ever said aloud. "How many others were arrested, along with her?" she demanded.

Siyon had been there too, swept up by the inqs who raided the Summer Club and carted all the alchemist members away. "A lot," he admitted.

But only three executed, Othissa one of them. Because for all her New Republic titles and personal wealth and alchemical skill, she wasn't azatani, nor in the direct service of one, and she didn't get their protections.

Jaleh produced her own candle, a deep rosy pink colour that Siyon didn't know the meaning of but could easily imagine Othissa wearing.

"I heard," Jaleh said, far too casually, as she used Siyon's candle to light her own, "you caused a circus in a sorcery trial yesterday and got the whole thing shut down."

"That's not—" Siyon started, shuffling farther out of her way and nearly tripping over a little potted palm someone had left in a nearby niche. He steadied himself on Othissa's shelf, then snatched his hand back; was that some sort of sacrilege? Jaleh rolled her eyes and went back to placing her candle. Siyon reconsidered what he'd been going to say. "That's not *exactly* what happened."

Maybe it had been a little bit of a circus.

"You shut it down anyway," Jaleh pointed out. For her, the words were almost soft; her fingers on the candle kicked up little eddies of gentle Aethyr. "And I know it's not the first time. I just wanted to say that I appreciate it, and now I have, and you can shut up about it." She reached out and ran her finger along the engraving of Othissa's abbreviated name and then gave him a sidelong look. "When I'm done here, I usually go and have a Seraph's Kiss in Othissa's memory. I suppose you could come along if you wanted."

Siyon blinked in surprise. "You're inviting me for a drink."

"One," Jaleh stated firmly. "And don't get used to it."

A Seraph's Kiss turned out to be djinn-wine and raspberry liqueur with a dash of Far Khanate pepper oil. It was pale pink and cloyingly sweet and scorched all the way down Siyon's throat; he nearly choked on his first sip.

Jaleh smirked as his eyes watered. "You never really knew her, did you? The Margravine Lyralina-Othissa de Ivrique Kortay the Third." The endless names trickled off her tongue like a slow pour of something syrupy. "She fluttered around like some sort of frilly jellyfish, and she had a sting like one too. Ink and ashes, but she could be a bitch."

"That why you signed on with her?" Siyon asked, before he could think better of it.

"Like to like, you mean?" Jaleh asked, lifting her eyebrows. But her smirk still lingered, though it twisted a little bitterly. "I signed on with her because she was the only non-industrial alchemist who'd take me. I didn't want to be tempering a dye bath or tinkering with bit-sharpening charms in some factory for my whole life. I wanted more. I wanted—I *want* to *know*."

Siyon knew it well. Jaleh's ambitions had featured heavily in their final, blistering arguments.

Jaleh shrugged, far too casual to be true. "And this is how the game is played, for the rest of us. The ones who aren't—" She waved a hand at him and didn't need to say it. *Who aren't prancing around pulling impossible shit.* She smirked. "Now *you're* the respectable one."

"Fuck off," Siyon grumbled, and as she laughed, he reflected that she wasn't entirely *wrong*, was she? Wasn't he working on helping the inqs? Trying to get in with the azatani?

Still smirking around another swig of her drink, Jaleh said unexpectedly: "So what was yours like? Izmirlian Hisarani. That's who you're really mourning, isn't it?"

Siyon's throat seized, like he'd downed the rest of his vicious drink in one go. "He's not—" he started, then wondered if he should finish that at all.

"Not dead," Jaleh finished for him. "No, I suppose not. I know what he wanted. Othissa was one of the alchemists he approached, before you, and she asked my opinion on the feasibility of his request, before she turned him down."

Siyon hadn't expected that, though possibly he should have. "What was your opinion? On the feasibility." Or on Izmirlian. Had she found him as fascinating as Siyon had?

Jaleh looked at him consideringly and then finished the last of her drink, pushing the empty glass across to him. "Your round," she declared, despite everything she'd said earlier.

The wineshop she'd chosen—a cozy little nook beneath University Hill—turned out to have apricot brandywine, though it was from one of the southern provinces of the New Republic and tasted more mellow, the sourness somehow gentler and rounder, than the bottle Siyon had once shared with Izmirlian on the roof of his family's townhouse.

Still, after the Seraph's Kiss it was sour enough to make Jaleh screw up her face at the first sip. That made Siyon smile, and then the words were coming before he really thought about it. "Izmirlian was sharp and unexpected too. Complex. Curious. He wanted to know as well." Siyon hadn't thought about that before now, this similarity in his last two lovers. "Not just know, but see and do. I've never met anyone so unafraid."

And Siyon missed him, so much. Ridiculous, for how little time they'd had together, but that felt like part of the tragedy. Siyon would never know what Izmirlian preferred to do at Salt Night, which parts of the city-wide party were his favourite. They'd never seen each other sick with winter sniffles, or shared the spring's first melons, or learned how the other cheated at checkers.

Siyon had known, from the outset, that Izmirlian wasn't his to keep. But there was so much more he'd hoped to share first.

The liquor was sharp enough to make Siyon's eyes sting. Across the table, Jaleh said, "I thought what he wanted was breathtakingly audacious—and utterly impossible." When Siyon blinked the blur from his vision, she was smiling at him. "Seems I was only half right."

To punish him for the apricot brandywine, Jaleh bought them a round of sickly sweet fig rakia next, and then Siyon retaliated with two mugs of the bitter Lyraec beer she'd been suffering through on the night they'd first met.

Maybe there were even more rounds after that, because when they finally tipped out of the wineshop, as the midnight bell was ringing, Siyon bounced off the doorframe and nearly knocked Jaleh over before he wrapped an arm around her to keep her upright. She elbowed him, and Siyon squeezed her tighter, lifting her entirely off the ground for three strides as she laughed so hard Siyon could see the bright motes of it dancing in the air.

It felt so familiar, like two dozen other nights when they'd been drunk and raucous and known to each other. So familiar that it felt natural for her face to tilt up toward his as she slid down to standing. Natural for Siyon to tip her chin a little more with a finger beneath it.

But the scent that lifted from her hair was all wrong—peat smoke and salt, not sandalwood and orange blossom.

Jaleh's head turned, and his nose bumped her cheek. "Siyon," she said, low like a warning.

"Yeah," he agreed, stepping back, letting her go entirely. "No. Right. Absolutely." He cleared his throat, looked around. They were in an alleyway that he thought he recognised, though someone had painted a symbol on the wall—for a moment he thought it was the baron-mark of the Shore Clan, but the baling hook was crossed over with a hammer instead. Wait, the Laders' Guild? Why was it painted up here?

Far better to pay attention to details like that. Like the corners of the alleyway, where to Siyon's vision, the shadows were pooling with a strange shimmer.

Actually, he'd never seen a planar emanation like that before.

"Look," Jaleh was saying, in that tone she got when she was drunk enough to think she could explain everything. "I just think that we should—who the *fuck* are you?"

Siyon whirled, and his vision sparked bronze and dark, and there *was* someone else in the alleyway with them, where surely there hadn't been anyone before. But the guy was clearly a real person—he cast a shadow and took a step that sounded on the cobblestones. He was shorter even than Jaleh, with close-cropped dark hair and deep, liquid eyes in a pale and boyish face.

To Siyon's eyes, he was also limned in the faintest burnished glow. It wasn't a scalding Empyreal orange, or a wisping soft Aethyreal shade, or the creeping rust of the Abyss. What *was* it?

The guy looked at Jaleh without reply or even recognition, then turned to Siyon. "We have been waiting for you," he said. "But you haven't come, and time is running short."

"Hey," Jaleh snapped, stepping in front of Siyon, belligerent as ever. "I asked you a ques—oh, fuck me."

Because the strange shadow guy held up a hand, not threatening, merely palm-out, like he was asking her to stop.

And on his palm was a tattoo—or a mark, at least, Siyon wasn't sure how it was made. But he knew that shape, an almost perfect circle, with a short line cross-marked at the top.

The baron-mark of Midnight.

Jaleh stepped back so sharply she'd have trodden on Siyon if he hadn't also flinched away.

Midnight, the baron Midnight, one of the four criminal lords of the city. The one who was rarely seen in person, but whose underlings seemed more like *followers*, and who—it was whispered, among the city's alley alchemists—liked to collect practitioners. Sure, he might pay well for making the drugs and tinctures and poisons that his underlings peddled, but sometimes those who stepped into his tunnels were never seen again. It was said those tunnels burrowed beneath the city like the sticky tangles of a spider's web. It was said he could be in two places at once. It was said he could get *anywhere*, even into a locked room.

Supposedly he'd done just that, to kill the Bitch Queen and bring an end to the baron wars twenty years ago.

Midnight lowered his hand and said, "We are the one who waits in the darkest shadows."

Though he'd sobered up remarkably in the last few moments, Siyon was still *entirely* too drunk to make sense of that. "Well," he said, trying to keep up, "you can go back and keep waiting."

A frown creased down between Midnight's fine-drawn brows. "Keep waiting? For what? The awakening is upon us. Can you not feel the quickening? Can you not see the rising tide? Can you not hear her calling in your dreams? You may wait, but she will not. *We* will not!"

His voice was suddenly enormous, ringing from the alley walls, setting nearby dogs to barking.

It rattled Siyon's bones, but when he tried to clap his hands over his ears, suddenly Midnight was holding them, right in front of Siyon and staring into his face.

"You must come. It is your purpose and mine. We are but servants. Call, and I will come."

He pressed Siyon's hands together, with something small, and hard, and wickedly spiked between the palms.

Siyon winced, pulled against his grip—

And bounced off the alley wall, no one holding him.

No one here at all. The alleyway was dark and empty, Midnight gone as inexplicably as he'd come. But the burnished glow lingered a moment, settling slow upon the cobblestones, as wisps of mysterious Aethyr and fearful dark Abyss came creeping back in.

"What the *fuck*," Jaleh said, her voice catching.

"*I* don't know." Siyon turned around. No sign of Midnight anywhere. No sign he'd been here at all, save . . .

Siyon opened his hand, and on his palm sat some dark little figurine, the carved spikes of it glinting bronze, but not enough light in the alleyway to see anything more.

"What was he talking about?" Jaleh demanded. "What quickening? What's waking? *Are* you having dreams?"

"No!" Siyon said, as he'd deny *anything* she asked him in that tone of voice, and only after the word was out of his mouth did he think about it. About dreams swamped in darkness and stone, with a distant and steady beat like a summons. They were better than the dreams of Izmirlian dying, so Siyon hadn't thought much about them, but now...

Jaleh saw his hesitation and jabbed a finger at him. "You *are*!"

"They're dreams!" Siyon shouted right back. "Don't make out like it's some moral failing. Can *you* control your dreams?"

From somewhere above them, a voice shouted back, "Can you shut the fuck up?"

Siyon and Jaleh flinched in unison, and then—of course—she glared. "I'm not the Power of the Mundane," she hissed at him, and he hated that she had a point. "Ink and ashes, Siyon. *Midnight.*"

"I know." Siyon glanced down the alleyway, where even the last burnished marks had been scrubbed away. He closed his hand around the figurine and, despite his instincts, put it in his pocket.

Jaleh sniffed. "You'd better figure out what's going on."

Like he didn't know that as well.

There weren't so many properly challenging carrick games in the Flower district that Anahid could simply avoid play at one, no matter how unpleasant the House manager had proven himself to be.

And, as Selsan whisked them both into the back room at Sable House, Anahid reasoned that possibly Stepan Zinedani had been having a bad day at the races and would not be that odious tonight.

He wasn't. If anything, he was worse.

The table was the three of them—Anahid, Selsan, and Stepan Zinedani—along with the Captain, the elderly Azatan Josepani (who had retired from society three years ago, but apparently not from the gaming table), and a hefty Khanate man who introduced himself only as Bo. He looked like a caravan guard, dressed in a plain vest and trousers with his long black hair plaited simply down his back, but the rings climbing the shell of his ear looked like gold, and the bands on his bared arms were studded with well-cut gems. If the game turned away from tokens to more tangible collateral—which it often did, at these private tables—he was well provided for.

Zinedani himself, Anahid decided after the first half dozen hands, played like the brat he was. He drank more rakia the more he lost, which did his acumen no favours. When the third losing hand in a row left him with a bare handful of tokens, he blithely bought more.

They were carried in by one of the House attendants, a slender girl of perhaps eighteen, with the strawberry-blonde hair and freckled skin of the North. The black banding on her robe, Anahid now knew, meant she was still in training and not yet a Flower, but she couldn't be far from finished. She had a willowy grace, a winsome tilt to her nose, and a watchful slant to her eyes as she attended her master.

She was only one of many distractions, hustling in from the House proper in a little burst of music and chatter with messages and matters for the House Master's attention. Between all that and learning the styles of Stepan and Bo, Anahid knew she wasn't playing her best. Each missed opportunity or risk unlikely to pay off wound her irritation a little tighter.

The Vidama Selsan dealt out the cards—at a private game like this, there was no separate dealer, but rather a complicated rotating roster of who shuffled the deck and who dealt from it. Her hands were brisk—two cards facedown in front of each player, and two in the centre of the table, faceup. "Ana, darling, buy the game."

Anahid ran her thumbnail down the milled edges of her stack of tokens. She had fewer than she'd like, when she was being called upon to set the rules and pace of the hand to come. But she'd been dealt the six of Abyss and the Alchemist. With the centre cards—the nine of Aethyr, and the Arch Dominion—she had a pair of Powers, at the very least. A very good chance of a significant winning hand, if she took the risk to capitalise on it.

"Oh, come on," Stepan muttered. "We're playing cards, not choosing a new dress."

Anahid grabbed a handful of tokens and dropped them into the pot. "Two more for the centre, buyer's market."

With a low and delighted laugh, Selsan dealt two more cards faceup—the ten of Mundane and the six of Empyre. Anyone who wished to get more cards into their hand would have to match Anahid's initial wager to do so, and that was on top of any further play.

Her set play conditions were a slight risk, suggesting as they did that Anahid had a starting hand she considered strong. Bo folded immediately, adding no more tokens to the pot—and Anahid's potential winnings. But Selsan (Anahid knew) always loved a challenge. She bought in merrily, as did Azatan Josepani. Stepan glowered, but couldn't bear to be left out; he not only bought in, but raised the bet. The Captain even bought an additional card, though he then wrinkled his nose and folded entirely.

Anahid's tokens were running low, and she couldn't buy any more in the middle of a hand—not that she'd want to. Gambling debts had been Tahera's terrible secret; Anahid preferred to keep her losses cinched tight. But if she needed a little more support for her hand, she'd dressed this evening with a careful eye to what might be useful for play. Her earrings were heirloom turquoise from the North, won at a previous game, and she also wore a string of black pearls. Any one of those pieces could supplement her bets amply.

So she counted in sufficient tokens to match Stepan's raise and then tossed in the remainder of her stack.

"Oooh," Selsan cooed with girlish glee. She danced her fingers over her own stack of tokens—rather more significant than Anahid's had been—and carefully counted in the requisite amount and then, with a sly glance across the table, added two more.

Just over what Anahid could supply.

But over what Stepan could muster, as well. He scowled and tossed back his glass of rakia. The pale House girl stepped forward to refill it as he flung his last token into the pot and snarled, "All in."

Selsan beamed at him. "Might I suggest that ring of yours as additional collateral? It's hideously vulgar, but I'm sure someone could—"

"The House," Stepan growled.

They all stopped, Bo looking up from tamping down his bronze pipe. Selsan raised her eyebrows. "Which House?"

"*This* House." Stepan waved a hand around the wood-paneled room.

Oh.

He'd managed to shock even Selsan into speechlessness. Anahid had no idea what a House like this would even be worth.

"I fold," Azatan Josepani said into the silence.

A tiny, hysterical giggle tickled at Anahid's throat. Well, of course he did. Who wouldn't? Against *that*. Could all her jewels together possibly match it?

But it was *enraging*. She had a pair of Powers, for pity's sake. And a lesser pair of sixes, but who cared? This was her *chance*, and he was buying his way out of the hand.

Buying her out of the game. A game he didn't think she should be at in the first place.

"That's ridiculous." Anahid hoped she sounded irritated rather than desperate. "And you bluff terribly."

Stepan sneered at her. "I wouldn't expect a spoiled society wife chasing a thrill to understand the harsh realities of serious play."

Bo snorted. The Captain said, "Uncalled for, za."

"He's no azatan," Anahid corrected, and she knew her voice was icy and her chin had come to that sharp angle she'd been told, so many times, made her unflatteringly severe. From the clench of Stepan's jaw, he *hated* this, her looking down her well-bred *society* nose at him.

It burned that he had an azatani name, but no azatani respect.

Right now, she *wanted* him to burn. More than that, she wanted him to lose.

"I call," she said. "State your price."

Convention, if not the actual rules (Anahid was unsure of the difference, or even if there *was* a difference, at this level of the game) dictated that he had to accept *something* within her power or possession as a match for his bet. It wasn't possible to entirely buy your way to victory.

His gaze skittered over her earrings, her pearls... and farther down her body. His smirk slanted toward a leer. Anahid was already tensing before he said, "You're not without assets. They'd fetch enough, to the right buyer. From the right seller."

"You *can't* be serious," Selsan snapped.

It took Anahid a moment longer to realise what he meant. "I'm married!" she gasped.

In name only, but still.

Stepan shrugged, his smile stretching like a lizard in the sun. "You wouldn't be the first woman in Bezim's history to come to a District auction block with a full life behind her. And yes," he added to the Vidama, "I am quite serious. That's the stake. One auction, for one night. Goes for both of you, if you're still in the game."

"Absolutely not." Selsan slammed down her cards. "And I'll not be sitting down at a table again with *you*. This is a disgrace."

His face twitched, but the challenge was back as he looked to Anahid.

Who was still reeling. The auction block. Not a physical thing, but a concept. They called it a Flower Night, the first time someone's physical charms were made available to the highest bidder.

The cards were crumpling in her fist; Anahid made herself lay them facedown on the table, avoiding Stepan's avid gaze. He was watching for her reaction to his suggestion that she be *pimped out* from his House.

She wanted to scream. She wanted to claw his face off. She wanted him to *lose*, so badly it burned like bile in her throat.

He was bluffing, he had to be. Just a different sort of buyout, raising the stakes beyond what she could afford, chasing her out of the entire game. He *had* to be bluffing; what were the chances he had a hand better than her?

It wasn't impossible, even if she wanted it to be. She wanted it so badly she couldn't trust her own judgment. He could have one of the other Powers, the ones that weren't in her hand or already on the table. He could have *both* of them.

Stepan smirked at her and hooked his finger over the edge of the centre pot, tokens clinking as he tipped it toward himself.

"Fine," Anahid snarled, yanking the pot out of his grip to slam it back in its place. "I'll see your stake. Show your hand."

Shock flitted across his face, and he looked away quickly. But Selsan had already folded, and there was no one else left in the game. Stepan shrugged and tossed his cards down one at a time.

First was the Demon Queen, Power of the Abyss, and Anahid's heart stopped. The sudden silence of it shook her body like another Sundering.

He had a pair of Powers, and what's more, his was the balanced pair—his Demon Queen against the table's Arch Dominion. His pair beat hers.

Then he cast down his second card negligently: the two of Aethyr.

Anahid's life restarted with a lurch. She dragged air into her lungs and pulled the pot away from Stepan's reaching hand. "No," she croaked, like she couldn't believe it.

She almost couldn't.

Anahid flipped over her cards, both of them at once. She watched Stepan watch them land. The Alchemist, making a pair of Powers, though lesser than his. And then the triumph drained off his face as he realised she also had the pair of sixes.

It had seemed meaningless, that second pair. Until it was the thing that tipped her hand over his. Satisfaction sank its teeth into her. She'd beaten him. He'd *lost*.

She'd won.

She'd won *the House*.

The Vidama Selsan fell back in her chair, laughing so hard she rocked it on two legs.

Azatan Josepani lifted his tufted white eyebrows and said mildly, "Oh my."

And the Captain knocked his knuckles against the table. "I call this game finished and suggest we all accompany Zas Zinedani and Joddani to the former's office to witness the transfer of winnings."

"Wait," Stepan gasped.

"Yes." Bo rose from his chair. He was even more hefty when standing. Almost menacingly so.

Stepan paled as the other chairs scraped out from the table. "No, wait, I can't, my uncle—"

His uncle, Garabed Zinedani, one of the city's crime barons, was surely likely to be very unimpressed with his nephew gambling away one of their Flowerhouses.

The Captain said, "Then you shouldn't have bet in the first place. You, girl, which way to the office?"

It was only as they all bundled out of the private room that it really hit Anahid. She was about to own a Flowerhouse. This Flowerhouse. A House full of gambling and entertainments and Flowers like this one, leading them along with a graceful sway to her hips.

She couldn't possibly. She'd be shunned as the Zinedani were. Azatani might come to the District for discreet entertainment, but they didn't *run* the place. They were merchants, not *shopkeepers*. To trade was noble; to serve was tawdry.

Then they were in the office—Stepan's office, with his poor taste visible in every ostentatious decoration, from the Archipelagan shell-beaded curtain over the doorway to the collection of Northern turquoise adorning the walls in the sort of cheap, tacky settings that smugglers always seemed to use.

Stepan was protesting—had been protesting the whole way here, but Anahid had barely heard it over her own panic. The Captain wasn't paying any heed, steering Stepan behind the desk—a hulking box of black walnut—and shouting for the House clerk to be fetched.

Selsan draped herself along a red-velvet chaise, apparently enjoying all this tremendously. Bo lit his pipe, sitting in the window, and watched with implacable disinterest.

But when Stepan kept repeating, "I can't! I can't!" the large Khanate warrior took the pipe out of his mouth to state, "You made a promise."

The words sliced through the room. Stepan swallowed hard and turned wide and desperate eyes on Anahid. "Surely," he gulped. "Surely, you cannot *want* this House."

She didn't. She desperately didn't. There was already gossip about her in the Avenues, about where and how she was spending so many of her evenings. This would be an outrage.

"Perhaps," Azatan Josepani said quietly, "Azata Joddani might be satisfied with an equivalent monetary sum."

Stepan looked desperate. "I haven't the faintest—you." He pointed behind Anahid; a serious middle-aged man dressed in all-black livery had just brushed his way through the curtain of beads and shells. The House clerk, Anahid presumed. "How much would the House be worth in money?"

The sum the clerk named—remarkably promptly—was so significant that the Captain dropped the ornament he'd been examining. It made a heavy thud on the desk.

But after a blanched moment, Stepan said, "That sounds reasonable."

There was a wild light of hope in his eyes. He wanted this way out. He thought that price, be it ever so exorbitant, would be less trouble to him than his uncle's reaction to the loss of the House.

Anahid remembered how he had looked earlier, over the table, as he suggested that she be sold on the block for some man's pleasure. For *Stepan's* pleasure, to see her at his mercy. To see her humiliated.

He'd have done it, had the cards fallen differently. She could never have begged or bargained her way out of it.

"No," she said, and watched Stepan Zinedani's face fall.

Like playing her cards all over again. Like *winning*.

Just as great a thrill.

CHAPTER 4

Siyon hadn't been retired from the Little Bracken bravi for that long—barely two months, since he'd become someone too controversial, and too busy, to run the rooftops. Only two months, and yet there was some young punk he didn't know at the door when he showed up at the Chapel, the Little Bracken safe house in the quiet corner of the city between the river and University Hill.

More importantly, the guy didn't know Siyon and absolutely wasn't letting him in.

Arguing was made harder by the racket from inside—a skirmish party had returned from an early raid on the Bleeding Dawn, and the celebrations were in full swing. But eventually Siyon managed to persuade him to send for the Diviner Prince.

With the door guy still watching like he thought Siyon might be a one-man counterraid, Siyon made an exaggerated show of leaning against the stone wall to wait, tucking his hands in his pockets—

And found there was something in one of them. It was hard, and spiky sharp, and even as Siyon pulled it out, he remembered the tight clasp of Midnight's hands over his, pressing something into his palm.

It was a little figurine, made of something black and glassy that sucked light into its depths and only reflected on the edges and tips.

Siyon had to tilt it this way and that to really make out that this curve was a neck, and that a tail, and these two spreading wings.

A dragon. It was a tiny, perfectly carved dragon.

These weren't the trousers he'd been wearing last night. How had it got into the pocket?

The double doors burst dramatically open and Daruj came swinging out, bellowing, "No, you can't come in, you're too fucking sober!"

It had been weeks, Siyon realised, since he'd last seen Daruj. There were new baubles threaded in the tight braids of his hair, and a new scar cut across one cheek, paler than his dark skin. All of them new stories that Siyon hadn't been a part of, when nearly every story for the past eight years had included both of them, side by side.

The pang was brief, crushed in Daruj's hug, with laughter bright in Siyon's ear. "Here." He thrust a raffia-bound flagon of rakia into Siyon's ribs, as though to remedy his mocking complaint, and steered him past the bemused doorman.

Inside, the vaulted wooden rafters echoed with merriment. The only quiet corner was where the injuries of the recent raid were being salved by a brusque Tein Geras. Siyon used to mix up that salve for the tribe. He wondered where they were getting their alchemical pastes and charmed stitching thread these days. But Tein had plenty of back-alley alchemist contacts, from his pre-bravi days, when he'd been a runner for...

For Midnight. Siyon was almost sure of it.

"I just want to have a word with—" was as far as Siyon got before Daruj yanked him in the other direction.

"Nope!" Daruj called, lifting his voice over a nearby group singing a victorious opera aria very badly. "Important business first!"

Siyon had to tilt close and shout to be heard. "You invited me down here to celebrate a raid?"

Daruj laughed, a flash of white teeth in his dark face. "Trust me."

Atop the raised dais at one end of the Chapel, the Little Bracken sergeant was holding court. A woman as short, sharp, and weathered as her favoured sabre, Voski Tolan looked more like a back-alley bruiser than the popular image of a dashing and daring bravi. She plucked a tiara from the winnings her victorious skirmish party laid out for her and set it sparkling atop her bravi tricorn with a flourish.

"All hail the Bracken princess of the New Republic!" someone shouted, and someone *else* started blowing a fanfare on a horn.

Tein Geras appeared out of the crowd, apparently done with his nursing duties, to step up and whisper in his sergeant's ear. Siyon knocked knuckles against Daruj's shoulder, getting his attention, and nodded up to the dais. "Hey, you remember who Geras ran for before he signed up with Bracken?"

Daruj frowned. "That was *decades* ago. Was it Midnight?"

Up on the dais, Voski Tolan stood on her chair, bracing a hand on her quartermaster's shoulder and lifting the other to whistle—sharp and piercingly—for attention.

"Savani!" she bellowed in the new quiet. "Where is she? Zagiri Savani!"

"She's trying to leave!" someone shouted, from back near the door.

Laughter, and cheering, and then—Siyon could just see over the crowd—Zagiri was hoisted up atop someone's shoulders and passed along atop the press like a piece of cargo being loaded. Siyon clapped and called with the others; he had a notion of what was afoot now, and he was pleased to have been asked to witness it.

"I have a thing in the morning!" Zagiri called, but she was laughing as well, then yelping as she nearly fell into a gap in the crowd, before being safely deposited on her feet near the front.

"Well, if your beauty sleep can spare it…" Voski said mockingly, snapping her fingers at Geras.

Who passed up to her a sheathed sabre, wrapped up with black ribbon. Voski tugged at the securing knot, and the ribbon fell away, revealing a basketwork hilt glittering with platinum and diamonds, and a tooled leather scabbard in a blue so dark it was nearly black.

Not just any sabre. A Named Blade.

Little Bracken hooted and hollered, then calmed down toward silence as Voski lifted the shining blade over her head. "The Star Whisper!" she declared, her voice ringing from the pillars. "A Blade of Bracken that was, and will be."

The assembled tribe shouted, dozens of voices shaking the rafters: "Brave the knife!"

Voski drew the sabre—the showy way, making it ring and flash in the light. It was a *beautiful* piece, the blade etched darkly with intersecting points of a star map, filled in with whispering swirls. Holding it high, Voski started her recitation:

"A blade that knows. A blade that sees. A blade that remembers.

"A blade of the Old Kingdoms, of the first tribe, of Grand Bracken itself. Carried over the sea by Carmello in-ger-Hazy, this is the blade with which he duelled the sirens for the right to land. Passed in turn to Polinna Terretani, undefeated for a hundred and thirty-seven nights with this blade in her hand, and even then it took four blades to her one. Given then to the fiery Willand, the star who fell from the North to burn so bright and brief on the streets of Bezim."

It was a ritual—a remembrance of every hand that had carried this blade into battle for Little Bracken, and who had carried its name while they did so, their deeds adding to the legend of the blade, and the legend of the tribe.

This was part of the sergeant's role, keeping her tribe's history and guiding its future by selecting the next hand that would wield a blade. The next name to add to its lineage.

Siyon had seen dozens of these—including the ceremony when Daruj had been given the Diviner Prince.

This one seemed longer. Or maybe that was the strange ringing in Siyon's ears, like each new name from history struck a bell that layered itself into a resonating chime, almost visible in the air like a thickening mist...

He shook his head hard, momentarily dizzy.

"Passed now," Voski said in conclusion, "into the hand of Zagiri Savani, whose cunning danced Bracken through shadows to save those in dire need. Who has promised us one last season of her blade kissing air with ours, but in doing so reminds us of the true purpose of the bravi—to break shackles and run free, under the whisper of the stars!"

The Little Bracken *roared*. Siyon's head ached. Voski turned the sabre over her forearm, and the basketwork hilt glinted and glittered like the most beautiful potential.

Zagiri reached up to the grip, and lifted the glittering blade aloft. "Brave the knife!" she shouted.

And the answering roar nearly deafened Siyon.

It took ages, in the tumultuous celebration that followed, for Siyon to edge his way through the crowd to Zagiri. By that time, she was ruddy with drink and heady congratulations but still beaming fit to split her cheeks.

"Well done!" Siyon called over the noise around them. "You deserve it!"

She hugged him one-armed; Star Whisper was still in the other hand, though sheathed again now. "You're here! How are you here?"

Siyon wiggled fingers in her face. "Magic."

Zagiri laughed, and then Daruj came elbowing up behind Siyon, handing Zagiri a hideous gilt-and-jewels cup filled with bright-sparking liquor.

Everything was dissolving into chaos and jubilation, the air sticky with it and the noise a heaving blanket. The business of young people.

Siyon let the celebration press him out of its fevered heart, and he found Tein Geras behind the tall screen of the dais, perched in an alcove with his tally book open on his knee and a pair of half-moon spectacles balanced on his nose. He looked incongruous, a stocky brawler wielding a delicate pen on intricate calculations.

But the look he shot Siyon over his spectacles was sharp as ever. "I thought you were one risk I'd already got off my books."

Siyon waved a finger at his own eyes. "These are new, right?"

"I'm not immune to the ravages of time." Tein levered the spectacles off his face. In their absence, as though Siyon's eyes had been opened, other signs of age became visible. Lines shadowing the quartermaster's eyes. A hint of grey in his sideburns.

"Then I'm here to dredge up ancient history," Siyon noted. It seemed more respectful to just ask and not dance around the topic. "Did you work for Midnight once?"

Tein's eyebrows went up; he closed his tally book and tidied up before answering. "A long time ago. I'm sure I don't need to tell you that the decisions we make in our youth aren't always the wisest."

Some of Siyon's had been downright stupid, but everything had more or less worked out all right. "He's approached me." Far too innocuous a phrase to cover what had happened in that dark alleyway. He'd appeared out of thin air and disappeared back into it.

A stony wariness fell over Tein's face. "In what capacity?"

Siyon shook his head. "That's sort of the question. It wasn't clear. *He* was...very weird." He touched his pocket, where the hard little shape of the dragon was still nestled. *It is your purpose and mine*, he'd said. *Call, and I will come.* Weird barely began to cover it.

"You don't want to get involved with him," Tein stated.

"I don't," Siyon agreed. "But the more I know, the more I can avoid."

Tein allowed the truth of that with a little tilt of his head. "I wasn't that far in, you understand. That's the only reason I was allowed to leave at all. I was just a kid; I ran messages, I ran the money. Only ever saw Midnight himself the once, and that was at a distance, and briefly. But even so...you hear things. Things that made me glad I never got any closer. You know *those* stories, I'm sure."

Siyon did. The practitioners who went from being well paid to being nowhere to be found. Those who spent more and more time down in the tunnels, until they never came out again. "You say you saw him? This is, what, twenty years ago?"

"Closer to twenty-five. I got out before the baron wars really started."

But the man Siyon had seen last night, who'd been right up in his face...Siyon would have said he couldn't be much older than thirty. "Is Midnight a name or a title?"

Tein shrugged. "Could be a title. But the organisation...from everything I saw, and everything I heard since, there are never any succession struggles. Never any change to the flow of power. Just Midnight."

Just Midnight. Unchanging, for twenty-five years at least. Siyon couldn't believe it. But Siyon had seen all sorts of impossible shit in the last half year. And he couldn't deny that something very strange had happened in that dark alleyway.

Something stranger than could be explained by how drunk Siyon had been.

"Bastard's a mystery, right?" Tein shook his head. "When the wars really kicked off—when the Bitch Queen started killing the gang bosses that wouldn't swear to her—I knew I'd made the right decision in getting out when I did. But when it ended..." He shuddered—actually shuddered.

Siyon knew that story too. It was street legend. The Bitch Queen and all her inner circle had been found slaughtered in their locked and guarded stronghold, and the only witnesses—the latest batch of other barons' foot soldiers who hadn't been tortured or bartered or turned yet—had all sworn that it had been Midnight. He'd stepped out of nowhere, and the shadows had turned to knives, and then he'd vanished again.

It had happened the night after she'd first raided one of Midnight's operations. Up until then, she'd only targeted the barons who'd seemed more of a threat, the ones aboveground, who ran muscle and street-smart games.

After that, her entire war fell apart.

The moral of that story was clear. You didn't cross any of the remaining barons, the four left standing when the blood finally drained away. But you especially didn't cross Midnight.

We are but servants, he'd said to Siyon. *Call, and I will come.*

Siyon pulled the little dragon figurine out of his pocket. Tein's eyebrows went up. "Nice work," he said, with the professional assessment of the man who fenced whatever the tribe won—or looted, if a party raid got mean. "Is it obsidian? Carved like that?"

"Midnight gave it to me," Siyon told him, and Tein got *very* thoughtful. "Could you... I don't even know what I'm asking."

"See what I can find out?" Tein supplied, and, after a moment's hesitation, took the little dragon off Siyon's palm. He sighed, holding it up to the light, which sparked in bronze and orange from the points of the dragon's wings and spikes. "Yeah, all right, there are a couple people I could ask."

"Thanks," Siyon said.

And Tein shot him a wry look. "Don't thank me yet. This might all still get messy."

Siyon had a bad feeling that he was already in the middle of the mess.

Zagiri hadn't even wanted to come to Polinna Andani's post-season garden party breakfast. It wasn't required for Ball-sponsor preparation, and after her recent clerkship failure, being around all these bright young things with their futures arranged stung like sea spray on rope burn.

She could have stayed on last night, wielded her new blade in the circle, learned its balance and beauty. Star Whisper. A bladename of her own. At least she had that much.

But Anahid had *insisted* that there would be opportunities to explore at this less formal event. So Zagiri had scraped herself out of bed this morning and even remembered her net gloves…

And Anahid *wasn't here*.

Zagiri wasn't sure if she was more outraged—how could Anahid do this to her?—or intrigued. Anahid had once been nearly incoherent with the birchfever, and she'd still sent an elegantly penned apology to the hostess of the event she'd had to miss. *What* had happened this morning to keep her away without even a note?

It was obvious that Azata Andani was also dying of curiosity, but she'd sprained her ankle at an evening soiree last week. (Ironically, or so gossip said, because she'd been distracted by eavesdropping while descending the stairs.) As long as Zagiri stayed away from her, she wouldn't have to parry Polinna's insinuations.

To achieve that, Zagiri might even consider picking up a bocha ball.

Azata Malkasani was already at the games table, wreathed in the smothering pleasantness that made her both a capable organiser of the Harbour Master's Ball and a trial at this hour of the morning. It was essential to keep on her good side, so Zagiri prepared a smile and a pleasant greeting and tried not to feel as sharp and awkward as a sabre worn to afternoon tea.

There were two other women with her—the Northern women, who'd also been at the races, looking like they'd stepped out of an opera. Hair golden as a well-polished rivna coin, and skin pale as a shark's belly. They were both trussed up in heavily embroidered bodices laced over white skirts. It seemed incredibly impractical for a garden party; grass was already staining the hems.

"Ah, Miss Savani, how are you?" While Zagiri gawked, Azata Malkasani had spotted her.

The older Northern woman repeated, "Savani?" Her eyes were pale too, grey as storm clouds heading Zagiri's way. "You said this family is of the first tier, yes?"

It took Zagiri aback to hear it said so bluntly. Malkasani gave a little huff as well, before she said, as smoothly as ever, "Indeed. Miss Savani, would you join us for a moment? This is Madame Ksaia Bardha, newly arrived ambassador to the Council of Bezim from the Confederation of Northern Cities, and her daughter, Miss Yeva Bardha."

Zagiri understood now why she'd overheard those conversations at the races about the North, its violent upheavals, and the possible resumption of trade. Cousin Telmut—who oversaw the Savani family trading interests—had been whining for years about the various violent convulsions of the Northern cities, as the grafs put down revolutionary uprisings and the uprisings murdered the grafs. All of it had seemed very far away and unrelated to Zagiri's life.

Now it was being introduced to her. An ambassador? That must mean some sort of order had been achieved. Most importantly for the azatani of Bezim, *that* meant that trade could resume.

Malkasani was still talking. "And this is Miss Zagiri Savani, one of our sponsors for next year's Ball, and certainly one of our more mature and capable young ladies." By which she meant: *I've been hinting that she should be signing up for two years now.*

Zagiri smiled and gave a very respectful nod to Madame Bardha; she didn't need the gentle touch of Anahid's knuckles to hers to know that this was a situation that warranted all her manners.

Even if Madame Bardha seemed to have misplaced hers. "So you know your business," she demanded, "with this sponsoring and all the complications." The woman had a fierce frown; her daughter mostly looked bored, squinting across the grass to where the lawn games were underway.

"I've not sponsored before," Zagiri said carefully, "but I am very familiar with the forms through my sister, who presented me when I made my debut." And who had sponsored three times, increasingly if quietly desperate regarding her paucity of marriage offers. Zagiri certainly wasn't mentioning *that* to these strangers.

Malkasani nearly glowed with pride. "Miss Savani's sister, Anahid Joddani, is quite the burgeoning bloom of society. An azata of great propriety and discernment, who one day will no doubt guide our society as I do." She smiled at Zagiri and added, "I do hope she will soon recover from whatever malady deprives us of her company this morning."

Zagiri performed her best impersonation of Anahid's blithe society smile. "Thank you for your sympathy, which I will certainly convey to my sister." While she was kicking Anahid for stranding her here alone. Where *was* she?

"Zagiri Savani will suit your plan, yes?" Madame Bardha said to Malkasani, with a little flick of her fingers toward Zagiri. Now the daughter—Yeva, was it?—frowned at Zagiri.

Malkasani laughed in that way she had, when you were not quite behaving properly but she was overlooking it this once. "It was less a plan than an idea, but I'm pleased it seems to suit your needs. Miss Savani," she added, turning to Zagiri, "Miss Bardha—"

"Yeva," the younger Northerner interrupted.

Which Malkasani ever so pleasantly ignored. "—is obviously too old to debut but lacks the knowledge to properly sponsor and present on her own. But perhaps in partnership with another young lady…" She trailed off, her smile suggesting that the rest was quite obvious.

As though Zagiri didn't have enough problems without this girl, who looked prickly as a puffer fish, constantly needling at her. Gripping tight to a polite smile, Zagiri looked around the party for someone she could argue was a far more suitable candidate.

An awful lot of people were looking over *here*, Zagiri realised. Gossiping about Anahid?

No, wait. They were *looking at the Northern ambassador*. Thinking the same things Zagiri had. About trade. About possibilities. About the opportunities that a reopened North might hold.

Maybe there *was* an opportunity here for Zagiri. Those who couldn't approach the ambassador openly might try to come via her daughter. And if Zagiri was standing next to that daughter at every party, *she'd* get to speak to a lot of people she wouldn't otherwise.

It felt like something Anahid would have come up with. Zagiri felt wildly proud of herself for managing it on her own.

"Thank you so much for your confidence," she said brightly. "I will do my best to help in any way I can."

"Good." Madame Bardha gave a satisfied nod, as if that were all settled, and waved a hand. "Play this game, get to know each other, yes?"

Miss Bardha heaved a sigh and hefted up one of the boxes from the games table. "Come on," she stated with ill grace, and marched away.

Zagiri gave a hurried farewell and followed. "Miss Bardha, can I—"

"Yeva," the girl snarled.

Well, fine, Zagiri wouldn't help then. Not that Miss Bardha seemed to need it. She lugged the box as capably as any Dockside lader, dropping it in the spreading late-summer shade of one of the plane trees and tipping the lid open with her foot—encased in a sensible leather boot that surprised Zagiri beneath that spill of skirts.

Miss Bardha—*Yeva*—planted hands on her hips, squaring her shoulders like she'd rather be chopping wood than scowling at the polished balls lying in their velvet-lined dips. "I don't suppose we throw these at each other." Her accent gave the words harsh edges.

Zagiri couldn't help a little snort of laughter. "Unfortunately not."

Yeva's eyes—nearly a match for her mother's, just a little closer to blue—darted quick to Zagiri, perhaps more assessing now than dismissive.

But before she could say anything more, a young azatan appeared at her side. He had a round, cheerful face, hair cut unfashionably short, and was managing to carry three silver goblets at the same time, each nearly full and sprinkled with colourful flower petals. "Quick, grab one before I spill them all," he said, eyes on the drinks until Yeva slipped one from between his fingers.

He was about their age, and something about him seemed familiar, but Zagiri didn't think she knew him personally. Then again, he was clearly growing out a trade-voyage haircut—shorn close to avoid hygiene problems—so he might have been away from Bezim for half a year or longer.

He turned to pass Zagiri a goblet, the silver flashing as bright as his smile. "Been roped in, have you?"

Apparently nothing like proper introductions were going to be taking place over here. Anahid would hate it; Zagiri made herself at home. "Beats playing with the old gulls." She tipped a nod to the venerable azatas casting their bocha balls a little distance away.

The azatan's smile tipped into a grin at that, and Zagiri felt a sudden jolt, as though her boot had come down on a wobbly roof tile.

Yeva snorted into her goblet, raising a little puff of petals. "No one refuses my mother, Balian," she said, as though it were an ongoing joke, and waved a hand at them. "You two know each other?"

Zagiri opened her mouth to seize the chance for introduction, but the azatan—Balian, apparently—got in first. "You're Zagiri Savani, aren't you? You were involved with all that business with Siyon Velo over the summer."

"*Oh,*" Yeva said, as though the haze had burned off the horizon and she now saw clearly. "Of course Mother wanted you, then. The Sorcerer is the one she's really here for."

"What?" Zagiri forgot about Balian and his pretty smile—well, no, but she put him at the edge of her vision for a moment. "Why would you be interested in him? Alchemy's no one's concern but Bezim's."

Yeva shrugged a shoulder. "Before, yes. It only works here, everyone complains. But this Sorcerer Velo changes things, doesn't he?"

Zagiri had no answer for that. She had no idea. Anahid's husband, Nihath, and all his alchemist cronies were full to brimming with enthusiasm about how Siyon had apparently made the planes stable and *clarified the modes of intention* and all sorts of other gibberish. Had things changed *that* much?

"What's he like?" Balian asked, dragging her attention back to him. Zagiri must have looked confused, because he explained: "Velo, I mean. I've been up in the North since spring and I missed it all. Sounds like it was thrilling, but also rather troubling."

Far from the first person who'd come prying to Zagiri about Siyon and everything that happened. But Balian didn't seem like he was looking for an angle to get something out of Siyon. His eyes were bright with curiosity. And *thrilling but also troubling* was very close to how Zagiri felt about it all. She hesitated over her usual dismissal.

One of the venerable azatas screamed.

Zagiri whirled around, fruit nectar spilling sticky from the goblet in her hand. The older azatas huddled together, shuffling back from where their polished wooden bocha balls were clustered together on the grass.

With *something* standing over them.

It wasn't solid. It almost wasn't *there*, save in the sensation of movement, of shadow, of storm cloud twisted into a body, a head, two arms. A breeze blew into Zagiri's face—*toward* the sea—and tugged at the loose curls around her face. She could almost see the figure better from the corner of her eye.

Yeva snatched up a ball from their bocha set and hurled it at the disturbance. It passed straight through, with no discernible reaction.

"Huh." Yeva edged back. "What is it?"

Now she asked?

But Zagiri thought she knew the answer. "Djinn," she whispered. It had to be, even if it wasn't swelling up or zapping anyone with lightning like in an opera. It was just looking around, its eyes glowing orbs in the impression of its face, but still wide and avid. Like a debutante at her first rehearsal.

"Djinn," Zagiri repeated, more firmly. "At least, I'm pretty sure it is. The only other one I've met wasn't so...airy."

"You've met another?" Balian sounded somewhere between incredulous and impressed.

Which she sort of liked, but now was *not* the time. Thinking of Tehroun had given Zagiri an idea. She reached for her hip, but of course she wasn't wearing her sabre. "Do we have any metal?"

Even as she asked, she lifted her other hand, still clutching the silly goblet of floral nectar.

The *silver* goblet.

It would have to do. "All right," Zagiri said as Balian tipped out his drink and shifted his grip on the stem of it. She eyed the djinn, who had crouched down now to prod in delight at a bocha ball. "You circle around that way. I'll go this way. Yeva, come from here. We surround it, and I'll—" She'd *what*?

Balian said, "Abjure and banish it?"

"This isn't an *opera*," Zagiri hissed. But what was it? Siyon had never even suggested something like this was *possible*. "I'll think of something."

The djinn was now...digging up some grass? Dirt came up in a strange little spiral, and one shadowed possibility of a hand closed around a tuft of green, which then lifted into the air.

Oh, Zagiri heard, she definitely heard it, but it wasn't a *sound* so much as a...thing that appeared in her head separate from her own thoughts.

She sidled a little closer, holding the goblet in front of her and feeling completely ridiculous about it. Yeva edged closer from her side, her weight low and arms out, as though she expected the djinn to make a break for it. Balian held his goblet almost like a cutlass, which Zagiri supposed made sense, if he'd learned bladework on a ship instead of the rooftops.

Zagiri thought she'd just shout for its attention, show it the silver goblet, and then they could—

The djinn vanished. Simply gone, as though it had never been there in the first place.

Except a divot had been carved out of the grass, a little dip of bare dirt in the perfectly even lawn. The azatas wailed behind a nearby tree. Shouting from across the lawn suggested the inquisitors were on their way from the Palace of Justice—too late to do anything but overreact.

Yeva straightened from her bear-stalking crouch. "What in all the stars and darkness was that?"

Zagiri had no idea, not really. The djinn had looked so *interested*. It had taken something. Before vanishing.

In her head, she heard Siyon saying, *Get in, load up, get out.*

Had that djinn been *delving*?

CHAPTER 5

By the time Anahid accepted the finalised, notarised, rolled-up, and ribbon-sealed record of the transfer of ownership of Sable House, the dawn bell was ringing, and only Selsan and, for some reason, the Khanate man Bo were still waiting with her in Stepan Zinedani's office.

Former office. It was hers now.

Stepan had stormed out as soon as he'd thrown down the pen after signing his name. After Bo nodded his satisfaction, and Sel gave Anahid a delighted quartet of parting cheek kisses, and both of them left, the supervising staff of Sable House filed in. Lejman, head of security, was tall, broad, and solid, with the dark skin of the Archipelago and his hair in dozens of narrow, beaded braids. Qorja, who introduced herself as the stage mistress, had wild curls, warm brown skin, and a lilting accent straight from the Storm Coast. Both of them looked old enough to be her parent, and Anahid felt even more out of her depth.

From them, Anahid learned that Stepan had taken with him the manager of the gaming floor, three of the bartenders, and a good half of the security staff—"Zinedani thugs," Lejman said dismissively, "but they'll need replacing if we're to open tonight."

Tonight. Open. *We.* She was a part of this. It was her House now.

Panic clenched its fist around Anahid again. She couldn't run a

Flowerhouse. It would be a scandal. It was uncouth. It was not at all the sort of thing she was supposed to do.

She wasn't supposed to play carrick for such stakes either, but she'd done it anyway.

Anahid opened her mouth to suggest that perhaps they not open tonight, while she figured out what on earth she was going to do about all of this, but stopped at the sight of another face peeking through the shell-bead curtain across the office door. It was the girl who'd been waiting on Stepan at the table. The apprentice Flower. Just a young woman who lived and worked here. Who depended on the House for her livelihood, like so many others.

Of course they couldn't shut down while Anahid had an attack of nerves.

"What needs to be done?" she asked instead.

Her intention was to authorise them to take care of the essential business. To keep things running while she calmed down and figured out what she should do next.

But as Qorja started outlining the operations of the House—the games and the refreshments, the public spaces and the smaller chambers and the private engagements, the Flowers and the serving staff and the clientele—Anahid couldn't help but grow fascinated. Everything fit together in systems as intricate as trade networks or social hierarchies.

Or, for that matter, the nuances of carrick. Much as Anahid might shape her play to entice her opponents into indiscretions, so Sable House arranged its entertainments so as best to part guests from their money—and ensure they wanted to return another night.

It was complex, and absolutely enthralling, and Anahid was halfway through a tour of the House before she realised she was *far* too engaged with this.

She absolutely couldn't run Sable House. No matter how much her fingers itched to pick up the cards and play.

The upper levels of the House had been a warren of private rooms, and merely walking down those corridors had made Anahid's face heat, though curiosity tugged at her too. She'd considered, once or twice, as she left the District after a particularly profitable evening, about spending some of her winnings on a Flower's company. To see what all the fuss was about. But it had seemed so impersonal. She'd felt more of a thrill…

Well, she'd felt more thrilled facing down Vartan Xhanari in her parlour than considering paying for congress with a handsome Flower.

Downstairs, she was familiar with the black-pillared gaming hall, but there were also three well-stocked bars, an enormous kitchen, smaller entertaining rooms, and a large public dining hall with a velvet-draped stage in one corner.

"For Flower Night auctions," Qorja said casually.

It cut through the flurry of Anahid's other feelings. She would have ended up on that stage if the cards had fallen differently.

Anahid did not regret taking Stepan for everything he had.

The sun was well risen before she left Sable House, with its key tucked into her sash and her mind in turmoil. She had never seen the District at this hour, when the last dregs of the night before overlapped with the more prosaic business of the day. The narrow streets weren't quiet, but entryways were being swept, not full of enticements, and the balconies were draped with airing carpets rather than glittering Flowers.

As Anahid slipped quietly toward the gate, a flicker of shadow down an arcade drew her eye. There was no one there, merely the echo of a merry laugh and a faint hiss of scaled flesh.

Anahid hesitated a moment and called softly, "Laxmi?" The demon had lurked in this way more than once, before Siyon bound her not to stalk the city streets without him or his express instructions. But this laugh sounded brighter than the harpy's insinuating chuckle.

In any case, it didn't come again, and Anahid hurried on her way. She wanted to get home before too many people were awake enough to spot her and ask questions.

With the townhouse door firmly closed between her and the Avenues, Anahid leaned against it and sighed. Another reason she couldn't possibly keep the House. Was she going to scuttle home every morning like a schoolgirl late to class?

How many sensible reasons would she have to layer up before the scales of her heart stopped tipping stubbornly in the wrong direction?

"Oh," a voice said from the top of the stairs. Nihath peered down at her, over the open book he was holding and the glasses perched on his nose for reading it. "It's only you."

Anahid dragged her headscarf off, the pins snarling at her hair in points of pain. "Yes," she said. "Only me."

"I thought it might be Siyon." He turned back toward his study, then paused and frowned at her.

For a moment, Anahid thought perhaps he might say, *Isn't it rather late to be getting back?* Or even, *You look a little bothered about something.*

Instead, he said, "You didn't see him out there, did you? He was going to drop by."

Anahid squeezed her eyes shut and pinched at the bridge of her nose. "No," she sighed. "I didn't see him."

When she looked up again, Nihath was gone.

I'm married, she'd said to Stepan Zinedani. But she wasn't, not in any way that she'd so badly wanted when she'd spent three years seeking an alliance. Someone who knew her and valued her, Anahid had wanted. A partnership.

She'd spent half a year making the best of it. She'd spent the last two months finally thinking of alternatives. But none of the azatans of society looked any more appealing than they had when she was husband hunting, and in any case, changing one fish for another wouldn't get you a trumpet instead.

For a moment, she wished she could talk about it all with Tahera Danelani. Who'd laughed merrily and tucked her hand into Anahid's arm and known how it felt, to thrill to the cards in your hand.

But Anahid had burned that barge to the waterline. It would not float again.

Voices came from belowstairs, and Anahid pulled herself together. Stood up straight and folded her headscarf between her palms, gathering the pins. Not that Nura, the housekeeper, was inclined to gossip, but Anahid had her pride.

It wasn't Nura who came up the stairs, bounding two at a time and grinning to see her. "Ana!" Siyon cried.

"Oh." She hooked her headscarf through her sash, beside the heavy key to Sable House. "Nihath was just looking for you."

"He can wait." Siyon brushed that aside. "Are you only getting home now? Have you been carousing all night?"

He was one to talk; Anahid could smell the rakia on his breath as he came closer, and the collar of his plain brown coat was askew. "Are you still coming in by the yard like a delivery boy?" she demanded right back.

He laughed and waggled his eyebrows suggestively. "Must have been a good night at the tables."

Anahid couldn't help laughing. "You have no idea." She couldn't tell anyone, she absolutely couldn't let word get out, but this was Siyon. She fished the blackened-iron key out of the sash of her dress. "I won Sable House."

Siyon's jaw dropped, his eyes wide. "You—what? The whole House?" He looked at the key, and a cloud of uncertainty passed across the sun of his flattering amazement. "Isn't that a Zinedani House?"

"Was!" Anahid said, bright with false confidence, and then, "I know." She folded her fingers around the key, as though she could hide it. She *did* know, but she'd passed that fact by. "I know. I'll...sell it back, I suppose. I just wanted to hurt Stepan so badly."

"Shame," Siyon said lightly. "You'd make an excellent House Mistress."

That struck a spark in her stomach, where the fascination of all the House's details still lay like dry kindling. "Don't be silly," Anahid said harshly. "What do I know about running a Flowerhouse?"

Siyon gave her a skeptical look. "What did you know about carrick at the start of the summer? What did you know about managing the inqs before you danced Xhanari to your tune and straight out of his job? Of course you could run a Flowerhouse. Probably better than any Zinedani could."

"Thanks," Anahid said, keeping her voice flat. Trying to hide the way his words buoyed her up. "But the question's entirely academic. I can't possibly do it. It would be an utter scandal."

Siyon snorted. "An azata making money? Oh no, how awful. What?"

He didn't understand. "It's not the money, it's how you get it. The azatani, especially of the first tier, are traders. We aren't shopkeepers. We don't provide services."

"Plenty of you own factories over the river," Siyon pointed out.

"Own, perhaps," Anahid allowed. "We don't run them."

"So you *could* own the House and get someone else to run it," Siyon said, as though he was working his way through it, watching her face all the while. An understanding smile quirked at one corner of his mouth. "But where would be the fun in that?"

"I might as well sell it back," Anahid agreed. "Don't tangle with the barons, right?"

"Right." Siyon nodded, but his eyes had gone a little distant. Anahid caught his eye, lifting a querying eyebrow, and he flashed a smile. "Sorry. Had a run-in of my own the other night. With Midnight."

"Midnight?" The name still gave Anahid a little thrill of fear, left over from her childhood. She'd been all of four when the baron wars had come to their grisly end. But the tales lingered, bloodthirsty enough to thrill even azatani children. *Midnight will come for you,* they'd taunted one another.

"What did he want?" she asked.

"I'm not entirely sure," Siyon admitted. "I didn't really ask. Mostly I wanted him to fuck off."

"Fair." Anahid would likely have panicked herself.

"He said..." Siyon frowned, like he was still worrying at the problem. "He said the awakening is upon us."

"Awakening?" Anahid repeated. "Of what?"

"Yeah," Siyon said, slow and considering. "That's the question, isn't it? He asked if I could feel the quickening. If I felt it in my dreams."

"And do you?" It seemed the obvious question.

"I didn't think so. But there's been..." Siyon trailed off, considering again. "Something. Darkness. Stone. Something." He pulled a face. "I thought it was just that I wasn't used to sleeping in Auntie Geryss's old apartment. It probably is. Or bloody Laxmi."

"I thought you forbade her from visiting dreams she wasn't specifically invited into," Anahid pointed out.

"That's other people," Siyon clarified. "She said I don't count."

And Anahid could imagine the harpy's toothy grin as she said it. "Was she out and about tonight? I thought I saw her on my way home."

"Really?" Siyon smirked. "She does like the District. All that lust and desperation and make-believe. You know there's an alleytale that there's a naga down there? Supposedly she came over with a Storm Coast priestess fleeing an over-amorous chieftain's son, and you only meet her if you've won big." He pointed at her. "Which you have."

It seemed very appropriate for there to be a naga in the District— beautiful, strong, just unfamiliar enough to be alluring, full of prom- ises and danger. But such things were myth, not reality. "If the District had a naga, they'd make her the centrepiece of a spectacle." She waved a hand at his laughter. "Oh, go upstairs and see Nihath. I'm going to have some breakfast, and then I'm going to sleep."

"Hey." He snapped his fingers, pointing back at her even as he climbed the stairs. "Could I borrow one of your Flowers, before you hand them back? They use all sorts of alchemical charms and creams and stuff, right? I have a thing I'm working on that I want to test."

"They're *people*, Siyon," she chided. "But you can come and ask. Politely."

He grinned again and disappeared up the stairs.

Leaving Anahid feeling lighter. But that light only served to illu- minate the empty room of her life. She wasn't without friends, even if they were unorthodox. But who was she? What could she do?

Playing carrick wasn't quite enough. She wanted something more. She wanted something that mattered. It gnawed at her stomach like hunger.

Anahid laid a hand over it—on the hard shape of the key behind her sash—and for a moment, just a moment, she let herself want it.

There were a lot more people in Nihath's study than Siyon was expect- ing at half past sunrise. When he'd told Nihath he'd try to come by, he'd presumed it would be the two of them and, inevitably, Tehroun on the sofa apparently asleep right up until he said something weird.

Instead, there were three azatani practitioners on the sofa—Siyon recognised their faces but couldn't remember their names—all talking over one another. Master Unja and Miss Plumm—who Siyon did remember from his doomed attempt to join the Summer Club—were standing by the bookcase jabbing fingers at various spines as though that was all they needed to reference the contents in their heated argument. He definitely recognised the azata sitting at the desk, with her stately bearing and stern greying eyebrows and a heavily beaded scarf knotted over her hair in an old-fashioned style. Azata Markani— alchemist of the Summer Club, member of the Council, and under-secretary of the Working Group on Oblique Methods, overseeing the practice of the Art in Bezim.

And also, since Othissa's death, Jaleh's new master. Siyon was sure Jaleh hated it, answering to an azata, even if only for another season while she prepared her master working. She'd never admit it out loud, not to him. At Markani's elbow, she paused in her notebook scribbling to glare at Siyon, as though she could hear his thoughts.

"Ah, there you are," Nihath said from Markani's other side. He set a finger on the book he was perusing and considered Siyon over his spectacles.

Siyon was struck all over again at how much Nihath Joddani had unwound in recent months. His gold-embroidered evening longvest was half unbuttoned, and his dark curls were unoiled and growing overlong. Perfection, it seemed, didn't matter as much in the face of discovery.

Or maybe it was just that Anahid wasn't keeping him in line anymore.

Nihath brandished the open book and stated: "We can't afford to neglect the traditions of the Old Kingdoms."

Siyon blinked. "I don't know anything about the traditions of the Old Kingdoms."

"Because they don't *work*," one of the azatans on the sofa snapped, turning away from his argument with the other two. "It's merely superstition and folklore being passed off as rigorous investigation because they felt *left out*."

"The practice in Bezim derives originally from the Kingdom exiles—" Nihath started sententiously.

Another of the sofa azatans cut him off: "And I'm telling you, superstition is not as easily dismissed as you seem to—"

"Not this hysteria *again*," Markani said quellingly.

But the azatan wouldn't be quelled. "It's not only mud medallions and candles in lower city windows for the ghost of Papa Badrosani!" he objected, bouncing to his feet.

Siyon was astonished to hear some azatan in his lace and longvest even *mentioning* a mud medallion. It was a fisherclan ritual, supposedly protection against drowning and mermaids and other perils of the open sea; a coin-sized pendant of sun-baked mud would be hanging around Siyon's neck right now if he hadn't fled Dockside too young to make one.

The azatan was still going, shaking a finger like a scolding schoolmaster. "And if the revolutionary elements harness this fear—"

An azatan on the couch made a rude and dismissive noise. "It's agitating laders in Dockside. It happens every year; stop getting your knickers in a twist."

"Zas," Markani said from the desk in a tone of voice that cut through their bickering. "None of the reports of uncanny happenings can be verified. It's the effect of the events of the summer upon the impressionable minds of the less educated and more excitable. Not," she added smoothly, turning a look upon Siyon, "that I'm suggesting this is in any way *your* fault, Master Velo."

Somehow, when she put it like that, he rather got the impression that she *was*.

"Weird shit's happening?" Siyon asked. Unverified, she said, but what did that matter? Maybe *he* was less educated and more excitable, but he was also more willing to look outside the bounds of what others—especially azatani—accepted. After all, *he* was seeing strange things—the entire room was a tumultuous riot of storming Aethyreal energy sparking with Empyre and Abyss every time someone spoke—but he didn't think that's what anyone was talking about.

Can you not see the rising tide? Midnight had asked.

"The inquisitors are receiving superstitious reports," Markani corrected.

"Alleytales," Jaleh added. "Mermaids in the river, lights in the northern swamps, Papa B breaking up knife fights and dispensing justice, ghostly porters in the university colleges."

"A naga in the Flower district?" Siyon suggested, thinking of what Anahid had just mentioned. He'd been *joking*.

Jaleh shrugged. "That sort of thing."

The awakening, Midnight had said. *The quickening*.

Siyon wanted to dismiss everything he'd said. He certainly didn't want to get involved with any of the barons, and especially not Midnight. But Aethyr was spiralling around every scratch of Jaleh's pencil in her notebook, and the bickering over at the sofa was an endless sparking of Abyss and Empyre.

And maybe Siyon *did* feel something. He wouldn't have said a quickening. He would have said that the energy all around them felt like liquid sloshing in a bottle, like the bilge in a boat underway, constantly shifting in ways he wasn't quite expecting. Sometimes he caught himself wanting to put out a hand to steady himself, but what on?

Something was happening. Siyon had come here—had agreed to Nihath's invitation—partly to ask about it. But he wasn't mentioning his strange visions in front of this lot. Not when Miss Plumm was already watching him steadily from across the room like she'd quite fancy getting *him* into her workroom and experimenting on him. And not with Markani here, like the steady gaze of the Council looking over his shoulder.

They already thought Siyon was too much trouble to be allowed any say in matters. He wasn't letting them find out he was *seeing things*.

These weren't his people. They never had been. And even if they were willing to embrace him now, it didn't mean they understood anything of what was happening to him.

How could they? They weren't the Power. That was him.

Only him.

"My friends," Markani said, setting her hands on the desk and pushing up to standing, "thank you all for a most stimulating discussion, but the morning is advancing and some of us must be in Council at the Glory bell."

That set the azatans to scrambling off the couch and squawking about lateness. All three of them hustled out with hurried farewells.

Maybe they were all on the Council. It wouldn't surprise Siyon. There seemed to be hundreds of members. It was part of why the real governance was split up into smaller committees, though the whole thing still seemed utterly ponderous. But it certainly kept any one person from controlling affairs, and that seemed to be exactly what the azatani who'd overthrown the Last Duke wanted in their city.

None of it had been Siyon's problem, until now.

Last out, moving with the unhurried grace of a woman of experience and power, Azata Markani crooked a finger at Siyon. "A word, Velo, if you please."

Or even if he didn't.

She turned aside for a moment to speak with Jaleh, who was tucking her notebook away inside a satchel much like Siyon's. "Follow up those points for me, please," Markani said. "And check on the progress of the steeping silver grass, comparing against both the Negedic and Eastern traditions."

Jaleh nodded and flicked one last hard glance at Siyon, then left.

Markani turned back to Siyon with a serene smile, like some maternal relation about to bestow wisdom upon him. "An apprentice is a great gift," she said. "You should consider taking one."

Not this again. "And you know just the person to suggest, right?" Siyon was getting fed up with alchemists trying to slide in their cousin as Siyon's apprentice, to get secondhand access to his secrets. As though *Siyon* had any idea how he did anything.

Markani's smile suggested they were both in on this joke together. "I do happen to have a nephew at a loose end, now that he's been dismissed from his clerkship. But he'd make a terrible apprentice; he has no aptitude for the Art at all. A secretary, perhaps. Honestly, he made a terrible clerk as well; I'm not surprised at the outcome. But I wonder if something a little more unusual might prompt him to actually pay attention.

And you…" She paused, looking Siyon up and down in all his crumpled, unshaven glory. "You could perhaps use some additional assistance in coming to grips with the full responsibilities of your new position."

That stung, and all the more because Siyon couldn't honestly deny it. He was out of his depth, and flailing, in more ways than one. There was so much he didn't know—not about the other planes, but about the very city he lived in.

It didn't matter. Siyon wasn't letting some azatani brat stand at his shoulder and report his every move back to a councillor. Even one as connected to alchemy as Azata Markani.

"I'm doing fine," he declared, baring his teeth.

Markani sighed. "Velo, my only interest is in furthering the standing of alchemy in this city. This is difficult while you are a walking advertisement for carelessness. There must be some way—"

Fortunately, before Siyon could interrupt and tell her exactly what she could do with her interests, the front door crashed open downstairs.

"Hey!" a voice shouted, high and full of some emotion—perhaps panic, perhaps excitement.

Siyon knew that voice. He yanked the study door open, Markani following him out into the corridor, as feet thundered up the stairs two at a time. Zagiri crested the staircase, one hand holding her filmy blue dress up out of her way and the other hauling at the banister.

"There's been—" She had to stop to drag in a breath. "Djinn. In the gardens."

"What?" Siyon gasped, with Azata Markani's voice echoing his.

"Just—" Zagiri burst her fingers open, like a flower or a sudden puff of air. "Just there. Then gone."

"A djinn?" Nihath came out of the study behind them, shouldering the others aside in his excitement. "A manifestation? Or a projection? I must see this. Tehroun!" He hurried off up the corridor.

"I think," Zagiri said, stretching her side with a faint wince. "I think it might have been delving. It grabbed some grass and left."

"I need to get to the Palace," Markani snapped, her priorities clearly more practical. "You, girl, can you run to the annex and—"

"The inqs are already there," Zagiri interrupted. Her breath was evening out; it wasn't that far from the gardens, for a bravi, though clearly the dress and silly slippers hadn't helped.

"Fuck," Markani said, a neat little snip of a word. "Right. You—" She pointed to Zagiri. "Come with me. You lot—" and she waved a hand toward Siyon.

"*I'm* going down to the gardens to see this," Siyon stated. "Are you kidding me? A djinn?"

"I'm not going anywhere near it!" Master Unja declared dramatically. "What if it's imbalanced? What if there's some sort of open passage between planes? What if—"

"Great," Siyon cut him off. "More for me."

He strode for the stairs before anyone could intervene. After all, he was the Power of the Mundane. He was here to deal with the weird fuckery.

If he wasn't good for anything else, at least there was this.

CHAPTER 6

"Me?" Zagiri gaped. Lomena Markani, member of the Grand Council and undersecretary of the Working Group on Oblique Methods, was asking *her* to come along?

"Yes," Markani stated shortly, and strode off.

Zagiri scrambled after her, back down the stairs and out the door again. (No sign of Siyon; had he gone out the *back*? Was he still doing that?) The others from the garden party were streaming down the avenue now, hurrying in little wide-eyed clusters to spread the wild gossip even further.

"You saw this?" Markani snapped over her shoulder. She had a good turn of speed for a woman well past her prime, but Zagiri could keep pace, even while she tried to tidy her hair and straighten her dress after sprinting to get here.

"Yes," she answered. "I was there, at the party. The djinn appeared out of thin air, in the middle of a bocha game. I thought perhaps we could contain it with the silver goblets from the party, but it vanished again before we could really try."

"Silver," Markani repeated, glancing sidelong at Zagiri as they turned a corner. "Why did you think that?"

"Uh, just something I'd heard about." Zagiri probably shouldn't admit it was something she'd heard about from her brother-in-law and his fallen-djinn lover.

Especially not to a woman who had a lot of influence in certain parts of the Council and might be able to recommend Zagiri to a clerkship position otherwise closed off to her.

They crossed into the parkland, taking the most direct route to the Palace, which fortunately meant skirting well clear of where Polinna Andani's breakfast garden party had dissolved into a scrum of inquisitors, nosy onlookers, and Andani serving staff trying to clear away their mistress's silverware before anyone made off with it.

Markani's gaze slid from that mess to Zagiri. Who squashed the urge to smooth her hair again. She wished she'd kept her net gloves on, except they were sticky from fruit nectar. Then again, if she did look a little disarranged, she had plenty of good reasons. "You were involved in all that business over the summer, weren't you?" Markani demanded.

"Ah" was all Zagiri could manage for a moment. *I think we'd best try not to mention it*, Anahid had said, and Zagiri could see the wisdom. While she was trying to suggest she was responsible and respectable enough to be trusted with a clerkship was not the time to be reminding people of how she'd fallen off a major city monument and only survived through the possibly sorcerous intervention of Siyon Velo. Let alone any of the rest of it.

"In the thick of it, actually," Markani continued. She didn't sound critical so much as thoughtful, though Zagiri couldn't see her face. "Know Velo well, do you?"

Sometimes there was nothing for it but to make the attack and see if it worked out for you. "Quite well, actually, yes."

Markani turned just enough for Zagiri to see the edge of an approving smile. "That's what I thought. Stick with me."

They hurried up the wide front steps of the Palace of Justice.

Zagiri had been in here a lot in the past few weeks, visiting this councillor or that coordinator to ask humbly after the chance of a position. (And being told, in all cases, that they were quite full up for this year, but her name could go on the waiting list.) Every time she stepped into the entrance hall, it still stole her breath for a moment.

The entire building was grand—built by the Lyraec Empire in golden sandstone as their administrative headquarters and a symbol of their glory and domination, and then later, after the empire crumbled, commandeered by the ducal family as their palace before the azatani seized control of their own governance, thank you very much. Many of the salons and galleries had been carved up into offices and committee rooms, but the entrance hall still served its original purpose: to astonish and humble anyone who came through it.

The hall rose through five floors of open space—fringed by golden-railed galleries where clerks and councillors hurried about their business—to an enormous dome that soared like a sky of burnished bronze. Zagiri had heard Nihath describe the dome as the centre of the universe—the very place where the planes came together in crux—though that was far less interesting to her than what else the building held.

Power. And the chance to change things for the better. If she could just get a grip on it.

Markani didn't pause, striding to the grand marble staircase that curved up the outer edge of the hall. Zagiri hurried in her wake, slippers hushing against the mosaic floor that depicted the mythical founding of Bezim, with the newly arrived exiles from the Old Kingdoms (now the New Republic) casting out the shadows and snakes from the primitive caves on the crag.

"We'll need to move fast," Markani stated as Zagiri drew level with her elbow again. "I heard you've been knocking on doors after a clerkship; is that a whimsy or a serious endeavour?"

Zagiri gritted her teeth against the pang of embarrassment that hooked into her heart; how much of the Council knew she'd been scrambling around for whatever she could find? "I'm late to the realisation that I want to be involved, but I'm serious, azata."

"Good," Markani said crisply. "Because we're going to need a person with your sort of knowledge who isn't already tangled up in someone's pocket."

"We?" Zagiri repeated, with a little flutter of hope.

As though in response, Markani lifted a hand and her voice to a higher level. "Syrah!"

Zagiri looked up and clutched the golden banister against a sudden dizzy moment. Above them, a woman turned at the gallery railing, blindingly white in a patch of morning sunlight. Syrah *Danelani*. The prefect herself.

She waved a hand, and the two people standing with her drew off down the gallery as the prefect waited at the railing. "Lomena," she said, low but warm, as Markani came up the stairs with Zagiri half a step behind. Azata Danelani's gaze flicked over her, from Zagiri's disordered hair to her grass-stained slippers.

"Miss Zagiri Savani witnessed an interesting phenomenon in the parkland just now," Markani said, by way of introduction.

That drew a little snort from the prefect. "Interesting," she repeated, dry as Empyre. "It's going to *interest* up the whole bloody season, if we let it."

Markani settled against the railing with the prefect, close enough to speak in hushed tones. "We can hardly expect the Pragmatics to have been sleeping in this morning."

"I don't think they ever sleep." The prefect folded her hands in that way that Anahid sometimes did, as though she needed to hold on to her own fingers so they didn't do something violent. "Rowyani is actively avoiding me, so I assume he's planning an ambush in session."

There were too many councillors for Zagiri to remember all their names, but she knew that one. Azatan Matevon Rowyani was a pillar of the Pragmatic faction of councillors, who would prefer to see all matters of the city working in service to "the greater good of Bezim." In practice, that seemed to mean ensuring the azatani were able to make money off every opportunity.

Zagiri had *not* been knocking on any of their doors in her hunt for a clerkship. The only way the Pragmatics would reform anything, especially alchemy, would be to ensure greater azatani control.

Markani nodded, but she didn't look chagrined. In fact, if Zagiri had to lay money on it, she'd say the old woman looked a little smug. "This could be the chance we were talking about," she said, so quietly that Zagiri could barely hear her.

Azata Danelani frowned sharply, strong eyebrows knitting

together. "How so? They'll come in hard on Oblique Methods. And your bloody secretary will play right into their hands by bleating about due process and the technical definitions, and they'll whisk half the functions away into Indeterminate Planning by the end of the session."

Zagiri could barely keep up with this. The Working Group on Oblique Methods was the committee of which Markani was under-secretary, overseeing the practice of alchemy, and the Indeterminate Planning Committee was...no wait, she knew this. Strategic oversight of miscellaneous city resources not specifically covered by other jurisdictions? The vagueness of its remit had confused Zagiri during her research, but now she realised that it might also allow widespread meddling. If a faction controlled it strongly.

"They've already undermined Oblique Methods too severely," Markani said in a tone of disagreement. "This is an emergency, isn't it? We can—"

Danelani shook her head. "Too soon after summer. I'm still on shaky ground with the old guard; they think I should have a tighter grip on things. And one djinn at a garden party hardly constitutes an emergency."

"It could," Markani countered, "if it's merely the latest incident of new and unexplained planar rearrangements."

The prefect frowned at her. "You want to lean further on all these superstitious witterings and alleytales? Now, with the usual autumnal labour problems in Dockside as well?" Markani said nothing, merely lifting her eyebrows, and Danelani pursed her lips and hummed in an unconvinced fashion, and then she was looking straight at Zagiri. "So what *did* happen in the garden this morning, Miss Savani?"

For a single, panicked moment, the only words on Zagiri's tongue were *I threatened a djinn with a silver goblet*, but fortunately she swallowed them. This might be her only chance to impress both of these powerful women. "It looked curious, Madame Prefect. The djinn, I mean. And it took some grass with it, when it left. I think it was delving. Ah, that means—"

"I know what it means," the prefect snapped, her eyebrows drawing tighter, and Zagiri remembered belatedly that Siyon had breached the Abyss at Enkin Danelani's bedside, with the prefect herself holding the tether. Not, for once, to bring back ingredients for alchemy but, rather worse, to bring back Laxmi. "I thought that was what *we* did to *other* planes."

"Things," Markani said mildly, "may have changed."

That hung over them for a moment, echoing with her true meaning: *Siyon* might have changed things.

"Fuck," Syrah Danelani muttered, quiet and precise. "I wish I'd never heard of Siyon bloody Velo."

Zagiri didn't think it wise to mention that he probably felt the same.

"As I said," Markani continued smoothly, "this is an emergency, so we can use this as an opportunity to break off a task force. I can have a proposed membership to you by the time you rise to speak, and we—"

"No." Syrah stared off into space with thoughts turning like cogs behind her composed face. "No, not a task force. A select committee."

Now Zagiri was completely lost. But Markani looked disapproving. "If you break outside the usual structures, there will be a lot of potential for things to go wrong."

"That's why I'll be overseeing it personally," the prefect answered smoothly. She seemed settled now, serene as a swan, and just as capable of defending her territory. "And I can get Velo in there personally. I'll have you as an anchor, Lomena, for your expertise, though I imagine I'll need to let Rowyani choose the other anchor as a sop to his ego."

Markani's frown deepened. "I don't like this. It's too risky."

"You don't have to like it," Danelani replied. "You just have to do it. I'll have that proposed membership from you, quick as you can." Her gaze fell on Zagiri, and she smiled like a papercut, thin and sharp. "And I'll have the girl as well."

"What?" Zagiri squeaked. Couldn't help it.

Syrah Danelani raised her eyebrows. "That is, if you're willing to become special clerk to a select committee chaired by the prefect herself, for the emergency response to and management of planar breaches?"

There was a ringing in Zagiri's ears and a fizzing in her blood. She couldn't believe this was happening. She didn't know quite what *was* happening. But she knew the obvious answer.

"Yes, Madame Prefect."

Half the detritus of the garden party had been left behind. None of the *expensive* things, of course—the silverware and servingware and linen had all been vehemently tidied away by serving staff aghast at the notion of just anyone seeing their mistress's fine things. But the folding tables had been left where they stood or, in one case where people had panicked, lay.

Everything was overlaid, to Siyon's sight, with a wild and still-skittering array of Aethyreal emanations in shades of silver and pink and a pale, glittering turquoise. Aside from the headache knotting up his skull, it was rather beautiful.

The inquisitors had managed to be a little useful by sweeping the eager onlookers aside and keeping the site mostly clear. Of course, getting through the inquisitor perimeter was its own sort of difficult. Nihath got nowhere protesting that he was a practitioner and, moreover, an azatan.

"So's half the rest of this lot, za." The inq waved a hand at those avidly peering past the grey-uniformed cordon. "My orders say no one through until further notice."

"This," Nihath declared, tugging Siyon forward, "is the Sorcerer himself."

Siyon wished they'd stop calling him that.

The inq eyed him. "Nah, the Sorcerer's got a fancy purple coat and a pet harpy."

A crackling snicker curled down the back of Siyon's neck. Siyon muttered, "Do *not*." He didn't add to that. Laxmi might have to follow his orders, but she could be remarkably imaginative—and vindictive—in getting around them when she was piqued. And nothing piqued her like being ordered.

Meanwhile, Nihath continued his argument with the inq, who leaned back and hollered for his sergeant.

When she arrived, she was very familiar. "I expected you to be right in the middle of this already," Olenka remarked. She shot a filthy look at Tehroun, who sidled a little farther behind Nihath. Both of them were fallen beings, but their different origin planes seemed more significant than their shared experiences.

Laxmi's presence prickled across Siyon's shoulders, like the tips of phantom talons. The demon wasn't fallen, but here in fulfillment of a series of promises between her, her mistress the Demon Queen, and Siyon. She retained all her native dislike for Empyreal creatures, fallen or otherwise. Or maybe it was her dislike of anyone who thought they knew better than her.

All told, Siyon had enough trouble with extra-planar beings without *more* of them popping up in the middle of azatani parties.

"Disappointing as it is," Olenka said to the inquisitor, "this is indeed the Power of the Mundane. Might as well let him in to have a look. And his little friends too."

The inquisitor frowned at Siyon, as though he was reneging on some duty by not looking fancy enough, but let them past.

Closer to the innocuous divot in the grass, the air was a thick Aethyreal soup. Nihath kicked it up heedlessly like froth at the beach as he strode through. The emanations curled around Tehroun, following in his wake, in patterns that almost seemed to make sense until they shivered apart and slipped away.

Can you not see the rising tide?

Siyon scrubbed at his eyes—and the Aethyreal swirls were still there, overlaid by more prosaic dancing spots. "Laxmi, what *is* this?"

That sensation of claws again, and then there *was* a tugging at the collar of his shirt, as a large black lizard crawled out onto his shoulder. Out of the corner of his eye, Siyon saw her taste the air with a vividly red tongue and blink her golden eyes. "How the fuck should I know?" she asked. "Not my business how the djinn want to lark about, is it?"

"But it was a djinn. Not like that one—" Siyon waved at Tehroun, who was now lolling on his back, staring up at the bright blue autumn sky as though enraptured. "An actual djinn. Here. Like you."

"Nothing's like me," Laxmi purred, but the pinprick press of her claws shifted uneasily. "*You* brought me here," she pointed out.

For better or worse, yes, he had. "I think we'd have heard if someone at the party was doing deals with the Djinn Sultan."

But Zagiri had said she thought the djinn had been delving. It fit, didn't it? The djinn appeared out of nothing, looked around, grabbed a handful of stuff, and vanished again.

Was that what Siyon had looked like, delving the other planes?

"So it was delving," he said out loud.

"Can't do that to the Mundane," Laxmi said, quick as reflex, and sounding grumpy about it. As though she'd tried and was annoyed (as always) to be thwarted.

To the *Mundane*, she said. "You can do it to the other planes?"

No lizard had ever made such a scornful noise. "Of course. Did you think you were *special*, hopping over planar barriers like an imp stealing lies from the orchard?" Laxmi giggled. "The angels get *so* annoyed at the tiniest infringement."

Yes, Siyon could attest to that. He stared at the divot in the grass, which he could barely see for all the Aethyreal emanations, thick as the worst sea mists of midwinter. Waving his hand around did nothing to clear them; unsurprising, given they were hardly physical. He stepped closer, tensing as the tangle of energy crawled over him, even though there was nothing to feel.

Can you not feel the quickening? Midnight had asked.

On a horrible instinct, Siyon reached for his pocket and hesitated. He'd left the little dragon figurine with Tein Geras, in the Bracken safe house. He *had*.

And yet, when he laid a hand on the pocket of his trousers, there was a lump. Small and hard and with the muffled press of sharp points.

The bloody thing was back in his pocket. Unease coiled around the back of Siyon's neck like the ghost of Laxmi's tail. He shivered, and the Aethyr gusted aside enough to show Nihath, fishing that bronze-bound lens of his out of a pocket to peer down at the divot anew.

Siyon had forgotten he had that thing. He'd always used it to assess the various things that Siyon had fetched for him from the other planes. "What can you see?" he asked, on a leap of hope.

Maybe he wasn't the only one who could see the planar emanations after all.

Nihath looked up at him, one eye made comically large through the slightly nacreous lens. "Nothing at all!" He beamed as Siyon's briefly buoyed heart sank again. "Isn't it astonishing? There's no residue whatsoever, not like that which lingers upon delved material from its natural plane. Which suggests that everything that *came* with our visiting friend also *returned*."

Tehroun, still lying on his back, waved a hand in the air above him. "There's a memory," he suggested, barely above a whisper. "There's an echo when the voice itself is gone."

Laxmi sighed heavily. "Djinn," she said disparagingly.

"Zagiri suggested it was delving," Siyon ventured. "You told me once that it wasn't a one-way thing."

"There are ways between the planes." Tehroun fluttered a hand— he was an example of the fact. "But not delving. The Mundane won't hold still. At least—" He tilted his head, pale hair tangling in the grass. "That's the way it used to be."

Used to be. When the Mundane was out of balance with the other planes. There'd been no Power to hold it steady. But now there was Siyon. He changed things.

"It would be better to verify our suppositions." Nihath looked at Siyon with that eerily enhanced lens. "Could *you* delve across and check? Or have you felt a difference in moving between the planes since…" He waved a hand, as though everything that had happened over the summer was somewhere off to his left.

Siyon glanced around by reflex, but thanks to the inquisitors, it was only the three of them—four, counting Laxmi, who already knew what Siyon was reluctant to have overheard by anyone else.

In fact, Laxmi was cackling on his shoulder. "Yeah, you could say there's a difference."

Nihath lifted an eyebrow, so Siyon explained. "I can't delve at all. Not any of the planes. I've never been able to reach the Aethyreal plane, and I lost the Empyreal over the summer. Now I can't reach the Abyssal either."

"Ah." Nihath didn't seem bothered or disappointed by this new piece of information, just intrigued. "As the Power of the Mundane, I suppose it would make sense that you were rather innately attached to this plane. How interesting. *I* could go, but it would be my first attempt and thus no useful comparison can be provided."

He was the same wordy and pompous Nihath, even if he was now fixated on discovering things for himself rather than comparing the world against the framework laid down by Kolah Negedi. Good timing, as the world revealed itself to be larger and stranger than ever.

Thinking of it, Siyon's hand drifted back to his pocket, pressing a fingertip to the sharp point of the dragon's wing. "Hey, do you know anything about Midnight?"

He felt ridiculous about the question as soon as it was out of his mouth. Even more ridiculous as Nihath tugged the lens out of his eye socket in order to frown more fulsomely, like he couldn't see *how* this could possibly be relevant. "I am assuming you have not descended to the astrological lunacies of the Kalyrii twins and are referring instead to the criminal personage. But however skilled his underlings are said to be in the manufacture of recreational elixirs, there's no value there for the consideration of *proper* art."

Same old snobbery. Recreational substances had always been beyond Siyon's precision or equipment, but he didn't see the difference between the tinctures for mood improvement that some azatani acquired from discreet shopkeepers, and the little pick-me-ups Midnight's runners peddled. Save, perhaps, for the price.

Nihath waved an airy hand, his attention already back on the grass, and added: "And I'm sure those practitioners who claim to have lost their apprentices to his organisation are merely covering their own inadequacies in instruction."

That prickled uneasily at Siyon. "Wait, what? Lost apprentices?"

"Hmm?" Nihath blinked at him again. "Oh, yes. One or two, over the years. Just stories, you understand."

The Alchemist had been just a story, until it was Siyon. He wasn't sure he trusted *just* when it came to stories anymore. And especially not when Midnight was already proving wreathed in other strangenesses.

An awakening. A quickening. A rising tide.

Call, Midnight had said. *And I will come.*

But what would be the price?

CHAPTER 7

Unfortunately, it was only after Anahid woke up—in the middle of the afternoon—and beheld the veritable mountain of notes and cards that had accrued throughout the day that she remembered Polinna Andani's breakfast party.

Exciting as the event had turned out, her absence—without apology—had not escaped notice. It had been not merely noticed but commented upon, dissected, analysed, and used to generate some truly outrageous speculation.

Anahid splayed her hands over the notes of polite inquiry, false sympathy, and blatant scandal-mongering and breathed through the urge to tear them all to shreds. She hated this; she hated how familiar the walls of society closing in around her felt.

The tightness in her chest. The clamour of imagined voices in her mind. The urge to snarl, and snap, and *bite*.

Last time, when she'd lost her temper and slapped Avarair Hisarani in public, she'd been bothered enough to consider fleeing the city altogether. She'd stood in her father's private study and stared at his map of Savani family trade routes, all those little notations on the map that marked other places Anahid could be that *weren't here*.

But there were still azatani there, weren't there? That's what the notations meant, the proprietary lines, the little markers of ware-houses and contacts and arrangements. *The reach of Bezim is even so far as this.*

This time there was Zagiri to think about. Zagiri's struggle to carve out the life she wanted would only be made more difficult by Anahid dropping upon her a full-laden cargo of scandal. Which it certainly *would* be, if anyone found out that Anahid had missed the garden party because she had been winning a Flowerhouse at carrick.

Anahid needed a fulsome, respectable, and *public* response to quash this quickly. Which unfortunately meant she needed help.

She looked for Nihath first in his study, but though the books were splayed out all over the furniture as though thrown in an explosion, he was not at their epicentre. From the window seat, a pale voice said dreamily, "In the workroom." Tehroun blinked at her. "Are you quite all right?"

Maddening, that *he* was the one to look closely enough to ask the question. What a ridiculous collection of nonsense Anahid's life truly was. "Not really," she admitted, "but I'm making do."

Nihath had closed the workroom door, as she'd always asked him to do. Of course, there was less reason than ever now for secrecy. The inquisitors weren't arresting azatani practitioners for sorcery—not when any they *did* pick up just called for Siyon to attest the lack of risk from the newly balanced planes—and in any case, the inquisitors seemed loath to set foot in this house entirely since the violent events of the summer.

Anahid had never raised an official complaint against Vartan Xhanari for bursting into her home and committing violence. Yet she'd received a stiffly worded letter of apology from the superinten-dent of the inquisitors himself, assuring her that Xhanari had been punished, demoted, and shuffled off into some lesser function in which he would never cross her path again.

She'd received another letter from Xhanari himself, very proper and also, it had seemed to Anahid as she read it through—more than once, if she was honest—very sincere. He had apologised for causing her so much trouble. He had claimed to regret causing difficulty to a woman whose capability, propriety, and composure he considered admirable.

She hadn't raised an official complaint. Had Xhanari reported himself? Or had the gossip mill of the Avenues simply turned in its usual inexorable fashion?

Anahid was startled from her thoughts when Nihath answered her knock; he in turn was distracted and disinterested and reacted as she'd anticipated to being told they needed to promenade that evening.

"What?" he said. "No, I can't possibly. Too much to do. It was *delving*, do you understand?"

Not in the slightest. If they'd understood each other, they probably wouldn't have ended up here. "It's something married couples do," she told him sharply. "And we haven't in weeks."

He pulled a face, said "Fine," and shut the door again.

But he did show up in the front hall before sunset, shaven and styled and in a longvest appropriately sparkling with gilt embroidery and coloured beads. Anahid had trodden a careful line between becoming modesty and appropriate finery, with a headscarf beaded in blue and green waves with sparkling silver froth that matched the embroidery on her grey dress. They weren't likely to be the fanciest couple parading the Avenues, but they made a respectable showing, and that was almost all Anahid needed.

Almost. She hesitated with her hand on the door, as Nihath checked his watch. "I can't loiter about for half a bell or more," he warned. "I've got to prepare for this select committee."

Whatever that was. Anahid took a breath. She didn't *want* to tell him about all the rumours they needed to fight—that awful tower of notes, the well-wishes blooming like flowers with snide insinuations slipped between their petals. That Anahid had been with a lover, that she'd known the djinn would visit, that she was kidnapped to another plane herself, or even that Siyon had whisked her away for an extra-planar tryst. None of them, thank goodness, were anywhere close to the truth, but they were still slippery in their own way.

If she said any of that, Nihath would probably suggest again that it would be all right if she *had* been with a lover, and that Siyon was quite a fine chap, really. And then she might scream at him.

Instead, Anahid said, "If anyone asks, I was at home this morning."

"All right," Nihath said absently, tucking his watch back in his longvest pocket. He frowned at her. "Weren't you?"

He'd seen her come in. But why would he bother remembering that? She was only his wife.

Outside, the sun was setting over Bezim, dying in fire in the dusty hills to the west. In the Avenues, the promenade was getting under-way, azatani stepping down from their townhouses to make stately procession along the tree-lined streets, to chat and gossip and scheme, to see and be seen in the elegant dusk hour before dinner.

Anahid had rarely hated anything more than this meaningless, empty ritual. But she tucked her hand into Nihath's elbow and gave a little wave to Azata Malkasani, who was descending from her own townhouse across the road, as they started their perambulation.

The hand on Nihath's arm was necessary; he wanted, as always, to walk far too fast. Promenade was not anything so coarse as *exercise*. The appropriate pace slipped beyond sedate into outright dawdling. All the better to show off your finery, exchange empty witticisms, and take thorough stock of who was walking and talking with whom.

The Andanis were their neighbours on one side, so Anahid steered Nihath the *other* way. She wanted to turn the tide of gossip a little before she confronted the unpleasant source, and while her ankle recovered from its unfortunate injury, Polinna's participation in the promenade was limited to sitting on a stool in front of her town-house and chatting with passersby.

No one they exchanged pleasantries with along the first block seemed inclined to ask pointed questions—far more interested in ask-ing Nihath about the djinn who'd appeared at the garden party—but Anahid watched them notice her hand on her husband's arm and knew the point was being taken. At the corner, she hesitated, think-ing they might turn up toward the Palace.

"Ana!" someone called, before she could decide, and she turned away from Nihath to see Zagiri, hurrying through the slow-moving crowd with one net-gloved hand holding in place the filigree gold decoration braided into her dark hair.

Anahid blinked. That delicate decoration matched the embroidery on her sister's gown. "Are you—dressed for promenade?"

Zagiri shot her a look all the sharper for the kohl that had been applied to her eyes. "I do know how, you know. I got your note. I thought you might like support."

Anahid's note, where she'd apologised for letting her sister down and promised to come and say it in person, after the promenade.

Anahid let go of Nihath to throw both arms around her sister—though carefully, to avoid crushing either of their finery.

"I have news," Zagiri murmured in her ear, as she returned the hug. "Quite a lot of it, actually. But I want to hear yours first."

Panic pinched at Anahid's lungs. "What news?" she squeaked.

Zagiri pulled back enough to give Anahid that familiar look—like she had no idea how Anahid could be so strange. "You might have convinced everyone you spoke with so far that you *just forgot*, but I know you better. I very much *hope* you didn't stand me up for cards. I want to hear a better reason than that." She grinned wickedly. "Like a lover-shaped reason."

She'd kept her voice down, at least. "Giri," Anahid sighed.

Zagiri shrugged. "I know, I know. Scandal, propriety, more to life, a silly waste of your time—but you seem to have the scandal anyway, and you deserve some fun."

"I have fun," Anahid snapped.

She sat at the carrick table and her blood thrilled as she watched Stepan Zinedani *lose everything*.

Zagiri leaned to the side to say, "Good evening, Nihath, you're looking very fancy."

He snipped his watch closed and sniffed. "Surely this has been sufficient."

They'd *barely* covered half a block, but Zagiri waved a hand and said, "Off you go. I'll keep her company from here."

Nihath didn't need any further encouraging to abandon her for his work. Anahid couldn't help a short, sharp grunt of frustration. "Giri," she snarled quietly, "I *need* him here. It's your chances I'm thinking of."

"Don't worry," Zagiri declared cheerfully, and tucked her hand into Anahid's arm, much as Anahid had to Nihath. Zagiri's grin widened. "I have a clerkship. A special clerkship, to a select committee chaired by none other than the prefect herself."

Anahid blinked. "You—*what*?"

"I know." Zagiri wriggled a little, close to dancing with glee. "I *know*. It's some special function, outside the entire structure, the prefect wrangled it out of Council today in response to this djinn popping up. Since I was there, and since I know Siyon, I'm the perfect candidate, apparently." Her slow pacing got a little strut as she added, "Oh yes, *and* I was given a named blade last night."

Anahid barely stopped herself from gaping in astonishment. "Zagiri!" she cried, quickly lowering her tone as they earned a curious glance from across the road. "That's wonderful. Congratulations! All of this at once... Have you freed a dolphin from some net recently and not told me about it?"

"Amazing, isn't it?" Zagiri agreed; her grin showed no signs of dimming, and nor should it. Everything she wanted was being presented to her, like the Salt Festival had come a month early, just for her. "And—oh, good evening, Azatan Kozetani."

Of course, they were still in the middle of promenade, and Anahid had work that still needed doing. But walking with her sister turned out to be a blessing. Even those who opened with sympathy— and curiosity—about Anahid's absence this morning soon turned to Zagiri.

"So," Azatan Kozetani said, smoothing down the layers of his frilly cravats as he smiled superciliously, "my husband tells me you'll be assisting Danelani with her new select committee on this whole djinn business. Awfully convenient that you were on the spot like that, wasn't it?"

Anahid tightened her grip on Zagiri's hand in anticipation of the umbrage her sister would take at that tone, but Zagiri just smiled prettily. "Oh, I only hope my experiences can be useful to ensuring the safety and prosperity of Bezim."

He pursed his lips and gave them the appropriate nods, then continued on.

"That's a load of old fish scales," Anahid noted quietly.

Zagiri snorted a laugh, but at least she did it behind her hand. "I know. But it makes them so annoyed when I say it. Who cares what they think? I have a real chance with this. I'd been resigned to taking something—anything—and working away at meaningless tasks for years before I could really make a difference. But this might—oh! There's the Northern ambassador."

"The *who?*" Anahid turned to look.

It seemed there was another opportunity from the garden party that Anahid had missed, and soon Zagiri was introducing her to Madame Ksaia Bardha and her daughter, Yeva, who Zagiri had been invited to take on as a co-sponsor for the Ball. Both Northern women were handsome—golden and pale and even taller than Anahid. Promenade was no place for proper conversation, and they moved on shortly after introductions and a few vapid pleasantries.

"You *have* been busy," Anahid noted.

"Maybe you should miss more events," Zagiri said, a smirk hiding behind her lofty expression. Her eyes slid sidelong to Anahid. "Maybe you should get a lover to loiter with."

Anahid gave the long-suffering sigh that she was clearly supposed to, pleased to see Zagiri dissolve into happy giggles. So pleased that her life seemed to be coming out the way she'd wanted it.

If not quite in the way that it *should* have been done. They'd followed all the rules, in the last few weeks, and caught nothing. But then this opportunity had thrown itself into Zagiri's boat, a direct product of all her least appropriate behaviour.

Once, Anahid might have resented that. Now, it made her thoughtful. Interesting that the rules could perhaps be stepped around, in the right circumstances. If you were careful.

Anahid thought of the locked drawer in her desk, where she had hidden away the key and the deed of ownership. She couldn't possibly have that, of course. She couldn't court a scandal that would cut all of these achievements out from under her sister. She'd have to go down there—not tonight, but soon—and set it all to rights.

But she could have *something*, perhaps. Something that fired her imagination like that. Something that made her fingers itch—like carrick—to play the game, and win.

Something that lit her up like Zagiri. With purpose, and with pleasure.

Anahid looked across the azatani promenade, at the hollow conversations and placid people she'd spent her whole life among.

There was nothing for her here.

"This inaugural meeting of the select committee for the management and mitigation of interplanar activity will come to order."

Zagiri was impressed that Syrah Danelani could manage to say all that in a single breath and with a straight face. Then again, the woman had had a lifetime of experience. *She* hadn't been fumbling her way into her first clerkship at the age of nineteen; she'd been two years on the job by then, and negotiating her own, very advantageous, marriage.

But Zagiri didn't want to be prefect. She just wanted to make the city, and the practice of alchemy within it, a little fairer. A little better, for *everyone*, not only the azatani.

And this select committee might be how she did it.

Danelani added, "Are we all here?" Which caused a ripple of amusement.

The room was absolutely full to bursting. All the seats around the long table were taken by the named members of the select committee—including, way down at the bottom, Nihath and Siyon. (He'd grinned so wide upon seeing her here that Zagiri had had to look quickly down at her notes to keep her decorum.) But around the outside of the room, between the backs of the chairs and the thick patterning of the wallpaper, was a thick swaddling of onlookers like every single member of the Council had sent a clerk to observe.

Zagiri didn't get a seat, as the administrative clerk of the select committee. The role earned her a desk wedged into a dark corner of an ancillary antechamber of Syrah Danelani's crowded office, and a place here standing against the wall behind the head of the table, where three seats had been arranged for the chair and the two "anchors" of the committee.

Danelani, as chair, was in the middle. On her left was Azata Markani, officially here to ensure all matters relating to the practice of alchemy were within the parameters established by Oblique Methods. Behind Markani's shoulder was a clerk, managing her papers as Zagiri was doing for Danelani, but Jaleh Kurit was also there, looking unimpressed about it.

They actually weren't all here; the chair on Danelani's right was still empty. The chair for the second anchor, that Markani and the prefect had agreed they'd leave to Azatan Rowyani and his Pragmatic faction to fill.

Maybe they were going to show their disapproval for the whole concept by abstaining entirely?

But as Zagiri let that thought flutter hopefully through her mind, a voice from the crowded doorway said, "Ink and ashes, is this a committee or a circus?"

Oh shit, she knew that voice.

The crowd at the door parted in a flurry of snippy apologies and hissed imprecations, and Avarair Hisarani elbowed his way inside. Clearly he'd waited to make a dramatic entrance, and now everyone was watching as he worked his way up to the empty second-anchor seat.

Everyone except Zagiri. She was watching Siyon, who looked like a ghost had kicked him solidly in the stomach.

It was uncanny, Zagiri reflected, how much the older Hisarani brothers looked alike. Had looked alike. It had unsettled her too, when she'd seen Avarair at the hippodrome.

And she hadn't felt for Izmirlian half of what Siyon had.

"This is ridiculous," Avarair stated as he sank into his waiting chair. He waved a hand at the general assembly, now back to shifting and muttering like the evening sea. "How can we possibly get anything done like this? Clear the room."

It had the sharp snap of an order. *You just wait,* Markani had said to Danelani on their way here. *Whoever Rowyani sends will raise full sail straight out of the harbour. We'll be lucky if we define terms in today's session.*

Zagiri hadn't expected it to start quite *this* immediately. Then again, she hadn't expected Avarair Hisarani.

"Such an unprecedented occurrence is justifiably of interest to a great many of the Council." Markani smiled genially past Danelani at Avarair. "But if you've an order closing the committee's workings to observation in your pocket, by all means whip it out."

A titter of laughter unwound a little of the room's tension, but Avarair smirked, and Zagiri—who'd been reading up on the procedures and conventions of a select committee, trying to find her feet—knew what was coming next.

Sure enough, he said, "By all means, Azata Markani. I move that the meeting be closed to observation on the grounds that feeding constant speculation in this dangerously nebulous area will only damage the already troubled equanimity of the city and her ventures."

It ran off his tongue very easily. Zagiri wondered if he'd practiced. It was nonsense, of course. Possibly Avarair really would like to kick out the observers so fewer people saw him being as obstructionist as possible. But the real point of it was to demonstrate immediately the support that the Pragmatic faction could call upon in the select committee.

Syrah Danelani knew it too. She gave Avarair a flatly unimpressed look but was already lifting a hand to present the motion for voting.

Nihath interrupted from the other end of the table. "I can't think what seems nebulous to the good za in the circumstances. The djinn was clearly delving in the Mundane, something now made possible by the planes returning to proper alignment. It's all quite straightforward and—"

The shouting drowned him out—not only from the committee members, but from the assembled onlookers who, strictly speaking, were not allowed to contribute at all. "You mean this will *keep happening*?" one azatan demanded amid dozens of similar sentiments.

It took a little time to get the chaos under control, with Avarair smirking the whole while since Nihath's comments—and the reaction—effectively had proved his point.

In the end, two-thirds of the members voted to close the meeting to observation, though Zagiri didn't think that was an indication of the usual numbers Hisarani could command. They'd compiled information on all the members, including expected voting patterns on various themes and issues. The membership arrangements had been a wrangle. At least a third of those seated around the table—not ushered grumpily out by white-sashed stewards—could be counted on to follow the Pragmatic faction. Just shy of half the members were likely to support the prefect in all but extreme motions. The rest were more changeable.

Zagiri had been particularly interested in the numbers because of the sorts of things she hoped to sneak in around the edges. But there were no existing indications on who might support alchemy reform. No one had asked the question yet. That was half the problem.

But Zagiri was here now. *She* could ask it. Which felt surprisingly thrilling. Like lining up for a bravi all-blades. The fight wasn't really starting now; it had been running every day leading up to this and would go on long after this skirmish was done. But this was *her* chance to draw her metaphorical blade and engage.

If she could spot the right moment. Probably not this first meeting. But when?

"Now that things are a little quieter," Danelani said as the doors swung closed again, and she nudged proceedings into the scheduled business, establishing the select committee's area of work, fleshing out the brief definition that the Council had agreed upon. With its hundreds of members, the Council itself was not at all the place for fine detail.

As though his point had been made, Avarair Hisarani was remarkably untroublesome through the process, and the meeting moved along quickly. There was some wrangling about special terms, and the positions of the committee, but the prefect did carry some executive power—especially with an order from the Council to create this select committee—and the choppy seas were swiftly cut through.

"Which brings us to the first official order of business," Danelani continued, turning a page in the papers Zagiri had prepared for her, "which is the investigation of the incident in the gardens."

"I object," stated an azatan halfway down the table. He spoke clearly and without hesitation, but he also darted a glance at Avarair Hisarani, and Zagiri wondered if he'd been prompted in advance. "The first order of business, for the safety of all Bezim, must be to ensure that the city is made safe against any further such depredations from the other planes."

"Depredations!" scoffed an azata across from him. "It was one djinn grabbing a handful of grass. Kozetani, you're overreacting."

"And next time?" he countered. "When it is more than one, making off with..." Kozetani tilted his head, as though inviting them to imagine the worst.

"The investigation of the incident in the gardens," Danelani repeated sternly, "which has *already begun*, will allow us to understand whether we need worry about further incidents and any consequences that might qualify as *depredations* for those of more delicate sensibilities among us."

There were a number of smirks at this subtle dig at Kozetani, but others around the table looked troubled. One azata pointed down to the end of the table. "He just said this might now be normal."

"Oh yes," Nihath confirmed, with earnest but unhelpful enthusiasm. "Not something ever recorded before, but now we may be on the brink of genuine and sustained exchange between the planes. We could learn so much. The possibilities are endless."

Given the muttering and frowning going on, that was not generally viewed as a good thing.

"I thought the Sorcerer was supposed to have things under control!" an azatan harrumphed into his moustache.

"I'm right here," Siyon said.

"And what are you doing about all this?" Kozetani demanded.

"First, all manner of reports of strange beasts and beings scuttling about our alleyways, and now a djinn in broad daylight! What's next? Demons stepping out of any shadow?"

Siyon's mouth twisted a little, and for a moment Zagiri braced herself for the chaos that would surely erupt if a demon—or a harpy— *did* choose that moment to step out of a shadow. It was the sort of thing Laxmi would enjoy.

"This committee was not formed to squeak and quail at superstitious alleytales," Syrah Danelani said, scornfully enough to earn a few sheepish expressions around the table.

Azatan Kozetani was not one of them. "But could we perhaps," he said, "have some alchemical specialists who *haven't* been arrested for sorcery?"

"Yes," Markani said crisply. "You've got me."

There were a couple of surprised blinks at that, as though they'd forgotten that she was a member of the Summer Club, as well as a member of the Council.

"And no one," Avarair interjected, so smoothly that Zagiri itched to preemptively punch him. "No one could possibly raise any concerns about your own behaviour, inclinations, or likelihood to take risks. However, let's skirt around the nonsense and get to the heart of the matter. You, Azata Markani, are not the Power of the Mundane. That—or so we are all invited to believe—is Siyon Velo."

No honorific. Zagiri knew that the appellation of *Master* made Siyon antsy, but she was annoyed at the lack of respect.

Avarair continued: "And *his* behaviour, inclinations, and risk-taking is rather a matter of common knowledge, is it not?"

Siyon bared his teeth in a feral grin. "I hear someone's writing an opera about me and all." He seemed to emphasise the word *opera*, for no reason that Zagiri could understand. "What exactly is your problem, Hisarani?"

How was that for getting to the heart of the matter?

But Avarair smiled, thin and cold and barbed as a fishhook. He hardly resembled Izmirlian at all, like that. "Your colleague here has informed us that this sort of attack—"

"I never said attack," Nihath scolded.

But Avarair talked over him. "—has not occurred in centuries. Until *you* came along. My *problem*, Velo, and indeed the entire city's problem, is that no one understands what you've done, and no one knows what might come next, including—and please disabuse me if I am mistaken—*you*."

That hung a moment, as Siyon opened his mouth, looked at Avarair like a crab eyeing the pot, and closed his mouth again.

"Or is there some other reason you did not mention to anyone that such things as this might be possible?" Avarair asked, gentle as a shark arrowing in on an overturned boat. Siyon's expression turned sour, as Avarair smiled. "It's understandable. You are but one man, and one who, through no fault of your own, has scant experience in such responsibility. The Council has been remiss in not supporting you better. I move that this select committee immediately form a panel for the consideration of daily reporting from and formulating of daily advice to Master Velo."

Zagiri frowned and paused in the scratching of her notes. That sounded . . . supportive. And yet—

"You want to tell me what to do," Siyon stated starkly.

"You want to tie up everyone's time with endless paperwork," Markani snapped.

"Of course not!" Avarair objected with patent insincerity. "A panel, only, of those most suited to the consideration of alchemical practice and its applications, to assist Master Velo in better fulfilling his onerous role. None of us, surely, want him to fail."

The faint emphasis on the last word had half the committee looking sidelong down the table, to where Siyon slumped in his chair, wearing a patched coat and a surly expression that did nothing to counteract his general air of being intimately acquainted with failure.

If Zagiri had a blade to hand she might have run Avarair Hisarani through.

"Daily seems onerous and moreover unnecessary," Syrah Danelani declared, as though she recognised that Avarair had carried this round, and she could only try to minimise the damage. "Weekly should be ample."

"But this *is* an emergency, is it not?" Avarair countered, almost innocently. "Let us settle on every three days."

The motion passed at three days.

When the meeting had finished, Zagiri stood with Syrah Danelani near the door as she spoke with the departing members. Everyone paused for at least a word of farewell, but finally the ordeal was over and the room nearly empty. Markani was at the other end of the table, in avid conversation with Nihath, and Siyon was lolling in his chair again, half slid under the table. He watched them approach from under his eyelashes.

"Well, that could have gone better," the prefect stated. "I wasn't expecting the eldest Hisarani. He's a little junior for this sort of appointment."

Siyon snorted. "I could have told you he'd sign up to haul oars if I was the prize." He hauled himself upright, dragging a hand over his face. "You seriously want to hear a daily little update on whatever the fuck I'm thinking about?"

"Every three days," Danelani corrected. "And *I* don't want any of this." She sighed and planted her hands on her white-robed hips. "I don't suppose you were withholding anything there?"

Siyon patted his coat, as though he were searching his pockets, and his mouth twisted a little. But all he said was, "I wish I knew anything useful. It's not like there's an instruction manual."

"Of course," Danelani muttered, flipping a dismissive hand. "Well, do your best. Try not to destroy anything, including my standing with any more of the Council."

And she stalked out of the room.

"You know," Markani said as she stood to follow, "this reporting business might be something that your secretary could take care of. If you had one."

Siyon slumped lower in his chair. "Yeah, all right, I give in. Send your bloody nephew to see me." His eyes slid sideways, landing on Zagiri, and his mouth crooked up toward a smile. "Hey, little clerk."

"That's Miss Clerk to you," Zagiri returned, but she couldn't help smiling back. That faltered a little as Markani and Nihath headed for the door as well. Zagiri took the chance to say, "Weird, isn't it? Seeing…" She waved a hand toward the doorway, where Avarair Hisarani was long gone.

Siyon picked absently at the edge of the table with a thumbnail much rougher than the varnished surface. "I really thought it was him. Just for a moment." He looked at the doorway too, like he was seeing another time. Another man. "This would be easier if he were still here."

Zagiri didn't think he was only talking about the committee.

CHAPTER 8

The distant clangour of the gate bell dragged Siyon from the depths of sleep, buried in stone and darkness, lulled into eternity, and he blinked in the strange light of morning slanting across his ceiling.

"What?" he said aloud, and his own voice sounded strange to his ears. What had he been dreaming about? But already it was evaporating, leaving only a long-burning ember of frustration and discomfort, as though Siyon was tangled up in something inescapable.

He *was* tangled up, but he flailed his way out of the sheets, reaching out to the bedside to haul himself up and wincing as his hand came down on something hard and prickling sharp.

The little dragon figurine, sitting on the box beside his bed, where he definitely hadn't left it. With a snarl, Siyon knocked it off, sending it clattering away into the corner of the room.

Anahid was waiting in the workroom when Siyon finally staggered downstairs, still trying to get his shirt straight on his shoulders. One corner of her mouth quirked just a little, and a teasing spark kindled in her eye, and Siyon almost looked forward to the mockery lining up on her clever tongue.

But she stiffened, as the shadows lurking behind her thickened and coiled into a blunt-nosed snake. It came tipping over her shoulder, nudging at her chin, slithering down across her chest, all glistening scales and heavy inference. "Coussssin dearessst," Laxmi hissed, tongue tasting the air.

Anahid pulled at the scaled weight of her, until the snake dissolved into shadowed mist and the echo of demonic laughter. Siyon grinned. "You did name her such. In front of witnesses."

"One of my many mistakes," Anahid said absently. "I am on my way to take care of another, and you mentioned wanting something with a Flower before I did...?"

After all the mess of the last few days—the djinn and the committee and Avarair bloody Hisarani—a protective nullification charm seemed like someone else's preoccupation. But all things considered, Siyon could possibly use the goodwill of the inqs more than ever right now.

"There'll be coffee, right?" he asked.

"It's the Flower district," Anahid pointed out. "There can be anything your heart desires."

Not that the Flower district would be operating at this time of day—somewhere not long after the Glory bell, judging by the slant of sunlight and the rumbling of the last, late delivery wagons on their way back down the Kellian Way to the Swanneck Bridge.

A pastry from a bakery cart and the crisp autumn morning chased the last dusty shadows of Siyon's strange dream away. "So you're definitely giving it back?" he asked around a mouthful.

"I have to." Anahid sounded far firmer than she looked, something wistful in the distance of her eyes. "I'd make a mess of it for everyone, not to mention the outrage if I was found out."

Siyon shrugged. "What's life without a little scandal?"

"This wouldn't be a *little* scandal," Anahid corrected. "A first-tier azata involved in the provision of services would tarnish my whole family, impact the Savani trading concerns—"

Siyon snorted at that; trust the azatani to get in a tizzy about someone making money *the wrong way*.

"And it would make a mess for Zagiri," Anahid continued.

Siyon laughed. "Like Zagiri cares. Isn't she the one constantly at you to get a leg over?" He laughed again at the exasperated look she gave him.

Though Anahid wasn't laughing. "This isn't merely propriety. It could ruin Zagiri's presentation sponsorship, let alone this new committee business. She's finally getting somewhere. I won't scupper it." She looked at him sidelong. "You're involved in this committee too, right? How did it go?"

Siyon let her change the subject, though he didn't much like this new one. "Yeah, I was there, for all the good it did me. It went fine for her. She was up there at the prefect's shoulder, handing her papers and taking her notes like she'd been doing it for years."

That got a brief and proud smile out of Anahid. "But for you?"

Siyon pulled a face. "Avarair Hisarani is helping run it."

"Oh," Anahid said, which...yeah, that about covered it. *Oh.*

"They want me to *make the city safe from the depredations of other planes*," Siyon said, squinting off into the morning sun. It wasn't just the wanky phrasing that bothered him. "*We've* been raiding *them* for generations. As long as there's been alchemy here."

Anahid considered that. "But have you—when you were doing that raiding, I mean. Did you ever come out in the Abyssal equivalent of a garden party?"

Siyon was distracted by a brief mental image of Laxmi playing lawn games. Siyon and Izmirlian *had* come out in the middle of the Demon Queen's court, hadn't they? But the court had been out in the wilds, hunting. Usually, Siyon had slipped in and out without seeing more than a lone patrolling angel.

Anahid shrugged. "Perhaps the other planes don't have cities like we do. Though there's always one in the stories. Pandemonium, or that castle of the angels."

Siyon had also been to Pandemonium, right inside the whalebone-vaulted hall of the Demon Queen herself. Another unusual event; he hadn't been raiding that time, but delving specifically *to Laxmi.*

"You're onto something," Siyon mused. "There's...The other planes must have some protection around their cities—or whatever they have at their hearts. When I delved, I always slipped into the

fringes, until I had something to pull me in closer. But that djinn..."
He'd just taken *grass*. There was grass everywhere. Why had he come
through *here*?

Perhaps because the Mundane plane—and Bezim—had none
of the same protections. Because *Siyon* didn't know how to make it
happen.

This is your *problem*, Avarair Hisarani had said. Being annoying
didn't stop him being right.

At least now Siyon had an idea to pursue. He could turn it over.
Chase down implications. Consider things to try.

He could report it to the panel, like he was a new blade who kept
breaking line. The whole thing left a sour taste in his mouth.

The grand main gates of the Flower district closed with the rising of the sun, but the delivery gate around the back was thronging
with wagons and the denizens of the District running their own
errands. Inside, the rubbish of last night was being swept away, the
Houses tidied and aired, tradesfolk working on repairs, maintenance,
improvements. No one was wearing House livery, the laughter was
more raucous, and the only music Siyon heard was someone bawling
a washersong.

Sable House was tucked into a quiet little square with a fountain
at its centre and two other houses at the edges. A heavy three-storey
building of dark stone, it was softened a little by star-jasmine vines,
their flowers closed tight as a drunkard's eyes in daylight, spilling
from a line of window boxes along the top floor. A large pair of double doors in some material as glossy and black as Siyon's annoying
dragon stood propped permanently open, too heavy to move; a grille
had been drawn across the opening and fixed with a large, glittering
padlock. Charmed, probably. A lot of them were, both to show off and
stay safe.

The delivery laneway down the side ended in a gate propped open
and half blocked by an unloading cart. Beyond was a large courtyard, crowded with crates and barrels and a dozen children engaged
in a noisy makeshift game of tip and run. Each shot earned applause
from a high balcony, shaded by colourful awnings, under which the

Flowers of Sable House were taking their leisure—eating and drinking, mending clothes or playing cards, one strumming an oud.

"Mistress!" someone exclaimed, and a brown-skinned Storm Coast woman came hurrying over from the kitchen entrance. She was middle-aged but still glowingly beautiful, with a figure that defied the shapelessness of her simple dress. Her pleasant expression didn't slip at all upon hearing Anahid's wish to speak with the Zinedani, though she did get a little spark of bright-eyed interest when Anahid introduced Siyon. "I assume you are not here to discuss the provision of our cosmetics and prophylactics."

Siyon knew, from some of the alchemists he'd provided ingredients to in his previous life, that some of the creams and powders the Flowers made use of went beyond mere *cosmetics* and toward the sorts of things that opera might have called *glamours*. "I sort of do," he admitted. "I'm working on a way to switch them off."

"Rude," Qorja commented with a little smirk, then waved a hand. "I know someone who'd love to speak with you. I'll see if she's awake. Why don't you both wait in the dining hall?"

Inside, Anahid's attention seemed to snag on the curtained stage in one corner of the velvet-draped dining hall. Siyon glanced at it— and at her, one hand gripping the sash of her dress. "It's where they do the Flower Night auctions, right?" he asked.

Her eyes had a sharpness that Siyon didn't think was really for *him*. "So I'm told."

Soon a young woman joined them, lithe and cheerful with freckles the same colour as her orange hair sprinkled generously across her pale cheeks. She introduced herself as Imelda, "who will be known, when I'm known, as the Dawnsong." She bit at her lip and added unnecessarily, "I'm not a Flower yet, is that all right? I did bring my charms." She dangled a little drawstring bag from one finger and smirked. "At least, the ones that aren't natural."

She might not have been a Flower yet, but she was clearly ready to take it on.

As she opened the bag and set out her little vials and jars and pots, she asked, "Are you from Dockside?"

There was a bright innocence to the question that Siyon didn't believe. He considered her colouring and her accent—even with Flower training smoothing the edges out—and made a guess. "You recognise my name."

She smiled in a flash of dimples. "Only in passing. Though one of my brothers married into the Doti fisherclan. All the others are laders."

From across the table, Anahid asked, "Are they mixed up in this current unpleasantness?"

"The dock disputes?" Imelda shrugged. "Probably. There's something every autumn, isn't there? It doesn't seem so important up here, so I don't really pay attention." Siyon snorted at that; she wasn't the only one.

Siyon pulled a few things from his satchel as well—salt seemed likely to be useful, and a jar of dust from quenched ashes—and they got to work. Imelda wiped a cream over her nose and cheeks that made her freckles fade away to nothing, then dabbed a drop of oil on a finger that could twist her strawberry hair into curls. That one made Anahid's mouth drop open a little in what Siyon thought was some sort of covetous surprise.

"And then to take them off I usually just..." Imelda dipped a finger into another vial—with a whiff of alcohol—and to Siyon's surprise she drew a circle on her cheek and slashed a line through the middle. The curls fell from her hair, and her freckles were suddenly back in full strength on her cheeks.

"You know the nullification sigil," he said in shock.

"The what?" she asked, blinking. "Oh, the mud sign? Yeah, of course. Taught all the others as well. It's so useful for making sure your drink hasn't been tampered with. Don't you..." Imelda trailed off, frowning at Siyon. "Do fisherclan boys not play with that? There's a skipping game too. And a rhyme. It's really about Bezim, I guess. Like, the city's history? The mud and the mountain, the two sides of the river, the lives above and the power buried."

Siyon had never heard of *any* of this, and he wasn't sure if it was something the mud kids didn't share with fisherclan kids, or whether it was women's business that his cousin never would have deigned to share with him.

"The mud and the mountain?" Anahid repeated. "Isn't that what the first Old Kingdom exiles said was here when they arrived? Fisherfolk on the flat, and the wild men up in the caves on the crag..." She trailed off, brows wrinkling as she tried to haul memory from the depths. "Mourning something? I can't remember."

Siyon had never known to begin with. And yet, this had lingered, a scrap of history, a skipping game, and a symbol that actually happened to be the same as the alchemical nullification sigil. That couldn't be a coincidence.

But here and now, none of this was what Siyon was investigating. "Right." He tried to gather his thoughts again. Even with Imelda's cheek still wet with the drawn symbol, she could reapply the freckle-fading cream. If the inquisitors were going to have some reassurance that they couldn't just be batted aside with sorcery... "We need a way to prevent a charm from taking hold."

Drawing the symbol in salt and ashes didn't seem to have any additional effect; it was the drawing itself that snapped the thread of the charm.

"Draw it over and over?" Imelda suggested, immediately frowning. "Oh, that would be...inconvenient."

Siyon frowned and considered this. "Would you mind if I used a spark of extraplanar energy?" He wasn't sure which. They all came easily, these days. He didn't even have to reach across the planes; he could pluck it from the soup of energy all around him. He was still dithering as he snapped his fingers—

The world *twitched* around them.

Siyon hurried to trace the symbol on the back of Imelda's hand, and this time his finger left a faint bronzed smear behind, looping into a glowing circle and still lingering as his finger lifted to start the cross slash.

The door opened suddenly, and Siyon jumped, losing track of the sigil still undone. Imelda startled, with a little squeak.

"Mistress?" Qorja said from the doorway, and Anahid hurried over while Siyon looked down at the mark.

The glow was fading, the cross slash barely started. It looked—he suddenly realised, especially glowing burnished-bronze like that—like Midnight's mark.

Imelda's eyes were wide. "That felt..." She flexed her hand and then reached for the pot of freckle cream. She smeared it over her cheek, and Siyon stared.

Every little dot stayed clear and dark.

"Well?" Imelda asked excitedly.

But even as she said it, the freckles started to fade. Siyon looked at her hand, holding the charm pot, and the sigil there had vanished.

But for a moment... it had worked. *Something* had worked.

Something Siyon didn't quite understand. An energy he couldn't quite name but had still summoned.

The same burnished energy he'd seen around Midnight.

When Anahid joined Qorja outside the dining hall, the stage mistress was chasing away a trio of other Flowers—a tall Lyraec man called back, "Fine, keep him all to yourself!" and Qorja laughed merrily.

She sobered a little as she noticed Anahid. "Apologies, mistress. They are very curious about Master Velo."

The salacious edge to the male Flower's remark had not sounded like *curiosity*. Anahid hesitated a moment, but this might be her only chance to ask. "I would have thought, given the nature of the work..." But then she couldn't find a delicate way to continue.

Qorja smiled. "That we wouldn't be so interested in sex for fun?" She made indelicacy seem elegant and tantalising; that was the magic of Flowers, Anahid supposed. "Mistress, every encounter has its own conditions. Its own unique collection of elements, its own exchange of power and favour. Its own contract, whether or not money is involved." Her smile widened. "I'm sure I needn't tell an azata that the best deal is one where everyone walks away satisfied."

Anahid could feel the blush rising in her cheeks. But even as she was embarrassed by the discussion, she was still curious. The art of the deal was central to the azatani trading philosophy, an exchange of power and benefit and favour. A deal had its own rhythm, like the shift of tensions over the carrick table, except that yes, as Qorja noted, *everyone* could win, in a deal.

She wondered how it worked—the negotiation, the give-and-take—when it didn't really matter. When it was only for fun. She wondered—

"Mistress," Qorja said, her voice delicately casual. "We have the usual restrictions on in-House liaisons here, but there *are* reciprocal arrangements with other Houses that may be to your interest."

It took Anahid a moment to realise that Qorja meant she was banned, as mistress of the House, from soliciting sexual favours from her *own* Flowers, but she could sample the wares of other Houses for free.

And for another moment after that, Anahid was tempted. Or at least curious.

She cleared her throat. "Something that will soon no longer apply to me."

Qorja's smile slipped. "On which note, the Zinedanis will be here by the midday bell, but, ah—" She hesitated before adding. "Master Zinedani requests that you meet him in the yard."

Anahid frowned. "There's a perfectly good office, though I assume it *is* still hung with Stepan's awful decorations?"

That made a corner of Qorja's mouth tweak up, but she said carefully, "They will not enter the House while ownership is under dispute."

A spark of anger struck in Anahid's heart. "There is no *dispute*. The House is mine." Or it was, until she gave it back. She took a breath and forcibly smothered that spark. "My apologies. It's not your fault. I'll meet them in the yard, when they get here."

When Anahid went back into the dining hall, Siyon and Imelda had packed their things away. Siyon was frowning at his own hand, deep in thought, while Imelda practiced a graceful curtsy on the corner stage.

When she saw Anahid, she beamed. "Will you be conducting my Flower Night yourself, mistress? I'd hoped to hold it before Salt Night."

Anahid nearly flinched at the reminder of the fate that might have been hers. But for Imelda, it was a choice, not a punishment. It would be the culmination of years of training, and the beginning of a career that might bring her wealth and fame.

"I hope you can," Anahid replied. "But it won't be me. I'll be returning the House to the Zinedani today."

Imelda's good cheer faltered for a moment, like a cloud passing briefly over the sun, before she rallied. But Anahid had seen it. The girl played happily at being auctioned off to sleep with a stranger, but at the mention of the Zinedani...

Anahid remembered the way Imelda had watched her master at the carrick game, so careful as she refilled his rakia time and again.

"Imelda," Anahid said carefully. "Was Stepan Zinedani a good master of the House?"

Imelda's smile now was placid and polished. "On the Path of Flowers there can be occasional thorns, but every life has its unpleasantries. I'm sure the Avenues are no different. It's merely a matter of working around them."

She drew herself up, her smile golden and confident. A child wearing the aplomb of a woman.

She should be kept safe. Not thrown back among the thorns.

"I should be going," Siyon said suddenly. "Thanks, Imelda, for all of that."

Anahid went along with him, out through the yard and along the alleyway and into the front square. She didn't realise they'd come all this way in silence until Siyon broke it. "You're having second thoughts."

"What?" She blinked at him. "No. Of course not. I have to give it back. There's no other sensible decision."

He grinned, like a man whose life was built upon very few decisions that could be called sensible. Anahid shoved at his arm, rolling her eyes.

And her attention was snagged by a glint of gold across the square. Two women stepped out of another Flowerhouse, one with her golden hair braided atop her head, wearing trousers and a shirt and an unusually cut vest. "I know her," Anahid murmured. But where from? Her memory conjured up the Avenues, but this was no azata.

"Who?" Siyon asked as he absently followed her gaze. "Not Aghut's bruiser, I assume."

Anahid realised he was right; the other woman, talking with the Northern girl, wore a canvas vest that bared muscles and tattoos in equal measure. Including, Anahid recognised with a faint thrill, the mark of Aghut's Shore Clan.

The Northerner turned to leave, giving Anahid a full look at her face, and *now* Anahid remembered her.

Why was Yeva Bardha, daughter of the Northern ambassador, meeting with the underling of a crime baron?

"Hey." Siyon nudged at her shoulder, dragging Anahid's attention back to him—and his encouraging smile. "Good luck with the Zinedani. Wring 'em out for a good price. They can afford it, and then you can buy something more acceptable with that, right?"

A rosy little plan. Anahid thought about it more, after Siyon had gone and she was waiting in the office. The problem, really, was that she'd considered all the acceptable options already. She'd tried to make the best of them. And she'd ended up here.

She stewed on it, and she glared at Stepan's awful smuggled turquoise, still cluttering up the walls of the office, and the longer Anahid looked, the more problems she found, from the cheap gilded wood to the way the pieces didn't quite line up flush.

By the time Qorja came to tell her the Zinedani had arrived, Anahid was quite cranky. She did her best to swallow that, as she came downstairs on Qorja's heels. This wasn't about her feelings. This was about making a sensible decision.

In the yard, the game had been abandoned, the children now clustered in the corner, curiosity balancing caution. Lejman stood at the gate with his arms across his chest and his face impassive. Nearby, though pretending this was coincidental, was Stepan Zinedani, even less impressive in the light of day, and an older man with a great deal more dignity to his excellent posture and careful barbering. He even wore a longvest, though in a plain dark grey that no Avenue azatan would countenance.

This could only be Garabed Zinedani, though he looked more like a merchant than one of Bezim's criminal barons.

"Gentlemen," Anahid said in greeting. "I suppose we will speak here, if you decline my hospitality."

Garabed drew himself up, though if he was trying to look down his nose at her, he was foiled by her height. Anahid had been told by more than one azatan—some of them possible suitors—that she was unforgivably tall. For the first time, she found it a little pleasing.

"I am made distraught by my nephew's poor decisions." Garabed's voice was low, and a little rough, but well modulated. "A woman of your standing should never have been put in such a position. Accept my apologies, and those of my intemperate nephew, and we will pretend this interlude never took place."

Surprise cracked a door for Anahid's anger to come creeping back. Never took place? Not a word about the other *position* his nephew (intemperate hardly covered it) had been eager to put her in. And no apology for dragging her out here to conduct the business.

"My nephew," Garabed Zinedani continued, laying a hand on Stepan's shoulder—a heavy hand, wearing its owner's wealth in gaudy, overlarge rings. The same bad taste as the turquoise upstairs. "For all his faults, he knows this business. Leave this to him, and you can go back to—" He waved that hand dismissively, up toward the Avenues. "Whatever it is you do."

Whatever it was she did. Battle meaninglessly with barbed gossip. Parade in idle circles for no good purpose. Attend endless carefully orchestrated gatherings that achieved absolutely nothing.

Play cards at games where men like Stepan Zinedani could threaten her and not lose a thing.

Leave this to Stepan. *Occasional thorns*, Imelda had called him. *Unpleasantries* to be worked around. This wasn't a world Anahid understood. She was here to make the sensible decision.

Anahid looked at the children, still huddled in the corner. They watched with a wariness similar to Imelda's, waiting at Stepan's elbow. They were too young to be apprentices, but perhaps they were the children of Flowers. All of them being raised with this *thorn*. Anahid looked at the balconies above, which were lined with curious Flowers. Lives and livelihoods that Anahid didn't understand.

But she understood that Stepan Zinedani was a bully. His uncle seemed little better, only more polished about it.

She understood that she was *angry* about it.

Why did they get this, to be *thorns*, and not her? *Why not her?* So many reasons, so many very good reasons, and in this moment Anahid couldn't hold on to a single one, as they washed away in the surge of her anger.

She turned back and said: "No."

Garabed continued as though he hadn't noticed. "I will, of course, compensate you for the winnings that are yours by rights."

"I have my winnings," Anahid said.

He noticed that. "I beg your pardon?"

"I don't want the money." She even managed a smile, though it felt small and tight on her face. "I admit I was a little startled at first, but on reflection, I think this will be fun. I only invited you to come and collect the rest of Za Stepan's personal things."

There was a flutter in her chest and a thrill in her veins, like sitting down at the table, like seeing the first cards dealt. Even if she was going to have to learn the rules as she went. She'd done it before. She could do it again.

And she was *not* simply stepping aside and letting them win.

Stepan lurched forward, snarling, "Azata—"

Anahid flinched, recoiling barely a step before she bumped against something solid.

His uncle's hand on his shoulder dragged Stepan back as she heard a noise like the hiss of a tile edge against the game board; Anahid realised that Lejman, now standing at her shoulder, was holding a naked blade.

"But thank you for your gentlemanly concern," Anahid managed, as though she wasn't trembling. She folded her hands tightly in front of her. Manners. Manners always helped. "You are, of course, always welcome in Sable House, but in the future remember that the courtyard is only for the staff of the House."

They all stood there for a moment, in dramatic tableau, and then Garabed turned to march out of the courtyard, Stepan at his heels.

Lejman slid the blade—a distressingly heavy-looking long knife—back into the sheath at his side. "Thank you, mistress."

Anahid pressed her hands against her middle, pressing the iron key behind her sash into a stomach that felt filled with little fish. "Don't thank me yet. I don't know what I'm doing. I might yet ruin everything."

"Not for that. Qorja owes me five rivna. I knew you wouldn't give us back." An actual smile curved at his mouth. "And we're here to help."

Here to help. Here to help *her*. In running her Flowerhouse.

She would have to keep it secret. She would have to be so careful. This was *not* the sensible decision at all.

But all the Powers help her, Anahid was excited to begin.

CHAPTER 9

Siyon jerked awake, lurching in his chair where he'd slumped over the book he was reading. The pages had pressed lines into his face; he rubbed at the marks and turned to tell Izmirlian—

There was no one next to him. That had been a dream.

When he looked down at the book, there was something nestled in the valley of the splayed pages. Of course. The little obsidian dragon.

Siyon picked it up, thumb and fingertip spanning its wings. When he'd got back from Sable House the other day, there'd been a note waiting from Tein Geras, apologising for losing Siyon's little dragon, but possibly it was just as well, since his contacts had all got very nervous about it. Something about a direct line of communication with Midnight himself.

Call, and I will come, Midnight had said as he'd pressed Siyon's palms together around the little figurine.

Siyon had so many questions. What was the awakening? What was that bronzed, glowing energy? What did Midnight *know*?

What did he want from Siyon?

That was the thorniest of them all. He was Midnight. Even the other barons didn't want to mess with him. Every instinct Siyon had told him to run away, and being sure that the dragon figurine would follow him did not lessen the urge.

"I'm not fucking interested," Siyon said to it. "So stop asking."

He flicked it off the table, and it went clattering beneath the workbench. It'd be back again soon enough.

"What *is* that thing?" Laxmi stretched one set of talons up over the edge of the table, then the other, pulling herself up to crouch on the edge. It shouldn't have been possible, for human limbs or anyone subject to gravity. She wrinkled her scaled nose. "It prods like a tine of Her Majesty's trident."

That was interesting. "Prods how?" Siyon asked.

"Proddily." Laxmi dug her claws into the edge of his book instead. "What's this?"

One of a whole stack Siyon had borrowed from Nihath; he tried to tug it back without causing any damage. Mostly the books were histories of Bezim, though also some early forays into alchemy, and even some ancient Lyraec poetry where the metaphor got a little mystical. Siyon wasn't quite sure what he was looking for.

The lives above and the power buried, Imelda had said. Skipping-chant myth about what had been here before there was anything like Bezim. The city was centuries old. There was so *much* buried, by time and layers of history and new stories. There were strangenesses that had become accepted simply for having endured.

People kept suggesting that Midnight didn't age…but how old *was* he? The idea that he'd been here from the start seemed wildly implausible. But so had Siyon becoming the Power of the Mundane.

Siyon didn't know where to start looking for the impossible that might just be true. All he had was a mess of ideas, and no aptitude for untangling them. He sighed and flipped the book closed. "I wish—" But he stopped himself, hard, with the words burning on his tongue, sweet as apricot nectar.

Laxmi smirked. "You wish?"

I wish Izmirlian were here, Siyon had been going to say. When didn't he? He missed Izmirlian's smile, and his sarcasm, and his curiosity. He missed the smell of him, and the whiplash of his handwriting, and the way his eyebrow had quirked like he was skeptical, but interested in being proven wrong.

Siyon missed him more sharply than ever, since looking up at the select committee and thinking he'd just walked in the door. A swoop of hope, and the plummet of reality.

But Izmirlian had also been clever, and well-read, and knew a surprising amount about a surprising array of topics. He'd seen things differently from Siyon. He would have looked at all this—at the demands of the select committee, at the tangle Siyon was making of everything—and had some new suggestion for Siyon to try. Right now, *that* was what Siyon wished for.

That and everything else.

Laxmi chuckled, shadow coiling around him as though she were luxuriating in his emotional turmoil. Siyon shrugged against it and snapped, "What, don't you miss Enkin?"

Enkin, who went to the Abyss for love—and left again for lack of it. Enkin, who had been nearly killed by the strength of the love Laxmi still held for him in turn.

The shadows clenched around Siyon for a moment, before evaporating into a sharp reek of sulphur. No one conveyed annoyance quite like a harpy.

Siyon coughed his way out of the workroom and spread out the sailcloth on the living area floor. The canvas was stained and marked from the various things Siyon had wrapped up in it before he'd shaken it out of his satchel last night in a fit of inspiration. Maybe, he'd thought, if he pulled his spark of energy into the twine and then stitched the almost-complete nullification sigil…

It had seemed like a good theory. The stitching would give the sigil permanent shape, and the twine could hold the energy, and the whole thing should work together. Except Siyon could barely sew a button back on his coat, and messy stitching and thumb-prick bloodstains didn't seem to be helping achieve the effect.

How did Siyon think this was going to turn out? Were the inqs likely to let him embroider their tunics? Maybe, if the thing *worked*.

He sat back on his heels and put his fingers together, ready to snap. Ready to summon a spark. He let his eyes fall out of focus with the physical world, looking instead at the energy swirling around him. Aethyreal wisps and Abyssal coils and Empyreal swipes.

Something else as well, if he looked more closely. That bronzed and burnished glow underpinning it all. He reached carefully, teasing it out, and then ran the twine between his fingers and thumb. It took on the faintest shimmering glow.

The gate bell clanged; the twine fell from Siyon's startled fingers, coiling on the sailcloth over one of last night's failed attempts. The fallen twine had a better shape, a loop almost making a circle by itself, and still with that undisturbed bronze sheen.

Siyon stared at it. What if he didn't need to sew it down? Could he just knot the symbol out of twine? Then he could—

The gate bell jangled again, and Siyon growled. He shook out his hands in sparks of energy, dragging himself up. He'd been expecting Laxmi to deal with it—which was all that people deserved, for coming ringing—but she, of course, had disappeared in a puff of stink and pique.

Siyon stomped down the stairs and glowered through the vines-and-flowers tangle of the alley gate. "Yeah, what?"

He certainly wasn't expecting a stately woman with golden hair wrapped around her head in braids, wearing a strange cross-laced dress of burgundy velvet. She didn't so much as raise an eyebrow at his rudeness, but said, "You must be Siyon Velo."

"Must I?" Siyon tugged the collar of his shirt a little straighter, at least. "Who are you, then?"

He got all sorts at his gate. It *wasn't* any secret, where to find him. Some people were after knowledge, or gossip, or a souvenir. Some of them just wanted to talk. And talk, and talk, and talk.

None of them really came to see *him*. They wanted to see the Sorcerer.

"My name is Ksaia Bardha," the woman said. Her Northern accent was slight, but Siyon didn't think he'd be able to get the same sharpness to her name that she did. "I bring to you cordial greetings and respectful congratulations upon your station from the Unified Citizens' Council of the Confederation of Northern Cities."

Siyon stared at her, trying to figure out what all of that *meant*. There were so many words to untangle (what, *all* of the citizens?) that it took him a moment to realise: "You're some sort of Northern ambassador?"

Here? Visiting *him*? With cordial greetings and respectful congratulations—that sounded *official*.

Shit, he had enough trouble with one government. He didn't want another taking an interest.

Madame Bardha gestured to the twisted iron vinework between them. "Do you usually conduct your business through the grate?"

"It's a nice grate," Siyon said.

"Master Velo," Madame Bardha said, like a stern older female relation whose patience was running thin; Siyon started to tense up reflexively.

But before she could say more, footsteps came ringing down the laneway, and a new, cheerful voice said, "What a surprise seeing you here."

The faintest hint of a frown twitched briefly between those golden eyebrows, before Madame Bardha said, "Balian."

Balian was clearly azatani by colouring and the quality of his tailoring, though he wore no longvest, just a plain blue coat over shirtsleeves, and his dark hair was cut oddly short, framing wide, honest eyes and an almost plain face. "I'm so glad you're getting out and seeing more of the city, though—" His sunny face clouded over into concern. "Shouldn't you have an escort? For appropriate respect, of course; the city is quite safe!"

"I must have left them behind somewhere," Madame Bardha said, almost smoothly enough to be believable. "Please excuse me, both of you, and I will go and find them."

She strode back down the lane.

In her wake, Balian—whoever he was—snorted, then muttered, "Left them behind, my eye. Gave them the slip." He fixed Siyon with a sudden sharp look through the grate. "Did she offer you a job?"

Siyon blinked. "A—what? Why would she? Alchemy doesn't work outside the city."

"So we've always been told," Balian agreed. "But I understand you've changed a few things. Why not that?"

It hadn't occurred to Siyon—not that particular possibility. He thought suddenly of the sorcery trial he'd stopped. The *foreign sorcery* trial. And Balian seemed to think Madame Bardha might want him to make alchemy work in the North? Like he didn't have enough problems right here. "Who are *you*?" Siyon demanded.

"Oh." Balian seemed to realise he'd skipped over some parts of the conversation. "Yes. Sorry. Azata Markani suggested you may have need of an assistant for handling some matters."

Markani? Memory heaved itself into the boat of Siyon's awareness. "Oh. You're the nephew." Siyon rubbed at his face, unsure if he could deal with this today. "Look, I don't know that—"

Balian kept talking, unrelenting and sympathetic. "I heard about some sort of reporting requirements? Sounds like you're being buried in gullshit by someone who wants you out of their way. There's a process through the Livery Committee where you can lodge a complaint if we file three consecutive reports without panel amendment, and if it's upheld you can have the entire requirement suspended pending review."

Siyon stared at him. Balian smiled again. He'd dispatched Madame Bardha quite handily as well. Siyon said, "I guess you'd better come up."

The scent of sulphur still lingered in the workroom, but in the living area, the twine had lost its burnished energy. Siyon bundled it aside for later consideration.

When he turned around, Balian was frozen in the middle of the workroom, shadows looming where they'd burst from the corners, coiling around him. "Who's *this* tasty morsel?" Laxmi's voice buzzed out of thin—or rather, ink-thick—air.

Impressively, Balian managed to say, "Um."

"What?" Siyon was unable to help a bit of amusement. "You hadn't heard that I had a harpy bound to my every whim? Laxmi, behave yourself," he added. "Balian here is apparently going to be my secretary."

"I assumed that was exaggerated gossip," Balian said carefully as Laxmi giggled, evaporating into nothing. He touched delicately at his neck; maybe there had been claws in that amorphous shadow or, knowing Laxmi, possibly teeth. Siyon had ordered her to *harm no humans*, but she maintained that terror wasn't harm. And it was apparently delicious. Balian tugged his coat straight. "Is all the rest of it true, then?"

Siyon snorted. "Depends on what *it* is."

"Fair." Balian smiled ruefully. "I was away over the summer. Trading venture up in the North. So all I have to go on is what people tell me and...well, I prefer to see things for myself. I can't say you seem much like the outrageous mage of gossip, hell-bent on dominating the universe."

Which part of Siyon's crumpled clothing, unshaven face, and no doubt bloodshot eyes might be causing that doubt? But Balian was still looking cheerful, and Siyon found it hard to hold on to distrust. "Trading venture in the North," he repeated, then thought of something. "Didn't your aunt say you'd been fired from a clerkship?"

Balian gave a little wince. "Having trouble adapting."

Siyon could relate. "And that's how you know Madame Bardha."

"Use her full name," Balian advised easily, making it sound like a friendly tip, not at all condescending. "If you want to be formal. They don't like titles in the North, not since the revolution. Even a *madame* can get you in trouble. It's still a bit...fraught."

Balian had spent the summer learning the North's foibles, no doubt getting the tone as just-right as he'd managed here. A trading venture, he'd said; Siyon suspected this guy, with his easy manners and easier smile, could clean up at the negotiating table and still leave the other side happy.

Surely he could handle this reporting, and whatever else Avarair Hisarani might come up with to throw at Siyon, trying to shove him back into the box Siyon had dared climb out of.

A thought occurred to him. "Wait. Do I have to pay you?" Weird concept, *him* paying *someone else*. Could he afford it? The Council paid him a stipend for *services rendered to the city*, which was more reliable money than Siyon had ever been able to scrape together, so probably actually a pitiful amount.

But Balian shook his head. "If I can't find profit in this role, I shouldn't be allowed to have it. Don't worry. Secrets can only be sold once. There are far more sustainable methods."

"Oh," Siyon said. "Good." He teetered again. Maybe this *wasn't* a good idea.

Balian looked to the side, where the stack of books was still sitting on the worktable. "Oh, the van Dorryt history of Bezim." He chuckled. "I practically knew that by heart at one point back at school. I do prefer him to the official Lyraec version, even if—" He looked up, caught sight of Siyon, and froze. "What?"

Siyon swallowed. He hadn't even considered this angle. He'd been wishing for Izmirlian's input, and he couldn't have it, but Izmirlian hadn't been the only educated azatan in the city, even if he had been unique in many other ways. This could be... "Do you know anything about Midnight?" he asked, barely daring to hope.

"Not a thing," Balian declared. "Beyond the usual alleytales, of course. But I could ask. The university library is just up there—" He waved, in totally the wrong direction, but Siyon got the idea.

All right. Siyon had a secretary now.

Zagiri had known a clerkship would be a lot of work—it was a *job* after all, and she wasn't completely heedless—but she hadn't realised quite how much would be involved. Syrah Danelani had a dozen other clerks already in her office, and every one of them rolled their eyes when Zagiri had to ask something—how to get the select committee meetings on the official schedule, or where the records needed to be filed.

Whenever she could, Zagiri asked Jaleh instead. For all the woman was an alchemical apprentice, she seemed to work out of Markani's office in the Palace more days than she didn't. Her scorn was less for Zagiri's ignorance than for the Council—or perhaps the azatani—as a whole. "Of course they wouldn't explain anything to you," Jaleh muttered as she pulled Zagiri's paperwork out of its folder and reordered it properly. "How dare *you* get this chance, rather than someone's cousin's recommendation."

Her flat look felt strangely like commiseration.

Between dealing with all of that, and walking all over the bloody Palace delivering reports and records and notices, and the notes to take, the names to learn, the connections to remember, the strategy to consider…Zagiri was as tired at the end of the day, finally making it out of the Palace as the sun flirted with the horizon, as she'd ever been after a night on the tiles. She even *ached*. How was that possible?

She'd only been out once with Bracken since she'd been given her named blade. Every evening, Star Whisper reproached her from where it hung off the post of her bed. The diamonds on its basket hilt deserved to sparkle in rooftop moonlight. The star-maps etched on the blade deserved to be bared beneath their namesakes. It deserved to shine—and carve new legends for its name.

But Zagiri couldn't earn any glory slipping off a roof peak from fatigue. Leaving the Palace tonight, all she wanted was to go home and sleep.

Instead, she went to Siyon's.

Laxmi must have told Siyon she was here, because he was calling down, "Come on up!" before the peal of the gate bell had faded from the alleyway. The grate opened under Zagiri's hand, though she was pretty sure it had been locked before she rang.

As she crested the stairs, a strange voice with the faint edge of an Avenue accent said, "You can just—" and a hand waved, and actually, Zagiri did know that voice.

"Balian." What was *he* doing, sitting at Siyon's workbench with a half-drunk glass of tea in front of him?

"Miss Savani." He smiled as though he was pleased to see her, which set a pleasant little flutter in her stomach. He was far less formally dressed than he had been at the garden party, and the whole plain-with-occasional-moments-of-very-handsome-smiling thing was working well for him.

Siyon came out of the other room, with a book in each hand. "You two know each other already? Azatani." He shrugged and waved one of the books in Balian's direction. "Markani sent her nephew to be my secretary."

Zagiri considered Balian, who just kept smiling. He didn't look much like his aunt, who was sharp and pointed where Balian was genial and rounded. Maybe she was only related by marriage. Had Markani taken her husband's name, or the other way around?

She wasn't *asking* for his full name. That seemed somehow like admitting defeat, at this point. She went and found the pitcher of tea instead, and as she poured herself a glass, she said, "So I suppose I should be telling *him* that the process for reporting to the panel has been finalised?"

"Let me guess," Balian said cheerfully. "It's the standard observation form with an additional question about alchemical repercussions?"

His smile invited her to be inside the joke with him, and it almost annoyed Zagiri how easy it was to just go along with him. "Actually, we persuaded them to bundle that under the possible risks section."

"Even easier!" Balian shuffled some loose papers into his notebook and wrapped the whole package up with a leather thong. "I'll submit a first report tomorrow," he told Siyon, even as he stood up, pulling a plain blue coat off the back of his chair, "in line with what we've already discussed. And then I'll chase up those things at the library. See you later."

He might have been talking to Siyon, but he smiled—again—at Zagiri as he left.

A shadow peeled away from the wall and draped like a scarf around Zagiri's neck. "Someone," Laxmi crooned in her ear, "is getting a bit bothered, aren't they?"

Zagiri shrugged her off, and the shadow evaporated along with the sound of Laxmi's laughter. Siyon had amusement lurking in the corners of his mouth. "What?" Zagiri demanded. "We met at the garden party. He saw the djinn too."

Siyon looked surprised. "He didn't mention that."

"What did he mention?" Zagiri demanded, slurping at her tea and beckoning. "Come on, you know so much more than me. I met him for a handful of moments and then we faced down a delving djinn together."

"And you've already got designs on his bowsprit?" Siyon's laughter had a tinny echo, rattling around the shadows of the ceiling.

"The pair of you are very childish," Zagiri told them. "I want to know who's getting involved in your business, is all."

Siyon shrugged and set down his books atop another stack. When did he become such a reader? Nihath was a bad influence. "He asks a lot of questions. Doesn't know that much about alchemy and was up in the North over the summer, apparently. Not questions about what I *did*. About the planes, about traditional Negedic alchemy, about what I do differently."

Zagiri didn't like the sound of that. "So he *is* trying to get at your secrets?"

"I don't have secrets," Siyon objected, throwing up his hands. "I don't *know* what I do differently. Not enough to tell anyone about it. But—" He rubbed at his face. He looked tired, now that Zagiri was paying attention. Shadows under his eyes. Zagiri could relate. "I think he's just curious."

That word, and the pause before it, and the look on his face. Zagiri would bet all the rivna she had that he wasn't thinking about Balian whatever-his-name-was anymore.

"And the other one's here," Laxmi declared out of nowhere, a moment before the gate bell rang.

Siyon waved a hand and called out again, and a moment later Anahid was climbing the stairs. "Who's that I passed in the alleyway?" she asked in greeting. "He looked familiar. Oh, hello, Zagiri."

"That was Balian," Zagiri told her. "Siyon's new secretary."

"Markani's nephew," Siyon added, "so I assume you know him."

Anahid frowned. "I thought her nephews were Soljan and...the other one."

"Balian," Zagiri pointed out. "Clearly."

Anahid frowned at *her* then. "Or he might be on the *other* side, who are only second tier, and if you'd had a proper introduction—"

"Not my fault!" Zagiri objected. "I met him with Yeva Bardha,

and those Northerners are all weird about names and titles and formality." And she'd been trying to figure it out for herself, but Balian
was too common a name.

Siyon nodded thoughtfully. "He mentioned the Bardha woman. I
thought her name was something else. Sky?"

"Ksaia," Anahid corrected absently, and now she was frowning
in earnest. "The mother. Yeva is the daughter. I'd forgotten until you
mentioned her—but, Zagiri, I saw your friend Yeva the other day."

Zagiri pulled a face. "Friend might be a little strong."

Anahid ignored her. "She was in the Flower district, talking
with—" She hesitated, looking at *Siyon*, for some reason.

Siyon said, "Oh, the one with Aghut's thug?"

Zagiri nearly inhaled the last of her tea. "Aghut the *baron*?" she
managed to croak. "Are you sure?"

"She's quite distinctive," Anahid pointed out. "Oh, you mean the
other one. Well, she had the mark." She gestured to her shoulder,
where the laders and other heavies of Dockside often advertised their
allegiance.

Siyon nodded. "It's not the sort of thing people imitate. And
she had fish down her arm"—he jabbed at his own elbow, as though
in illustration—"that suggest she's killed at least five people in service of—"

Zagiri groaned. "I get it. Fuck." And Yeva Bardha was meeting
her. "She must be making some sort of mistake."

"That's what I thought." Anahid nodded. "You should have a quiet
word to her about it."

"Damn right I will," Zagiri said firmly. "Before anyone else finds
out about this and I lose my position with the committee."

Anahid's eyes widened. "You don't really think—"

"That the prefect of Bezim, who's already under political siege,
might want to distance herself from even a hint of additional scandal?" Zagiri sighed. "I wouldn't blame her at all. Things are very delicate right now. Not just your stuff—" And she nodded at Siyon, who
looked surprised, like he'd forgotten there was any alchemical business going on, or perhaps like he hadn't realised *alchemical* business

was also *political* these days. "The Laders' Guild is being particularly troublesome this year, and apparently it seems like Aghut might be involved in that somehow. And the Northerners are getting a lot of attention, including me for co-sponsoring with Yeva, so it's going to look really messy if she's carrying on with the barons."

Anahid looked very troubled, exchanging a quick glance with Siyon. Maybe she hadn't thought about it like that. Hadn't realised quite how tangled things were right now, or what Zagiri's position was like.

Zagiri wouldn't have thought about it herself, if she hadn't been in it. "You guys have no idea what it's like, up at the Palace," she added. "The Pragmatics gained so much influence over the summer, and I'm not saying Danelani didn't make some bad calls, but they're *fearmongering*." Zagiri waved a hand, grievance starting to fizz in her veins. "Making out like the whole city's under threat from uncertainty, not just azatani profit margins, and so many things are playing into their hands. All these alleytale reports, and I heard today that people are trying to blame magic to get out of criminal charges like theft or negligence, and—it's not funny!"

"It is," Siyon countered, still giggling. "Just a little. That's Bezim, isn't it? We'll try anything to get ahead."

He did have a point, but so did Zagiri, dammit. "The prefect is still the best chance we have for making Bezim a little more fair. Especially with this select committee."

That wiped away Siyon's mirth. "Yeah, because it's been a regular Salt Night of freedom and opportunity so far."

"I know," Zagiri told him, and she did; that first meeting had been rough, and all the back-and-forth with Avarair Hisarani since had only proven the git was going to keep fighting. But there was a *reason* for that. "It's because the select committee sits outside the usual structure and reports directly to the Council itself."

Anahid's mouth dropped open. "You mean resolutions out of the select committee go straight to a general vote without passing through the usual weighing, costing, and approval structures?"

Zagiri nodded. "So for instance," she said pointedly to Siyon, as her excitement started to bubble. "I think we could push through a change to the sorcery law."

His confusion melted into astonishment. "You can just bypass Oblique Methods and that whole mess? Seriously?"

Zagiri was grinning so hard that it made her cheeks ache. She could *do* it. All the fear that had mired the city streets over the summer, when the inquisitors had been cracking down on practitioners who had no shelter, not from the law or from wealth and status...she could make sure it never happened again. "We'd have to convince the committee members," she said. "The sorts of non-azatani practitioners we'd be talking about admitting don't exactly get to speak in Council. But if we can frame the argument right, and show the value of non-traditional approaches..."

Siyon huffed a little laugh. "You mean I need to look like I have answers." He grimaced and rubbed at his rasping chin. "Fuck, I need to *have* answers."

"But you *can*, right?" Zagiri wasn't too bothered. Siyon *always* looked like he was making it up as he went along, but he'd still caught her when she fell. He always figured it out. "There's no one else who can. You just need a bit of space and time to concentrate on it. I can make sure you get it." After a moment, she allowed, "Balian can help too."

Siyon didn't look convinced. In fact, he looked downright troubled. Zagiri glanced at her sister, and Anahid was frowning at him; she'd noticed it too. "Something's troubling you," she stated. "And it has been since the other day, with Imelda."

"Who's Imelda?" Zagiri asked.

"It's not important," Anahid said quickly, without even looking away from Siyon.

Whose eyebrows went up, glancing from Zagiri back to Anahid. He grimaced a little. "Yeah, there was an energy...I saw it with Midnight too."

"Midnight?" Zagiri repeated. "As in the *baron* Midnight? Didn't I just *say* this wasn't the time to be messing with barons?"

"Not my choice!" Siyon insisted. "*He's* the one who...never mind.

The point is: I think things might be a little more complicated than they look. There might be something *more* happening."

Exactly what they didn't need right now. Shit, what *else* was going to pop out of thin air? "Then you need to fix this fast," Zagiri said. "Before anything else goes wrong. So we have a chance at getting things moving. Right?"

Anahid shrugged one unconcerned shoulder. "If anyone can, it's you."

Siyon gave her a sour look, dragged a smearing hand over his face, and heaved a sigh.

But in the end, he agreed: "Right."

CHAPTER 10

Anahid left Siyon's apartment with unease still niggling at the back of her mind, over Zagiri's vehement reaction to Yeva Bardha's indiscretions.

The prefect of Bezim might want to distance herself from even a hint of additional scandal, she'd said. If Anahid was discovered personally running a Flowerhouse, it wouldn't be only a *hint* of scandal.

She hadn't thought Zagiri would care so much. Had hoped that Siyon was right, that Zagiri and propriety had never been too cozy.

They were all changing, it seemed.

Anahid stopped in the street, laying a hand on the wall overlooking the fruit market like she was admiring the view rather than trying to catch her breath.

She wasn't being *careless* about it. She'd stressed to Qorja and Lejman the need for discretion about her identity, and the Flowers had immediately set themselves on the project of creating a disguise. They'd produced a black lace widow's mask from the Old Kingdoms and been three generations into the elaborate family history of "Lady Sable" while Anahid laughed helplessly.

It didn't seem all that funny now, with only a mask and an obviously false story standing between her and the ruin of Zagiri's dreams. It could cause problems for Siyon too, if Syrah Danelani's precarious influence was the only thing keeping the Pragmatics from chaining him to greater profit. Madness to think that a prefect may fall because Anahid Joddani won a game of cards. And yet she'd *seen* stranger things tangle the intricate rigging of Bezim's politics.

What could Anahid do? Go sheepishly back to the Zinedani, like some silly girl who'd been swept away by a fit of pique? No. *No.* She could make this work. She *would.*

But perhaps she should let Zagiri know about the risk, at least.

"Azata?"

Anahid spun around, heart in her throat like she'd been caught out. She needed to be calm.

She needed it more than ever, when she saw who had addressed her and was now giving her the most scrupulously polite nod, nearly a bow.

"Captain Xhanari." No, that wasn't right any longer. "Lieutenant Xhanari." A rung back down the ladder he'd surely struggled to climb, without an azatani name.

Vartan Xhanari, who'd raided her house and searched through her life. Who'd done violence in her parlour and watched her as she'd lied and pretended and deflected him. Whose apology letter had called her admirable, or at least named so her capability, propriety, and composure.

Anahid was surprised to find her feelings a tumult. But one thing she was quite sure about. "You are not supposed to approach me."

He inclined his head again. "I will be reprimanded severely, should you wish to report me."

That sat between them, like a winning card he was passing to her. She remembered, wildly, Qorja saying that *every encounter has its own exchange of power and favour,* and shoved that ridiculous thought aside.

"Then why," Anahid asked, "are you approaching me at all?"

He looked straight at her, as he always had. Straighter and keener than anyone she'd ever met, and she'd always wondered just what he saw when he looked at her.

He'd said he admired her.

Now he said politely, "I don't wish to keep you from your business. May I escort you down to Sable House?"

Her heart froze. A moment later it resumed beating, fast and panicked, stuttering the breath in her lungs. He knew, and he was here; did he intend to blackmail her? Was this how he clawed back the rank she'd had stripped from him? Was he going to—

"No," he said, quick and gentle as a flower furled between them. Took a little step forward that she was too shocked to retreat from; close enough that their toes nudged and he could all but whisper as he added, "I am here to ask for your help."

He held up a calling card; her fingertips brushed over his as she nearly fumbled taking it. VARTAN XHANARI was simply printed on the plain card. No title. But below the name, it read: SPECIAL CRISIS TASK FORCE.

She couldn't help her surprise, and from the tightening of his mouth, Xhanari had seen it in her face. He stepped back again, to a more circumspect and proper distance.

Anahid's mind unclenched from its panic. Xhanari's fall from grace had been particularly ignominious, to go from Alchemy to the Specials. The task force had been created at the height of the baron war, and while the official story credited their keen effectiveness for bringing the combatants (those remaining alive) into a truce, Anahid knew from the gossip at the last prefectural election that they were merely the front for the clandestine deal hammered out by Syrah Danelani.

The task force was a shadow now. A polite fiction of enforcing laws that the barons kept for themselves.

But Vartan Xhanari had never struck Anahid as a man who would be satisfied doing nothing.

The sunset bell started ringing, down in Tower Square. Anahid was late. Qorja had asked for time before trading started tonight, to go over the House's accounts and explain the intricacies. Specifically, she'd said, with reference to the barons' shares. The tithes paid, and influences allowed, and the services and opportunities enjoyed in return.

Anahid looked at Xhanari. At the clench of his jaw and the tap of his toe and the new lines that feathered his eyes since summer.

"I could explain as we walk," he suggested, almost hopefully.

"Tell me first." Anahid turned his card over in her fingers. "Which of them are you going after?"

Which of the barons, ostensibly untouchable, fictitiously policed by his new office, with whom Anahid was, thanks to Sable House, somewhat entangled.

A smile twitched at one corner of Xhanari's mouth. She might have missed it if she hadn't been watching his face. If she hadn't watched it, grown to know it, over the fraught summer. "All of them," he said, plain and simple.

It almost took her breath away. One man, against the four figures who ran the criminal side of the entire city. The four who'd remained standing from the dozens of gang leaders the Bitch Queen had carved through before she was finally stopped. The four who'd controlled the shadows ever since. Aghut, Midnight, Zinedani, and Mama Badrosani, who it was said ruled the lower city like she owned it.

"That seems..." Anahid swallowed, searching for the right word. "Rash."

Xhanari gave a little tilt of his head, not disagreeing. "So was taking Sable House from the Zinedani."

She wondered, briefly, how he knew about that. But he had always preferred to be thorough. If he was stalking the barons, he would be gathering all the information he could arrange.

Anahid shouldn't be listening to this. But after everything they'd shared, she was curious why he would approach her again. And he wasn't, after all, wrong.

Perhaps both of them could be a little rash, on occasion.

Anahid tucked his calling card into the sash of her dress. "Walk with me," she said, turning on her heel. He caught up quickly. "You would seem to be exceeding the remit of your role."

"I disagree." He had his poise back, stiff as armour. Though he'd stopped cutting his hair so short, Anahid noticed. It was long enough now to show that it was straight, starting to fall in his eyes without an azatani curl. Xhanari glanced at her; Anahid looked ahead. "The barons are not keeping to the bounds of the agreement, but no one cares. Because the stability and order that the agreement brings, even compromised, is seen as good for the city."

Anahid thought of the Pragmatics, in the Council. Of their increasing power, according to Zagiri. "You mean good for the azatani."

"It has been an interesting autumn, so far," Xhanari said, and Anahid was not fooled by the apparent change of topic. "In Dockside, the Laders' Guild seems more agitated than usual, but also better supplied, and with a lot of extra muscle. The denizens of the lower city outdo one another with tales of seeing Papa Badrosani patrolling the alleycanals, though he's been dead for twenty years, and the family left alive are strongly encouraging remembrances at his crypt. And the shadowed crannies where Midnight's followers lurk have been seething with a strange eagerness in the last two months.

"In your experience," Xhanari continued, without pause, "are the Zinedani good for the District?"

Think of Imelda—her care, her thorns, her determination to make the best of it. Think of Zinedani with his heavy rings and heavy manners and heavy hand upon his nephew's shoulder. "My experience is still very narrow," Anahid demurred.

"It's going to get wider," Xhanari pointed out. "You are a fish in the school now. The sharks will be curious." It might have sounded like a threat; he seemed almost kind about it. "The Zinedani have steadily pushed out all other interests in the Flower district over the last twenty years. There have always been stories about what goes on unseen in Midnight's hidden tunnels. The Badrosani organisation keeps the lower city on a very tight line. And the Shore Clan has always meddled in the workings of Dockside for their own benefit, even before Aghut took over." His voice had firmed as he was talking; his chin rising again with purpose. He looked at her sidelong. "All I ask is that, if you see anything useful, hear anything useful, you consider bringing it to me. Privately, if you prefer. That will likely be safer. I have put my home address on the back of the card."

Anahid laid a hand against her sash. They had turned downhill, nearing the District. The evening breeze brought the sharp scent of the conifer hedge. She couldn't walk into the District alongside an inquisitor. *Safer*, he said. He had thought of it.

Anahid stopped, and Xhanari stopped beside her. "Do you think I'm in danger?" she asked.

It genuinely hadn't occurred to her before. She was azatani. But an azatani would not run a Flowerhouse. She had stepped outside the bounds of safety.

"I think," Xhanari answered, "it would be a very foolish person who underestimated you. But bullies are often fools." He gave that little bow again. "I hope to hear from you."

He went back the way they had come, striding up the hill with purpose.

Anahid almost envied him that.

Sable House was busy when Anahid slipped in, with black-liveried waiters and attendants rushing about in the first flurry of opening. Qorja passed her on the stairs, with a smile that seemed bright and pleased to see her, and promised to join her in the office as soon as she'd finished with the scheduling.

The office was almost bare. Stepan Zinedani had cleared everything out, or at least he'd tried to, but the enormous black-walnut desk simply wouldn't fit through the doorway. Maybe they'd built the House around it in the first place.

Anahid would need to bring her own things. Make it hers. The thought curled a tendril of excitement in her stomach, despite the uncertainty Zagiri's reaction had seeded, and the nervous twist Xhanari had added.

I think it would be a very foolish person who underestimated you. Anahid ran her hands over the big black desk. Her desk. Her office. Her House.

She would make this work. She would. That nervous twist in her stomach curled tighter still, into anger, or perhaps fear.

As she hauled out the centre drawer of the desk, something rolled to the front; a little cylindrical case, not even the length of her hand,

enameled in bright greens and yellows. Anahid knew this sort of
thing. They'd been all the rage in the Avenues when her father was
young, and he still kept his upon his desk at home.

When Anahid pulled the ornate cap off one end, it revealed a
sharp-polished blade of barely three inches. A penknife, a beautiful
trinket, an elegant fancy.

Anahid put the cap back on and tucked it inside her sash, alongside Xhanari's card. It pressed against her rib with her breathing.
Which slowed just a little. Anahid felt stupid; it was barely even a
knife. What could it protect her from?

She felt stupid, but she left it there.

Olenka looked askance at the twist of twine on Siyon's palm. "That's
supposed to protect me from sorcery?"

Siyon had to admit, it didn't look particularly impressive. Even if he
was quite proud of having—*finally*—done it. It had been extremely fid-
dly work, to keep a thread of that bronze energy bound with the twine
while he looped and knotted the nullification sigil not once, but thrice.

It came smoother if he stopped thinking about it entirely and let
his fingers work, let them catch the tension in the twine and that
energy that glowed just like Midnight had in the alleyway.

Only then, as his mind wandered and his fingers twisted and the
charm finally came into fruition, had Siyon realised what should have
been obvious to him all along.

That burnished energy, shifting bronze at his fingertips along with
silvery Aethyr, sparking Empyre, shadowed and seething Abyss…it
must be the energy of the Mundane itself.

The crossed-circle twist of twine still had a faint sheen of it, a too-
metallic shimmer to the machine-made string. It was almost over-
whelmed by bright sparks of Empyreal energy as Olenka plucked it off
Siyon's palm.

Almost, but not quite.

"Huh." Her sharp hawk eyes slid consideringly to Siyon. "Aren't
you supposed to be working on other things?"

Yes, he absolutely was. Zagiri was right; he needed to fix the sudden-djinn problem quick, before whatever was going on with Midnight went ahead and awoke. But the fact that even Olenka admitted he'd done something here made him grin. "What if," Siyon suggested as she frowned at him, "what I did with *this*, I could perhaps do…" He spread out his arms as wide as they could go.

If he bound up the whole of Bezim in Mundane energy, like the twist of twine, couldn't he keep *out* everything else?

Olenka considered that. "*Perhaps* isn't a word that the Council likes very much."

Wasn't she entirely fucking correct about *that*? "The Council," Siyon muttered, "can kiss my—"

A sudden clamour interrupted from down the corridor—shouting, and running feet, and the bang of a door. Didn't sound like an obstreperous arrest.

Olenka strode off without hesitation, and Siyon hurried after her. There was a solid chance that anything that made the inquisitors shout this much was something to do with him.

A crowd of muttering grey-uniformed bodies barricaded the waiting area, but Siyon stuck close behind Olenka, who carved a way through with sharp elbows. An inquisitorial runner with a flushed face and his hands braced on his scrawny knees gave a report through heaving breaths.

"Fell out of the sky," he gasped, and had to pause for a moment. Clearly not bravi, this one. "Saw it myself. Bright flash of light. Over the fruit market. Like the sun falling."

It was another delver; Siyon knew it by the panic. Another planar incursion. Another thing for the azatani to get their collective knickers in a twist about. Bright flash, falling from the sky… Siyon jabbed at Olenka's side. "One of yours."

She grabbed his wrist and hauled him toward the exit. Behind them, orders were being shouted, forming up pairs and plans. Siyon didn't imagine any of them could run fast enough to get there in time; the djinn, according to Zagiri, had stayed in the Mundane for scant moments.

But as they burst outside, Siyon could still see a spot of light coruscating in the sky over the commercial district by the fruit market. They might just make it, if they ran like the wind.

"Hey," Siyon called after Olenka, "shouldn't I write up my intentions in a report and post it in triplicate to the—"

"Shut up," Olenka growled.

They ran.

As they came off the Boulevard and down the back of the commercial district, Siyon realised it wasn't only a patch of light where the gate was; a blinding and golden line snaked out of the sky into the depths of the fruit market. When Olenka stopped suddenly and he ran into her back, Siyon grabbed her arm and pointed. "Is that the tether?"

"What?" She looked up absently, then frowned at him. "No. What are you talking about? Only you poor skewed Mundanes need an artificial tether. For the rest of us, the soul is a natural tether."

"Then what's—?" Siyon started, then stopped again.

She couldn't see it. That golden path crackling down from the gate in the sky, like a short leash of lightning, was invisible to everyone but him and his weird vision.

The street patrol inqs had put up a roadblock, shoving back a crowd of shoppers, traders, and general street traffic who now pressed forward, keen to stickybeak or just get back to their business. They showed no sign of moving, even for a fallen angel.

"This way." Siyon pulled her down a side street.

Not far along, the buildings gave way on one side to a stone railing and a sharp drop into the fruit market. From here, Siyon could swear he *heard* the angelic tether snapping and crackling like some cranky cookfire. He stepped up onto the stone railing, teetered for a moment, and jumped down to a shop roof. Bracing a hand against the roof's peak, he called back, "Not scared of heights, are you?"

Olenka was already climbing up onto the railing; Siyon hurried to slide down the other side of the roof before she landed on top of him.

From here, he could swing down off the gutter, get a foot to the upper floor windowsill, hop onto an awning beam, and take a running leap down into the market.

It was still teeming with people, most of them sensibly shoving *away* from where the golden sparking string came to earth. Siyon struggled to swim against the tide, ducking and dodging and losing track of Olenka completely. He had bigger problems.

Like what he was going to *do* when he sprinted around a stand of melons to find the angel in a cleared and scorched ring of cobblestones.

It was clearly an angel, all shattering white light and an impression of feathers and sharp edges. It didn't seem to have the flaming broadsword that Olenka had carried or, come to think of it, wings. But as Siyon hesitated, the angel screeched—like a hawk on the wind, like a blade passing just beside your ear—and lashed out with one dazzling limb, shattering a nearby stall and leaving the broken wood smouldering.

A little part of Siyon wondered if that constituted angelfire. There was good money in that. It was how he'd first got into all this mess.

Then he forgot all about that, as a figure leapt off the awning of the damaged stall, straight at the angel. They were visible only as a smudge against the blaze, but as Siyon squinted, he could have sworn they threw something—a rope? It tangled around the angel, a faint darker thread made of bronze and shadow.

Wait. What was Siyon *seeing* here?

Nothing and no one was going to wait while he figured it out.

The angel struggled, as though impeded by that rope, and each twist and shake sent stray tongues of flame licking out to kindle in the nearby wreckage. That shadowed figure reached the top of their leap and seemed to hook a hand around the golden lightning strike of the angel's not-tether.

Siyon stopped dead in shock as the shadow-figure swung off the golden tether and somersaulted away, somewhere behind the angel that was now tearing free of the shreds of that dark-burnished restraint. Siyon pushed himself back into motion; he could worry about who that shadow was, and what they'd done, when they were all on the other side of this.

Before he'd taken two steps, Olenka came charging out of the market rubble, her dropped shoulder hitting the angel in what might have been its ribs with a very human-sounding *thud*. The angel staggered, and Olenka staggered with it, grappling for a good hold. Siyon hoped none of the other inquisitors were seeing this, or there'd be a lot of questions Olenka didn't want to answer about just how the fuck she could go toe-to-toe with an angel.

She slapped a hand against its shoulder—or where a shoulder might be if this blinding light were slightly more person-shaped—and the angel *screamed*, like something was being torn apart.

Siyon staggered, covering his ears, and realised distantly that Olenka had been holding his nullification-sigil twine twist in that hand.

It was the advantage she needed, apparently; Olenka gripped the angel by its shoulder and waist and heaved it up into the air. The effort sent her sprawling, but even Olenka, with the strength of a fallen being, shouldn't have been able to throw a person that far, not all the way back up to its blazing delving gate. That golden tether recoiled like frayed fishing line, pulling the angel up and into a vanishing speck of Empyreal ire.

It lingered in Siyon's vision—the lightning of the tether, the now-gone blaze of the angel—like the whole thing had scalded itself upon the world.

Through the juddering afterimages, he saw the shadow-figure running, laced in the same bronze-and-shadow of whatever they had thrown. That familiar burnished energy.

This person, whoever it was, was wielding the Mundane.

Siyon ran after them, leaping over Olenka, taking off into the tangle of damaged market stalls. He blinked furiously, trying to get his vision back to the real world and yet also clinging to that burnished trace. The shadow became a person, wearing black leathers, looking back over their shoulder—just a glimpse. They saw Siyon; he saw them.

He knew that face. Had seen it in a courtroom. Mayar el-Kartou. Just-Mayar.

Mayar put on a fresh turn of speed, leaping past the inqs barricading the base of the staircase, up onto the railing, racing up it as the crowd hooted and cheered. Siyon, already feeling his months away from bravi drills, slowed to a halt.

"Is that the Sorcerer?" someone in the crowd shouted, and there was a little welter of shouting and maybe even a cheer.

Siyon ignored it all. He might not be a bravi anymore, but he did have *other* tricks. "Laxmi," he hissed, his breath heaving. And again, louder, "Laxmi!"

Shadow poured down from behind a straggling banner. "I am *not*," it snarled as it twisted itself into a raven shape, "fighting a fucking angel, not even for you."

"It's gone," Siyon huffed. "Follow that person!" He pointed to the top of the stairs where Mayar was leaping from the railing and disappearing into the curious crowd. "Find where they go, who they talk to, where they end up."

"And kill them?" Laxmi asked eagerly.

"Don't touch them." Siyon nearly shouted it. "Just report back to me."

With an aggrieved sigh, Laxmi launched onto big black wings and clawed up into the sky.

CHAPTER 11

Everyone at Madame Bardha's party was talking about the angel in the fruit market.

Did you hear? Did you see? Were you there? I hear it killed fifty people, I hear it destroyed half the markets, I hear it fought tooth and claw with the Sorcerer's pet harpy in the skies above the city.

"Two stalls were damaged when it landed," said Zagiri, for the fifth time, fighting to keep her pleasant smile. "And their owners sustained some injuries. It was dealt with by Master Velo in concert with the inquisitors. There's really no cause for such alarm about the whole business."

That was the official line from the select committee, and therefore from the Council, though Zagiri had to agree with those who scoffed at her final remark. No cause for alarm? It was just an *angel* in the *fruit market*. No one seemed to know what it had come to get, or see. As soon as it had crashed down out of nowhere, the stallholders had started pelting it with invective, fruit, and whatever else came to hand. Apparently things had only deteriorated from there.

The formal request to Siyon for a report had returned with a page far too elegantly written to be anything but Balian's work. In very formal, bordering on florid, terms, it had basically said: *Working on it.*

It made Zagiri laugh, and Syrah Danelani sigh, and she hoped it made Avarair Hisarani grind his teeth, but she feared it would aid whatever attack he was preparing for the next full meeting of the select committee. Unless Siyon could produce some results.

Nothing she could do about it here, at the party Ksaia Bardha was throwing in her rented townhouse. It was allegedly a Northern autumnal festival, what they had instead of a Salt Festival. This one was all about celebrating the harvest, which Zagiri supposed would be a pressing concern in a climate where there might only be one in a year, and most food didn't come from trade and the sea.

The party had wooden mugs of some hot and heavily spiced sweet drink, and large orange pumpkins with all sorts of designs carved into them, and sharp-smelling boughs of conifer over every window and door. Presumably no one had told the Bardhas that that smell was associated mainly with the Flower district here in Bezim.

Of course, Yeva should know. She'd been gadding about with the barons there.

Zagiri had been hunting for Yeva all over the party, to talk with her about that. Ksaia Bardha had introduced her to a number of people so far as her daughter's co-sponsor for the Ball, and Zagiri was grateful for the opportunity to talk with people who'd otherwise not have been at all interested, but it *did* make the whole matter of Yeva's indiscretions a little more pressing.

She couldn't let everything she'd worked for be put at risk.

"Zagiri!" someone called, and she spun around eagerly, but it was just Anahid.

"Here," Zagiri said, holding out her mostly full mug of spiced whatever. "Have you tried the seasonal Northern—oh, you've got your own already."

Anahid cradled her mug between her hands and smiled. "Awful, isn't it?"

Zagiri giggled. "Absolutely awful. So *sweet.*"

"I was with the hostess as she was explaining it and I had to keep drinking as she mentioned the various ingredients; I think I'm a little dizzy." Anahid smiled. "And Yeva was suggesting—"

"Oh!" Zagiri interrupted. "Where is she? I still need to speak with her."

"I think in the back parlour." Anahid glanced that way. "But, Giri, I was hoping we could chat about—"

"Definitely. But I need to catch Yeva." And Zagiri hurried away down the corridor.

Yeva was not in the back parlour. Her mother was, apparently teaching a small group of azatani a traditional Northern song that involved lifting their mugs and shouting. Zagiri surreptitiously left her mug on a side table, then ducked into a neighbouring sitting room, and nearly ran into Balian.

"Miss Savani! How nice to see you. Have you tried the mulled mead?" And he offered her a wooden mug.

"Do not!" Zagiri put her hands behind her back as though they were ten years old and playing touched-it-last. She froze for a moment, horrified on Anahid's behalf at her own manners.

Balian laughed, his eyes merry, and it was downright unfair how handsome that made him. "It's an acquired taste." He took a big swig from his mug as though in demonstration. "Can I get you something else, Miss Savani?"

This was getting ridiculous. "Please call me Zagiri," she said, which would at least level the informality. He smiled as though that invitation delighted him, and her stomach gave an irresponsible little flip. "Hey," she added, "you wrote that report from Siyon, didn't you? What's he up to?"

Balian pulled her into the sitting room. It was empty, save for them, and Zagiri was ridiculously aware of the warmth of his hand on her arm, drawing her further into solitude. She missed it when he let her go. "I don't know," he said, though she couldn't remember what he was talking about. Oh yes, what was Siyon up to. "I haven't seen him, not at all, since he left this morning to go talk to someone at the Palace. Though I did get a message asking me to find out about alchemy in the Khanate."

Zagiri frowned. "*Is* there alchemy in the Khanate?"

"I don't know," Balian admitted. "I'm on my way up to the university to find out now that I've fulfilled my duties here." He hesitated, looking at her a little sidelong. "Want to come along?"

Zagiri couldn't think of anything more boring than spending the evening pawing through books. But spending the evening with *Balian* was a different matter.

She still hadn't spoken with Yeva. "Maybe next time. I've further duties of my own. Actually, have you seen Yeva?"

Balian thought Yeva was probably bored of the party already— common for her, apparently—and suggested looking for her upstairs. Poking around in the private rooms seemed like something Anahid would disapprove of, but fortunately as Zagiri neared the stairs, she spotted a flash of golden-blonde halfway up.

"Zagiri." Anahid caught her hand from behind. "Can I have a moment? There's something I think we should—"

"I'll be right back," Zagiri insisted, shaking her off, and rushed upstairs.

It *was* Yeva, stopping at the top of the stairs when Zagiri called her name, and beckoning her up. "*Don't* tell me," Yeva declared, "that I still have to exchange silly gossip with more people. I am done. All they want to talk about is nonsense in the fruit market."

"It was an angel," Zagiri pointed out.

"As though that is the only important thing in the world." Yeva rolled her eyes. "Come. I have firewater instead of that mead."

The firewater was not at all the sort that Zagiri was used to seeing from the Republic—this was clear, rather than tawny brown, and it tore down her throat like iced lightning, leaving her coughing and Yeva laughing. "Better, yes?"

"Different," Zagiri managed to gasp. She set the little glass down on the low table in Yeva's private sitting room. This was clearly the best chance she was going to get, as Yeva kicked off her slippers and tucked her legs up beside her on the couch. "Listen, I—I heard you've been seeing some more of the city."

"I have been seeing lots of things," Yeva agreed. "Though I have not managed to go down the Scarp. Perhaps you could convince my mother to let me?"

Zagiri blinked at that. "Down into the lower city?"

"Yes." Yeva leaned forward, her pale eyes intense. "It was written about in a revolutionary tract. The author called it the perfect allegory of the city, fallen into the ruin of its hubris, the many scraping a living amid the discarded grandeur of the few." Her eyes had gone distant, like she was pulling the phrases from polished memory.

"I... suppose?" Zagiri had never thought about it like that. She'd gone down the Scarp a time or three, when Little Bracken went to raid the Observatory, the safe house of the Bower's Scythe, once the very tip of the promontory and now an island low enough that the waves lapped against the building's stones at the highest of tides. She didn't remember much of the lower city itself save the mud of the alleycanals, the ramshackle density of the tenements, and the children lining the listing balconies to whistle as the bravi ran past.

She supposed those alleycanals *had* once been pleasant, busy streets. Those tenements once grand apartments. The whole of the lower city had been the centre of trade and grand living. The Avenues had only become fashionable after the Sundering.

Wait. "Revolutionary tract?" Zagiri repeated. "About Bezim?"

The revolution had happened in the North. And it was *over*.

Wasn't it?

"Why wouldn't there be?" Yeva asked, like she genuinely didn't understand what Zagiri was asking. "Especially now, when the Sorcerer has shown the world that the azatani do not know everything. How are you so surprised? Are you paying no attention? There is an uprising already stirring in the Dockside!"

"Just Dockside, not the Dockside," Zagiri corrected absently, even as she gaped. "Wait, what uprising? You mean the laders? No, that happens every autumn. The laders or the warehouse workers or the refitters get together and agitate for higher wages." Everyone said so. But looking at the scorn in Yeva's blue eyes, Zagiri was suddenly unsure.

"Every autumn," Yeva repeated, "and you throw them crumbs, while you eat cake!"

"*I* don't..." Zagiri objected, and trailed off. It was true that she didn't have anything to do with it, but her family used the guilds for their trade voyages, didn't they? And her father sat on the committee that oversaw the table of standard pay grades for manual labours.

She didn't. But indirectly, she did.

Yeva leaned forward, her smile curving dangerous as an invitation to duel. "This year, crumbs will not be enough. This autumn, things are different. The laders are not alone. There are those, in Bezim and elsewhere, who will stand with them."

Her words struck a spark of fear in Zagiri, but her tone conjured a greater thrill. Did she mean the North? Had Ksaia Bardha been sent here to encourage revolution? But who were the others here in the city?

Even as she asked herself the question, Zagiri realised the answer. "*That's* why you were meeting with a baron's underling."

This wouldn't be the first time the laders of Dockside and the thugs of Aghut's Shore Clan had a lot in common. Yeva's meeting hadn't been about anything criminal. Just revolution.

Just.

Yeva frowned. "I thought you don't have nobility here."

"What?" Zagiri blinked at her. "Oh, not that sort of baron. The woman you met—in the Flower district—she works for a criminal. A gang leader. A *leader* of gang leaders, really." She wasn't even sure what the Shore Clan did, except that surely it involved smuggling, and some of the Dockside bravi had mentioned beast-baiting rings and other illegal entertainments.

She honestly didn't want to think about it too much.

"You see," Yeva said, lifting a finger like Zagiri had made her point for her. "Where you have such inequality, such a gap between people, that is where you get crime. We saw it in the North as well. The corruption of the grafs and of the streets are like a mirror, yes?" She pressed her hands together, palm to palm, and smiled like Zagiri was with her.

Zagiri wasn't. She couldn't be. This would be as scandalous and damaging as Yeva taking up with criminals. More so. This was revolt.

And yet, Yeva had a point, didn't she? There was a great soaring cliff of a gap in Bezim, carved across the city, and Yeva had barely been here for long enough to know up from down and she could already see what so many of Zagiri's fellow azatani seemed blind to.

This wasn't fair.

Yeva nodded, like Zagiri's hesitation was visible on her face. Maybe it was. "Yes, you agree. I know this, from when we first met. And Balian tells me you want to make change." Oh he *did*, did he? "But this way—with the council and trying to drag them along—this won't work. You must realise that. Trust me, we have tried. In the North, we tried. There were those who believed the grafs—not all, but some—they could be reasoned with." Yeva's face crumpled a little, until she smoothed it resolutely flat. "My father was one. He served a graf. He believed in him. He tried to explain, to reason with him. He was hanged as a traitor, and my mother and I were forced to flee."

Zagiri gaped at her. "I'm so sorry," she said. "I truly am. But Bezim... This is not the North. The azatani are not your grafs. Our government is built differently; we made it that way on purpose. To be more stable, more balanced, more fair."

"Fair," Yeva repeated, and sniffed. "When you bring your ideas to your government, what do they do?" She lifted her eyebrows, like a demand, but didn't wait for an answer. "When I bring *my* ideas to the revolution, I am made a part of it. We all work together. We are none of us more important." She slumped back on her sofa, arms crossed over her chest, and glared at Zagiri. "Are you going to turn me in? I will not name any of the others involved. I could not, if I wanted to. I know none of them."

Zagiri pressed her hands over her face. This was a nightmare. "You and your mother can't—"

"My mother!" Yeva made a rude noise, and Zagiri dropped her hands to stare at her. "She is full of fear, after what happened in the North. She brings us here to hide. But I will not hide."

A little of Zagiri's panic unknotted from her throat. This wasn't some foreign incitement. Just an overexcited young woman burning to make a difference. Zagiri could understand that; she felt it in her bones. And perhaps that meant none of the rest of it was as big or as bad or as bold as Yeva believed.

She was a little disappointed. But it was better this way.

"Don't be silly," Zagiri said, settling her shoulders back the way

Anahid had taught her. "Of course I'm not turning you in." None of the azatani so eager to reopen trade with the North would thank her for the diplomatic scandal—nor would Syrah Danelani, with whom she was linked. "But you need to be more circumspect, or you'll be found out."

Yeva's glare softened a little. "You are sensible. I can respect that."

As though that settled everything.

But Zagiri's mind was a whirl long after she went back to the party.

Anahid had only attended the Bardha party in the hopes of speaking with her sister, and had instead spent most of her time evading Ksaia Bardha's persistent and refreshingly direct questions about Siyon. In retrospect, it would never have been the best situation in which to have a conversation about Sable House—reassuring Zagiri that she understood the risks, and was managing them, and wouldn't let them cause problems, not when she was so proud of what Zagiri was achieving.

Perhaps it was for the best that Zagiri had been so distracted by chasing after Yeva. There would be another—a better—opportunity for them to talk. Anahid couldn't stay longer at the party. She had business in the Flower district.

Even an angel in the fruit market wouldn't stop tonight's auction.

Imelda was getting her wish—her auction held before Salt Night, and run by the House Mistress herself. Little as Anahid wanted to draw attention to herself, it seemed that avoiding the usual duties of the House Mistress would only increase curiosity.

"But we tell *our* story," Qorja had declared, "and that is what they will see."

So *two* new figures of the Flower district would take the stage this evening in Sable House. Imelda the Dawnsong, with crushed beetles sparkling on her toenails and pink-dyed ostrich feathers crowning her coppery hair, would be put up for auction by Lady Sable, in her black lace Old Kingdom widow's mask and layers of confected mystery.

Imelda's excitement had her almost wriggling; when she had to sit still to let Qorja paint her face, her fingers drummed impatiently on her freckled knees, bared by the flimsy little shift she was wearing for the auction. She seemed so *young*—almost younger than Zagiri, for all they were both nineteen.

After this night, she would be a proper Flower, able to conduct her trade in the House under full rates and with full rights. She could make her own decisions, choose her clients, and craft herself a career that might span decades, or catapult her into enormous wealth and influence. The most celebrated Flowers of the city rivalled the fame of Gayane Saliu, and it didn't matter at all that Imelda had been born in Dockside.

"Can we discuss the contract binding?" Anahid asked as Imelda hooked the golden twist of an earring into one lobe.

Flower Night contracts could be made *bound* or *unbound*, depending on whether Imelda would entertain the notion of dismissing the standard contract of behaviour for sufficiently high bids.

The standard contract listed some things as unacceptable that many Flowers found laughable. A little play with rope or feathers or wax, Anahid had been assured, was no one else's business. But there were other clauses that made her blood run cold. Breath shall not be forcibly deprived. Participants shall not be struck with either body part or implement. Any act must have the consent of both parties.

An unbound girl could expect double her usual price, or even more. An unbound girl might suffer indignity or even injury. Killing a Flower was always a crime. But scars could be left, visible or otherwise.

"Hmm," Imelda said absently, considering her reflection; she held herself with a confidence any Avenue debutante would love to have. She was only nineteen. Knowing there were thorns couldn't prevent you being scratched. "I appreciate your concern, mistress. But this is how it is done. No one would mar a Flower Night girl. The gossip would be tremendous. He would be barred from the Houses."

She was so calm about it. Anahid felt tied in knots. Gossip and barring seemed flimsy protections.

"You," Imelda added, turning to look at Anahid straight on, rather than in reflection. "You should remove your headscarf."

Anahid touched her scarf, just over her ear. It was one she rarely wore, black and beaded, suitable for Lady Sable. "I couldn't," she objected breathlessly. She hadn't been out of the house without her headscarf since she first sponsored a presentation.

Qorja, coming in with a heavy velvet over-robe for Imelda, said: "Exactly. An azata would *never*. And thus Lady Sable could not be an azata." Her smiled widened as she reached for the pins holding the headscarf in place. "Let me show you."

She turned Anahid away from the mirror and wouldn't let her see while she gently unpinned and unwound the scarf. Anahid felt jittery and nervous, and she fought the urge to flee with words. "May I ask a strange question? About the baron Midnight?"

Siyon's situation, and his converging oddities, had been teasing at Anahid. And they were far less personally thorny to consider than Zagiri's new propriety or Xhanari's unsettling invitation.

Surprise dropped into Qorja's face like a stone into a deep pool, the ripples soon gone but the cause remaining. "Strange questions are the most appropriate, with them," the stage mistress replied as her deft fingers touched at Anahid's hair.

Her *bare* hair. "Them?" Anahid asked firmly.

"The whole organisation is weird," Imelda said, more of her attention on watching what Qorja was doing. "The other barons are all about business. Midnight's…" She pursed her lips, not finding the right word.

"Midnight looks after his people," Qorja said, with a sort of bland care Anahid couldn't decipher. "When I was younger, I had a regular client among his crew. She spoke very highly of Midnight. Very… fervently." The word was delicately neutral. "She was promoted to lieutenant. And I never saw her again."

A chill stroked down Anahid's spine. And this baron had set his sights on Siyon. Could it possibly be benign?

"There!" Qorja said brightly, but Anahid's new worry distracted her until she was turned to face the mirror.

There was *someone else* standing there. A tall woman, mysterious in her silver-embroidered tabard. Her eyes seemed dark and secretive, and her hair was a knot with a few stray curls softening its severity.

The door opened behind them, and Lejman rumbled, "Mistress."

But Anahid couldn't look away from the mirror. From Lady Sable. A woman wreathed in mystery and mastery. Who had left behind all the rules. Who could do whatever she pleased.

"Mistress," Lejman said again.

Out in the dark, curtained-off stage space, he twitched aside one edge of the heavy drapery to show Anahid a slice of the gathering audience. There was a lot of animated conversation—concerned frowns and eager speculation and wild-eyed gossip in equal measure as everyone discussed today's angelic visitation.

Stepan Zinedani had a table near the front.

Lejman let the curtain fall closed again. "Auctions are open events. Refusing him entry would have been an insult to his family. I didn't think…"

"Quite right," Anahid murmured. Of course they shouldn't insult the Zinedani any more than Anahid already had. But what was he *doing* here?

Anahid set a hand to her stomach, where beneath her costume tabard she still carried the pen knife, and Inquisitor Xhanari's card, in the sash of her plain grey dress. Both of them ridiculous, useless aids, but she'd cling to any small comfort. She was a small fish swimming with sharks.

Lejman wasn't done. "And I have admitted at least one of Aghut's lieutenants, and Mama Badrosani is here herself."

Anahid felt dizzy. "No one from Midnight?"

"Not that I've seen," Lejman said, which wasn't all that reassuring. "But Midnight's priorities are not those of the other barons."

It was bad enough. Three of them. *Stepan.* "Do the barons usually attend Flower auctions?"

"No," Lejman confirmed.

They might be here to see Imelda. Or they might be here to see *her*.

Imelda reached past Anahid toward the curtain. "Good crowd?" she asked, with a smile made tight with anticipation.

Anahid knew when Imelda had spotted Zinedani by the hitch in her breath. Her pinkened lips pressed tight together. But she didn't say anything. She'd already said it. *On the Path of Flowers there can be the occasional thorns.*

They didn't have to make it easy to get scratched, though. "I won't specify the contract," Anahid said. "If an unbound bid is made, you can decide if you wish to accept it."

Imelda's eyelashes fluttered beneath the weight of paint and tiny, glittering flower petals. "The money is important," she said, as though convincing someone. "People take note of the price a girl gets on her Flower Night. And *he* always wanted as much profit as possible."

The House took half the money, when they'd trained the Flower. But Anahid was in charge now. "I am not him. And I will not barter your safety."

There was no more to say, and no point putting this off any longer. Anahid checked her headscarf by habit—and felt a flutter in her stomach as her fingers encountered bare hair.

Lady Sable slipped out between the curtains, and the crowd fell silent with daunting alacrity. They were crammed into the room, crowding the tables, standing in the back. Mama Badrosani must be the magnificent woman in furs and glittering jewels, smoking a long-stemmed pipe at a table of her own. Perhaps Aghut's lieutenant was among the rougher-looking types in the far corner.

All of them were looking at her. But behind her mask, Anahid didn't have to smile. She willed her voice calm and clear, like she was facing down gossip, like she was bluffing at the table. "Good evening. I am Lady Sable, and you are welcome in my House for tonight's auction." Stepan's expression soured, and satisfaction twisted in Anahid's heart. "I present to you Imelda the Dawnsong."

The curtains whisked back, and Imelda stood ready, with the confidence of a woman twice her age, but the challenging smirk of youth. Beneath the lights, her pale skin shimmered like some Northern winter queen in an opera. She accepted the applause as her due, blew kisses into the corner, and seated herself with her oud upon the waiting stool.

She played beautifully, with deep feeling and haunting harmonics, with caressing fingers and a knowing smile. Yet when Anahid risked a glance, it seemed half the audience was watching *her* instead.

The song was a beautiful demonstration of Imelda's elegant House-acquired skills, a haunting opera classic of love all the sweeter for being forbidden. As it soared into its finale, Anahid felt her heart lift with the music. Felt it tug at her memories of girlhood dressing up, pretending to be the heroine. There was a magic here.

Indeed, Imelda looked even more golden, and a haze seemed to shimmer out from her fingers upon the strings, stretching out over the audience as they all sighed together...

The music shimmered away into completion, and Anahid took a sharp breath. What had *that* been? From the slightly stunned fall of Imelda's mouth, she didn't think it was usual, or planned.

There was no time to falter now. The audience applause had been eager and extended, but it was trickling away. It was time for business.

Anahid knew her words. "For Imelda the Dawnsong, a cultivated Flower of Sable House, the reserve mark is fifty rivna. Bidding will begin at twenty."

A bidding marker immediately lifted in the back corner, and a voice called, "Fifty."

Imelda gave a little show of demure surprise, but the hand over her mouth covered a pleased smirk. The reserve was the price at which the Flower unrobed, but after Imelda shrugged out of her velvet over-robe, she still stood with brazen confidence as the hem of her flimsy shift fluttered around her knees.

"Sixty," Stepan announced from his front table, and Anahid nodded without looking at him; his bid was immediately beaten by seventy from the middle of the room, and then eighty from the back.

As the price continued to climb, Stepan raised his marker again, and again. He wouldn't be driving up the price of a girl whose winnings were no longer split with him. Did he mean to win? To take out his frustrations on Imelda, because he'd failed to put Anahid in this very position?

"Two fifty, unbound," Stepan snapped.

A whisper slithered through the room. It was a seventy-rivna jump, yet no one knew if unbound bids were valid. Anahid looked at Imelda, who was staring at Stepan. After a moment, her gaze shifted to Anahid. She didn't say no.

But she didn't say yes either.

Anahid said, "The House will accept bound sales only. I have one eighty in the back."

Stepan stood abruptly, his chair scraping against the floor. "I said two fifty, unbound."

"And I said—"

"It's not your service I'm bidding for."

The whispering simmered louder, and Anahid itched to slap down this challenge to her authority. This was *her* House. But not her decision.

She looked back to Imelda—as did everyone else.

Imelda's chin tilted; she seemed pleased at all the attention. "A girl cannot give everything away all at once," she declared. "Bound, or not at all."

Stepan opened his mouth, raising his bidding marker as though he might throw it, but a new voice cut across the hubbub, as rich and dark as molasses, frayed around the edges through hard wear. "Two sixty, bound as the lady pleases."

At the centre of everyone's attention, Mama Badrosani smirked around her pipe stem.

It took a moment for Anahid to recollect herself enough to say, "Do I hear any further advances?"

She didn't, and Imelda the Dawnsong's Flower Night sold for two hundred and sixty rivna, bound to contract, to Mama Badrosani herself.

Back in the dressing room, Anahid left Imelda crowing in triumph with a delighted Qorja—it was the highest Flower Night price in three years, apparently—and made her way back out into the room. Only dregs of the audience still lingered, but Mama Badrosani sat at her table like a queen holding court; she patted the chair next to her welcomingly. "Sit, Lady, and let's see that face."

Anahid sat but said, "You bought the girl's disrobing, not mine."

Mama Badrosani laughed, loud if rusty, tossing back her head. "Interesting things afoot in this House tonight."

Anahid remembered in a sudden spark the strange magical haze of Imelda's music, but shoved it aside again. She was conversing with a baron. She needed to pay attention.

The other woman held out a hand to shake; a looming opal ring eclipsed the knuckle of her middle finger. "Shakeh Badrosani, but you might as well call me Mama like everyone else. Since you seem to be staying." She tucked her pipe stem back between her teeth, and around it said, "Little advice, one lady o' business to another: Don't think you've seen the last of Stepan Zee."

That seemed pointed. "You think he's a threat?"

"You don't?" Mama leaned closer, smoke rising between them like a veil. "Lady Sable, in this business, we're *all* threats."

"Including Midnight?" Anahid asked lightly, thinking of her questions earlier. "I didn't see *him* here."

Mama gave a little cough. "You see *him*, you know you've fucked up." She grinned; her teeth were cracked and blackened. "And before you ask, all pretty and pert, yes, including me. *Especially* me. Nothing personal, my little gullchick. It's just the business. It's all sharks and minnows here."

Sharks and minnows. Anahid swallowed hard and laid a hand on her sash.

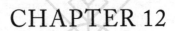

CHAPTER 12

The select committee for the management and mitigation of interplanar activity was still closed to members only, but the corridor outside was crowded as Salt Night with agitated conversations and frantic questions. Siyon edged his way through with speculation foaming in his wake; he wasn't listening, but the occasional word leapt out. *Untenable*, and *insupportable*, and *outrageous*, hissed with vitriol.

At least Nihath seemed pleased to see him, down at the kids' end of the long table. "I've been doing some reading," he said unnecessarily; when *wasn't* he reading? "I think there are allegorical—"

But the prefect of Bezim, in her white surcoat of office and looking like she'd had about as much sleep as Siyon recently, applied her little mallet to the table surface, calling the meeting to order. On one side of her, Azata Markani tidied her papers. On the other side, Avarair Hisarani lay in wait like a stingray.

Siyon should have been used to it by now, but he still had a moment of dizziness over just how much Avarair looked like his brother. Or maybe that was left over from the dreams whose clinging, claustrophobic shadows Siyon had dragged himself out of far too recently. He hadn't *seen* Izmirlian in the dreams, only heard his voice, sardonic and almost fond, echoing strangely in a deep stone cavern. That made it worse, somehow. Siyon had been desperately searching for him, racing down tunnel after tunnel. And now here he wasn't.

That night, on the roof of the Hisarani townhouse, Izmirlian had talked about his brother. A twist to his mouth bitter as the apricot brandywine as he listed off his brother's exploits: *fencing, picking winners at the hippodrome, and politics.*

Siyon couldn't be this distracted here. Not when the exclamations were already rising around the table, hysteria interrupting the fuzzy business of opening the meeting. An angel in the marketplace. Demons murdering us all in our beds. The room was filled with whirling sparks of vindictive Empyre and Abyss.

"Let's be clear." Avarair's voice—too crisp, too cutting, lacking entirely that thread of sharp amusement at the entire world. "These incursions from the other planes can and will continue. Indeed, yesterday's visitation in the fruit market is but one of the many incidents reported in the past week." Avarair lifted a page—oh, it was multiple pages, shaken in display. "Unexpected lights, sightings of non-human beings, things moving or vanishing, including cobblestones, materials from factory yards, and an entire delivery box of scarlet heartsease."

Siyon couldn't help but snort; scarlet heartsease was what university students used to stay awake all night cramming for exams, so he doubted that had been filched by demons. And especially in autumn, surely factory-yard pilfering was more likely to be disgruntled workers.

The noise got him skewered by Avarair's sharp look. "You find the invasion of our homes amusing, Velo?"

So many stern and outraged frowns around the table; even Markani had her lips pursed like a disapproving aunt, and behind Syrah's shoulder, Zagiri was glaring like she'd have words to say later, a lot of them very rude.

But who at this table had ever approved of him in the first place? Dockside brat, gutter grubber, one step sideways from a message-runner. They'd thank the Sorcerer for saving the city, pay him to shut him up, and shove him into a corner. Until there was something to fear. Something to blame on him. Something to demand he fix for them.

Siyon fought a sudden urge to stand up and walk out. At least if someone tried to stop him, it'd be a clean fight.

Nihath's hand touched lightly at the back of his wrist, and when Siyon glanced sideways, this frown was more worried.

Fancy that; *Nihath Joddani* didn't disapprove of him.

Siyon took a breath and stayed put, then opened his mouth to respond.

But Avarair Hisarani hadn't been waiting to hear his answer. Now he was brandishing another set of papers. "And the single paltry report you have handed up to the panel says only that you are *pursuing manifold angles of inquiry to ensure a thorough understanding of the underpinnings of the matter at hand*—Master Velo, in the circumstances, do you really think this is satisfactory?"

In the circumstances, Siyon thought they were fucking lucky to have that at all. *He* certainly hadn't written it; he wasn't even sure what *manifold* meant. Balian was an *excellent* secretary.

"Sorry," Siyon drawled, before Avarair Hisarani could just keep fucking talking. "If anyone here has a *better* idea of what I should be doing, maybe *they* should have been in the fruit market facing off with the angel."

Like Mayar el-Kartou had been. Siyon drummed impatient fingers on his knee. If he didn't have to be here, he could have been hunting for just-Mayar. Actually learning something relevant.

"We are merely asking," Avarair Hisarani said, "what you have been *doing*, Master Velo, while this emergency deepens all around you."

"Us," Syrah Danelani corrected in a cold tone. "We're all in this together, Azatan Hisarani."

He allowed that with the faintest tilt of his chin.

"Actually," said a new voice from halfway down the table. Just some azatan, no one Siyon recognised, but the guy had a stern and no-nonsense face, and his longvest was plain grey.

"Yes, Superintendent Kurlani?" the prefect said.

Oh shit. Siyon's gut instinct was that the superintendent of the inquisitors could not possibly have anything good to say about *him*.

But Kurlani opened his mouth and reported: "The sergeant who assisted Master Velo with dispatching the angelic incursion reports that it was made possible only by the application of an experimental device of some kind."

Siyon barely stopped himself gaping in surprise. He certainly didn't manage to scrape together a response before Avarair Hisarani leapt back in with a demand: "Why was this not mentioned in the report?"

"I think you'll find," Markani said, flipping through her own set of pages, "that an item under *other activities* mentions sundry further explorations of preexisting projects that have not yet proven related."

Siyon needed to get hold of a copy of this report. Everyone knew what he'd been up to except him. But scrambling through by the tips of his fingers was a habit he still hadn't lost. "That's right. I've been trying to develop a way to negate the effect of alchemical charms, so that the inquisitors can—" *Stop wetting their pants about sorcery*, had been how he was describing it, but this hardly seemed the audience for that remark. If only Balian and his fancy words were here. "Ah, maintain full confidence."

"And it is very much appreciated," Superintendent Kurlani chipped in supportively.

Siyon might have felt like he was dreaming, if his dreams had been anything like good recently.

"But *how*," an azata on the other side of the table nearly wailed, "are we supposed to maintain *our* confidence without a clearer understanding of what is going *on*?"

Another azata immediately snapped, "As though *you* would have any clue about alchemy even if it was laid out for you."

The first azata lit up with umbrage, but Danelani hammered the meeting back to order before things could get really entertaining.

An azatan up toward the top of the table took advantage of the sudden quiet, leaning forward to address a question to Siyon: "Couldn't you make one of these devices for the entire city, then?"

Exactly what Siyon had been wondering about, though obviously he couldn't quite tie up all of Bezim with imbued twine.

Beside him, Nihath said with some agitation: "But if the charm is for the negation of alchemical effects, wrapping up the entire city might well cancel out all alchemy."

There was a stunned moment and then an explosion of alarm. Not just from the other practitioners at the table, but *everyone* seemed very upset about that idea. Siyon could see that the Flowers—with their charms and glamours, not to mention their alchemical contraceptives—would be worried, but the azatani outrage was more confusing.

"My factories!" the azatan nearest bleated. "You can't—oh, ink and ashes, it would shut down *everything*."

Oh. Oh, of course. Siyon knew—and had provided alchemical material to—a lot of the industrial alchemists who made their livings maintaining the processes that ran in the factories and workshops across the river.

"A disaster!" the azatan wailed, clutching Siyon's hand imploringly. "You mustn't!"

Another hammering of the mallet, and the quick raising of a motion, and a unanimous vote: Siyon was not to conduct any such nullification of Bezim without express direction of the Council.

Because Powers forbid—or rather, *Council* forbid—anything should get in the way of azatani profit.

"This is why," Avarair Hisarani insisted, making a last press at the issue, "we need more fulsome and specific reports."

"This is why," Siyon countered, "I need to be—" What had Balian written? "—understanding the underpinnings of the matter at hand. There's more in play here than we—"

"In *play*?" some snooty azatan repeated, like Siyon had started passing around the rakia bottle. "Velo, I don't think you're really approaching the matter with due seriousness."

Someone else jumped in to carp about all these interruptions, and everything devolved quickly into a dirty little brangle.

Leaving Siyon a moment to reflect that probably, trying to explain to *this* bunch that the problem might be bigger, and stranger, and scarier than they realised hadn't been a good idea to start with. Siyon might find it exciting that Mayar had been doing something he didn't understand, but the azatani might find the involvement of an alleged foreign sorcerer less invigorating.

He'd wait until he had some *answers*, not just questions.

"If that is everything," Syrah Danelani called over the last dissipating mutters of the argument, "we shall proceed as previously outlined and—"

"No," Avarair snapped, "that is not everything. Velo must be brought properly to task. We must see evidence that he is addressing the matter with his full attention and all appropriate resources."

It was possible Danelani's patience was fraying. "Like what?" she snapped.

"Where," Avarair asked, with alarming relish, "is his pet demon?"

Another explosion of noise around the table, though some of it seemed rather eager and anticipatory this time. "Yes!" an azata—the one who had been accused of not understanding alchemy—exclaimed. "She could fight off the angel!"

The superintendent of the inquisitors seemed offended at the notion. "We do not need demonic assistance to protect Bezim."

"Better her at risk than our people!" an azatan challenged him.

"You're welcome to ask her," Siyon called over the babble. "But she won't do it."

From the flash of satisfaction on Avarair's face, that had been the wrong thing to say entirely. He turned almost triumphantly to Syrah Danelani. "Does not this select committee have the power to compel reasonable compliance from the citizens of Bezim?"

"The demon's not a citizen," Siyon snapped. Though Siyon was. For a moment, he wasn't sure what he'd do, if Avarair wanted to compel *him*. He'd been trying to stay within the lines. But there were limits.

But Avarair sneered: "Then perhaps, in such a dire time, she should not be enjoying the amenity of our city without contributing to its defense."

A different rage spilled cold through Siyon's veins. Of course it came to this. When fear tightened its grip, of course the azatani would turn on anyone who wasn't *them*.

"You think *you* can make her leave?" Siyon demanded with a tight smile at imagining that exchange.

But he looked at Syrah Danelani—whose son had been dying, his soul ground against the planar barriers, until that demon had been brought back from the Abyss. It had been two months since then; Siyon didn't know if Laxmi and Enkin were still bound together, but he didn't think Syrah Danelani would risk it.

Sure enough, the prefect smacked the table with her little mallet again, and her voice cut through the hubbub. "This matter is moot. The city will not lay its hope in the talons of a harpy. If there is *nothing else*—" And she fixed Avarair Hisarani with a sharp look. "Then I declare this meeting concluded."

Hisarani was out of his seat in a moment, papers bundled in the crook of his elbow as he strode around the table, calling, "Kurlani, I'll walk with you."

Siyon watched them go, Avarair Hisarani and the inquisitor superintendent, and suspected that nothing good could come of *that*.

But he'd survived this meeting. It was *over*.

Which meant the *real* work could start.

According to Laxmi, Mayar's flight from the fruit market had been fast and circuitous enough to have lost another bravi, but not a harpy on the wing. Nor did they seem to have spotted the trailing demon, though clearly there was more to them than just another dabbling bravi.

Mayar had flourished that burnished bronze Mundane energy. Siyon was sure that was the key to all of this, and he wanted to know more.

As Siyon left the Palace of Justice, Balian leapt up from where he'd been waiting among the stone monsters that flanked the stairs.

"What?" Siyon jerked his thumb over his shoulder. "Did you get fired so bad they don't even let you in the building now?"

Balian's eternal equanimity might be annoying if he weren't so cheerful about it. "I didn't want to miss you. Again."

Faint stress on that last word; Siyon refused to feel guilty. He'd been *busy*. He was still busy. "Talk while we're walking. Laxmi tells me I have pressing business out at the Western Hill depot." Balian fell as easily into stride beside Siyon's longer legs as Izmirlian ever had, which Siyon absolutely was not thinking about. "Thanks for the report, by the way. What does *manifold* mean?"

"Many and varied," Balian responded easily. "Technically not required yet, though I thought it would look better to hand one in. Of course, I don't actually *know* what you're doing…" The sentence trailed, like a hook in water.

Siyon wasn't biting. *He* didn't know what he was doing. Though perhaps he was starting to pick shapes out of the shadows. "It helped. But Hisarani is clearly out to get me."

They skirted around a pack of azatani youths, dawdling along the shade-dappled paths of the Palace parklands. Balian waited until they were out of earshot before he asked diffidently, "Is that to do with his brother?"

Siyon should probably have been expecting that. "Gossip mentions him too, does it?"

Balian shrugged. "Gossip says Izmirlian Hisarani ran away with an opera singer. Or got stabbed in a lower city bordello and dumped in an alleycanal. Or perhaps set out to find the lost capital of the Grand Khanate that the desert swallowed up."

Siyon couldn't help a faint chuckle. "That one sounds more like him."

"So you did know him?" Was that surprise, or satisfaction, or something else in Balian's voice?

Siyon was having enough trouble with his own feelings. "Yeah, I knew him. All too briefly." Enough wallowing. "What did you not want to miss me with?"

"Oh, yes." For once, Siyon had managed to catch Balian almost off-balance, but he rallied quickly. Even as they stepped out onto the Boulevard, heading west toward the city gate, he said, "That matter you asked me to research. With Midnight? I assumed you meant the crime baron, but I wanted to double-check. My friend at the university library found a mention in the Lyraec annals of the Cult of Midnight, which isn't quite right, honestly, the Old Lyraec is more like the Darkest Shadows—what?"

Siyon had stopped dead; Balian turned back to face him. *We are the one who waits in the darkest shadows*, Midnight had said. Maybe it was a coincidence. Except Tein Geras had suggested that Midnight didn't age. Except Imelda had linked the nullification sigil, which looked a lot like Midnight's mark, to myths of the founding of the city. Anahid had known it too. Wild men mourning something.

"Were these cultists up in the caves on the crag?" Siyon asked, feeling strange and numb.

"Oh." Another question Balian hadn't expected. He pulled out a notebook and flipped through its pages. "I don't think so? The Lyraec annals say *underground*, though I don't think that's literal."

Siyon was less sure. Everyone knew about Midnight and the tunnels. Something was buried in Bezim's history, and it seemed to be rising.

"Find out everything you can. On all of it. Midnight, the cult, the caves, the tunnels, anything that seems related, however weird." Siyon hesitated, then added, "You can access the Summer Club library too, if it'll help. Though they're still sorting it after the inq raid."

"Really?" Balian huffed a strange little breath. "My brother would haunt me if I didn't grab that chance. Yes please, and I'll see what I can do." He scribbled a note, then his gaze slipped past Siyon's shoulder, and he frowned. When Siyon started to turn, Balian snapped— sharp but quiet, "No. Don't. There's a clerk back there that I know. Very junior, but reports to Avarair Hisarani."

Did Balian know *everyone*? Wait. "Do you think he's following me?"

"She," Balian corrected absently, closing his notebook. "I'll find out, either way. Make sure you're back in the city before sundown." He brushed past Siyon, heading back the way they'd come, crying out, "Usha! What a surprise!"

Siyon ducked down a side street, cut through a quiet fountain yard, then looped back to the Boulevard near the gate. It seemed surprising that Avarair Hisarani might have him followed. Didn't that suggest Siyon was somehow important?

Maybe a buzzing fly felt important, before it got swatted.

He shivered as he passed through the city gates, like a shark had shadowed where his bones would one day lie. Siyon wasn't going to let himself be easy to swat.

The hills outside the city made Siyon's skin prickle with exposure. There weren't even planar emanations out here, save a few faint wisps on the wind. Nothing but a tumble of rocky hillocks from the gate down to the hippodrome and the little encrustation of other buildings that had sprung up around it.

The Western Hill depot was a tight knot of markets, warehouses, guesthouses, and rakia gardens, clustered around the hippodrome and avoiding the thornier tolls of business in the city proper. In the heart of the warren, the solid stone bulk of the caravanserai squatted. It had been here even before the Sundering had spooked every horse in Bezim and made the new hippodrome necessary. A home away from home for generations of traders from the various remaining Khanates, who didn't feel comfortable—or perhaps weren't welcome—inside a city their briefly united clans had once tried to conquer.

The massive stone arch at the front was worn by time and the wind over the hills, but the painted decorations were fresh. Inside, shouts and singing and ringing bells and the cries of animals echoed and redoubled off the buildings that bounded the central square. There were pens and strung convoys of oxen and donkeys and a strange humped beast that Siyon realised must be a camel. He loitered, goggling at the dusty train of animals, until someone bellowed at him to get out of the way and he danced aside to avoid a couple of men staggering along with a heavy trunk between them.

"What you want?" One of them looked Siyon up and down. They were both from the Khanate, with blue-black hair and high cheekbones and leather banding their tawny arms.

Siyon, obviously, was not. "I'm looking for Mayar el-Kartou?"

"Kartou clan?" The other one jerked his chin. "Up there."

The second level of the caravanserai was lined with a long, covered veranda. Many of the doors were open, and the noise of the stock-yards competed with raucous chatter and laughter and the clattering of crockery.

"Kartou?" he asked, and was pointed farther along.

The next time he stuck his head in the door to ask, a woman looked up from her stove and demanded, "Who's asking?" She had a massive frying pan that Siyon could barely have got his arms around, but she flipped grains with practiced twitches of her wrist. Her face was age-lined, and her grey-streaked hair covered by an elaborately beaded cap.

This seemed promising. "I'd like to talk with Mayar el-Kartou," Siyon said.

She snorted. "You and everyone. They go, they come, they go again." She spoke quickly, her accent clipped, and Siyon wasn't sure who she meant; were other people looking for Mayar? The woman shouted at an ear-ringing volume, "Yalla!"

A girl of maybe ten elbowed Siyon aside in the doorway. "What?" she bellowed back.

The old woman spoke quickly and incomprehensibly, the words twisted and half swallowed. One of the Khanate dialects, Siyon realised helplessly.

The girl ran off. The old woman eyed Siyon. "Who are you?" she demanded again.

"Siyon Velo," he admitted.

"The Sorcerer?" The voice came from the back of the room. Siyon hadn't realised there was anyone there, amid the woven hangings and smoke haze, until the man leaned forward. He was hefty, broader than Siyon if not as tall, and the muscled arms bared by his leather vest spoke to heavy work, though not necessarily in trade. There was the stillness of violent potential about him, and as he came forward into the light, Siyon could see a scar or three on his arms, between the gem-studded bands. He peered at Siyon. "Are you as I've heard?"

"Depends what you've heard," Siyon hedged.

"Oh, the Sorcerer." The old woman cackled. "Twelve feet tall. Rides fire. Seduces pretty young men. So you're safe, Bo."

The man ignored her, still watching Siyon. "Or some say a charlatan. Street tricks. Not properly taught. Causes problems."

Siyon shouldn't feel so bitter about the truth.

"But you look like a mage," Bo said, like he was commenting on the colour of Siyon's eyes. He reached out, and Siyon flinched back, but the Khanate man merely rubbed his fingers together near Siyon's ear. He sniffed, then frowned over at the stove. "You added too much cumin."

"What do you know about cooking *or* mages, Uncle Bo?" a new voice asked from behind Siyon.

It was just-Mayar—or perhaps, considering where they were, Mayar el-Kartou. Or maybe not. Mayar was clearly among their own people, but with a freshly shaved scalp and no bands at all on their bare arms, Mayar was also clearly different.

Siyon knew a bit about belonging, and not, at the same time.

"This guy," Uncle Bo said, "says he's Siyon Velo."

"He is," Mayar responded easily. They were looking Siyon over just as closely. "You need some way for people to recognise you, if you want to throw your name around. Didn't you have a purple coat, when you did your shit over the summer?"

Something came whistling past Siyon's ear to ping off Mayar's forehead—a hot toasted grain, he realised, as the woman behind him said, "Tscha! My daughter didn't raise you to talk like that!"

Mayar scowled, rubbing their forehead, and Siyon leapt in. "I came here looking for you. Back in the fruit market, with the angel—"

"Angel?" Bo frowned like a thunderstorm. "What have you been doing? Your *meekash* did not let you ride the wind here to go getting involved—"

"Uncle!" Mayar nearly shouted, rolling their eyes, and dragged Siyon back out onto the veranda by his elbow.

Siyon wondered if he'd overestimated how old Mayar was. Inside, the old woman started shouting at Bo, and Bo sniped right back, but neither of them seemed inclined to follow.

Mayar huffed and folded their arms. "You have family?" they asked.

Siyon shook his head. "Not anymore. Not really."

"Good and bad, I guess." Mayar shrugged, looking Siyon up and down, lips critically pursed. "Yes, I stepped up to the angel in the market. I didn't realise—well. If you're claiming all the city as your territory, I guess that's fair, you quested for it. I can go; my uncle will be glad to take me home."

"Wait," Siyon nearly yelped. "No. What?" What had just happened? "I want your help. What you did—you could see the tether too, right? You tangled the angel up in Mundane energy."

The more he said, the more Mayar's frown deepened. "See?" they repeated. "No. I *feel*. What is Mundane energy?"

"Like..." Words were getting him nowhere. Siyon lifted a hand and pulled together a pinch of burnished glow. It came grudgingly, thick and sluggish, sullen as a glowing coal between his fingers.

But Mayar took a sharp breath, eyes going wide...though *not* looking at Siyon's hand. "Mother Sa," he breathed. "Uncle is right, you *are* a mage."

What had Siyon stumbled into here? Excitement bubbled up in him like water through a breached hull; for the first time, he didn't feel like he was entirely alone in this mess. The pinch of Mundane energy slipped out of his fingers, and Mayar's shoulders relaxed a little. They'd said they *felt* it. "What's a mage?" Siyon asked.

The tilt of Mayar's head suggested they were suddenly unsure about a number of things, but they answered readily enough. "You. Me. One who can lay hands on the essences of the world and bend them to their will." They shook their head. "None of the others, not even in Haruspex, they had no idea...You say you *see* it?"

"All the planar energies," Siyon confirmed. "It took me a while to notice the Mundane. But maybe it's getting stronger."

Mayar nodded thoughtfully. "Usually all I can grab is sparks. Enough to do little tricks, like a street show. But when I reached out in the market, with that angel, there was so much. Like it was rising in response."

This was fascinating. This was exactly why Siyon had come. Nihath would probably love it too. "There's some people I'd like you to meet. I think this Mundane energy might be the key to what's going on. Between the two of us, we'll be able to find a solution, and then the Council—"

"The *Council*," Mayar repeated, scalding with derision, and Siyon remembered that he'd first seen Mayar in the accused circle of an aza-tani courtroom. "Yeah, that's not happening. My uncle's not the only one who's heard about you. Seems like you really are on an azatani leash. Just another dog guarding their warehouse."

"Hey," Siyon snapped, half by reflex. But that was unfair. "I'm not apologising for being sensible. They're in charge. I need to work with them."

"With." Mayar gave a sharp little bark of laughter. "You know what got me arrested? I was growing flowers out of a handful of fire on a street corner, for small change and to make the kids squeal. And I'm a danger to Bezim. Fuck *with*. It's only *for*. They only want things they can control."

"It's not about *them*," Siyon insisted, a little desperate. He thought he'd grasped an answer, or at least a possibility, and now everything was slipping away like water between his fingers. "Something's happening here. We're a part of it."

"Not my city." Mayar smiled, flat and brittle. "That's been made clear."

"It's my city," Siyon insisted.

"Do they think so?" Mayar challenged, and they left Siyon alone on the veranda.

Siyon couldn't help thinking of the committee meeting today. Of Avarair Hisarani, entirely willing to deny the city to those who wouldn't do as he wanted.

But Avarair Hisarani didn't get to make decisions for Siyon Velo. Bezim was his city too, and he was going to make sure it came through whatever was happening. All of it, not just the azatani.

He'd do it alone, if he had to.

CHAPTER 13

Sitting down to her breakfast—that was really a late lunch—Anahid gave thanks for her housekeeper, Nura, who had once again included a pot of coffee without being asked.

This wasn't sustainable; Anahid couldn't keep racing the dawn back to her own bed and then hauling herself out again to pay a couple of afternoon calls. But there was so much to do at Sable House; whenever Anahid thought things were going well and she'd be able to leave before the Deep bell, some small matter would go awry—a client staying overlong with a Flower and pushing out the schedule or a streak of luck at a gaming table that deserved the commendation, and distraction, of the House Mistress herself.

It would be easier to shirk if things were not so fascinating. If each system of the House didn't turn so intricately and compellingly with the others. If each part didn't snare Anahid's attention like a cunning lure.

There was no give in the other direction. Afternoon calls were necessary to avoid even more gossip. Society relaxed a little, in the weeks after the social season and before the Salt Festival, but *someone* was always watching.

Already, more than one azata had asked delicate questions about the company Anahid might be keeping, or told a whimsical story about the extra-marital romantic affairs of an aunt or grandmother. Some of those stories were a little risqué for azatani society, and once Anahid might have been among those hiding a blush in her teaglass. Now she listened with calm curiosity, comparing against the overheard chatter of Flowers.

And perhaps she cast a newly contemplative eye over the azatans parading peacock-like at promenade. None of them seemed particularly worth the potential scandal—faint as it would be beside all the other trouble Anahid was already juggling—and certainly not worth adding more commitments to her crowded daily schedule.

As for Nihath...

Nihath drifted into the dining room, where Anahid sat at her late breakfast. He poured himself a glass of tea and only then looked up from the book he was reading. For a wonder, he actually noticed her. He even closed his book over one finger marking the place, and said, "Have you seen anything untoward in the Flower district recently?" When Anahid stared at him for an astonished moment, he added, "Are you still going down to play carrick?"

"Not to play carrick," Anahid admitted. She hadn't sat down to a game since she'd won the House. She hadn't felt the lack. There was more than enough in the running of the House to keep her fully engaged. "Things have progressed somewhat from there. In fact—"

"Other games, then." Nihath waved the book dismissively. "Have you seen anything strange? In the Houses or the arcades? Are there alleytales about the District?"

Anahid pressed her lips tight against a sharp frustration; of course he wasn't actually *interested* in what she was doing. Except as it related to whatever it was that *he* was doing.

"Are there?" Nihath pressed.

Anahid sighed and drained the last of her coffee. She thought of Imelda's auction, and the strange golden haze as she played, but couldn't really find the words to describe it. There was an easier example to hand. "I thought I heard something, one morning, close to dawn. Like scales on stone, and laughter. Siyon mentioned a tale about a naga in the District."

"Yes!" Nihath seemed very satisfied. "Just like that."

He hurried out of the dining room.

Sometimes—in fleeting, heedless, impossible moments—Anahid wondered why she bothered coming back to this house at all. Everything she was most interested in was elsewhere.

Every step down the hill, away from the Avenues, felt like turning her face into the wind. As though she were on a trade voyage of her own, travelling into possibility. All the petty matters of society fell away behind her, her mind slipping easily into the problems of Sable House.

They badly needed someone to run the gaming floor, since the last manager had walked out with Stepan. Qorja couldn't keep doing both jobs at once; even her capability had limits. The best candidate so far—one Anahid had actually spoken with, and been impressed by the credentials of—had been far too entangled with the Zinedani. Anahid didn't want to descend into paranoia, but she also didn't want to put her House at risk of him carrying information, or even doing something underhanded. Perhaps Anahid could—

She paused in her thoughts as she turned a corner and Sable House came into view. The big black doors were open, of course—they were always open—and the grate was pulled across to secure the entranceway. All business and access went through the side alley and courtyard during the day.

But there was a knot of people outside the doors. Lejman was there, and the skinny little Lyraec man she recognised as the House's usual alchemical provisioner, and—as Anahid hurried over—she could hear Qorja from inside, saying, "What do you *mean*, alchemically fused?"

The sun slanted obliquely across the courtyard, lancing between two other Houses. Their upper levels were lined with curious faces, off-duty Flowers with their hair in rags and turbans sipping drinks and gossiping as they watched. The Fade bell had been ringing when Anahid left the Avenues, so they had perhaps half a bell before sunset, when clients would start arriving and the House needed to be open.

"What," Anahid demanded, "is going on?"

The little Lyraec alchemist looked up at her and gulped. He had one black-smeared hand wrapped around the padlock that fastened the security grate, and more black smudged up his bared forearms, and across his cheek, like he'd wiped his face absently.

"The lock has been tampered with," Qorja said sharply from inside.

Anahid grabbed for the lock, heedless of the black gunk. Where the key would go—the big black key she had a copy of on a chain around her neck, under her dress—the hole had been plugged up with something that looked like...stone? She prodded it with a thumbnail. It was hard, glossy, black. Like obsidian.

"Fuck," Anahid snapped, letting it drop again. The Lyraec alchemist handed her a rag to wipe her hands. "Can you break it?"

"The lock's charmed against damage," Lejman rumbled. "And the grate as well."

But this had got around both.

"I think I can dissolve the substance," the alchemist offered. "A colleague mentioned dealing with similar tampering on Dockside warehouses recently, probably the Laders, and..." He trailed off as Anahid turned a sharp look on him.

"How long?" That was all she cared about.

"Um." He glanced at the setting sun.

All the answer Anahid needed. It would take more time than they had before opening.

Anahid drew in a breath, and her chest swelled with more than merely air. Rage *seethed* in her. This was clearly not an accident—nor anything to do with the arguments the laders and other unhappy workers of Dockside were currently having. But if the wherewithal to achieve this was being passed around by the disgruntled and potentially violent, she knew who might have been eager to use it upon Sable House.

She saw again in her mind Stepan's face as he lost the auction on Imelda's Flower Night. Screwed up like a thwarted child. This was just his sort of vengeance, petty and childish and dirty.

A taunt. A threat. *We're all threats*, Mama Badrosani had said. *Sharks and minnows.*

Anahid wasn't going to be a minnow to anyone's shark. Especially not Stepan Zinedani. She wouldn't let him get away with doing this.

But first and foremost, she needed to *fix it*.

"Get started," she snapped at the provisioner, and looked up at Qorja through the grate.

All her own misgivings were echoed on the stage mistress's face. "Would your friend be able to fix it faster?" Qorja asked quietly.

"My friend?" Anahid repeated, then realised—Siyon. She hadn't even considered it, but now that she did, glancing back at the sinking sun, she shook her head. "There's no time, even if he *is* able to be found."

"Mistress." The voice came from Anahid's elbow, where Imelda had sidled through the crowd, wrapped up in her dressing gown. "What about the thing he was working on the other day? The mud sign?"

For the cancellation of alchemical effects. What had Siyon called it? "The nullification sigil," Anahid said to the Lyraec provisioner. "Have you tried that?"

"What?" He looked up from the glass bowl he was carefully measuring various liquids into. "That's for temporary workings and flimsy charms. For something like this, you'd need a prepared solution to balance the planar influences, and that would take even longer than what I'm already attempting."

"I just use rakia," Imelda said with a sweet smile, producing a pretty little chased-silver hip flask from her pocket.

"Let her try," Anahid ordered. "What can it hurt?"

The Lyraec alchemist's ego, apparently. He sulked his way aside barely enough to let Imelda crouch daintily beside the lock. The sun sank lower with every moment, and Anahid clutched her hands together to stop herself fidgeting.

Imelda took up the lock, and it nearly filled the whole of her slender palm. Holding it flat, she carefully doused it in rakia and tucked the flask between her knees to have a hand free for drawing. She traced a circle on the side of the lock, and then she took a sharp breath in and slashed a line down through the centre of it.

The padlock sizzled, and Imelda squeaked and dropped it, tipping over backward. The lock swung, clanging against the gate, and all of the stony substance turned to melted wax, dropping away with a sound like an oyster being shucked to plop into a steaming little puddle.

The padlock sprang open and fell away from the grate. "Oh," said Imelda, from where she'd fallen. "It's wiped away *all* the charms."

"Still, that's one problem solved." Anahid smiled. "Well done, Imelda. Please go and get ready. It seems we'll be opening as usual."

The Lyraec provisioner stared at the mess like he'd never seen anything like it. "What just happened?" He sounded bewildered, looking up at Anahid. "That shouldn't have worked. It certainly shouldn't have worked *that* strongly. I've never seen—"

"But now you have," Anahid pointed out. "Get this cleaned up, please, and we'll need a new padlock charmed by sunrise."

Because if Stepan was inclined to cause them problems—and it seemed that he *was*—Anahid wanted a new lock and a sturdy one. She didn't want to descend into paranoia, but if the threat was real…

They were all threats. Just the business. Nothing personal.

Anahid was going to *make* it personal.

Word had come in from the late-night streets that the Bower's Scythe bravi were on the move, swarming up the Scarp to raid Little Bracken. Finally, Zagiri could cry her new blade's name in proper battle.

If they ever showed up.

Zagiri loitered with Daruj and another four Bracken down a narrow street with a good view of the square out front of Bracken's chapel. They were supposed to be the ambush, and Zagiri had been thrilled to be chosen, keen to let the night air and the clean slice of a sabre sweep away the worries and concerns that tangled up her daylight hours.

They'd been waiting half a bell, and all those questions were creeping back into her mind.

How could she use the select committee to introduce reforms to the policing of alchemy? If Siyon couldn't get to the bottom of this latest trouble, would angels and djinn and demons keep appearing? Would every chance of progress be stymied just because the azatani felt threatened?

Was Yeva Bardha right? Was revolution the answer?

"Hey." A pebble pinged off the wall beside Zagiri's head, and she jumped, banged her elbow on a windowsill, and glared across at Daruj and the starlight glint off his grin. "Some pretty young za have your head in the clouds?" he teased in a whisper. "We've got business here, and you're away across the whitecaps. Where you sailing?"

The night was still empty of whistles and running feet. "We've got business?" Zagiri asked pointedly.

The other four had withdrawn into a whispering knot, comparing blade boasts or Flower tales. She didn't doubt they would leap into action the moment the whistle sounded. *They* weren't being pulled in two directions.

The other day, in the select committee, Zagiri had caught herself getting angry at Siyon for rocking the boat. For not keeping his head down and letting the tide of Avarair Hisarani's antagonism wash over him. Couldn't he just trust in the prefect, and Zagiri, to manage the political strategy?

But why should he? When had sitting quietly worked out for Siyon, or those like him? Why should he *trust* in anyone with a name like theirs?

It was far too easy to slip back into azatani thinking up there. In the Avenues, in the Palace, in their comfortable position at the top of the city.

"There you go again," Daruj whispered.

Zagiri put up a hand to catch this pebble. Where was he getting them from? "Some of us are *busy*," she snapped.

Daruj snorted. "Whereas I spend all day eating grapes peeled by Gayane Saliu."

That made her hesitate. Zagiri had never thought about Daruj's life, outside running the tiles. He was the Diviner Prince, one of the tribe's best-known assets, day and night. He might earn a living in bravi prize money—he was certainly good enough with his blade—but that was because he worked damn hard.

This was his job, and he'd chosen *her* in his six, and Zagiri was repaying that by getting distracted.

"Sorry," she whispered, glad the shadows covered her blush. "It's only...I really want to change things. Make the city fairer. And it's hard."

"Change always is." Daruj shrugged in the dark. "You've been trying, what, two months?"

Much less than that, with the chance to really try. "I hadn't appreciated how much mud I'd have to wade through," Zagiri admitted, then hesitated before she added, "And there's another opportunity. Maybe."

"What opportunity?" he asked. Of course he did.

Zagiri dithered for a moment, glancing out into the square, but the Bowerboys stubbornly weren't showing up. "You hear anything out of Dockside recently? About what the Laders are up to?"

"Same shit as every year, isn't it?" Daruj shifted a little, against the other wall. "When I went down there with Siyon, back in the summer, we met his brothers, and they...they were angry, about a lot of things. Some of Dockside doesn't look too favorably on the bravi."

"What?" That pulled Zagiri out of her revolutionary thoughts. "Why? We accept members from all over the city. We're egalitarian!"

A low whistle floated across the square; the *keep quiet* from the doorman. Zagiri hunched.

"We're paid entertainment at azatani parties, Savani," Daruj pointed out quietly. "Yeah, we stalk each other around the city, mount raids and public challenges, and earn names and fame. But the money that keeps this whole thing afloat comes from your lot. From party games and playing at security and raiders for idle entertainment. And there's not a lot of it. Nearly everybody has to work a job as well."

Nearly everybody. Zagiri wasn't special—except in the ways that she was. The ways that meant she hadn't even thought about a lot of this before.

They were angry, about a lot of things, Daruj had told her.

She wasn't the only one.

Feet in the night; Zagiri's hand dropped to her sabre hilt, but she hissed in frustration at the whistled signal for *runner incoming*. Not the Bowerboys. A runner blitzed across the square and into the Chapel.

They barely had long enough to shift uneasily before Voski Tolan came striding out, shouts and a mass of blades churning behind her.

"Change of plan, Bracken!" she hollered into the night. "Seems the Bowerboys think they can tell the town they're coming for us, then raid Haruspex instead. What do we say to that?"

A jeer rose from the crowd, and Zagiri bounced on her toes with anticipation.

Daruj cupped hands around his mouth to shout back: "Take 'em both!"

Voski pointed at their dark side street. "Ambush party," she called, "take point. Let's run!"

Zagiri didn't waste time cheering, just tucked in behind Daruj as they burst out of the side street. Behind them, sixes were being hurriedly formed, but they led the way, proud and open. Straight down to the Kellian Way, their boots drumming on the paving and their Bracken ribbons fluttering. An arrow, flying to battle, with more mayhem in their wake.

As they passed, curtains twitched, windows knocked open, shadows hurrying to look. People ducked aside in the streets, calling back into teahouses and wineshops. Some fell in behind, bringing drinks and merry songs, eager to bear witness to whatever spectacle was brewing.

Zagiri ran, with her named blade strapped to her hip, with her tribe, and left behind all her worries, her options, her strategies.

Over the Swanneck Bridge, in the industrial district where it was never quite dark or still, whistles rose shrill and sharp as the Bower's

Scythe rearguard scouts spotted them coming. Too little, too late. Bracken boiled up through the streets like a flood tide.

The Haruspex safe house was a tall tower, long taken over from its industrial purpose. In the yard out front, the Bowerboys formed themselves up, three sixes arrayed against the incoming Bracken, and another two formed up in the rear. They'd come here in *force*; Zagiri wondered how many had been left to hold their own safe house against any counterraid.

For a moment, there was stillness, as the first Bracken sixes formed up warily, not liking the numbers.

Then the doors of the Shot Tower rolled back, and Haruspex fell upon the Bowerboys from the rear. Bracken surged forward; the fight was *on*.

Not much audience here, aside from what had been brought merrily along in Bracken's wake. At the first clash of blades a shout rose from a nearby yard, and curious heads appeared over the wall. All of Bezim loved a show.

No money in this, but plenty of glory, and the most important audience of all: other bravi.

Who better to appreciate the Bowerboy somersaulting between two Bracken, then leaping up in surprise attack? Or the Bracken trio who covered one another so strongly they drove a wedge clear through the Bower ranks? Or the Haruspex blade who leapt from a comrade's shoulder over the fray, with moon glinting off a shaved-bald head and a hand full of bright fire?

Even Zagiri stopped to gape—she'd seen Siyon call fire to his snapped fingertips, but never in the middle of a fight—and got a stinging slice down her arm for her inattention.

Afterward, when the furious melee was done, the crowd ambled away, chattering and laughing. The defeated Bowerboys totted up their forfeits while injuries were treated and refreshments wheeled out. Zagiri's arm wasn't so bad, the bleeding already stopped, so she went and dipped herself a cup of Haruspex's spiced wine before heading for the corner where Tein Geras had set up with his little leather-bound chest of alchemical supplies.

As Zagiri took the folding stool in front of him, he frowned after the previous patched-up bravi. "What?" she asked. "Bad tally tonight?"

Tein shook his head but gave a sharp whistle—*sergeant needed*—before taking a look at her arm.

The slice really wasn't that bad—barely three inches long, and not very deep. Tein passed over the bobbin of charmed thread and reached for a pot of salve instead. His finger scraped the bottom as he scooped some up.

"Getting low on that," Zagiri noted.

"Still looking for another supplier." Tein's mouth twisted wryly. "Velo was handy to have around. Now hold still."

It burned, as always; Zagiri gritted her teeth against it. Burned and then itched, and she fought that moment of dizziness, then retched at the foul sensation in the back of her mouth. She already had her cup of spiced wine to wash away the taste. By the time Zagiri rinsed her mouth and swallowed, the gash on her arm had closed to a—

"Huh," Zagiri said, lifting her arm as though more light would show the raw pink line she was expecting to see.

A hand reached over Zagiri's shoulder to grab her wrist, tilting so the thin white scar glittered in the moonlight. "You do that just now?" Voski Tolan demanded. The sergeant didn't wait for an answer before she pressed her callused thumb to the centre of where the wound had been.

Zagiri braced for it to sting—it usually did, for at least a day or two, but then again it didn't usually heal up *this* fast. It was like she'd got the cut months ago.

"It's been like that all night," Tein reported quietly. "And the thread too. The other quartermasters have been reporting greater effectiveness, but this is something else."

Voski chewed at her bottom lip. "And the other week, when I did your blade," she said, with a nod to Zagiri. "That history? Some of that I'd swear wasn't in what I memorised from the sergeant before me. It showed up in my head as I went. Like the blade was telling me."

Zagiri blinked. "You do…At the start, you say that bit about the blade remembering, right?"

"That's the ritual. But it's never actually *worked* before." Voski looked wry but also uneasy. "There is some strange fuckery afoot right now, and it's not bad, but…" She trailed off and exchanged a look with Tein.

Not bad. Not *yet*.

"Siyon was talking about something *more* happening," Zagiri remembered. "With the djinn and angel showing up. What if this is part of it?"

Neither of them looked too happy about that, and Zagiri knew how they felt. *You need to fix this fast*, she'd told him. What was going on? How much worse was this going to get? And how was the Council going to take it?

"You're still kicking around with Velo?" Voski asked, shaking Zagiri out of her endless questions. "Come with me."

Across the yard, a whip-thin woman all in black propped against the barrel of spiced wine, an old scar on her face tugging her mouth into a perpetual sneer. "Slender," Voski greeted the sergeant of Haruspex. "One of your blades was asking about Siyon Velo earlier. The Star Whisper here would be the one to talk with."

Slender gave Zagiri a brisk once-over and then turned to shout, "Mayar!"

A bravi slipped out of the milling pack at once—the one who'd made that mid-fight leap, hand full of fire. They were shorter than Zagiri had realised, with high cheekbones and a swagger to their walk. They didn't look azatani, but Bezim was home to many, wherever they'd been born. It didn't matter—not to the bravi, and not to Zagiri.

"Nice work in the melee," she offered as they stepped aside from their sergeants, into a quieter corner of the yard. "With the—" She snapped her fingers.

Mayar smiled, a tight and satisfied expression. "Something a bit different. More effort than it's worth, but good for a distraction. You practice?" When Zagiri shook her head, they frowned. "But you work with Velo?"

"We're on a committee together," Zagiri said. Mayar's lip curled, like that *really* wasn't what they'd meant, and Zagiri hurried to add, "And he—well, I'm the one who fell off the clock tower." She always felt foolish admitting to that.

Mayar huffed a harsh little laugh. "There you go," they commented. "Not even gravity applies to azatani in this city."

What was *this* about? "*Siyon* saved me," Zagiri snapped. "Not my family name. He didn't get anything out of it. He did it because he could. No, not even that, because he didn't *know* he could do it. He *tried*, because it was the right thing to do."

Her breath was coming quick again. A couple of nearby Haruspex glanced their way, like they were wondering if there was going to be another fight.

Zagiri was curious about that too.

But Mayar's head tilted, more curious than belligerent. "What's he trying now?"

"What do you care?" Zagiri demanded, and got a shrug for answer. A shrug, and Mayar still watching her. It seemed unlikely this person—with their battered leathers and foreign blood—could be a spy for the Pragmatics. "He's trying to figure out what's going on," she said. "He's trying to get a handle on it before some people use it as an excuse to start twisting the screws again."

"Some people," Mayar repeated. "Some of *your* people."

Zagiri bristled, but it was only the truth. "Yeah, some of my people. But not me."

Mayar considered that. "You know where I could find Velo?"

It wasn't a secret, though Siyon was bad at answering the bell. Unless it was Zagiri or Anahid ringing. "Why?" she asked.

"He came looking," Mayar answered. "Everyone else has just told me I'm wrong, but he came looking."

That sounded like Siyon. "I'll take you," Zagiri told Mayar. "And if you mess him about, I'll kick your arse."

Mayar grinned, sudden and bright in the moonlight. "You can try."

The dreams were growing familiar now; Siyon recognised that sensation of sinking down, down, down, like he was falling into the centre of the earth.

The rest of it was less clear. He was searching for something, or perhaps something was searching for *him*. Maybe it was Izmirlian, and that made Siyon hesitate, even in dreams. Yes, he wanted to see Izmirlian, wanted to stamp memory more firmly over Avarair Hisarani's similarities, but this was a dream. It would only be Siyon's memory that he was meeting anyway.

He needed to move past this.

And yet, when he heard a voice, whispering in the dark, he whirled around, reaching out for it.

He was in a labyrinth of stone now, with shadows closing in... except Siyon could still see clearly, his surroundings faintly limned with that burnished energy he was coming to know well.

Siyon trailed his fingertips down the bronzed stone sweep of the cavern wall. It flexed gently beneath his fingers.

Not a wall. It was *breathing*. It was—

Shattered by the clangour of a bell.

Siyon grabbed at the sheets around him—but there weren't any. He'd fallen asleep on the living room floor, and his grasping fingers found only the rag-twisted rug. He was wedged in between the couch and the rubber fig, and he ached like...well, like he'd fallen asleep on the floor. His throat felt dry as stone. Everything still shimmered bronze in his vision. "Laxmi, who is it?" he croaked, and there was no answer.

He was alone. In the drum of his frantic heartbeat against his aching ribs, Siyon felt more than just alone. There was being the only one in a boat, and then there was being stranded in the middle of the ocean. No one else could even start to understand what was going on, let alone help him unravel it all. Siyon was unreachable, even if anyone had cared to try.

He heard the faint creak of the alley gate opening, so it must have been either Zagiri or Anahid, for whom the gate was charmed to unlock. Friends, who tried to help, which wasn't nothing. Siyon should get up, greet them properly, but hadn't managed it when footsteps came into the workroom. "Siyon?"

Zagiri, then. Siyon cleared his throat and managed to call, "In here."

A voice he didn't recognise, with a faint accent that tweaked at his memory, said, "What's going on? It feels... strange."

Siyon put down his hand to push himself upright, and something bit at his palm, something he'd been holding without even realising it.

Of course. Of course it was.

Siyon opened his hand to reveal the fucking dragon figurine. For a moment, he had the urge to fling it out the open window behind him, but what would that achieve? It'd be back the next time he wasn't looking.

"What's that?" asked a voice from the doorway.

It was Mayar, standing at Zagiri's shoulder and frowning down at the dragon in Siyon's palm.

Zagiri was frowning too. "Were you asleep?" she demanded. "On the floor? It's only just gone midnight."

To top it all off, there was a sudden flutter of wings at the window and the scratch of talons, and Laxmi cawed, "Finally."

"That's not a talking bird," Zagiri said to Mayar. "That's—"

"A demon," Mayar finished, looking far more curious than afraid.

Laxmi stretched out of bird-shape, and into her own—hardly less disconcerting, perched on the windowsill with her hooves demurely crossed at the ankle and her horns glinting. She looked down her nose at Siyon, still on the floor. "When you dream like that, it gets fucking uncomfortable."

Siyon gaped at her. "What?"

"Mother Sa," Mayar said, like agreement.

Hadn't Siyon heard them say that before? When Siyon was talking with them out at the caravanserai, and had pulled up a pinch of the Mundane?

Before they got in a snit about azatani and walked out on Siyon. Why were they here now?

Mayar waved a hand around, glittering with heavy silver rings. "The energy was very strong when we came in."

When he'd first been dragged out of the dream, everything had looked bronze to Siyon's sight. He'd thought it a lingering effect. Maybe it was, just not on *him*. He blinked up at Mayar. "What are you doing here?"

Mayar's face screwed up in a fleeting expression Siyon couldn't name—maybe reluctance, maybe regret, maybe just indigestion. "When I calmed down," they said, "that's what I asked myself. What was I doing here, in Bezim? I came for a reason. I came to find something, following a whisper on the wind. I shouldn't let the azatani stop me looking for it."

"I don't know what that means," Siyon admitted.

"You don't have to," Mayar replied, almost haughty. "It's not your business."

Fair enough. Siyon rubbed at his face. The room no longer looked overlaid in bronze, but other emanations were only starting to creep in at the edges—wisps of curious Aethyr lifting off Zagiri's skin, and a steady beat of the Abyss coming from Laxmi at the window. Like those emanations had been pushed out as well by whatever had been going on with Siyon's dream.

He certainly wasn't going to turn down help. Not when Mayar was the only person Siyon had found who even came close to understanding.

"I'll make tea," Siyon said.

Even that nearly got away from him when he snapped his fingers for a spark of Empyreal energy to heat the water, and the samovar flared briefly red-hot. He yelped and leapt back, and though the metal ended up slightly sagging out of shape, it seemed like maybe he'd got away with it.

Zagiri was halfway out the door, having said her farewells (because some of us, she'd said pointedly, had to work in the morning) but at that she stopped. "Is that happening a lot?" she asked.

"Fuck you, I know what I'm doing," Siyon grumbled, even as he shook out his stinging fingers.

She gave him a look. "Because I got a slice earlier tonight that's already healed up perfectly, thanks to your salve. Which isn't where the weirdness ends." She told him what Voski had to say about the recitation of named blade history. "And I thought," she finished up, "of what you said about something *more* happening."

Siyon didn't know what to make of any of this. "They're not the same thing, though, right?" he considered. "*I* made the salve; that's alchemy. But if bravi tribe blades *do* have their own memory, that would be..." Allegedly, some of those blades had come from the Old Kingdoms. "That's *centuries* old. That's more like..." He trailed off. It was something else. Like Anahid possibly seeing a naga in the Flower district. Something older and stranger and beyond alchemy.

At least as they knew it.

"It's magic," Zagiri suggested blithely, just leaving him with that whale in his nets.

Magic. It made him laugh. Kolah Negedi would be outraged.

Speaking of older and stranger, once Siyon had actually managed to make tea without melting anything, Mayar told him a little about the Khanate understanding of the world behind the world. It hadn't changed much since the Lyraec Empire was young.

"Everything in the world is braided together out of multiple..." Mayar pulled a face, one heavy-ringed hand wavering as they weighed up words. "*Essences* is not quite right, but neither is *energy*, and I hate the word *spirit*. Every time the Khanate showed up in ancient Lyraec stories, it was all about the *spirit of fire*—" They put on a grand, theatrical voice. "And there isn't one. Fire isn't only one thing. It's a tool, and it's a friend, and it's hungry, and it's implacable. Those things— those concepts—are where the essences lie. Water can have a violent change, the same as fire."

Siyon wondered if he should be taking notes. "And a mage is someone who can manipulate those essences?"

"Mages don't exist." Mayar's little smile tweaked wider at Siyon's confusion. "Not in the Khanate territories. Not anymore. We have all the stories, we have all the theory. My *meekash*, she—" A pause, as they considered. "Yes, I think you would say *she*. She is the shaman of my clan, teaching me to listen to the wind, to the essences all around us, and to help guide the clan to easier paths among them.

Once, there were mages too, and she passed that to me as well, what they do, how they do it, but it was just a story from the time of heroes. Until I came here."

Until they came to Bezim. This was the only place in the world where alchemy worked, or so Siyon had always been told. The only place where other things worked as well, it seemed.

"The essences were faint at first," Mayar continued. "Difficult to grasp, slippery to hold on to. But they grew firmer."

"Let me guess," Siyon interjected. "In the summer? Around two months ago?"

When he'd become the Power and brought the Mundane plane back toward balance.

"Since then," Mayar continued, "maybe I am getting better with practice, but I think the essences are growing stronger all around us."

Like everything else. Waking up. *Magic.*

"You say it's a story from the time of heroes?" Siyon asked. "There used to be mages even in the Khanate?"

Mayar smiled, a sharp expression not without bitterness. "Our stories go back a very long way. It could be hundreds of years ago. Longer, maybe. There are stories of mages performing wondrous feats, before Mother Sa fell asleep and pulled all the other essences into slumber alongside her."

There was that term again. Siyon leaned in. "Mother Sa. That's what you said when I manifested the Mundane energy. When you came in here, just before. Who is she?"

From the expressions that passed over Mayar's face, Siyon felt like he'd asked for an explanation of the sky. Something beyond the real capacity of language—especially a foreign one—to encapsulate. But Mayar tried. "She is oldest. Strongest. The essence of stillness and solidity, but also…death? No. Fate, perhaps. A thing that cannot be evaded. She is *everything*, you understand?"

Siyon thought he might. Everything. Everywhere. The bronzed energy that he could reach out and grasp. The Khanate term for the essence of the Mundane plane.

"But also…" Mayar tilted a hand this way and that. "Also, she is the deepest asleep, and in the stories...maybe that is a good thing? In the time of heroes, there were also wild monsters, who caused all sorts of disasters. So when something could be an opportunity, or could be a problem, we say, *Be careful, you'll wake Mother Sa.*"

That trickled a chill down Siyon's spine. *The awakening is upon us*, Midnight had said.

It was just a story. Just the sort of thing older relations told their young folk, trying to urge them to a caution unnatural for their years. It wasn't the same.

He pushed ahead. "And you know how to manipulate these essences. You were taught by your meer—er..."

"*Meekash*," Mayar supplied. "My teacher. But you know how as well. You did it in front of me." They pinched their fingers and thumb together in demonstration.

Siyon huffed a little laugh. He'd summoned a pinch of it. He'd barely managed to tease out enough to imbue a thread. "You tangled an angel up in a great big rope of it," he countered.

Mayar allowed the truth of that with a tilt of their head. "All right. I teach you, you teach me." They glanced at the window, open on the depths of night, the midnight bell long since rung. "Now?" they asked uncertainly.

Tiredness still dragged at Siyon's bones and scratched at his eyes, but there was nothing waiting for him in sleep but more of the same dreams, disorienting and disturbing. Izmirlian wasn't really there. The answers weren't really there.

"I don't have anywhere better to be," Siyon said. "Do you?"

Mayar shrugged and settled more comfortably on the armchair, drawing their feet up to sit cross-legged. "All right. First, always, we listen. You know meditation? Sitting quietly?"

"I am not known for it," Siyon admitted, but this was about learning, after all, so he copied Mayar's posture, closed his eyes, and reached out into the plane around him.

His plane. His power. And for the first time, he felt like he might be doing the right thing with it.

CHAPTER 14

The address on the card Xhanari had given her led Anahid to a wineshop in a neighbourhood up near the old hippodrome. Once stiffly respectable, now these streets were too close to the Scarp, though not quite close enough to draw the thrill-seeking sort who had taken up in the cliff-top mansions. Here, the once-elegant houses had long been sliced up into cramped apartments and crowded in by newer buildings around tangles of narrow streets.

Anahid had heard ghosts walked these streets—pale and filmy echoes of the elegant lives that had played out here. She didn't see anything like that, but then again, it was the middle of the afternoon.

The wineshop might once have been a carriage house, in an age when horses were still comfortable within the city bounds. The bar was broken up with pillars wound with boneleaf vines, and the woman behind it nodded at Xhanari's card, poured Anahid a glass of wine nearly as pale as the foliage, and bid her wait a moment. She left Anahid loitering uncertainly at the bar.

The wine was too sweet—a late harvest blend from Lyraea—and the shop was too quiet. The only other patrons were a couple cuddled close in a corner booth, two women giggling into each other's shoulders. An assignation, Anahid realised, a little warmth touching her cheeks. That was why people drank in the afternoon, with no one else around.

Anahid watched the women wind their fingers together, with smiles and whispers even sweeter than her wine. No one had ever behaved like that with Anahid, not even in that first week of her marriage, before she'd realised where Nihath's true preference lay. In truth, she wasn't sure she wanted it; to her, the softness seemed more swaddling than sweet. Perhaps that was why no azatan had ever courted her assiduously.

All Anahid wanted was to be valued for who she was. For what she was capable of. If only anyone would look, and see her.

"My usual, please," said a voice beside her, on the far side of the pillar.

Anahid startled, knuckles bumping her wine glass. She grabbed for it at the same time as a hand reached across the pillar and caught it. Their fingers closed together around the stem, his over hers, warm and callused.

Anahid looked up into Vartan Xhanari's black eyes. He was leaning around the pillar, almost as close as he'd been that day on the street, though today he wasn't in uniform. His shirt was dark red, open at the collar, and suited his colouring far more than inquisitorial grey.

"Apologies," he said, barely above a whisper. "Would you meet me outside?"

He took up the pewter flagon the wineshop tender had poured for him and walked out a back door Anahid hadn't noticed.

Anahid's heart still beat fast from the startlement, that was all. She looked at the woman behind the bar—who lifted her eyebrows as though asking what Anahid thought *she* had to say about anything.

So Anahid followed Xhanari into the back courtyard.

There was a low bench running along one of the stone walls, but it showed far more signs of being used by the staff for their personal breaks than by wineshop patrons. There were barrels stacked against the near wall, and a gate to the laneway, and a staircase clinging to the side of the building that presumably led up to the apartments in the rest of the building.

Xhanari spoke from its shadow. "I'm sorry. I thought—perhaps best we not be seen together."

He was, after all, a member of the Special Crisis Task Force. That was why she'd come to see him.

Anahid glanced back into the wineshop—and through it to the quiet, sunlit street beyond—and couldn't see anyone interested in what she was doing. She'd taken care in coming here, and as far as she knew no one had followed.

Would she know? She was so out of her depth. But she wasn't simply going to accept being the minnow to Stepan Zinedani's shark.

There was more boneleaf growing beneath the staircase, out of the harsh light of the sun. Anahid stayed clear, as though stepping over that line might mean something. She'd left the too-sweet wine on the bar and now regretted it; she folded her hands together over her sash. His card was tucked back in there, next to the little penknife.

"I didn't think you'd come," Xhanari said. "You have always seemed very capable of solving your own problems."

Ridiculous, that it should lodge like a warm coal in her chest. *Your capability, propriety, and composure*, his letter had said. The things that he had admired. About her.

Anahid looked down again. The sleeves of his red shirt were rolled up a little, showing his wrists. His hands wrapped around the pewter flagon, nearly full with some dark liquid. This close, a rich scent of molasses and spice tickled Anahid's nose. "Is that seawine?" she asked before she could think better of it.

His hands shifted on the flagon. "I'm surprised you recognise it."

She couldn't help but smile and looked up to find him smiling as well. "Any azatani family, be it ever so high up the tiers, is still a trading concern. We all set sail at least once."

He watched her as closely as anyone ever had at the carrick table, without any attempt to hide it. An inquisitor, after all, needn't play coy. But here that prickling sensation of his scrutiny felt closer to her skin. A thing for them alone.

"At least once?" he repeated.

She shouldn't tell him more. But then again, he shouldn't want to know. He'd asked. So she told him. "Only once, in my case. Revarr and back, and never again."

Is this how he looked when he was trying not to laugh? The light in his eyes, the twist of his mouth; she found she liked it. Liked that she had caused it. "Revarr, as in the free city just to the north? That Revarr?"

Anahid nodded. "Barely three days each way. I was outstandingly sick for every moment of it. They tried everything." She nodded to his flagon. "Including seawine."

"I doubt it helped." He lifted the flagon and took a swallow. Watching his throat work, Anahid remembered the thick, sweet taste of it in her own mouth.

The thought struck her that she knew how he'd taste, if she kissed him now.

Anahid looked away, heat bleeding into her face. It was too warm, in the sun, but stepping into the shade with him seemed...unwise. She cleared her throat. This wasn't why she was here. Whatever this was. "I have something of a difficulty, Lieutenant Xhanari, with which I hope you can help me."

"I heard—" He paused; Anahid glanced at him as he chose his words. "I heard there was some small difficulty with Stepan Zinedani at a recent Flower Night. And possibly other troubles."

He'd heard? Anahid turned back to look at him properly. "Are you having me watched?"

His chin lifted a little, but otherwise he didn't seem abashed. "Not well enough, unfortunately. I don't know who tampered with the House gate."

He was watching for her reaction, but Anahid wasn't sure how she felt. Of course he was watching her; he wanted to get at the barons, and all of them—save Midnight—had been represented at Imelda's auction. Anahid—or Lady Sable—was a point of interest. A way he could achieve his goals. She knew he was thorough, systematic, persistent. She'd watched him as well. She knew him.

At least a little.

In the end, she ignored that matter completely. The question of the gate tampering was more important. "One needn't know the fish personally to recognise the taste," she pointed out.

Vartan inclined his head, one corner of his mouth quirking up. "Stepan is making quite a name for his temper, and his lack of moderation. Still, he seems to be the heir apparent. Garabed's daughters are respectably married, one out of Bezim, and the other into a lower-tier azatani family. I believe Garabed favours what he sees as Stepan's boldness. But Stepan could also be a weakness, if there were something sharp enough to come between him and his uncle's protection."

That matched almost exactly with what Anahid had seen of the Zinedanis, elder and younger, and with what she'd been thinking, though she hadn't known about the daughters. She eased a little closer, dipping into shadow in her eagerness. "What if I could tell you that Stepan has in his possession a collection of smuggled Northern turquoise. It was on display in his office at Sable House; I had quite some time to consider it while he was caviling against the transfer of ownership. The settings were—"

"Gilded wood," Vartan interrupted to guess; he knew what smugglers often used as well. There was a light in his face, leaning closer to hers. A possibility.

Anahid nodded. "And not the more elegant weathered and carved sort."

"He's not an elegant man," Vartan chipped in.

Anahid smiled; that had been her thought as well. Vartan smiled back. "Thank you," he said.

She liked it. She liked his smile, the warmth in his voice, she liked that it was hers, she *wanted* it.

A tread sounded on the steps above them, and Anahid startled; Vartan reached out, a hand on her elbow, as she looked up. Just one of his neighbours. Someone descending the stairs from their apartment to the street. There was no reason to hide.

No reason to step closer, to crowd under the staircase alongside Xhanari. But Anahid did it anyway, Vartan's hand sliding up her arm, a sharp catch in his breath.

Her heart was beating in her throat. This felt like carrick, like the pure thrill of the first cards being dealt. When anything was possible, and it was hers to grab.

She wanted to *know*.

The footsteps descended; someone went into the wineshop. Silence settled in the courtyard again.

Anahid didn't step away again. Neither did he. Her eyes seemed caught on that top, unfastened button on his shirt. She couldn't look any higher.

Not as she said: "Lieutenant Xhanari—"

"Please," he said with a breathless little laugh. "I'm hardly on duty here."

Here, so close she could feel his breath, fast and warm, against her cheek.

Anahid looked up—at his chin, at his mouth, at his nose, at his black eyes watching her. "Vartan," she said. His name on her lips.

He liked it. She didn't need to be a Flower to see it, in the twitch of his mouth, in the darkening of his eyes, in the way he leaned a little closer, barely a sway…

And hesitated.

Anahid curled her fingers in the collar of his shirt and tugged him down to her mouth.

She kissed him and took his little gasp as her winnings and went looking for more. For his hand settling on her waist, for his fingers brushing at her chin.

And then easing her gently away. "You're married," he murmured.

Anahid couldn't help the harsh laugh that fell from her too-sensitive lips. "Am I?" she demanded. Met his gaze, those black eyes that saw so much. "Vartan Xhanari, how many times have I shown you through my home—my *life*—and you say to me that I am—"

She lost the rest of the words in his mouth as he kissed her again, and Anahid responded fiercely. Buried her fingers in his hair and opened her mouth to him.

He pressed her back into the boneleaf, the scent of crushed flowers rising sweetly around her as he kissed her—demandingly, devouringly, desperately. Kissed her as Nihath never had, as Anahid had never, in all her desultory courtships, been kissed.

As though he saw her. He valued her. He *wanted* her.

Anahid grasped at his collar, his shoulder, his neck. Pulled him closer, and bit at his lip, and when he shuddered under her hands she felt alight with exultation. Like winning the House all over again. Like the sweetest, wildest, most heedless victory.

Vartan Xhanari's control was coming apart in *her* hands.

She pulled back just enough to mumble, "Do you have an apartment upstairs?"

He was breathing heavily against her cheek. "A—" He started, and for a moment she thought that even here, pinning her to the wall, he was going to call her *azata*. But then he tried again. "Anahid. I—yes. But I couldn't possibly—"

"I could." Anahid leaned back, took his hand, smiled at him. "Vartan. Take me upstairs."

And he did as she asked.

Meditation was working about as well as Siyon had anticipated.

Mayar had laid out the steps like preparing to put to sea: close your eyes, calm yourself, settle into the moment, just feel.

Cast off, set sail.

Drift, Mayar had suggested. Like a hawk on the wind, they said, which Siyon translated to seaweed in the current.

Not that it helped. Siyon didn't drift. The moment he loosened his hold on himself, the world opened up around him. It was heavy and heady as it had been since he'd come back from the void, dragged back into the Mundane and his Power. Like the whole world was waiting to embrace him, to swallow him up. It was roiling, and churning, and it stretched forever not only in the directions of the compass, but up into the farthest stars, and down, and down, and down...

Siyon shook himself out of the trance in a flinch.

Sinking was easy. Siyon wasn't seaweed; he was a stone. He was fourteen years old again, thrown into the harbour wrapped up in a sack, plunging down into the depths.

There was something waiting there. Like death, or fate. Siyon wasn't going quietly.

But despite all the problems, meditation seemed to be helping. The burnished Mundane energy came more readily to his call; he could swipe it out of the air now. Even after he wiped his fingers down a length of twine, sticky bronze glow remained on his fingers. He could twist it up into a little coil, grasp the ends delicately—

Oh. *Oh*, he'd been a fool. So busy with his twine that he hadn't really thought. Could he make his continuous negation sigil out of Mundane energy alone? Could he imbue that directly into the inquisitors' badges?

And if *that* was possible, could he—

The gate bell jangled through his thoughts.

Siyon turned his head, though not enough to lose sight of his glowing fingers, and shouted, "Yeah, what?"

Voices rose faintly up the stairs, like waves on a distant shore. Didn't seem to be talking to *him*.

Siyon held tight to his twist of Mundane power, and the end of his escaping thought. Other things he could do with energy that was entirely of this plane, that was native, that was natural, that would gently nudge away the energies of other planes all by itself if he just—

The gate bell rang again. The voices grew louder, overlapping and braiding together into an argument. Siyon wished he could send Laxmi down to scare off whoever it was, but when he'd sat down to meditate, she'd reacted like he was trimming his toenails and fled.

Siyon shook the Mundane energy off his hand and clambered to his feet. The voices came clearer with every step down.

"—not as though anything can be done right now." That was Balian, all calm and reason, and possibly Siyon should modify the gate charms to open for him as well. He'd certainly proved his usefulness, taking care of Siyon's reports, deflecting all sorts of requests for Siyon's time, and chasing off that Hisarani clerk.

"But if we prepare now, we'll be ready when the time comes." Why was Zagiri arguing on the doorstep instead of coming in?

"Wait, are you arguing *for* paperwork?" There was a warm note in Balian's voice that Siyon hadn't heard before. Was he *teasing* her?

Siyon stumbled down the last few steps as Zagiri shoved at Balian's shoulder—far more gently than Siyon had seen her slug her fellow bravi—and said, "I want to be *doing* something."

Just as well Laxmi wasn't here; Siyon didn't want to see a harpy vomit over this display.

He yanked open the gate, and both of them jumped. "There a reason you kids are doing your flirting on my doorstep?" Siyon demanded. They both blushed, he was absolutely sure of it, though Balian pulled his composure taut almost immediately. Siyon grinned. "Come on up."

He stepped back to let them in, but Balian yelped "No!" and threw an arm in front of Zagiri. "No, you have to come to the library," he insisted, even as Zagiri whacked ineffectually at his elbow.

"He said come in," Zagiri argued. "We can talk about sorcery reform and *then* you can show him the stupid book. Where's it going to go? It's a *book*."

"It'll go back on the shelf," Balian countered, still restraining her, "under lock and key in Antiquities. This is our only chance."

"What book?" Siyon had to lift his voice over the scuffle of their childish little wrestling match.

They both looked at him like he'd been forgotten already. "Oh." Balian pulled his arm back and tugged his coat straight. "There's a report from the first Lyraec explorer to reach the River Kell. It—well, I think it might mention Midnight. I could take notes, but there's a picture as well."

Siyon didn't even have to check his pockets to know that Midnight's little dragon was with him. Always with him, like a vague but threatening breath at the back of his neck.

"We're going to the library," he told Zagiri. "But you can talk on the way, if you want."

The afternoon stretched late and golden, the streets crowded with the overlapping bustle of day's end and evening's promise. They passed packed teahouses and bakery carts selling their last wares at half price. Some of the shops already had signs about Salt Festival orders; Siyon had lost track of the days.

"Balian was saying we should start readying our proposal," Zagiri declared.

This looked like news to Balian. "I was *suggesting*—"

Siyon wasn't letting them get distracted again. "I thought we were waiting until I had answers before we pushed for legal change."

"I just think we should be prepared," Zagiri said, with a good impersonation of Anahid's aplomb.

But Siyon remembered what she'd been saying when he'd come downstairs. That she wanted to be doing something. *That* was the Zagiri he knew.

"What sort of change are we talking about?" Balian asked, casual as considering where they should go for a glass of tea.

"Proving the risk," Siyon said, plainly and firmly.

As Zagiri said, just as firmly, "Opening the register." She frowned at him as they crossed the Kellian Way. "What? Proving the risk? What does that even mean?"

"It means the inqs have to prove there's a risk to the city," Siyon retorted. "Instead of insisting every non-Club practitioner is guaranteed to cause another Sundering. It was never true; it's even less true now. You want to—what?"

"All those people who came to Bracken to flee the city." Zagiri looked distant and haunted when she talked about it. "They were only in trouble because they weren't registered. So we register all practitioners in the city."

"*All* of them?" There was a certain simplicity in it.

Balian steered them up the Bankers Stair, strewn with peddlers and buskers, teeming with students and clerks. "Arguments could be made," he said consideringly. "Economically, logistically, practically, it would bolster practitioner numbers for aboveboard trade and services. Greater opportunities, just what the Council favours."

Zagiri beamed at him. "Exactly, and we—"

"They can't all do the work, though," Siyon interrupted, getting a matched pair of perplexed azatani expressions for his trouble. "No back-alley, two-knuckle hedgewizard can cause the Sundering, but they can't do the work of a registered practitioner either," he explained. "Nor does it mean they're safe. Unlicensed practitioners pull plenty of dodgy stunts and have plenty of accidents. They blow things up, they poison themselves or others, they create unstable products—"

"I could poison people by tipping turpentine into the party punch," Zagiri snapped, "but that doesn't make painting illegal."

Siyon lifted his hands, like he was yielding a duel, and she grimaced and stopped dead in the middle of an arcade. Balian carefully steered all of them to the side, out of the way of the flow of oblivious students. Compared to some of *their* arguments—one pair actually screaming at each other over fluid dynamics, whatever they were— Siyon supposed this little discussion hardly warranted attention.

Zagiri folded her arms over her prim striped dress. "Why does this have to be so *hard*?" she demanded in a tight voice. "I only want to fix it. I want it to be *fair*."

Fair? In *this* city? But Siyon liked that she cared.

"Get a copy of that section of the law," Balian suggested, "and we can go over it together, see where the easiest alterations would be."

Sounded to Siyon like an excuse to spend more time together. But Zagiri shrugged her shoulders like she didn't want comfort to settle on them. "Sure. I guess. You guys go on and do your book thing. I'm going to..." She turned back the way they'd come.

Balian watched her go, a frown clouding his usually sunny face. Siyon wanted to tell him to go after her, but there was a reason they were here, at the edge of the law school cloister. "You said something about a book?"

"Scroll, actually." Balian straightened his coat unnecessarily. "Yes, come on."

The scroll wasn't in the library, but rather in the basement of a grand grey-stone building with some ponderous phrase in ancient Lyraec carved over the pillared entry. "Department of Antiquities," Balian explained as they wriggled through a warren of narrow corridors inside. "A friend told me the archives were open for cataloguing today, so I came for a look and—well."

Well indeed. In the promised basement, shelves lined up in ranks, crammed with bits of stone and age-altered metal and all sorts of other rubbish. One aisle had row after row of staring stone heads, which frankly gave Siyon the creeps.

At a table tucked away in one corner, Balian fussed about with a pair of rolling pins, with some sort of thick paper stretched between them. He shuffled the handles, the paper rolling off one side and onto the other, and eventually Balian stopped muttering to himself and said, "Here. Look."

Siyon stopped watching sluggish wisps of Aethyr chasing the basement shadows, then glanced down at the stretched section Balian was showing him.

Midnight glared back at him, one hand raised—as he'd been in the alleyway, with the same symbol on his hand. *His* symbol, the circle and the little line, not quite the nullification sigil.

"Fuck," Siyon gasped, taking a quick step back and nearly knocking over a dusty stand holding a Lyraec legionnaire's uniform.

Balian winced, but his hands were full, and he had to let Siyon steady the stand. "I'll take that as confirmation that this is indeed Midnight."

The drawing was scratched with pen and ink, but the likeness was uncanny. Boyish face, intense eyes, demanding posture. Midnight held a staff in his other hand, with a long clawed serpent twined around it, and he was surrounded by gloom.

"What is this?" Siyon asked, his voice a rasp.

"Copy of a painting found on the wall of a riverside cave," Balian provided promptly. "The original was lost in the Sundering, probably underwater now. But this was considered a faithful rendition."

"And you said this is the report of the first Lyraec explorer to reach here." Siyon couldn't believe it. That was *Midnight*. And it had been painted on a cave wall before there was even a city here.

Balian looked nervous as well. "I'm not really up on the barons' marks," he noted. "But that sigil on his palm..." He winced at Siyon's nod. "Right. Can I just ask...what's going on?"

Siyon didn't know. He had absolutely no idea. It was possible that the only person who *did* know was Midnight.

If *person* was even the right term.

"I could ask Midnight," he said aloud, to test the idea.

Balian's frown deepened. "Is that wise? He's a baron. And possibly centuries old. One of those would be bad enough."

Never mind the burnished glow that Midnight had been wreathed in the last time Siyon had seen him. The energy that might be the key to a lot of things.

Siyon's mind turned back to the realisation he'd had, before Balian and Zagiri had rung his bell bickering. He could make his ongoing nullification sigil out of Mundane energy. It seemed to have a natural tendency to repel the energies of other planes.

Perhaps he could make a binding for the entire city. Not the nullification, but something else. An imbuement of Bezim with its own power?

It *felt* right, to Siyon, settling into his mind like a puzzle piece. Surely that would calm the ructions he felt in the energy all around him. Surely that would settle the uneasiness that clutched at him.

Perhaps it would even bind Midnight. Make him something like safe. Make it so Siyon could ask him some questions without fearing he might regret it.

"I have an idea," he said aloud.

Balian didn't look entirely reassured.

If Zagiri had stayed with Balian and Siyon a moment longer, she might have screamed.

She strode with no destination in mind, only *away* from all their sensible and realistic points, driven by frustration with reasonable compromise.

Of course she needed to deal with the concerns and the priorities of the azatani council. And of course the azatani weren't going to make changes just because the current situation was unfair.

But part of Zagiri kept thinking, louder and louder until it shook the inside of her skull... that they *should*.

She finally stopped in the middle of the parkland, unwilling to take a step closer to the Palace itself. Tomorrow, she would. She'd go back inside, do her job, and make the compromises.

Today, she fled to Anahid's.

The house was quiet, Nihath's study empty as Zagiri went past.

She had a pang of nostalgia for the frantic days of summer, crammed into this house with Siyon and Izmirlian besides. It had been awful, desperate, scrambling, but not *all* bad. Now they were scattered. Still desperate and scrambling.

Upstairs, in her private sitting room, Anahid was still in her dressing gown, hair braided over one shoulder, sipping tea as she sifted through correspondence at her desk.

"Wow," Zagiri declared, half falling on the chaise, twisting up her day gown. "Are you at home at *all* to morning callers these days?"

"Who'd wish for a private interview with me?" Anahid asked, and she had a point. She wasn't involved in trade and had no dependents whose marriage or career disposition might require the delicate intimacy of a morning call, and she'd never had the sort of gossipy friends who spent the mornings rehashing last night. Anahid shrugged one shoulder, her robe slipping a little. "And Nura knows she can wake me, if something urgent presents."

Zagiri had a teasing joke about the quality of play at the card tables all prepared, but that fled her mind at the sight of Anahid's bared neck. "Ana," she breathed, sitting up straight. Anahid tugged her robe back into place, but Zagiri yanked at the sleeve again. It *was*. "That's a *love bite*."

Anahid twitched away, her lips pressing together. But Zagiri knew her sister's expressions, and this wasn't disapproval. In fact, she thought her sister might be hiding a smile.

"You sly piece," she crowed, slumping back on the chaise. "Oh my goodness, I didn't think you'd actually—who is it? Am I going to have some asshole smirking at me in the Palace corridors?"

That little cough might have started as a laugh; Anahid gave her a stern look. "As though I'd get involved with someone who would behave like that."

A fair point. But Zagiri—for all the encouragement she'd offered toward just this sort of behaviour—had never actually thought Anahid *would* take up with a lover. Not her proper and upright and *boring* sister. Then again, she'd never imagined Anahid would spend most of her nights in the Flower district.

Oh.

"Is it a Flower?" Zagiri was so curious. What was it like, and what sort of tricks might he know, and—

"No," Anahid said, quickly and firmly. "I don't—" She cut herself off, looking at Zagiri as though she was weighing something. "No," she repeated finally.

"What?" Zagiri demanded.

But Anahid shook her head. "Trust in my discretion. Trust I know what I'm doing."

"Of course I do." Zagiri needn't even think about it. This was Anahid. Zagiri trusted her more than she trusted herself. "I'm glad you're having a little fun. You deserve it."

That curved Anahid's mouth into a faint little smile; she sipped at her tea, and the scent of it drifted across to Zagiri.

Her second shock in as many minutes. "Is that kumquat tea? You haven't drunk that since..." Zagiri couldn't even remember. The smell was bundled up in so many childhood memories, both of them at the Savani townhouse, long before Anahid married Nihath. Possibly even before her first presentation.

Anahid smiled faintly in the steam wisping from her glass. "I've never really cared for the mint, you know that."

Though no one else would, from how many glasses Anahid drank in polite society. Kumquat was so old-fashioned; nobody served it these days, and to ask would be making oneself awkward, which Anahid never did.

Even Zagiri had thought that her sister's tastes had changed. That she'd grown up. That she'd compromised, because that's what one did, to be a part of the world.

"What about you?" Anahid set down the glass again. "Are you having fun? Or, I suppose, getting what you deserve?"

Just like that, Zagiri's tangle of emotions tightened to choke her. Frustration, and anger, and the depressing certainty that this would never happen. It would *never* be the right moment to introduce the question of reform. Whatever solutions Siyon found would come with their own problems, and Avarair Hisarani and his Pragmatic faction would keep twisting at the Council. Nothing would get better. It might even get worse.

"Neither," she admitted, tilting back in despair. The geometric patterning on the ceiling stared back at her, resolutely regular. "I know I can't expect things to be quick or easy. That isn't how a ship turns, let alone a city. I *know* that. But this select committee is such an opportunity, Ana. This whole situation with Siyon. I feel like we're poised on the brink of possibility. And we're just treading water. We're reacting, we're keeping everyone happy. What if—" She pressed her mouth firmly against a horrifying urge to cry.

"What if?" Anahid prompted gently.

Zagiri stared at the ceiling and made herself say the words. "What if it never happens? What if I spend all my life in the corridors of the Palace until I'm Azata Markani, old and stiff and very carefully trying to defend the little I still have left?"

It sounded awful, the moment it was out of her mouth.

"Lomena Markani is a councillor of long standing," Anahid pointed out. "She may be personally responsible for alchemy being as readily practiced today as it is."

"I know." Zagiri pressed her eyes closed.

In the darkness behind them, Anahid was still talking. "And you've only been doing this for a few weeks. You can't—"

"I *know*," Zagiri interrupted, curling up on her side on the chaise. She knew, she *knew*. It was unreasonable. She was impatient. She wasn't *right* for this sort of job, not at all.

But no one else was going to do it.

She opened her eyes, and Anahid was watching her with awful sympathy. Zagiri hated needing it. She hated how much better it made her feel that her sister understood.

One corner of Anahid's mouth curved gently upward. "I'm proud of you, you know. Of everything you've achieved already and everything you are still trying to do."

"Ugh." Zagiri wrinkled her nose. "Shut *up*."

But she felt better for hearing it.

Anahid smiled properly, the sort of smug that she never allowed herself in public, where too many whispers had commented upon it.

For a sudden burning moment, Zagiri was fiercely proud of her sister in turn. For taking back so many parts of herself, in defiance of all the things she'd tried so long to become. However badly things had ended with Tahera Danelani, Zagiri could kiss the woman for showing Anahid the first steps of this new and wonderful path.

"You'll find a way," Anahid said with that calm confidence that had once irritated Zagiri but now stroked like a balm over her frustration. "You're determined, and inventive, and you won't be told no."

"I won't," Zagiri agreed. "I'll figure out a way. Balian's going to help me."

Oh, that had been a mistake. She knew it the moment the words were out of her mouth, long before Anahid cut short her sip of tea and set her glass down primly. "Oh, *is he*?" Anahid said. "And do we have a family name for this useful young man yet?"

Zagiri pulled a face, like that could stop the warmth spreading in her cheeks. "Why? It's not like you can invite his mother for a morning call if you're never here."

If she'd hoped to shock Anahid, she failed. "But *our* mother could. Don't look like that, Giri. You're sponsoring in the spring, and it's nearly Salt Night. Already, across the Avenues, your name is in lists and dossiers measuring the Savani worth and your personal merit as a spouse." The teasing light fell from her face, brows drawing closer. "If you don't want it, say so now, Zagiri. I'll fight for you, you know that. A marriage is not made better by less consideration."

Zagiri opened her mouth to insist she hadn't even *thought* about marriage, and the words wouldn't come. She wasn't some giggling debutante floating rose petals in a fountain to spell her future partner's first initial. But Balian was fun and filled her with energy even when they were arguing, and her stomach still flipped over at that ridiculous smile of his. He was capable and intelligent and not at all fussy.

There would certainly be *worse* husbands.

She cleared her throat. "This is all entirely beside the point. The work is what matters."

Anahid nodded, as though in understanding, though Zagiri didn't trust the smoothness of her sister's face. She was unsurprised when

Anahid said, "So you should find this Balian and schedule in all this very important work you'll need to do together."

"I take it back," Zagiri declared, even as her sister's laughter lifted her own heart. "A lover was a terrible idea. You're running wild."

"Well, we are sisters after all," Anahid noted lightly.

That lightness stayed with Zagiri, buoying her steps as she left the Avenues again.

It wasn't a terrible idea, going to check with Balian to ensure they *could* go over the details of the sorcery law together. That was all. This was about the work.

Though on the way to Siyon's apartment, Zagiri's attention was snagged by a strange crowd in one corner of the fruit market. No alarm or outrage, just an eager curiosity shuffling people to crane and peer. Zagiri drifted over to check what was happening.

Beneath the bulge of the old wall, beside the tea shop that Siyon had once told her to visit if she needed to find Geryss Hanlun in an emergency, there was a fountain, one of the really old ones topped with fancy statues. This one had a woman lifting a pitcher from which the water poured; she was wreathed in snakes.

And right now, her eyes glowed ever so faintly green. As Zagiri stared, they faded back into plain stone again.

"That's a yes!" someone called from the front of the crowd. As people shifted, Zagiri caught a glimpse of him, with a tea shop waiter's apron and his damp sleeves rolled up. "That's your lot; she only does one question. One at a time, folks, form a line, have your coin ready."

Coin ready? For what?

The woman next to her—with the neat grey dress and hair-kerchief of a prosperous shopkeeper—smiled at her. "The statue's telling the future, dearie. Think about your question, toss in a coin, and if her eyes light up like that, the answer is *yes*."

Zagiri gaped at her. "Are you serious?"

The clerk next to her chuckled. "I know, sounds like something out of an opera, doesn't it? Probably a stunt. Alchemical paint or something. Still, bit of fun, isn't it?"

The crowd shuffled along, and Zagiri realised she'd been added to the queue without realising it. They moved forward to the steady *plop* of a coin into the water, and the statue's eyes would glow, or not, and they'd all shuffle up again.

It probably *was* a stunt. Alchemical paint.

Or something. There were strange things waking in the city, right now. Magic sprouting and growing.

Zagiri dug in the sash of her dress for a coin.

When it was her turn, she weighed the five-knuckle piece in her palm and thought, *Will I find a way to bring fairness to this city?*

Her coin dropped into the water with a heavy *plunk*. Zagiri stared at the statue's downturned face.

And whooped as the eyes lit up with a vivid green glow.

CHAPTER 15

Mayar tilted their face toward the sun like a contented cat. "I didn't think this city even knew how to be peaceful."

Siyon had to admit, up here in the hills was probably the only place in Bezim that could ever earn that description. The little knot of hillocks skirted the southwest corner of the city, crammed in between the wall and the cliff coast and the encroaching quiet suburbs like a swept-up pile of rocks. The noise of the city—the rattling of wheels and the shouting of stallholders and the clatter of domesticity—blended into the hush of the ocean, carried by the breeze that toyed with the branches of the olive trees and thorn bushes that clung to the outcrops.

Frankly, it had always seemed a little eerie to Siyon.

"You're supposed to be keeping watch," Siyon reminded as he squinted up at the golden expanse of the wall, rummaging absently in his satchel for something hard enough to chip at it.

Centuries old, of course, but the Lyraec Empire knew how to build to last. Out here in the hills, the golden sandstone didn't even have generations of initials carved into it by bored street brats and young couples in love.

"Keep watch for what?" Mayar demanded, sprawling on a rock halfway back up the hill behind Siyon. "A goat?"

They'd seen a couple on the hot and sweaty climb to get here.

Siyon found a small pry bar—that he'd entirely forgotten he had—in the bottom of his satchel and used one end of that to scrape at a promisingly rough block. The sandstone grit fell into the canvas he'd laid down, ready for collection. All he needed was enough to—

"Hey!" someone shouted from the top of the wall.

Siyon didn't waste time with swearing. Just dropped the pry bar into the canvas, swept up the whole bundle, and legged it back into a gully between hills. Out of sight of the wall, he clambered awkwardly up the slope and nearly dropped everything when Mayar slid down from behind a rocky outcrop to join him.

"That!" Siyon snapped. "You were supposed to keep watch for that! The wall is still patrolled, you know."

"Patrolled?" Mayar repeated, brushing reddish dust off their leathers. "Why? We're not coming back to try again!"

Siyon shrugged. "Probably to stop people doing what I just did." He carefully peered into his canvas bundle; looked like he had plenty of sandstone grit in there. "Or to stop people messing with the ballistas they still have up there."

Mayar peered into the bundle too. "Couldn't you have formally requisitioned this? You're their fancy sorcerer, aren't you?"

Not tempting. "I'd have to tell them what I wanted to do." And they'd have poked holes all through it. Siyon wasn't even sure it would work, but he had a good feeling. A right and balanced sort of feeling, and he hadn't been having many of those recently.

Try explaining *that* on the paperwork.

Much better to give it a go and then saunter back into the Palace as though he'd always known he could fix everything that easily.

Hey, a guy could dream. But he had to actually make it work first.

"I need a base," Siyon said, looking around. "Something stone."

Mayar flourished a hand, rings glinting in the sun, at the rocky hills around them. "Take your pick."

Siyon shook his head. "Something flat. Preferably made so by people. Come on, I know just the place."

The old Lyraec fort hadn't lasted quite as well as the wall, but even if Siyon didn't want to get too close to what remained of the walls for fear they'd fall on him, there was still plenty of paved courtyard, under the spreading and fluttering shade of the thorny wishing trees. The branches were adorned with dozens upon dozens of scraps of rags like strange flowers. Some were new and colourful, others faded and worn away to mere threads.

Mayar lifted a hand toward the trees, fingers shifting as though they were feeling a breeze that certainly wasn't blowing here in the stifling hills. "There's a...shimmer."

Siyon could see it, like each rag-tied wish had caught up a fragment of burnished Mundane energy, along with the curling wisps of wistful Aethyr.

He'd tied a scrap of his own, years ago now, up here with a six of Little Bracken and far more booze than was good for them. Daruj had wished—shouting at the night sky as though in challenge—to meet Gayane Saliu. Siyon had wished—silently, to himself—to become a proper alchemist.

He supposed *improper* wasn't so bad.

Was this waking up too? Were the new-made wishes coming true?

Today Siyon started getting a handle on what was happening in Bezim. He hoped.

He swept clear one of the big paving slabs the long-dead Lyraec army had laid in the yard of their fort. With the broken edge of another stone, Siyon scratched out his best attempt at a map of the city. No details—he couldn't use this to show someone how to get from the low market to university hill—but the basics. The approximate wobble of the cliffs along the south of the city's headland. The bulge of the lower city, where it really didn't matter if he was vague because so was the coastline, shifting with each tide. The curve of the coast around Dockside, out to the northern lighthouse, and then back across, through the marshlands, to the river, and the crag on the other side of it. A slash down the left side for the wall.

Utterly wonky. He had the curve of the river totally wrong. It didn't matter. The more important part was what came next.

Siyon shook his new-scraped sandstone grit along the line that represented the city wall. He set the stub of a grave candle—filched the last time he went to Othissa's memorial—where the crag blocked the northwest corner of the city. Along the top, where the brackish and desolate marshes clustered against Bezim's tenuous margins, Siyon smeared a line of mud from a little pot in his satchel. He'd used to trade for this, unwilling to go back down to Dockside himself. And finally, around the approximate lines of the east and south coastlines, he shook out a trail of sea salt.

Mayar watched him do all this in a silence that felt skeptical. "Even working in miniature," they commented, as Siyon recorked his vial of salt, "that's a lot of distance. A lot of energy."

"I'm not going to do a proper sigil," Siyon said. He was still figuring out what he *was* doing, but he knew that much. "Something's waking up, right? I'm just giving it a gentle nudge. A reminder of where the boundary is. This is my plane. My city." He fixed Mayar with a look; Siyon wasn't accepting the challenge on that one.

But Mayar only looked thoughtful. "It's a lot of energy," they repeated. "It has to come from somewhere."

"It's waking up," Siyon countered. "It's rising. It's...unsteady; can't you feel it?" Mayar frowned but didn't confirm or deny it. "It wants direction. It wants to be used. This is right."

Siyon wasn't sure who he was convincing. But it didn't matter. This was the best idea he'd had, and the only way to find out whether it worked was to try.

He looked at his little map of Bezim, fixing it in his mind, and then closed his eyes.

The autumn sun beat down, laughing at the idea that it was supposed to be getting cooler. Salt Night wasn't even four weeks away; Siyon shouldn't be sweating like this. He tried to ignore it.

He reached—not through the barrier to another plane, but out across the Mundane. With his eyes closed, every direction felt the same; maybe he reached down instead, into the earth. It was all the same, right? There was energy all around him, slow and glowing, oozing out of the world like it had been waiting for this.

Siyon pulled his fingers closed and opened his eyes to a fistful of power. It came so easily. It wanted to be used. It went where he wanted, when he cast it like a handful of chum onto the water, falling only inside the boundaries of Bezim that he'd scratched on the rock and marked with intent.

Those borders started to glow—the stone grit, the mud, the salt. The wick of the candle stub sparked for a moment in vibrant bronze, then went out again. A wisp of dark, shadowy smoke coiled, drifting over the little map of Bezim.

Something settled, heavy as a reassuring blanket, over Siyon's senses.

And then a voice behind him snapped, *"What is this?"*

Siyon startled, and the last of the Mundane energy spattered out from his hand, droplets disappearing in the air. His foot kicked out, smearing grit into mud, scattering salt.

It didn't matter. It was done. He could still feel it—a new clarity, a faint and watchful hum.

Mayar leapt to their feet, hand dropping to a sabre they weren't carrying. Siyon twisted around, coming into a crouch, snatching up the rock he'd used to scratch his map.

Midnight stood in the long shadow cast by the remnant wall of the Lyraec fort, overlapped by a wishing tree's shade. In the plain light of day, he looked almost entirely the same. No taller, draped in the same black robes, hair still shorn close to the skull. But his face seemed a little longer, his shoulders broader. The same person. Probably.

Siyon was no longer sure of anything, when it came to Midnight. "What are you doing here?" he demanded.

"You—" Midnight started, then hesitated. Something like uncertainty crossed that implacable face. "You pulled me here," he finished, though with no real conviction.

The energy has to come from somewhere, Mayar had said. Siyon had reached. Had grabbed. Had drawn.

"Who are you?" Siyon asked, but that didn't quite feel like the right question. "*What* are you?"

"I told you." The conviction was back in Midnight's tone, each word a defiant statement. "We are the one who waits in the darkest shadows."

Siyon was sober, this time. And he had all Balian's unsettling research to help. "The Cult of Midnight," he said. "That was you? Hundreds of years ago?"

Surprise flitted over Midnight's face, like he'd reached into a pocket and found a handful of rivna he'd forgotten about. "Some of me. Yes. It has been a long time. The details fall away. What is buried remains. *She* remains. And she is waiting for you."

Midnight held out a hand, and though it was palm up, like an offer, everything else about his stance reminded Siyon of the picture in the scroll. Midnight forbidding. Menacing, even. Midnight, centuries ago, before the city was founded. Midnight in a cave, beneath the city. Far beneath, now.

Siyon shifted, and something nudged against his toe. The stub of the grave candle, for those dead and buried.

What was buried. Who was *she*?

Unease crawled down Siyon's spine. He straightened slowly, not letting go of his rock. "Did you kill the last Power?"

"No!" Midnight almost shouted it.

And yet there was that light of uncertainty again. It had been a long time. The details fall away.

He wasn't sure.

"What do you want from me?" Siyon demanded. He took a step sidelong, out of the shade of the wishing tree. Into full sunlight.

Midnight flinched back, deeper into shadow. "You must come," he said, but the demanding edge was gone from his voice. Instead, it was almost a plea. "You *must*. There is... I have been waiting... So long." He looked up, and there was an anguish in his eyes. Something lost so long ago it had been lost again in time.

Then his face twisted into anger, so abrupt and complete it was like Midnight was suddenly another person. "Enough!" he snapped. "Long enough. You will come, if I have to drag you there myself."

He strode forward, and should have stepped into the sun, but the shadow dragged with him, looming and bronze-edged. He reached for Siyon's arm, fingers pale, eyes hard.

Siyon lifted his rock. "No!"

With the word, something pushed out of him, felt rather than seen, a force that shoved Midnight away. He went flying backward, swallowed by the shadows in a shimmering burnished mist.

An instant later, the dazzle was clear. The ruins were empty.

The grasshoppers were still screaming in the thorn trees. A crow called, somewhere unseen. But the hillside was still—far more still than it had been. All the Aethyreal emanations were gone from the wishing trees, as though they'd also been blasted away by whatever Siyon had done.

"That was…" Mayar started, and seemed to find no way to finish it.

The rock fell from Siyon's nerveless fingers. He snatched up his satchel and left the remains of his little ritual where they had scattered. "Let's get the fuck out of here."

Like there was anywhere he could run that Midnight couldn't find him.

It was still three weeks until Salt Night, but tonight the Flower district—always eager for a party—was celebrating some imported Revarri festival. It seemed to require endless strings of little firecrackers and the exchange of kisses between strangers on the street.

The sun was just setting, but festivities were already well underway. Anahid dodged around knots of overexcited patrons eagerly lighting firecrackers from an alchemical taper.

Perhaps she could take one with her later, when she went to visit Vartan. Even if they were hardly strangers. Even if they hardly needed an excuse to exchange kisses.

Someone jostled her elbow—unsurprising, in the crowd—and said, "Excuse me, azata."

A man, tall and broad, looking at her. Oh. "No, thank you," Anahid said, with a laughing smile as she sidestepped around him. Her gaze snagged on the symbol tattooed on his bare forearm: a five-petal flower with a flourished Z across it.

He stepped with her, blocking her path.

Anahid didn't hesitate; she turned to run, but there was another thug beside her, blocking her escape, turning her toward a narrow arcade even as he wrapped one thick-fingered hand around her arm and said, "Pardon, za."

So polite. Anahid opened her mouth to shriek for help, but the man behind her reached around her face, pressing tight a bundle of cloth thick with a cloying scent that crawled hook-fingered into her head.

The street whirled dizzyingly around her, firecrackers fizzing in her head. She was lifted off her feet, and darkness swallowed her whole.

She fell, and she tumbled, and she rolled through the storm, seasick as ever.

Wait, no—

She wasn't on a boat, she'd been in the District, there were firecrackers and kisses and—

Darkness, and darkness, and queasy, roiling darkness.

An interminable time later, the world lurched, and Anahid struggled to open her eyes, her head *aching*, her body heavy, tossed on the sea—

The storm *roared* and washed her up on a hard wooden surface. She clung blearily to it, splinters digging under her fingernails, and the noise around her was shouting, wailing, cheering. Something *shrieked* and knocked heavily against wood. Where *was* she? Laughter brayed just above her head.

Turning her head took more effort than anything Anahid had ever done. Blobs of colour and shadow distorted like jelly, until they became, upside down, a large woman swathed in emerald satin and crowned with peacock feathers in her mass of midnight-blue curls.

Mama Badrosani's laughter trailed off, though the background hubbub continued. She tucked her pipe back between stained teeth as she looked down at Anahid. "Look who's back. Sit up if you like, child. Matters little if you hurl on the boards here."

For a moment, her smoke-scarred voice and easy manner were a relief, but other shadows shifted around them. They weren't alone, and cold dread curdled Anahid's stomach. Where *were* they?

And why had she been snatched off the street to be brought here? The bench was hard and rough beneath her; everything else was a blur. Noise hammered at her, rising up from somewhere below, beating at her head like surf on the beach. Feet stamping and hands clapping, tripping steadily faster until it spilled into more raucous cheering and...snarling?

Anahid tried to sit up, but the world spun and she only lurched sideways. She blinked again, and her vision resolved into the cold, grim face of Garabed Zinedani.

Below them, an agonised scream ended in a brutal wet gurgle; the crowd roared.

Anahid stopped fighting her stomach and threw up, bile scraping her throat raw. Garabed took a quick step backward.

Mama Badrosani waved a hand, and two strapping young men hauled Anahid up to sitting. A serving girl came with a threadbare blanket to wrap around Anahid's shoulders and a bucket to sluice away the mess. Anahid gripped the blanket tight, fingers trembling. It snagged in her hair. She'd lost her headscarf.

If only that were her most pressing problem.

They were all crowded on a rickety excuse for a balcony, one of many circling what seemed too crowded for a warehouse, but far too plain for a theatre. One wall bore a symbol painted in black—a baling hook crossed with a hammer.

But it was the people who demanded attention. Mama Badrosani reclined on a hard wooden bench as though it were an elegant chaise, and the young men at her sides looked similar enough that they were surely her sons. The elder Zinedani glowered at Anahid from one corner, though thankfully there was no sign of Stepan. The rest were strangers to Anahid, but that was hardly reassuring. Near the railing, two men and a woman loitered in a knot of muscle and obviously violent histories, all their hair shorn down to stubble. Beside them, two short and black-clad men waited with an almost eerie calm.

If Anahid knew two parties on this balcony for crime barons, she could hazard a guess as to the provenance of the other two. All the city's barons, gathered here with her. She shifted on her own bench, and the balcony creaked beneath her. Her knuckles scratched tight against the blanket. Hot white panic scrabbled at the inside of her skull.

Below, a clamoring mass of people surged at the barriers of a sunken and sanded ring. There was blood on the churned sand, and other oozings in black and even a thick green splashed about and muddled together. In the midst of it all, a Khanate draconet prowled, long as a shark, neck ruff flared as it hissed; the spikes of its tail were dark and wet with the blood of the tigrine whose carcass was being fished off the sand by a man with a long-poled hook.

This was beast-baiting. Anahid had heard of it; heard it was popular in Dockside, run by Aghut and the Shore Clan, for whom illegality was less of a deterrent. She'd never expected to see a pit firsthand. She'd never expected to be kidnapped either. She'd never imagined any of this.

But she could take a hint when it was paraded in front of her; in this place, her body could be cleared just as casually from the bloody sand.

Anahid pressed a hand to the sash of her dress, where the penknife still lay snug against her ribs. Either they hadn't bothered to search her or hadn't considered it a threat. Anahid could hardly blame them, either way. What good could it possibly do her?

She let her hand fall back into her lap.

"Let's get this over with," Mama Badrosani declared.

Anahid shuddered. "Get what over with?" she asked, voice a weak croak.

Mama Badrosani gestured with her pipe, trailing a wisp of smoke. "Zinedani, you know, of course—he's the one as called us here. These are my sons. That's Aghut and his people." She pointed the pipe stem at the group of three shaved thugs.

Which left the last pair of men. They weren't quite identical, but uncannily similar. Each was slender, with a boyish face and deep, liquid eyes that watched her unblinking. Their stillness went beyond unnatural into something that made Anahid uneasy.

"Consider this pair Midnight, for today," Mama Badrosani drawled, then beckoned to Zinedani. "All right, off you go, then."

"Yes," said the most tattooed of the shaven-headed trio. Anahid assumed it was Aghut himself, slouched like a bored tiger, with a scar that twisted down one cheek. "Why the fuck are we here, Zee?"

Zinedani stood, and the balcony creaked beneath him. "I request a death."

Aghut snorted. "What, hers?"

Anahid bit her lip. Sharks and minnows. She'd miscalculated.

"You can't be serious." Mama Badrosani blew smoke at him. "By the Demon Queen's tits, she's azatani. You think she won't be missed?"

"Given her recent unwise decisions," Zinedani said dispassionately, "it will look like a natural product of poor choices—and discourage further tampering in our affairs from that corner."

He was entirely right. It would be the perfect thrilling end to the scandal. If they ever even found out. No one knew where Anahid was; only Siyon might know where to look for her. She'd even had a chance to tell Zagiri what she was about, and decided matters were too delicate and dangerous now to risk her reaction. She could laugh—bitterly, hysterically—at the thought.

"Possibly," one of the Midnight pair said.

And the other added, "But why?"

Anahid could answer that. She'd miscalculated *badly*. Her breath came sharp and fast, still tasting of bile. The crowd below hissed, long and low, as Bezim's crime barons spoke of killing her as though deciding whether to pour more tea.

Garabed turned his gaze—flat and cold as a blade—on her. "My nephew is currently in the custody of the inquisitors—"

Aghut snorted. "So your fuckup has fucked up again."

Zinedani glared at him. "Have I ever shirked on acknowledging his errors? Have I ever given less than full satisfaction to any of you suffering loss or inconvenience as a consequence? Is there any—"

"Get *on* with it," Mama Badrosani snapped.

Zinedani drew himself up. "The charges are flimsy. An excuse. Related to some decorations my nephew had on display. Which they were informed about." He said *informed* as though it were a low and unpleasant act.

Aghut turned a frown on her. "You been carrying tales?"

Words stuck in her scalded throat, but Anahid forced herself to swallow. What did she have to lose? Killing her was already the topic of discussion. "I am not one of you," she croaked. "I have few means of defending myself. And Stepan Zinedani had made it quite clear that he would continue to harass my House."

Zinedani scowled. "A House you have no business owning."

"I won it!" She said that far more forcefully than she intended, but why not? Why *shouldn't* she shout? "You regret its loss? Take it up with your nephew, who laid it on the table."

Mama Badrosani laughed merrily around her pipe. She pulled it out to ask, "Who came for your boy?" She pointed the pipe and a wicked smirk at Zinedani and added, "I'll lay ten rivna I know the answer."

Zinedani's face twisted up, and he all but spat: "Xhanari."

There was an immediate reaction around the circle, Aghut and his thugs sneering in unison and one of the Badrosani sons growling, "*That* bastard."

Mama's smirk widened, nearly a leer. "*Such* a thorn in our sides, the last month or so. *Such* an interestingly upright man."

"Interesting." Aghut hawked and spat on the rough boards. "I'm *interested* in gutting him like a fish. Crashing in like a beached whale, rummaging where he's not wanted, making a mess of all our delicate understandings—"

"Refusing to be bought off like a reasonable man," Mama Badrosani added lightly.

"We'll get him," Aghut stated, crossing his arms with finality. "With money or the blade, we'll get him."

"In the meantime, he's making a mess," Mama pointed out, with something like relish.

"This is what I'm saying!" Zinedani burst in, like he felt this was getting away from him. "She's helping him, calling him down on us, we need to remove her from the whole business—"

But it *had* got away from him; Mama Badrosani was in charge now. "Or we need to use her." She looked at Anahid, eyes heavy-lidded and glittering like Laxmi on the prowl. "Because she's got a hook in him we can't buy, beg, or steal."

It was all Anahid could do not to gape at her. How did she know? How *could* she know?

Realisation hooked her like a fish. She *had* been followed. She had been watched. Just not by the baron she'd been expecting.

"That so?" Aghut looked Anahid over. "You doffing him?"

Anahid knew the term; had learned it from the Flowers' chatter. She couldn't have felt more exposed if they'd torn the dress from her back. Mama Badrosani had laid a hand on her life and turned it over to show everyone her cards.

Exposure wasn't the worst thing that could happen to her here. "Yes," Anahid admitted.

Aghut slapped one muscled thigh and chortled. "I didn't think he even knew how to use it!" He smirked at Anahid, sitting there bedraggled with the blanket wrapped around her, and added, "No accounting for taste."

The spark of anger that struck in Anahid was completely unhelpful right now. It didn't matter how much Vartan had wanted her—how hot his eyes, how hungry his hands, how burning his desire for *her.*

What mattered right now—and Anahid knew it without the significant look Mama Badrosani gave her—was what Anahid could use that desire for.

"You think," Mama asked, drawling the words out lasciviously, "you can give him something to pay attention to that isn't us and our business?"

Honestly? No. Anahid didn't think any power on earth could distract Xhanari from the pursuit of his aims. He'd always stayed focused, despite all her efforts to turn his attention aside. It had been an invigorating challenge.

But this was no place for honesty.

Zinedani cried, "This is ridiculous; she can't be trusted! What about my nephew!"

"Shut up," Aghut said. His eyes on Anahid like a cat watching a seagull. "Your nephew can dangle like bait on a hook for all I care, if this little za can pull that thorn from our sides."

Right on cue, the crowd roared below them. Two new animals were released in a flurry of violence. There were snarls, roars, a high-pitched scream. Anahid didn't look. It didn't matter what was happening down there.

Up here, they were all watching her—Zinedani glowering, Mama smirking—except for the Midnight pair, who seemed entirely uninterested. There was only one way out.

"Of course I can," Anahid said.

The crowd below applauded wildly, cheering and whistling.

CHAPTER 16

Siyon absolutely wasn't panicking.

He'd just been threatened, and maybe nearly abducted, by some mysterious, eldritch, possibly immortal, possibly *murderous* crime baron who was rumoured to be able to appear anywhere, any time.

All right, maybe he was panicking a little.

Of course, there was nothing he could do about it. No defense he could mount. No lock that he could charm up capable of keeping Midnight out. Possibly he'd somehow banished Midnight, up in the hills, but Siyon had no idea how, and certainly no certainty that he could do it again.

So he might as well ignore the whole thing and keep going.

Siyon wasn't sure if his little ritual, marking the city's boundaries, had actually worked. Everything more or less felt the same. He'd thought perhaps the seething emanations had settled down, but the next day they'd felt just as tumultuous, if not more so.

But the Mundane energy came more readily to hand. He barely had to focus at all, or to reach. Even if Siyon had felt more than a little nervous, the first time he'd pulled up a handful of burnished power. But Midnight hadn't leapt out of the nearest shadow again, and Siyon had managed to twist his power into a looping, twisting, continuous nullification sigil.

He'd dropped it straight into Olenka's badge, the whole silver candle momentarily gleaming like bronze. She'd glared at it like a grumpy hawk, turned it over in her hands, huffed and polished it, even tested her teeth against the thing. When she finally admitted it seemed good, she produced another half dozen badges for him to charm as further tests.

Admittedly, Siyon was far less worried about Midnight in the middle of the inquisitors' wing of the Palace of Justice. Though rationally, he didn't think Midnight—whatever and whoever he was—particularly cared about the petty laws of modern-day Bezim.

Alone in his apartment was another matter. Siyon was *supposed* to be settling down and figuring out how he could check whether his marked city boundary worked to repel extraplanar delvers. There had to be a better way than waiting to see if anyone else showed up.

Instead, Siyon kept twitching at every sound—and there were a *lot* from the street, where the snooty azatani teahouse on the corner was taking delivery of a load of mixed spices to start preparing its Salt Night special blends. Shadows kept lurking in the corner of his vision, no matter how many more alchemical lanterns he shook into full brightness.

Siyon's mouth opened for the fourth time, words on the tip of his tongue to ask Laxmi to stay close. To keep him safe.

Fortunately, she seemed to have decided that teasing him about being so twitchy was the best entertainment she was likely to find tonight. She lay spread out on the ceiling like she was floating on the sea, hair billowing like ink around her horned head.

So Siyon asked instead: "Do *you* know what happened to the last Power of the Mundane?"

"Rude," Laxmi crooned, smirking like he'd done something cheeky. "How old do you think I am?"

Fair point. She'd said something once, about having preferred Bezim before the Sundering, so clearly time flowed differently between the planes, or harpies lived far longer than humans. But there was long-lived, and then there was however many centuries they were talking, back to when Midnight did...

Whatever Midnight had done.

"Shall I ask Her Majesty?" Laxmi drifted down from the ceiling, all tendrils and insinuations. "Would you like me to beg for another favour, to make a pretty pair with the one you already owe for me?"

No, Siyon would certainly not. He had more than enough problems on his plate. He had a whole *buffet* of problems.

He leaned back from Laxmi's encroachment, then flinched and jerked aside when his hand came down on something sharp.

The little dragon figurine just sat there, like it was innocent. Like it wasn't the endlessly recurring reminder of an implacable demand.

You will come, if I have to drag you there myself.

Siyon startled as a serrated claw traced gently down his cheek. Laxmi pouted. "You never get this frightened of *me*."

He batted her hand aside, snatched up the dragon, and flung it out the window, into the night.

And then yelped—like a startled puppy—at the ringing of the gate bell.

Laxmi laughed, rusty and rolling like marbles in a tin can.

But over the noise came shouting from the stairs. "Master Velo! Master Velo! Are you there? It's Azata Joddani!"

It clearly wasn't—not Anahid's voice at all. But it also clearly wasn't Midnight. Siyon hurried down the stairs, eager to have something more tangible to wrestle with.

That Flower in training he'd met at Anahid's House—the one with freckles and a good grasp of both the nullification sigil and Dockside folklore—was shaking at the gate, her pale fingers clenched around the wrought iron bars, and her hair straggling loose of its elegant arrangement.

"I'm here!" Siyon pulled open the gate. The young Flower gaped at him; her makeup was streaked with tears. Siyon couldn't remember her name. "It was...the Dawnsong, yes? What's wrong?"

She huffed a strange little laugh, almost hysterical. Her breath heaved her ribs. She was no bravi, to run the distance from the Flower district without being winded. "The mistress of the House— she didn't come tonight. And there has been some trouble—before.

So we—asked around." She pressed a hand to her chest, like she could will herself calm. "There were men. With the Zinedani mark. We think she was taken."

This wash of panic felt clearer. It swept Siyon clean, and wrote him new purpose. "Taken where?" he demanded, and called up the stairs: "Laxmi!"

Imelda—not her stage name—couldn't run any farther, but she walked quickly, a hand pressed to her side, and explained as they went. About the trouble they'd been having—at her Flower Night, and since then, with the door of the House. "Azata Joddani said she had taken steps to dissuade Master Zinedani from troubling us further," she said breathlessly.

"Ineffective steps," Siyon commented as they turned downhill, the Flower district hedge rising ahead of them.

"Or perhaps *too* effective." Laxmi, who was riding Siyon's shoulder like a slightly too large and definitely too scaly raven, chuckled. "That's my girl."

Imelda looked sidelong at the disguised harpy but said nothing. Perhaps she simply didn't have the breath.

The Flower district thronged with laughing crowds, the night air alive with firecrackers—oh, was it Revarri New Year already? Imelda took them to the narrow arcade where Anahid had last been seen.

As Laxmi fluttered down, pecking at stray tapers and the stub ends of depleted firecrackers, Siyon looked around. This was a main thoroughfare of the District; there were two Houses opposite. "She was taken in full view, and no one said or did anything?"

Imelda shrugged her hunched and miserable shoulders. "Men with the Zinedani mark," she repeated.

And the Flower district was almost entirely owned and run by the Zinedani.

Laxmi clawed her way back up onto Siyon's shoulder. "Not enough here to find a trail," she cawed. "I'll need a stronger connection. Something she owns. Something that's part of her."

Imelda considered. "We have the mask she wears as Lady Sable, back at the House?"

Perfect.

But when they arrived at Sable House, the looming security man pointed them straight up the stairs. In the office with its shell-beaded curtain, Anahid was adjusting the fall of a stiff tabard of black lace that matched the mask waiting on the desk, as Qorja pinned up her hair.

"Mistress!" Imelda hurried to throw her arms around Anahid. "We thought that the Zinedanis…"

She trailed off, but Anahid nodded. "They did. Probably whatever you thought, they tried, at least. It's been a most unpleasant evening." She met Siyon's gaze, over Imelda's tumbling hair, and added, "Thank you so much for your concern. I am sorry to have put you out."

Imelda sniffed as she let Anahid go, then waved a hand at Siyon. "We didn't know who else to ask. In the circumstances, we thought, maybe not the inquisitors."

Anahid's laugh was a sharp-edged and brittle thing. "No, maybe not indeed. But now you should all get back to work. Me too. I'll be right behind you."

Qorja and Imelda filed out, the beads and shells clacking behind them, as Siyon looked at Anahid…and then wondered if he should. He'd seen her hair uncovered before, braided for sleep, but that had been in her own home. "Should I help with your headscarf?" he asked, looking around for one.

Anahid smiled and took up the black lace mask instead. "Lady Sable doesn't wear one. She isn't an azata, you see." She lifted it to her face, but fixing it in place was more complicated. "Could you?"

Laxmi curled her talons tight in Siyon's shoulder. "I'll help," she offered, with far more leer than a crow should have been able to manage.

When Siyon shoved her off, she flew laughing to the windowsill. Anahid laughed as well—faintly and briefly, but it was a reassuring sound. Siyon stepped up behind Anahid to tie the upper pair of the mask's trailing laces, then started on the lower.

A faint scent lifted from her hair, and it wasn't at all what he'd have expected. Pipe smoke, and something sweet and clinging, and a strange whiff of sawdust. "Where have you *been*?" he asked.

She shook her head, but only barely, not dislodging his hands at work. "In a mess," she admitted. "And I'm not out of it yet. I've woken trouble, and now I have to deal with it."

Siyon could relate to that. Though he hadn't been snatched by the Zinedani off the street. "I thought we agreed we *don't* get involved with the barons."

"They started it," Anahid snarled, then whirled around at Siyon's snort, fixing him with a sharp look. "What?"

"That sounds like something Zagiri would say," Siyon pointed out. "Or me." And they all knew how wise *he* wasn't. "What's been going on? What are these steps Imelda says you took?"

Anahid laughed a little helplessly, touching one hand to her hair, just above her ear, then almost flinched away. No headscarf, of course. Only the lace mask, now tied on firmly. Her shoulders squared themselves a moment later. Like that touch of bare hair had reminded her of who she was.

Lady Sable, not Anahid Joddani. Not right now.

"You don't want to know what I've been doing," she said, with a smile too complicated for Siyon to untangle. A little rueful, perhaps, but also maybe a little pleased.

She wasn't quite the woman he'd first met, up in the Avenues. Or maybe this was the woman he'd glimpsed, that night in her dining room, with her hair uncovered and a deck of cards in her hands. The one who'd insisted he teach her to play carrick.

"All right," he said. "Just know that I'm here if you—"

The squeals rose again from outside, but this time there was no pleasure or laughter in the sound. These were screams.

"What *now*?" Anahid growled, and stormed out of the office.

Laxmi fluttered back to Siyon's shoulder, smacking her beak with unpleasant relish as Siyon followed Anahid out. Quick down the stairs, hurrying out into the square. People were running in every direction. A bell had started to ring, in the heart of the District; the emergency bell. Siyon had only ever heard it rung for an outbreak of fire.

Faintly over the peals, someone screamed, "Monsters!"

"What?" Anahid gasped, and she stopped dead.

Siyon didn't stop. Siyon broke into a sprint.

He thought he'd *fixed it*. He really thought that ritual in the hills, as small and flimsy and slapped together as it had been, had done what he needed it to. It had *felt*—

Well, that didn't matter, did it? Not when there must be another incursion. Maybe not just an angel or djinn this time. *Monsters*. What did that mean?

"Laxmi," he called. "Find Mayar. Bring them to wherever I am."

She launched off his shoulder, in a gust of sulphur and feathers.

As Siyon ran, he plucked Mundane energy from the air—easy as lifting an apple from a passing cart—and started twisting it between his fingers.

Whatever this was, it wouldn't find them unprepared.

Shifting in her crouch next to the chimney, Zagiri scanned the street below again, letting her eyes drift lazily. In the dark, even with the light of the near-full moon, she was more likely to spot movement than see a person waiting.

Any other night of the year, she'd be relishing the anticipation. She enjoyed a good round of stalk-and-flee. It was excellent training for so many essential bravi skills—slinking over the rooftops, running across the city, spotting a target and avoiding being seen. And there was always the chance of blades kissing moonlight if the fleeing team took a chance on storming home base.

But tonight Zagiri was too frustrated to settle properly into the game. Maybe she'd picked the wrong lookout spot, but there was no action to drive the thoughts from her mind.

Thoughts that circled endlessly, fruitlessly around the select committee, and all the priorities of its members, and the sorcery reform that she probably couldn't make happen, whatever some statue in the fruit market had to say.

Zagiri couldn't stop thinking that there was one key piece that she couldn't see. Like trying to spot a creeping Bleeding Dawn bravi on the streets below.

As though summoned by her impatience, someone came around a corner, clinging to the shadows as they flitted along the row of houses. This little wedge of the city—between the Kellian Way, the river chasm, the Scarp, and the Flower district—was a good ground for the game precisely because it was a warren of twisty streets among sedate terrace houses tall enough to give excellent vantage.

Zagiri stayed out of sight as she shadowed the figure below. She'd only crept a little way along the row of roofs before she realised— frustration grinding her teeth—that whoever was skulking along at street level wasn't bravi. Moved all wrong, and wasn't wearing leathers and a tricorn, but some sort of strange pale hood.

No, wait. That was hair. *Blonde* hair.

Zagiri scrambled around the next chimney, scuttling along the far side of the roof quick enough to get ahead and verify her suspicion.

What was *Yeva Bardha* doing out here? Not visiting someone, not this close to midnight, not in canvas trousers and creeping along like she was trying to avoid notice.

At the end of the row, there was an easy descent—balcony, window box, garden wall, down to the street—and when Yeva slunk around the corner, Zagiri was waiting to grab her wrist and twist it up behind her back. Yeva squeaked, going up on her toes.

"I could be the inqs," Zagiri snarled in her ear. "I thought you were going to be *careful*."

"Zagiri," Yeva breathed, turning around enough that Zagiri could see her smile. "No, you couldn't be. They've been paid off or distracted elsewhere for the night."

That gave Zagiri pause. "Why?" she asked. Not at all the question she should be asking, not like that. But now she was curious.

Yeva heard it. "Let me show you."

They wound down and down through the twisty streets, with the rushing roar of the river growing closer, until they rounded a lantern-limned corner. The street was nearly blocked by two sleepy oxen and the cart they were hitched to; the cart was half full of narrow crates, and as Zagiri skidded to a halt behind Yeva, someone on the other side of the cart stacked another onto the load.

From where? There was nothing beyond the cart, quite literally. Zagiri could see the harbour, bobbing with the white anchor lights of the moored boats, and clear across to the pale green beacon on the far headland. Here, so close to the river, the Scarp wasn't as high as farther south, but it was still a cliff taller than Zagiri cared to fall.

But when Zagiri followed Yeva around the cart, there was a thick-twisted rope running from the cart between the half dismantled safety railing, through the hauling hands of two hefty-looking men, and over the edge of the Scarp.

The men looked up at their arrival but kept hauling, pulling something up from the lower city. "Bardha." One jerked his chin at Zagiri. "Who's this, then?"

"She's sound," Yeva declared. "And the law's looking the other way. We ready to roll yet?"

"Nearly," the first man on the rope said. "Two more cases."

Zagiri looked at the cart, at the crates already stacked there, and back at the men—pulling in easy rhythm, like they worked together often. Of course they did. They were *laders*, the disgruntled dock-workers causing all the trouble recently.

Trouble in Dockside. Warehouse locks damaged, deliveries delayed, ship repairs dragging on, equipment tampered with. *That* was the sort of trouble the workers made every autumn, using their seasonal importance to apply leverage. Sometimes, the trouble got up as far as the industrial district. It had been all of that recently. Zagiri had heard all the usual reports and complaints.

This autumn, things are different, Yeva had told her.

This year, she'd said, it would be revolution.

And now here were laders, in the upper city, smuggling something up.

Yeva stepped over to the cart, counting crates, checking that they were all secure.

"What's in there?" Zagiri hissed. "Explosives?" She was appalled.

She was thrilled. She couldn't believe it. Were they going to blow up the Palace?

Yeva gave her a look like Zagiri was talking rubbish. "What? Where would we—? No." She lifted one of the crates and shoved it in Zagiri's direction.

The smell that lifted from the wood sent Zagiri immediately into nineteen years of memories, of Salt Nights past and the spicebread she'd pilfered from the kitchen as soon as the cook started slicing it.

"Cinnamon," she realised.

Yeva smirked, putting the crate back in its place on the cart. "Whole lot of traders not going to make their contracted deliveries in the next few weeks. But bakers who deal with *us* will be all right."

"This..." Zagiri looked over the cart. Ink and ashes, was this *all* cinnamon? They must have emptied a warehouse. Locks damaged, deliveries delayed...just the same, and yet totally different.

This would mean shortages, not in Dockside, but in the upper city. On azatani tables. Worse, this would mean azatani merchants defaulting on contracts. A terrible thing, for an azatani family's reputation, to fail to deliver on a contract.

"A lot of businesses are going to lose out too," Zagiri pointed out. "Bakers who are just trying the best they can."

Yeva shrugged. "They deal with azatani, they can lean on those azatani. No change is made without pain. But it's going to be someone else's, for once, instead of theirs." And she jerked a thumb over her shoulder at the two hauling laders. There must have been something on Zagiri's face, because Yeva frowned at her. "What? You think we can make them change without a bit of mess? How's your bloodless revolution in the halls of power coming along?"

Frustratingly. Terribly. Not at all.

Zagiri was saved from having to admit it as whistles went up, somewhere nearby. Sharp and urgent, a short and strident pattern, repeated a moment later.

"What is that?" Yeva snapped. "Is it the inqs?"

Another time, Zagiri might have laughed. Right now, she was hurrying back up the hill, slipping past the cart and the oxen. "No, that's a bravi signal. The general alarm." The signal that all tribes had in common. The one that just meant *danger*.

What was happening?

Zagiri was halfway up the street before she realised Yeva was coming too, labouring along behind her. There wasn't time to wait, but Zagiri didn't have to go far. At the first crossroads, there was a main street, carving clean up toward the Flower district, and when Zagiri glanced along that, she came stumbling to a halt.

There was a glow of fire rising, farther up the hill. And against that glow rose a monstrous silhouette, scrambling on four legs across a distant rooftop, a pair of clearly feathered wings flared for balance. It paused, shook itself like a wet cat, and opened a massive hooked beak.

The scream tore across the night. It sounded like nothing so much as a very large—and very pissed off—parrot.

"What the fuck is *that*?" asked Yeva behind Zagiri.

She didn't have a good answer. She'd never seen anything like it . . . except no, she *had*. Crouched in stone at the side of the Palace steps. A lion body, eagle wings and head.

This wasn't stone. This was so much *bigger*. This was *alive*.

More bravi whistles in the night now, rising from the rooftops and the twisting streets. Zagiri heard Bracken signals—rallying blades, calling everyone to get up, to look out, to keep clear. There were other signals she didn't recognise, which must belong to the Bleeders, probably to much the same purposes.

Among them, from somewhere off in the distance, Zagiri heard cheers. Harder, for voices to carry—that was why they used whistles in the first place—but she picked out one word. "Velo!"

Siyon was out here, up there, coming to deal with . . . *that*. The monster scrambled along the roofline, disappearing from Zagiri's line of sight, and she found it a little easier to draw breath.

"Right," she said. "It's a big weird seagull. Cat. Both. Whatever. We can deal with this."

Yeva caught at her arm before Zagiri could get moving again. "Wait. Come with me. Let's get the rope. Maybe we can tie it up?"

Zagiri stared at her. Tie up *that*?

Then again, why not? It might help.

As they raced back downhill, more voices lifted into the night, shouting: "Bracken! Brave the knife!"

This city belonged to them—to the bravi and, perhaps, to the revolution.

No one and nothing else was allowed to trash it.

CHAPTER 17

The night sprang into new life all around Siyon as he sprinted out of the Flower district. Behind him, Zinedani men hammered on doors and rang the gongs, rousing the Houses and other denizens to emergency stations usually used for fighting fires, not...whatever this was.

Fire might not be out of the question; when Siyon left the shelter of the District hedge, there was a glow rising amid the quiet terrace houses downslope. *Something* was on fire, and in the dry days of autumn in Bezim, it was likely to spread.

Ash on the wind, and bravi whistles. Siyon wasn't running alone, as he sprinted down the slope, cutting down the alleyways and staircases between buildings. "Here!" someone shouted, standing on the wall that ran between two narrow gardens. Siyon could see the way up—one bracing foot on this building, bouncing over to that low lintel and then up.

The bravi—no one he knew, wearing the red sash of the Bleeding Dawn—jumped back as Siyon barrelled past. "Burn brightly!" he called, and the cry echoed from the rooftops around them.

From farther away, other cries. "Brave the knife!" and a faint and distant "Soul keen!" rising in the night, amid more whistles. Bracken out on the tiles as well, and Haruspex. For now, they all ran together.

Not the only thing alive and wild in the darkness. The very night air seemed to crackle around Siyon, the energy so heavy even he could feel it. Was the breach of the planar barriers so large, to cause this reaction?

Pulling a little Mundane energy free barely took any thought; Siyon twisted it into the nullification sigil as he ran. Lacking anything better to imbue with it, Siyon dropped it into the sleeve of his coat, and for a moment the whole thing hummed bronze.

A little garden opened up around him, probably once very elegant when this was a fashionable part of the city, but now given over to ramshackle neglect. The paths were still clear enough, and Siyon sprinted along one uneven with subterranean roots, through a tilting hedge—

Where he skidded to a shocked halt. In the centre of the garden, on a little raised dais long covered with lichen, sat the shattered lower half of a stone egg that had once been so large that Siyon might not have been able to wrap his arms around it. Now the broken remnant dripped some thick black ichor that clawed a rank, tarry taste down Siyon's throat; oozing black prints led away, still smoking faintly in the grass. Some were three-clawed and barbed at the back, like an osprey, and some had pads like a cat but were as large as Siyon's own.

"Shit," he said. "*Shit.*"

What sort of gate opening was this? What sort of *creature* had come through? He couldn't tell from the emanation residue; the entire garden was a tangle of shimmering Aethyr and dark Abyss and wildly sparking Empyre, all of it fluttering around like disgruntled seagulls. Around the prints themselves there was a boiling glow, almost too bright to look at, shimmering like fire but more metallic—

The corner of his vision flashed with sharp-sparked darkness, and something slammed into his side. Siyon staggered, tripped over a bit of eggshell (it *was* stone, ow, fuck it), and fell flat.

The person on top of him groaned and choked, scrambled off him (planting a knee in his stomach), and threw up not far enough from Siyon's left ear. In the next few dizzy moments, as Siyon shoved himself away and tried to drag air back into his body, he dimly recognised that this person was swearing in a Khanate dialect.

Mayar pushed unsteadily up to kneeling, looking like they weren't ruling out vomiting again.

"What the fuck," Laxmi's voice said from a patch of nearby darkness, "is *that*?"

"Never—" Mayar croaked, and lifted a finger, waving it wildly. "Do *not* do that again."

They'd come out of nowhere. Quite literally nowhere. Like Laxmi so often did, but she didn't usually *bring someone with her*. "Did you drag them between the planes?" Siyon demanded.

He turned and found Laxmi, crouched atop a trellis. "You said *bring them*." She shrugged and her wings flared a bit. Not so much for balance, but as though she was uneasy. "You have bigger problems," she added, pointing one taloned finger.

Siyon spun around, looking over the little copse of trees that tangled one corner of the park.

The monster clawed its way up to the top of a house two streets away. It looked half vicious sea-eagle, half confused cat, and all disgusting mess. It left smears of that black gunk where its back feet kicked up the wall; as it shook itself, droplets sprayed off its flared wings.

"And I repeat," Laxmi said, "what is *that*?"

The tar, the talons, the shriek it gave into the last shreds of the night... "Isn't it one of yours?"

But Laxmi said, "*No*," like she found the question personally offensive.

Fine. Empyreal, maybe, since it had those wings, though they didn't seem to be working too well—the monster bunched itself, leapt to another roof, and scrambled against the tiles to stay on. Or maybe this was some monster Siyon had never got to the Aethyreal plane to witness.

It didn't really matter. They had to get rid of it. Drag it back through its gate. Except Siyon couldn't *see* a gate. Couldn't see a tether. Just that seething glow around the prints, rising faintly from the puddle of tar. Was it buried somehow? Under the gunk? He scraped at some with his foot, but it was still so bright that he couldn't see clearly.

"I can't feel anything," Mayar coughed, staggering up to their feet, "but how *wrong* that was." They shuddered, all over, like a dog leaving the water, and dragged a heavy-ringed hand over their face.

"Here." Siyon caught the other hand and wound another sigil out of Mundane energy, snatching a scrap easily from the passing breeze; he dumped this one into the largest of Mayar's rings. "We follow it. We grab it. We drag it back here. Its gate and tether must be here somewhere. Can you climb?"

Mayar shoved at him. "Can you, old man?"

The monster had disappeared over the crest of a house, but Siyon didn't think it'd be hard to find again. The fire was between them and it, in a house half torn down by the monster's passage. Siyon and Mayar had to circle around, down toward the Scarp, before they could find a place to climb.

As they clambered up next to an ivy-wrapped chimney, the monster came into view, preening its shoulder feathers only one street away.

Mayar's eyes widened. "Griffin," they whispered. At Siyon's quizzical look, they added, "You know, like the— Maybe you don't. The western Lyraec legions had it on their standards. Called the stones their mangonels threw *griffin eggs*."

Siyon thought back to the stone-hard shattered shell in the garden. He looked again at the monster—at the griffin. It gripped tight to the roof edge, and those talons curled into terracotta tile like it was soft cheese. The whole griffin was glowing now, with a deep bronze sheen on every feather and sparking off its tail.

Oh. Oh shit.

"This isn't an incursion," he realised. "This isn't a monster from any other plane."

This was one of *theirs*. A Mundane monster.

Of course his binding of the city's borders with Mundane energy couldn't stop this. Would the nullification charms even matter? There was nothing to cancel.

"Azatani aren't going to care where it's from." Mayar nodded at the griffin, ripping up roof tiles now as it stretched.

It had only just hatched. How much damage would it do if they let it grow up? They had to get rid of it. But *how*?

There was always more than one way to win a fight on rooftops, but Siyon didn't think a fall to the street would be enough to slow this thing down for long. His eyes slid past its furred-and-feathered bulk to the darkness beyond.

Where the land ran out, plunging down into the chasm, at the bottom of which rushed the river, running *fast* here, and deep, churning and tumbling into the sea.

Siyon had an idea, and sort of wished he hadn't. "If I distract it," he said. "If I can get it a bit closer to the edge, could you use your thing—manipulate your essences—and give it a good shove?"

Mayar looked up at the griffin. "I guess?"

An awful plan. They didn't have time for a better one.

Siyon went one way, circling wide around the griffin up to the west, careful around chimneys and over high-pitched roofs. As he hopped from one to the next, a short, sharp whistle sounded farther along. A Bracken whistle.

Daruj came sliding down from the roof peak, with Zagiri and some nervous-looking blonde behind him.

"Brother." Daruj's usual grin was a tight and wary affair tonight. "What, and I wish to be clear about this, the fuck?"

"Fair question," Siyon allowed, returning his hug. "What are you *doing* here?"

"You don't get all the fun," Zagiri said, crouched and ready. "What's the plan?"

Siyon hated the plan all the more for saying it out loud. "We try to knock it into the ravine."

Zagiri glanced over her shoulder at the blonde woman, who looked uneasy about what was clearly her first time on a roof. "Would a rope help?" Zagiri asked.

That was unexpected. "Actually...yes."

The blonde woman frowned across the rooftops. "What is it doing?" she asked in a Northern accent.

The griffin launched off one roof but only managed to claw two beats in the air with its wings before it collapsed onto the next. Those wings splayed a little, looking uncomfortable. Something about the ungainly movement seemed familiar. "Its wings aren't working properly yet," Siyon realised. All that tar, from inside the egg. "But they're drying out."

If he wanted to drop it into the chasm, they needed to move fast. "Here's what we do," he started, as dread curled in his gut.

When he took off again, over the rooftops, it was with the bravi fanning out behind him, heaving a heavy length of twisted hemp rope up onto the tiles—and Siyon didn't know *where* it had come from, but he was glad of it.

Siyon circled down along the houses next to the river, even as the griffin cocked its head this way and that. "Hey!" Siyon shouted; he needed the thing's attention on *him*. He wished he had his sabre and laughed at himself for the thought. He didn't want to come close enough to this thing to prod at it. But as he ran, he snapped his fingers, conjuring up an Empyreal spark, to wrap it up in a furl of Aethyr.

As he crested the next roof, Siyon drew back his arm and hurled the handful of energy at the griffin. It smacked right into the back of that feathered head, and the griffin whirled around in a flare of wings to glare at him.

Siyon whooped, and ran in earnest, hearing the scrabble of claws behind him.

The blackness of the chasm came closer. The river roared from the bottom as Siyon skidded to a halt on the last row of houses.

Tiles crumbled behind him, under the griffin's bracing weight.

Siyon whirled around as it sprang. Fuck, but it could leap, clear across the roof and street between them. Siyon threw himself aside, but something yanked him back, and sharpness pricked at him; the griffin had grabbed the back of his coat in one talon. So much for the nullification charm on it. Siyon twisted, pulled one arm out of the coat, felt the other sleeve give way, and dropped to the roof. He staggered, and slipped, and fell on his arse, sliding down the roof toward the gutter—

The griffin's other taloned front foot came down on him,

slamming him against the tiles, smacking him flat. Siyon wheezed, then clutched at the claw that arched over his head.

From way up high, glowing bronze against the velvet night sky, the griffin's head lowered. Its beak was shiny black and its eyes golden; it tilted this way and that. Looking at Siyon, he realised. That beak opened a little, and the griffin made a quiet rattling sound deep in its gullet.

The talons scraped around Siyon, curling up. Grabbing hold of him properly. Oh fuck. Any moment now the others would come barrelling out of the night, stretching the rope to sweep the griffin off the roof, and Mayar backing them up with a shove of the essences.

And it'd take Siyon with it.

As the griffin gripped him, Siyon stretched out, into the air around him, into the city, into the darkness that was always with him, crawling out in his dreams—he *reached*, but did it sideways, inside the Mundane, not outside.

He laid desperate hands on the energy all around him, every little bit of it, and he shoved the griffin away as hard as he could.

It felt familiar. This, he realised, was what he'd done to Midnight on instinct, pushing him away.

With a squawk, the griffin hurtled back, and Siyon thumped down on the roof, suddenly sliding again. He scrambled to brace his heels in the gutter and looked up frantically.

The griffin twisted in the air as it passed over the edge of the chasm, too-young wings flaring and frantic. It slammed into the cliff on the other side, talons screeching at the stone, and plummeted.

There was a distant splash as it hit the water, and a forlorn and choking screech.

Siyon could barely hear it over the hammer of his heart in his ears, over the beating of the plane around him, over the shouts and whistles and the distant fire gongs. He lay back on the roof and laughed for the sheer relief of survival.

Zagiri came skidding in beside him on the tiles, patting furiously at his shoulders. "Are you all right?" she demanded. "Did it get you? Is this blood?"

"Let him breathe!" Daruj laughed, following a little slower. "Brother, you are a *maniac*."

Siyon let them haul him up to sitting, wincing at the pull at his shoulder.

"Can you make it to the safe house?" Zagiri asked doubtfully.

Much too difficult. "Take me to Anahid's Flowerhouse," he suggested.

Zagiri went still at his side. "Anahid's *what*?"

Oh. Shit.

As Anahid watched Siyon race off into the night, a woman marched into the square flanked by two heavy-shouldered men. She displayed a Z-crossed flower tattooed on her wrist, before saying, "Sable House, yes? Half function, send the extra staff down to Joyous Bounty. We're only preparing to receive the wounded, but that may change."

"What?" Anahid demanded, umbrage prickling sharply. Especially after the evening she'd already had—the stink of the beast-baiting pit still caught in her throat when she breathed in too sharply—she was in no mood to take orders from anyone with a Zinedani mark.

But Qorja grabbed her arm tight enough for Anahid to swallow her words. "Of course," she said.

The Zinedani woman nodded and headed for the next House.

"This is *not* their property," Anahid growled between gritted teeth as they turned back to Sable House.

"That's the emergency bell ringing." Qorja gestured toward the still-tolling gong. "When that rings, the baron marshals the District to best respond to whatever situation is at hand. It could be worse—the Joyous Bounty will have to close entirely! We'll send half of the staff down to assist, and we can still operate with the other half."

Anahid glanced over her shoulder, at the people still running through the streets, and...was that the glow of fire, staining the night from down toward the river? "You think there will still be patrons, in the face of this?"

Qorja laughed. "Oh, mistress, nothing makes people grasp for life like the risk of death."

She was, as always, entirely correct. Even as the emergency bell continued to toll, more and more patrons pressed into the House, clustering around the gaming tables that remained open, and competing for the favours of the Flowers. Some had come from other Houses that had closed due to emergency operations, but others were clearly recently arrived in the District, as though drawn by the very bell that should have warned them away.

With half of the staff dispatched to be nurses and haulers and potential firefighters, Anahid had no time to dwell upon the earlier events of the evening. She carried crates to the bustling kitchen, visited small chambers to reassure them that entertainment was on the way, and even stepped in for a brief period as the dealer at the gaming floor carrick table.

Even that couldn't hold her attention. Not tonight.

The costume tabard hung heavy from her shoulders, knocking reassuringly against her legs with each stride. In this dress, she wasn't Anahid Joddani—frail and out of her depth and flinching at every dropped tile, broken glass, popped cork.

Lady Sable was made of sterner stuff. Lady Sable had answers. Lady Sable was in *her* House, overseeing her staff, smiling benevolently at her clients' desire to defy death. Anahid drew it around her like armour and told herself she was safe.

Perhaps she even was. Zinedani had asked for her death and been rebuffed. She had won her way out. What more could they do to her now?

The question of what more *she* might have to do could wait for another day.

Gaming pieces clattered, the lottery wheel cackled to itself as it turned, bottles opened one after another. The crowd shifted around Anahid, simmering with speculation about what was happening right now, just a little way down the hill. *It's a monster*, everyone agreed, but everything else was wild conjecture. *The Sorcerer has harnessed it and flown away* or *It has killed a dozen bravi and eaten them* or *There isn't any monster at all; it's actually those Dockside troublemakers, getting serious this year.*

And then, after the emergency bell had stopped ringing: *The Sorcerer has been brought in bleeding* and *The Sorcerer has flown away into the night.*

When Anahid heard someone shouting, she turned toward it reflexively and then hurried to shove through the press when she recognised the voice.

Stepan Zinedani was in the entrance hall, face red and voice hoarse as he shook Imelda by one arm, even while he shouted at the doorman. "—Zinedani and I'll requisition what I damn well please!"

Lejman appeared at Anahid's shoulder, parting the last of the curious crowd. "Sorry, mistress," he began, but she waved him to silence. This night was beyond the control of any of them.

"Za Zinedani!" Anahid snapped, stepping into the clear space around this little tableau. "You will not speak to my staff in that manner."

He staggered around to face her, Imelda wincing as he hauled at her arm. Otherwise, she seemed quite composed. A professional, however young. *On the Path of Flowers there can be the occasional thorns,* she'd said.

That thought only stoked Anahid's anger to a white heat in her chest. How dare he come into her house, after all the trouble he'd already caused her. This was hers, it was *hers,* all the barons had agreed. She had *bought* this twice over, with her cards and now with her promise.

She would not allow this. Not here, not now.

"You." Stepan's pointing finger wavered, and his eyes were bloodshot; there was more than just rage in his veins. "You, *Joddani,* must submit to our demands."

A cold splinter stabbed through Anahid's heart—her *name,* said aloud, in front of so many avid witnesses.

But her rage swept that aside. "We have already provided our emergency aid as directed. I have nothing for a *brat* like you!"

Stepan let Imelda go then—the girl skipping quickly away—and took a step forward, lifting his hand. Anahid watched as though time had slowed to honey. The shifting of his shoulders, the movement of his balance toward her, the scything of his open hand. She could see the slap coming and she knew it would take her off her feet, would rattle her eyes in her skull, would hurt like nothing in life had prepared her to hurt.

Here, in her own House, she still was not safe.

Then Stepan stopped abruptly, wrist caught in a wide, dark hand. Behind her shoulder, Lejman asked impassively, "Mistress?"

Anahid took a half-gasping breath. The lace mask caught in her mouth, and she grabbed it, pulled it free to gulp air.

As steadily as she could, she said, "Stepan Zinedani, you are barred from Sable House."

Lejman and the doorman dragged Stepan out of the wide front door, even as he shrieked imprecations. The crowd all around Anahid came to a boil of exhilarated whispering.

So many of their eyes were on Anahid. The black lace mask was still in her hand, not on her face. They could see her. They had heard her name in Stepan's mouth.

Something was clawing at Anahid's throat. She wanted to scream in every staring face.

"Well," Imelda declared, tossing her coppery hair over one shoulder and fanning herself with a hand. "I don't know about anyone else, but *I* could certainly use a drink. Which way to the bar?"

There was laughter, and the crowd broke up to cluster around her, to drain away to other pursuits. When the entrance hall cleared, Anahid was alone.

Nearly alone.

One person remained in the open doorway, staring in slack-jawed astonishment. "Anahid?" Zagiri gasped.

Anahid started to laugh, rough and helpless. She couldn't stop, couldn't catch her breath. She clutched at her head, dug her fingers into her hair—her uncovered hair, around her uncovered face, oh ink and ashes, how had everything gone so wrong?

It was only when Zagiri's arms grappled around her shoulders that Anahid realised she was no longer laughing, but rather crying. She clung to her sister and sobbed into her shoulder, then the storm passed, leaving her tossed up on the beach of calm like driftwood.

"You'd better," she said quietly, carefully wiping her cheeks dry, "come upstairs."

Zagiri's shock seemed to have slipped away under the onslaught of Anahid's unusual emotional outburst, but every piece of familiar furniture in the office rekindled her outrage. She pointed at the low table between the couches—which a great-aunt of theirs had brought back from the New Republic—and hissed, "This is yours! This whole House is yours. How long has this been going on?"

Anahid propped herself against a corner of the big black desk and tossed her mask aside. "You remember when I missed Polinna's breakfast? It was because I won this House in a game of carrick." Zagiri's eyes grew even wider as she counted back the weeks that Anahid had kept this secret from her. "I was going to tell you," Anahid objected, before she could start shouting. "I tried to tell you. But you were so busy, and so concentrated on your goals, and then things grew complicated, and I thought...well, there was no reason for you to worry. I would keep this a secret."

Zagiri spread her arms, as though she couldn't choose *which* outrageous breach of secrecy to raise first.

She had a point. "Things," Anahid said delicately, "have not quite gone according to plan."

And then she waited. She deserved every shouted imprecation Zagiri could fling at her. She *had* jeopardised everything Zagiri was working for. She *had* lied to her sister. She *had* been entirely selfish.

She'd have to tell Nihath. The rest of her family. Tahera Danelani would hear eventually; might even feel relieved, that now no one would ever credit a thing Anahid might say about Tahera's own secrets.

Zagiri made a helpless little gesture. "This is what you've been doing all this time. Staying out all night, and ignoring all the social nonsense, and..." She looked a little alarmed, and pointed back out of the office. "Did someone here give you that love bite?"

Anahid couldn't help a gulp of laughter. "No, that—there are rules, about not making use of one's own Flowers." She smiled tentatively. "I'm so sorry, Zagiri. I don't want this to make a mess of all your work."

"Oh, *fuck* that," Zagiri declared, with a flip of her hand that was so familiar it made Anahid's heart ache. Standing here, in her battered leathers and pulling that face, this could be the Zagiri of a year ago, still disdaining any hint of responsibility. Anahid had always thought her exasperating; she didn't realise she'd miss her so much. "And fuck anyone who looks down their noses at you. These last few weeks, Ana, you've been..." She tilted her head. "Not happier, not that simple, but...you take up your own space again. You're *you*."

Anahid felt like she was going to cry again. She pressed her lips tight against the sensation, swallowing it down.

But Zagiri's words rang inside her like a well-tuned chord. She had found something here. Something *hers*. Something that made her life less hollow.

When she had her voice under control, Anahid said, "Can you help put my mask back on again? The night's still underway." Even if the sun was actually starting to rise now, bleeding gold over the horizon and slanting orange light across her office.

"And what a night," Zagiri said with a sigh as she picked up the black lace mask, turning it over in both hands. "Siyon beat the monster, by the way. The griffin. Threw it into the river. They patched him up at that Flowerhouse they turned into a hospital. He wanted me to let you know."

That was a relief. "Well, then," Anahid said, smoothing down her tabard. "It seems we've all come through all right."

And then the screaming started.

Zagiri dropped the mask, reaching for the sabre at her hip, but Anahid was already moving, out through the shell-bead curtain, racing down the stairs. Lejman was right behind her as they turned down the business corridor.

Qorja staggered out of a room halfway down the hall, lurching against the wall. Her face was haggard, slack with shock, but when she saw Anahid she straightened, putting out an arm to bar the doorway. "No, mistress," she cried. "You mustn't. Let Lejman—"

He was here too, and he'd kept her safe once tonight already. Anahid needed to know. She needed to see. This was *her House.*

The room was still lit low and pleasant from the evening, but a stink hung in the air—heavy, cloying, metallic, with a side note of overturned chamber pot.

Lejman's hand came down on her shoulder in the same moment that Anahid saw the body. It lay on the bed, facing away from the door on its side, but could not be mistaken for a sleeper. Not with the pale limbs splayed so unnaturally. Not with the long, copper hair a tangled mess. Not with all the *blood.*

So much blood, soaking sheets, staining hair, sprayed across the wall, spread over the chin and shoulder of the body.

Imelda's body. Imelda's chin, tacky with drying blood. Imelda's shapely shoulder. Anahid knew it even before she came closer, leaned over, smoothed the hair back from her face. The features were slack, her grey eyes staring.

Her throat had been slit. With a trembling hand, Anahid pressed on her shoulder, rolling Imelda over onto her back.

That was when she screamed, in pain and recrimination and sudden, burning rage.

Daubed upon Imelda's bare stomach, in bitter bloody capital letters, was the word: *mine.*

CHAPTER 18

Siyon turned the shard of eggshell over in his hands. Traced a finger along the patterns and striations that covered the outer side, avoided the shatter-sharp edge, let the nacreous black residue inside catch the light.

"An actual griffin egg," Nihath said excitedly, and not for the first time. He had another two shards of the shell on his workbench, and had been painting all sorts of things onto one part after another, watching the reactions eagerly.

It was so early it barely counted as morning, but there were a lot of people crammed into Nihath's workroom. Nihath and Tehroun, Jaleh and Siyon, Balian and Mayar. As strange a collection of people as Siyon had seen in one place since... well, probably since he'd become the Power.

Nihath set down his brush and frowned. "Do you suppose *all* the griffin eggs are real? They were very fashionable a century or two ago, after the Grand Khanate dissolved and the first trade missions went west, and that one in the park isn't the only surviving souvenir. I've seen a number in private collections, and I assumed they were either cunningly made, or naturally occurring geodes, but if they might *actually* hatch..."

Jaleh paused in her drawing of the stray feather that had also come into Nihath's possession. "It doesn't matter," she pointed out. "We can't shake all the questionable antiques out of the families that have them, and what would we do with them anyway? Dump them in the harbour? That thing did a proper number on at least two merchant vessels on its way out to sea."

Siyon winced. *That* wasn't going to make the azatani any happier. Most of them would overlook an imposition on their younger sibling's virtue more readily than any damage to their ships.

The workroom door opened, and Zagiri slipped inside. She was still in her leathers from last night and looked as haggard as though she'd been crying. Balian shifted aside at the bench to make room for her.

But it was Jaleh who spoke. "Are they convening yet?"

Zagiri looked confused for a moment, then shook her head. "I haven't been to the Palace," she said, voice subdued. "But the sun's only just up."

It was a reminder, though, that time was passing. The select committee *would* come knocking. They'd want answers. They'd want Siyon to have them.

Nihath squinted through his lens at the feather. "What's making this all happen?" he pondered aloud. "Is it energy coming from other planes, with varying results?"

The eggshell in Siyon's hands was limned with a burnished glow. "It's not that simple," he admitted.

Jaleh's eyes narrowed suspiciously. "Why not?"

"What do you feel on that?" Siyon asked, sending the eggshell spinning across the workbench to Mayar.

Who caught it with a wince, shaking their hand as though it stung. "Mother Sa. All the stillness of the world, so strongly it is almost—" They screwed up their face, looking for the right word. "Deafening."

Mother Sa, falling into a deep sleep to end the age of heroes. Mundane energy, rising anew.

An idea was coalescing from Siyon's suspicions. As so often recently, he didn't much like it.

Jaleh sighed. "Siyon, I appreciate that alchemical practice would greatly benefit from incorporating the wisdom that's been preserved and developed in other cultures, but you can't take it into a committee and expect—"

"It's Mundane energy," Siyon interrupted. "That's what's on the eggshell. That's what was practically *dripping* off the griffin."

"In all the chaos," Jaleh argued, "how can you be sure what you were feeling was the griffin?"

"What I *felt*," Siyon countered, "was..." For a moment, he didn't know how to put it in words. The crackle of power in the air all around him. The thickness of the energy, so much that it had been impossible, at first, to tell that the whole hatching site was drenched in it.

Can you not see the rising tide? Midnight had asked.

Siyon could now.

"There was so much of it," he said. "We were drowning in it. The griffin was part of it. I got a pretty good look at it when it ripped the coat off my back and tried to pick me up." He jerked a thumb over his shoulder, where he'd been graced with three parallel gashes that he'd barely felt, in the thrill of the moment. They'd certainly stung like consequences when someone in the Flower district's makeshift hospital smeared healing salve on them. "And I've seen that energy before."

"Where?" Jaleh demanded, still arguing. Never one to give up.

"Around Midnight," Siyon snapped back.

She frowned. "In the alleyway that night? You were *drunk*, Siyon!"

He hadn't been the only one, but that wasn't the point. "I can see planar energy, all right?" he cried, and waved a hand, stirring the thick Aethyr-heavy soup of Nihath's workroom. "Everywhere, but especially around workings. And our visitors from other planes—well, I can't comment on the djinn, but it left Aethyreal residue sparkling like someone had tipped over a scaling bucket, and the angel was full resplendent in the glory of its gilded wrath or whatever the fuck that poet actually said."

Everyone was staring at him. Nihath's lens dropped out of the socket of his widened eye. "How long has this been going on?" he asked faintly, then seemed to realise: "Since you became the Power."

"Since I became the Power," Siyon confirmed. "I thought it was

just lingering energy from what happened, with the void gate and"—
Izmirlian—"all of that. But it didn't go away."

"You can see planar energy." Jaleh's mouth got a funny little twist
to it. "What colour am I?"

"It doesn't work like that," Siyon argued.

"Uh-huh." That twist was definitely a smirk now. "But what colour
am I?"

Siyon looked at her—at the energy curling off her and twisting around itself. "Mostly a sort of dark blue. I'd say Abyssal. Bit of
Aethyr, couple of Empyreal sparks. People usually give off a mixture."

Perched on a workbench in the corner, Tehroun said, "I imagine
I don't." The fallen djinn smiled dreamily in, yes, a wisping cloud of
pure Aethyreal energy.

Jaleh's smirk fled again, leaving behind her serious thinking face.
"You say there was so *much* energy, last night. Is that the cause? Does
it…" She gestured, like the conductor of the opera orchestra. "Well
up until it overflows? Could we deal with it somehow? Flare it off
instead?"

The suggestion stole Siyon's words for a moment; he'd never
remotely considered that.

Nihath gave a pained whimper. "You'd have to flare the whole city.
Every working would have its energy burned up. And the size of the
flare would be insupportable." He was starting to sound intrigued by
the puzzle.

"We wouldn't do it as one." Jaleh turned a fresh page in her notebook and started drawing circles that overlapped at the edges. "A series
of smaller flares, covering all the territory required, synchronised
somehow, perhaps with a timed trigger, otherwise the energy will just
flow—"

"You'd shut down the entire industrial district," Balian pointed
out with a frown.

One of the azatans in the select committee had carried on about
that, when the question of nullifying the whole city came up. *That* was
never going to be acceptable.

Jaleh pulled a face. "Oh, by all means, let's ensure everyone *else*

has to suffer and accept inconveniences, but never the azatani."
She ripped the page out of her notebook, screwing it up into a ball.
"What's *causing* the excess energy, then? Why now? Is this a Power
thing?"

Demanding it of Siyon like it was all his fault, of course. Maybe it
was. "You were there," he pointed out. "With Midnight in that alleyway. The awakening is upon us."

Predictably, that just deepened her frown until she looked furious.
"What does *that* mean?"

"Awakening," Mayar repeated, and they looked somewhere
between hope and fear. "Of something or someone long asleep?"

This felt like Siyon's dreams, hunting for something half glimpsed
in buried darkness, grasping only the edges of some far greater, more
terrifying truth. "What if Mother Sa were the last Power of the Mundane?" he asked, testing the idea in the open air.

Mayar's eyes widened. They'd been with Siyon, confronting Midnight in the hills. Seeing his hesitation. "The one Midnight killed."

A sleep too deep to be woken from.

"And buried her here," Balian finished, like a light was dawning
inside him. He flipped through the pages of his own notebook. "There
are so many historical references to something buried or hidden. And
the Khanates all have their own stories, but they agree that Mother Sa
lay down to sleep where the sun rose from the sea, and—" He found
the right page, and quoted: "The lump of her arose like a stone overlooking the water. That could be our crag."

Mayar pulled a disgruntled face. "*Lump* is a very clumsy translation." But they didn't seem inclined to argue with the rest of it.

"This is flimsy," Nihath suggested, but he didn't seemed convinced
by his own objection.

Jaleh pursed her lips, thinking it through. "You're suggesting the
energy of the Mundane went to sleep when the last Power died—
however that happened. And now that you've taken on the role, it's
waking up." She shook her head. "Then how do we *fix* this?"

The faint victory Siyon had been feeling, of figuring something
out, trickled away again.

Far away, up in the house above them, a clock chimed. The day was getting underway. They were out of time.

Siyon rubbed his hands over his face. Scents rose from his skin: roof dust and his own blood and healing salve. For a moment, he'd felt like they were all pulling together, a group effort, but it all came back to this. He was the Power. He had to fix this.

Jaleh said, beyond the darkness: "Siyon, you don't have to present a solution today. It's a committee. They expect things to drag on. But I'd think twice about explaining any of *this*. I don't think they're the audience for it." There was a shuffle and a scrape as she packed up her things. "Coming, Savani?"

"I need to talk to Siyon for a moment," Zagiri replied.

When Siyon blinked his eyes open, wiping away the bleariness, she was watching him with concern. "You look like shit," he said, just to get in first.

She didn't even react. "There was a murder," she said quietly. "At Sable House. One of the young Flowers."

The unexpectedness of it dropped the bottom out of Siyon's stomach. For a moment, all he could do was gape. Around them, everyone else carried on, Mayar discussing translation nuance with Balian, Nihath showing Jaleh something on the eggshell through his lens.

"We have to—" Siyon started, then stopped himself. Zagiri watched him, exhausted beyond even a night spent out on the tiles.

They couldn't, either of them. They couldn't drop everything and rush down to support Anahid. They had the select committee. They had the fate and governance of the city. They had responsibilities.

"Is she all right?" Siyon asked.

Zagiri's mouth took on a bitter curve, nothing like a smile. "No," she admitted.

Yet they all had to carry on.

Jaleh was waiting outside Nihath's workroom, flipping through her notebook with a thunderous look. When Zagiri stepped out, that frown switched to her.

"Have you been home at all?" Jaleh demanded.

Zagiri glanced down. Her battered leathers were smeared with the griffin's tarry ichor and torn across one knee. Not exactly suitable for the Palace. "I should get changed. Can—" But she couldn't ask Jaleh to wait while she went home, found a dress—oh, and she'd probably have to wash first.

"You're a mess in all ways," Jaleh marvelled. She shoved her notebook into her satchel and hauled Zagiri toward the back door by an elbow. "Come on. We'll go to the Palace, you can earn the prefect's respect by having come straight to report, and then you can sort yourself out. You're welcome."

"You're going out the back door," Zagiri grumbled back, which had seemed a far more cutting retort in her head. "What is it with you and Siyon still doing this?"

Jaleh gave her a withering look. "This is quicker."

Only the truth. The laneway cut straight across two blocks to the parkland. Zagiri needn't even worry about anyone seeing her looking like she'd been dragged up the Scarp by her ankle. Not that it was very high on her list of concerns.

She hadn't wanted to come up here. Never mind that the Palace would be buzzing like a hive of bees, never mind her duties for the prefect. She'd had to leave Anahid in Sable House, clearly shattered by the murder and all its aftermath.

But Anahid had insisted. Of course she had. She might have won a Flowerhouse in a game of cards, started a feud with a crime baron, taken a lover...but Anahid would still make sure Zagiri fulfilled her commitments.

Zagiri could hardly believe what her sister had done. Grabbed her life. *Made* it what she wanted it to be. Taken the risk to do something real.

"You're pushing too hard at all this," Jaleh said suddenly. She glanced sidelong, and must have caught Zagiri's confusion, because she added: "Markani mentioned you're nosing around about sorcery reform. Which I'm in favour of, obviously." The pair of them had *met* when Jaleh came looking for a way out of the city, fearful after her first master had been executed for sorcery. "But it's like delving. If you try too much, you run out of support and float away on the breeze. But if you grab a little and run, you get to come back and try again another time."

Zagiri knew it was sensible advice. But she couldn't stop thinking about the laders, smuggling their cinnamon. Striking a blow. This autumn was different. This autumn might be the chance.

But it would be a long, vicious struggle from below. She knew the stories of revolution, out of the North. Fire and blood. Years of it.

The sun was burning the early mist off the parkland. The city felt strange, even up here. The last delivery wagons scuttled hastily along the nearly empty Boulevard, eager to get out of a city where monsters hatched and stalked the night. When Zagiri had come up from the Flower district, people were clustered on corners, telling wild tales about events only just passed. She'd been too tired—too heartsore—to stop and correct even the strangest lies.

The Palace was in a panic. Someone had dropped papers all over the entrance hall, and no one was stopping to gather them up. Everyone who rushed past Zagiri, as she climbed the stairs with Jaleh, seemed to have wide eyes or a fear-pinched mouth.

The prefect stood in discussion with Azata Markani outside the latter's office. Both of them said "There you are!" in unison and looked momentarily amused about it.

All of them bustled into Markani's inner office. Zagiri was going to have to report; her mind felt as battered as her leathers. There was so much that she couldn't possibly tell, not even—or perhaps *especially* not—to the prefect. Mentioning that the Northern ambassador's daughter was involved in smuggling and revolution would still cause a diplomatic incident. And Zagiri obviously wasn't going to talk about what Anahid was up to.

Oh, ink and ashes, her sister knew the prefect socially, didn't she? Anahid had definitely been invited to an occasional gathering in the prefectural apartments. If it came out—*when* it came out—Syrah Danelani was going to absolutely drop her anchor.

"Well," Danelani declared as she took the visitor's chair while

Markani sat behind the desk; clerks and apprentices stayed standing. "This is a fucking mess. Were you there, girl?"

That clearly meant Zagiri. "For some of it, yes. I don't know where the griffin came from—"

"Griffin?" Markani repeated sharply, like a great-aunt with faulty hearing. "You're sure about that?"

"That's what—" Zagiri thought better of naming Mayar in this company.

"The description from witnesses matches records both alchemical and historical," Jaleh said smoothly. "Indeed, there's a pair of similar statues flanking the stairs out front."

"Fucking Lyraec Empire," Syrah Danelani muttered. "You think they're just making up fanciful mythology to look good on their architecture and it turns out it's a real thing." She turned her keen eyes on Zagiri. "Some sort of Empyreal creature, was it? I heard it could breathe fire."

Zagiri was *extremely grateful* that wasn't true. "Not that I saw. There was a fire, but that was from a destroyed house that it climbed. Siyon said he thought it was a Mundane creature."

"We don't *have* monsters," Syrah snapped, like Zagiri was being purposefully dense.

"We never had a Power either," Markani pointed out, more reasonably.

Syrah grunted, which sounded like it had started as a curse word. "Don't say that in the select committee."

"You think I'll need to? Hisarani will write it on the walls." Markani pressed a finger to the deep line carving down between her eyebrows. "The only good thing about this select committee is that it's better than the free-for-all feeding frenzy we'd have without it."

"They're going to insist on some sort of action," Danelani sighed, drumming her fingers against the table.

"And if you don't want to play straight into the Pragmatics' hands and have Rowyani shouting about how you send everything into committee to die, you're going to have to insist right alongside them." Markani screwed up her nose, like a child being asked to choose between two equally hated vegetables. "Kurit, does this scheme of Velo's with the inquisitors' badges have merit?"

"Early testing indicates the charms are effective in protecting the wearers," Jaleh reported readily.

Which explained the good cheer of the flying squad of inquisitors who'd eventually responded to the emergency last night—albeit so delayed by chance, or possibly Yeva's intervention, that they only arrived in time for cleanup, with the griffin gone down the river. They'd specifically come to help take Siyon up to the Flower district.

Danelani pulled a face. "It's at testing. We can hardly roll that out as a grand plan."

They seemed to be looking for ideas. Maybe this was Zagiri's chance, faint as it seemed. "We should take the initiative," she suggested, trying to sound far firmer than she felt. "Push for a variance of the sorcery law to register hundreds of new alchemists to assist with—"

Markani barked a harsh laugh. Danelani shook her head. "I know you mean well, Savani," she said, awfully gently. "But the city is far too fearful to let unknown parties loose with alchemical power."

Zagiri knew she should let it be, even without Jaleh's sidelong look. But words seemed to have bunched themselves up in her mouth. "They're not unknown. These are people who live and work in Bezim every day. And they're *already* using alchemical power, it's just that they're doing it illicitly, so we can't have any oversight, or even *tax* them, or—"

"We *know* this," Markani interrupted, and the sympathy in her eyes was almost worse than the firm rejection in her voice. "This is the Council, my girl. We aren't talking about what's *right*."

"Why?" Zagiri demanded, and her voice cracked, like an upset little girl. She was too tired for this; she shouldn't have come. But she was here, and she wanted to know. "*Why* aren't we talking about what's right?"

Danelani smiled, faint and sad. "Because we can only afford to consider what is possible. This is the system we have. We have to deal with it the way it is, or we'll break our own hearts a dozen times before we ever improve anything."

She turned back to Markani, making some other suggestion, and Zagiri knew she should be listening. Jaleh touched her wrist, her eyebrows knotted in a glare that was almost concerned. Zagiri struggled to focus.

But tears were gathering behind her eyes—tears of frustration and disappointment and hot, impotent rage—and her clenched fists were pounding with the same beat that drummed in her ears. She was so *furious*, that this whole system could be so *broken*, so deeply entrenched, so completely immovable. That the azatani would blithely protect their own. Just carry on. Like Jaleh said, everyone was inconvenienced except the azatani. Even over the summer, when fear had been running rampant, none of them had stirred at all to protect alchemists until the arrests interfered with their factories. And now there was—

Wait.

No one had cared until it interfered with their factories.

Zagiri stared at Jaleh, whose eyes now narrowed in suspicion. Jaleh, who back at Nihath's had started planning a way to flare off all the energy in the city. Balian had pointed out it would shut down the entire industrial district.

All those factories, in which azatani wealth was invested, into which azatani-traded goods were poured and from which azatani-traded goods were produced... Even the Savani family had investment shares in two or three and relied on the business of others. All of them worked with alchemical assistance. In fact, they employed the vast majority of the currently registered alchemists in the city, just to keep things running.

"What?" Jaleh whispered fiercely.

There was no urgency to sorcery reform right now. There was no real *need* for more legitimate alchemists. But if something happened to those factories...

"Miss Savani? *Zagiri!*"

Zagiri jerked her attention back to Syrah Danelani, who was looking at her with a blend of exasperation and fond amusement. "My son all over again," she muttered to Markani, who snorted a little laugh, and then Danelani said to Zagiri: "Go home and rest. But on the way, please find Velo, wherever he's gone to ground, and tell him that they'll be waiting for him in the committee tomorrow. That's as long as we can give him, and he'll need to have some firm answers."

Zagiri nodded, with her hands folded like Anahid had taught her. "Yes, Madame Prefect." But as she turned to go, Zagiri caught Jaleh's eye and murmured, "I need to talk with you later."

It was time to change what was possible.

CHAPTER 19

The baker's cart on the corner of Glass and the Kellian Way was selling pastries and buns and amulets to protect from griffin attacks. The vendor seemed to be doing a decent trade among the slightly sluggish morning traffic.

When he saw Siyon watching—unfortunately recognisable in his purple coat—he cried: "And there he is! Get your amulet blessed by the Sorcerer himself!"

Siyon fled toward the Palace, cursing anew the griffin that had torn his plain coat—and his back—to shreds. At least the salve they'd used on him in the Flower district had been good; it might have smelled like a garland of star jasmine, but the gashes on his shoulder hadn't so much as twinged since.

Zagiri had mentioned the salve Bracken used had been working particularly effectively. An awakening. Siyon wished he could think of a word for *what* was waking that wasn't *magic*. The azatani in the select committee weren't going to like hearing that one. Siyon didn't much like thinking it.

The Palace was far more crowded than the streets, though the rushing clerks didn't seem too busy to stop and ogle him. Siyon hated this coat, he really did.

A pair of white-sashed Palace guards flanked the door to the committee meeting room. One of them caught Siyon's eye. "Good luck in there," she said.

He hadn't expected that. "What?"

With a tight little smile, she added, "My cousin's in the inqs. Street patrol. He says you're keeping them safe. Wants to buy you a drink sometime."

Siyon was still gaping at her when Zagiri called "Siyon!" from inside the meeting room, beckoning furiously. When he stepped closer, she looked him up and down. "At least you look better than you did yesterday morning."

Like she could talk. "Yeah, cheers," Siyon drawled.

Around the table behind her, discussion seethed like surf among rocks, quiet and furious and constant. It bothered Siyon more than if they'd all been shouting. This wasn't grandstanding. This wasn't performance. This was genuine fear.

He knew from past and personal experience that azatani didn't react well to being afraid. They weren't used to it. They didn't live with it daily, sleep with it and rise with it. When it showed up, unwanted and unannounced, they tended to overreact.

And it was Siyon and those like him who suffered for it.

"Look," Zagiri said, grabbing his arm for a moment. She looked grumpy, or maybe just determined. Stubborn, either way. "*Do* you have a big plan that's going to solve everyone's problems?"

He'd spent most of the past day trying to meditate. Trying to find the boundary he'd drawn around the city—he could *feel* it, but he couldn't quite grasp it, not without falling away into the depths and the maelstroms of the new-surging Mundane energy. If he could get hold of it, maybe he could find a way to calm everything down. Maybe.

"Sure I do," Siyon lied easily.

She nodded. "That's what I figured. Just..." That hesitation made Siyon even more worried. From the first moment he'd met her, Zagiri had been willing to jump into anything, sure of her ability to take it on and do fine, thanks. "Keep your head down, all right?" she said, very quietly. "Get through this. We'll sort it out on the other side."

Totally reassuring.

In the midst of everything, Avarair Hisarani sat in silence, watching Siyon take his seat. There was the faintest shadow of a smile loitering around his mouth; Siyon might not even have recognised it at all, if that face wasn't so much like Izmirlian's. Though he'd never seen Izmirlian look quite this coldly satisfied.

This was not the audience to explain what might really be going on, Jaleh had said. Siyon glanced at her, loitering against the wall behind Azata Markani. He glanced at Zagiri, waiting at the elbow of Syrah Danelani, who'd instructed him to have firm answers.

Siyon didn't know what he was going to do.

"All right," Syrah Danelani said, from the head of the table.

Avarair Hisarani opened his mouth.

And no, he didn't get to decide how this went.

Siyon stood up. "The situation has changed," he declared.

Everyone was looking at him, all these azatani faces surprised at his sudden interjection, like a fish had leapt onto the pier and started to dance. Behind the prefect, Zagiri was gently shaking her head; Siyon ignored her.

"I've done what you wanted," he stated, getting a jolt of hope from the flurry of whispers and impressed looks that provoked. "I bound the city's borders to prevent intrusions from other planes, and I'm pretty sure that worked." Maybe he should have left that bit out; too late now.

"Worked?" an azatan harrumphed from up near the head of the table. "Master Velo, that *thing* near scuppered my ship!"

Siyon wondered, briefly, where the griffin had washed away *to*. Was it going to become a hazard to navigation in the Carmine Sea? Was it going to crawl out on a beach in Lyraea?

Not his problem right now.

"That thing wasn't from another plane," Siyon corrected. No impressed looks now, just alarm, but Siyon didn't know what to do but press on. Try to get through this. "The Mundane plane is waking up. Returning to what it always should have been, maybe."

"Master Velo," the prefect interjected, with a thread of steel in her voice, like a warning that these were *not* the answers she'd had in mind. "Are you suggesting there will be *more* of these monsters?"

"Not if I can balance out the waking energy," Siyon replied.

At least, that's what he hoped. He thought he was pretty clever, using that term—*balance*. That was what he did, wasn't it? Balance the planes. Balance the energy. No worries.

Except the azatani around the table were shifting and muttering, teetering between unconvinced and very worried indeed.

"How?" Avarair Hisarani asked. Everyone looked at him; he lifted an unconcerned eyebrow, just like Izmirlian had always done when delivering a haughty challenge. "How are you going to do this?"

Siyon had no idea. He couldn't say that. "I'm investigating all the angles to find the best..." He trailed off, every useful word fleeing his mind's frantic grasp in the face of all these demanding stares.

Avarair's gentle, disappointed sigh fell like a bad omen. "Master Velo, I have tried—we have all tried—to be helpful in the past few weeks. We have extended our patience, and our assistance, and the benefit of our experience. In return, we have received only promises, fervent assurances, and progress reports that beneath their elegant expression are, fundamentally, empty."

Balian's reports. Siyon couldn't help wishing that Balian were here. He wished he had another note from Izmirlian in his pocket. He was still, it turned out, incapable of dealing with azatani by himself.

"You seem a master of pageantry," Avarair said, with a hint of distaste as his gaze passed pointedly over Siyon's purple coat. "You have dazzled and amazed. But the results themselves are lacking. Bezim needs reliable alchemy, Master Velo. Not outrageous feats. We need solutions." He sniffed and leaned back a little. "Or we need to pass authority for the city's alchemical security into more trustworthy hands. A committee from the Summer Club, perhaps. Practitioners whose workings might be quiet and unassuming but have always been consistent and reliable."

"Azatan Hisarani!" Nihath thumped the table in outrage, but he was the only one; everyone else was muttering and considering, and Siyon could see the prefect taking note of it as well. "You cannot possibly be serious. These are unprecedented problems, and Master Velo alone can solve them."

"Can he?" Avarair shot back, not looking away from Siyon. "We have seen no solutions so far. There are *monsters* on our streets, and nothing but empty plans. *Can* you work alchemy, Master Velo? Or can you only dazzle with empty spectacle?"

"Alchemy takes time," Markani said from the other side of Syrah Danelani. She looked stern and wise, and Siyon could almost see everyone remembering that she was a member of the Summer Club, a practitioner in good standing, and undersecretary of the Working Group on Oblique Methods. "I propose Master Velo be given until midwinter to conduct his working—"

"Unacceptable," Avarair interrupted, and one or two committee members rumbled in agreement. "It has been weeks already. Bezim cannot afford anything less than total commitment. Let us have an end to this, one way or another. A new beginning with the new year. Give him until Salt Night." He considered Siyon, and his chin lifted a little, and Siyon braced like he'd drawn back to swing. "And to ensure that you are undisturbed during your preparations, shall we say a permanent guard of two inquisitors?"

To ensure he wasn't engaging in *empty spectacle*, more like it. To ensure he couldn't get anything useful done. "That's hardly the best use of their expertise and people," Siyon tried, looking over at the superintendent, who was frowning but didn't seem inclined to object.

"On the contrary," Avarair said reassuringly. "You are apparently our only hope. Your protection is paramount. How says the committee?" He lifted an inviting hand around the table.

The motion carried. Of course it did.

And the moment it did—the moment Syrah Danelani's little mallet banged down on the table—Avarair was sailing out of the room like the victorious yacht at a regatta.

In his wake, the room exploded into furious knots of debate, of gloating, of negotiation, of recriminations. Zagiri shot a glare at Siyon, but the prefect was beckoning, and she had to lean over, take notes, be responsible.

Siyon leapt out of his chair and dashed after Avarair. No one stopped him, not the Sorcerer, in the coat and everything. The corridor was empty when he shoved out of the room, save for the two guards at the door. Siyon turned to the woman whose cousin wanted to buy him a drink. "Which way did he go?"

She pointed; Siyon ran.

This he could do.

He sprinted down the corridor, caught movement on the stairs, and dragged himself around by the banister, calling "Hey!" before he was really sure it was Avarair. But it was, halfway up and turning. So much like his brother, in posture, in bearing, in that mildly affronted surprise that someone like Siyon might *dare* to address him.

In Izmirlian, it had always been slightly mocking—of the world, of you, of himself. Avarair believed it.

"What?" this Hisarani said, here and now. "Will you call your demon down upon me?"

Siyon shrugged away the prickle between his shoulder blades that suggested Laxmi liked that idea. "There's no audience here," he pointed out, climbing up a few steps before he stopped, hands out, spread and empty. "Just you and me. So stop the grandstanding."

"You think this is playacting?" Avarair demanded. Not only haughty. Angry. Verging on incensed. "You think this is some sort of game? This is for the city."

"Is it?" Siyon challenged. "Is that what this is about?" He eased up another step, and Avarair's chin tilted up a little more. "Look, I'm sorry, all right? About Izmirlian. I miss him too. I wish he hadn't gone. But don't pretend, not to me, that you didn't know what he wanted."

Avarair's eyes were still and keen, taking in every detail. "Where?" he demanded, the word stiff as his spine. "Where has my brother gone?"

In truth, Siyon didn't know. "Where he wanted to." It was the best answer he could give.

It wasn't enough for Avarair, one way or another. "Don't give me that rubbish about running off with an opera singer," he scoffed. "Izmir never met anyone he loved more than his own wild dreams."

The words pressed on one of the more tender bruises in Siyon's heart, but he brushed them aside. "If you want to talk more about it," Siyon pushed on. Izmirlian was gone, but they remained, and the city remained, and there was more to do that couldn't be done if he was still haunting them. "If you want to hear more, or just talk to someone who also misses him, then maybe you and I could..."

But Siyon looked up, into Avarair's face carved from stone, and knew he'd got it all wrong.

Avarair came down the stairs now, one and then two more, until he loomed over Siyon. "You must have been quite the pair," he said, each word a chip of ice. "Both of you so caught up in what you *wanted* and expecting the world to play along. It would seem the consequences caught up with Izmirlian, and now they're catching up with you. If you're sensible, you'll disappear as well."

His words were stark and scalding, rushing into the careful gap Siyon had carved to reach out to Avarair, stinging like salt to the eyes. "Fuck you," Siyon snarled, and felt angrier still for the smug little twitch of Avarair's mouth, like Siyon had just *proven* himself the gutter brat they both knew he was. "Were you listening to what I said in there at all? This *is* for the city, you pompous git. Something is happening. Something is...is bubbling up. You can't squash it down and pretend—"

"I can," Avarair snarled, leaning forward, suddenly right in Siyon's face. "I can, and I will. I will squash it, and you, until you give up and stay down, in your proper place. I have the weight, and the patience, and the time. What do you have, Siyon Velo, aside from your fancy purple coat and *no answers?*"

Siyon could feel Laxmi coiling at the base of his spine, so eager for Avarair to lash out, so she could fulfill her vow to help him in the violent way she preferred. He couldn't tell if the eagerness for a fight beating at his temples was his or hers. For a moment, he didn't much care.

He forced himself to draw a breath. To hold it. To let it out.

"I have all the Power of the Mundane," he said, and stepped back. "It's mine, not yours. And I will use it."

Avarair had his composure back, cool and sleek and sneering. "You have until Salt Night," he called in reminder as Siyon stomped back down the stairs.

The sun rose, and the sun set; Sable House did not open, and everyone knew why.

A young woman—a Flower—murdered in one of the rooms. Didn't you hear? It was gruesome. And a total mystery, the poor thing. No client on the register. There was simply no way of knowing who was responsible.

Anahid thought it was quite obvious who was responsible. Stepan Zinedani had *wanted* it to be quite obvious. She didn't know how he'd found his way back into the House; she *wasn't* blaming Lejman, especially not when Lejman was so clearly blaming himself. In the busy chaos of the previous night's trading, with the euphoria of a monster vanquished and the entire district going wild, there were all too many ways it could have happened.

The inquisitors had come, of course; killing a Flower was always a crime. The street patrol treated Imelda's body with the utmost respect. They listened to everything Anahid had to say about the disruptions the night before and the significance of the writing on her body. They filled out their forms meticulously.

Is there any proof? they asked. *Did anyone see? There's no name on the register . . .*

They almost flinched when Anahid said *Zinedani*. It was quite obvious that the street patrol wanted no part in tangling with the barons, and she supposed she could hardly blame them for it. Here was cold, dead proof of what happened when people did that.

Or at least, what happened to the people around them. *Anahid* was the one tangling with the barons. Why was it Imelda lying cold on a slab?

The trainees and the younger Flowers were distraught; several had lived and worked with Imelda in the House for five years now. Some of the children were too young to understand why Auntie Imelda couldn't come and play ladders with them like she always did. Anahid hadn't seen Qorja cry yet, but the stage mistress's smile seemed shaky, and her eyes were red.

Anahid borrowed a headscarf from one of the Flowers and changed out of her Lady Sable tabard, back into the dress she'd been wearing when the Zinedani men had snatched her off the street. The stink of the baiting pit—sawdust and blood and fear and her own vomit—lifted faintly from the folds of it, sparking sharp memories, and yet it seemed like something that had happened to another woman.

She'd been so afraid. She'd been so satisfied at her own victory. She'd thought everything settled.

She'd been a fool.

Anahid could go home and change. Possibly *should* go home and let the House mourn in the absence of the azata who'd come in and ruined everything. But it was too late in the day now; she'd be seen on the Avenues by someone who knew her. There was a chance, bitter as it was, that Imelda's murder would eclipse the news of an azata unmasked as manager of a House. She should remain circumspect. Like it mattered.

More importantly, Anahid didn't want to speak to anyone who would ask questions, who didn't know, who didn't care, at whom Anahid couldn't possibly scream about this fucking injustice.

Nineteen. Imelda had only been nineteen.

She slept on the chaise in her office instead, uncertain she'd slept at all save that the sun's slant at the window had changed when she opened her eyes again.

She'd been woken—by a young trainee, barely fifteen and with his face swollen from weeping—because Imelda's sisters had arrived to claim her body.

A rickety handcart waited in the yard, looking more like something that would fall apart comically in the second act of an opera than a suitable way for Imelda to be carried home to her grieving family. Everyone who could bear it was clustered in the kitchen, sad and muted outside the cold store where they'd cleared out space for Imelda to rest and wait.

Two living women inside, and neither of them looked all that much like Imelda. Both of them were of a height with Anahid, and their ages were impossible to guess; older than Imelda, younger than Qorja, but their faces were hardened and worn by the paths their lives had taken.

Every life has its unpleasantnesses, Imelda had said.

One had hair of a similar orange tinge to Imelda's, but hers seemed dry and faded, hauled ruthlessly out of the way into a single plait down her back. The other had dark curling hair and the same pale grey eyes as her sister, but in her they were the flat colour of overcast skies and dead fish scales.

Anahid didn't want to intrude, but she wouldn't hide from them either. Not when this was her fault. She was the one who hadn't understood the depth of the water, or what lurked within, when she leapt from the pier.

They both looked at Anahid with a measure of blank unease. "Sorry, za," the dark-haired one said. She sounded a little like Imelda, but without any Flowerhouse training brushing the mud from her drawl. "We'll be gone right quick."

"Woulda been up sooner," the red-haired one chimed in, "but the cart were needed for the salvage going on from that monster."

"No," Anahid said, and both women frowned, twitching a glance at each other. "*I'm* sorry. About Imelda. I should have taken better care of her."

The one with the faded red hair snorted. "Immy always done just fine taking care of herself. She knew the risks when she come up here."

"There are risks and then there's this," Anahid objected. This was more than merely a thorn on the Path of Flowers. She took a breath; her anger still simmered inside her, where it had bubbled since this morning. "I am going to make sure the person responsible is brought to justice." Even if she didn't know how.

"Oh yeah?" The red-haired one jerked her chin to the door behind Anahid. "Them out there says as how it were likely the Zinedani nephew who done it. Don't see no justice coming for the likes of him."

"And that's hardly your fault," the dark-haired one added. "No one cares for a Dockside girl, not the inqs, not the barons. Just her family."

"Even that ain't sure," the red-haired one muttered, "if she ain't fisherclan."

"I care," Anahid said.

"Well, ain't you special." The red-haired one smiled; even that had a twist of bitterness.

"We appreciate it, za," the dark-haired one said firmly. "And like I said, we'll be gone right quick."

Or they would be, if Anahid left them alone to get on with it; she could take a polite hint.

The crowd was still waiting in the kitchen, other Flowers, and trainees, and the serving staff all clustered together. Some of them offered Anahid watery smiles as she passed through the kitchen. None of them made demands. None of them asked what she was going to do to make Stepan pay.

None of them expected justice either.

Abruptly, Anahid's anger surged within her, like a ship whose sails had filled with freshening wind. It carried her out of Sable House, into the quiet of the daytime District.

Everyone knew where Garabed Zinedani made his headquarters. He owned or at least oversaw the majority of the District's Houses, but there were some gems that sparkled more brightly in his baronial coronet.

The Banked Ember was the centrepiece.

Anahid hadn't been there before; they didn't have carrick tables, and even if they did, the establishment was designed to appeal to an azatani clientele, and Anahid had never cared to spend time with the people she fled the Avenues to avoid.

It looked, from the outside, more than a little like an Avenue townhouse—tall and plain, with glimpses at the windows of elegant furnishings and tasteful decorations. Everything for the azatan who wanted the comforts of home, with a little extra spice. All the trappings of an elite society that would not accept Garabed Zinedani among its ranks, whatever his name.

The wave of Anahid's anger carried her only so far as its front step, and there it stranded her, ankle-deep in uncertainty.

What was she going to do? March in there and demand justice for her Flower? Rage at him like a helpless woman with no other weapons at her disposal? Demand Stepan's life, as Garabed had demanded hers?

She wasn't a baron. She *wasn't* a part of this world.

Anahid looked up at the House and saw a figure standing in one of the upper windows, framed by lemon-yellow drapes and wearing a cross-patterned longvest.

Garabed Zinedani. Watching her watching his House. He lifted a hand in a jaunty little wave.

Anahid folded her hands carefully over her sash, to stop them clenching into fists, and felt the hard line of the penknife pressed against her ribs.

She entertained a brief, vivid fantasy of having her sister's skills, her sister's boldness. Imagined that she could run straight at the building, climb up the frontage, burst through that window to slice her tiny, ridiculous blade across Garabed Zinedani's throat, as his nephew had done to Imelda.

She couldn't.

But this was not her only weapon, was it?

Anahid turned on her heel and walked away. Not back to Sable House, but out of the Flower district entirely.

CHAPTER 20

Siyon's threatened entourage showed up remarkably promptly, ringing the gate bell early the next morning.

One of the pair of inqs was Olenka. "Aren't you too important for this, Sergeant White?" Siyon asked nonchalantly.

"I'm head of your detail." Not a hint of amusement in her stone-hard face, but Siyon still got the impression that she was laughing at him as she added, "So think long and hard on how difficult I could make your life."

The other of that initial pair was the cousin of the Palace guard who'd spoken to Siyon. Ehann had volunteered for this task; he was still enthusiastic about buying Siyon a drink sometime. He showed Siyon his badge, which looked exactly like any other inq badge. Not even Siyon could see the Mundane glow of the charm he'd put in there, but when he brushed his fingers across the polished surface, it whispered to him from the depths of the metal.

Feel, Mayar had told him, *not just see.*

His guard detail, as laid out brusquely by Olenka, was ten inquisitors, in a rotating arrangement of shifts so that there would always be two with him, like embarrassing younger cousins constantly following him around.

All of them, allegedly, were volunteers. A couple of them wanted out of their previous squad, and a few were wildly curious about the Sorcerer of Bezim, and all of them were keen to get their badges charmed as well.

"Our instructions are to report back at the end of our shift on any notable incidents or actions," Olenka said with a lift of her eyebrows like a challenge.

So there was at least a shift's worth of delay on word of what he was doing getting back to the Council. And even then, it depended on an inquisitor's discretion regarding *notability*.

Siyon could make the leap from one rooftop to another. He *had* this escort, but—weird as it seemed—they might be on his side.

Testing it out, Siyon said, "I want to go out and survey the city to inform my planned working." It was even the truth, though he doubted he was planning a working anything like Avarair Hisarani wanted.

Olenka shrugged, like she'd accompany him to a lower city bordello—probably without a change in expression—if that's what transpired. But Ehann said helpfully, "Up the clock tower is probably the best vantage. You can see the whole city from there. Or, um, so I've heard."

They didn't stop Siyon. Ehann held the gate open for him.

It was chilly this morning, autumn starting to crisp the air, but Siyon did not regret leaving the purple coat behind. His escort was getting enough curious looks, and with things as strange as they were, Siyon didn't want to be recognised. Sure, they passed street corner vendors hawking the little purple-coated dolls again, now with a rat-looking monster for a knuckle or two more. But they also passed a blue-robed beardy bloke atop a crate outside the Eldren Hall, shouting about how the vile Sorcerer Velo was the godkiller as prophesised in the holy book, and everyone must now repent and become true believers before the end of days. The streets were quiet, but he was drawing a small and cheerful crowd; Bezim loved a spectacle.

Siyon was fine passing unnoticed, thanks.

Ehann glowered at the bearded berater. "Inciting panic?" he suggested hopefully to Olenka.

But the sergeant shook her head. "Not our beat. And not worth it."

Did an inq just consider arresting someone for being mean about Siyon? The world had turned upside down. As they continued down the Kellian Way, the opera house came into view. Siyon turned away from it to ask Ehann, "What do you think about everything that's going on anyway?"

"I, er, what?" The inq glanced at Olenka, got absolutely no help, and said, "Um, about what?"

Good question. Siyon wasn't sure what he was asking. He waved a hand around. "About the city. About beings coming from other planes. About monsters. About all the other weird things."

Ehann shrugged uncomfortably. "It's Bezim. Everyone comes here, from everywhere. Why shouldn't they? We have a lot of strange stuff—alchemy, bravi, a cliff through the middle of the city…I don't know, I've never been anywhere else, but this seems fine. Even if it's getting stranger."

"Getting stranger?" Olenka prompted, before Siyon could.

That made Ehann fold up like an unpromising hand of cards, but eventually he mumbled: "My little sister loves Old Kingdom fairy tales. She's always left milk out for the pixies. The skinks used to drink it, you know, the tiny little ones? I see them when I'm leaving early for my morning shift. But recently, well…" He was *blushing*, Siyon would swear to it, right here on the Kellian Way. "Some of them have grown wings. Is that what pixies really are? Skinks with wings?"

That was *adorable*. It wasn't a naga in the Flower district, or the seventh runner on the rooftops, or alchemy working more strongly. It was a tiny sprinkle of wonder.

"What does your sister think?" Olenka asked.

Ehann smiled. "She loves them. She's knitting them little dresses."

Siyon coughed to cover his laughter, but then they rounded the last corner before Tower Square and saw the crowd.

Bigger, this one, than the blue-robed guy had drawn. People were clustered at the end of a row of shops, where a large sheet of paper had been pasted over the usual bills announcing the forthcoming opera season and the special events of the Flower district. The new poster, drawing all the attention, was headed with a symbol Siyon had seen painted on other walls recently: a hammer crossed with a lader's baling hook.

Beneath that, in large print: MANIFESTO OF THE RIGHTS OF THE PEOPLE OF BEZIM.

"Fuck," Ehann muttered, "another one? I thought they cleared 'em all off before dawn."

Siyon caught the first line of the close-printed text on the poster—RISE UP, BROTHERS AND SISTERS OF BEZIM, IN SOLIDARITY WITH THE LADERS' GUILD AND ALL OTHER—before Olenka nudged him onward down the hill. "Keep moving," she advised, "unless you want to get caught up in the response to this."

The Council would presumably take a very dim view indeed of the usual autumnal Dockside unrest spilling over to this side of the river. Siyon glanced back as they cut across Tower Square. The crowd was only getting bigger, people at the back calling for those at the front to read the text aloud.

Bezim always loved a spectacle.

Then the base of the tower closed around them. Siyon had his own business to attend to. And a lot of stairs to climb.

He hadn't been up the tower in years. He and Daruj had gone up with some other Bracken shortly after they'd joined the tribe, and looking out from behind the clock, at the wide sweep of the city all around them, had been the first time Siyon realised how much bigger Bezim was than he'd realised.

Ehann was right. You could see the entire city from up here. From the beacon away at the northeastern edge of the bay, to the golden sweep of the city wall disappearing into the hills off to the southwest. From behind the clockface, Siyon could pick out the little dark spots of the burial caves on the crag, and through the slow-turning cogs on the other side of the tower, he could see the dome of the observatory burning golden in the sun, way out at the tip of the sunken headland.

All of it glowed to Siyon's sight with a burnished energy beyond the morning light. It was difficult to see much past the wall, or into the marshes stretching up the northern coast, but the low coastline of the lower city made it clear that the bronze glow stopped just offshore.

It stopped at the bounds of the city that he'd defined. *That* had worked, though not to prevent the griffin hatching. This rising Mundane energy... could that have *helped* cause the egg to hatch?

Rising. As Siyon stared out over the city—vaguely aware of the sounds of Olenka and Ehann making themselves comfortable behind him—that was the word that came to him. The energy was *rising.* Awakening. Quickening. But also coming *up.* Bubbling up, like a spring, like a leak in a boat.

Was there some way he could push back? Not smother it, not *stop* it, but equalise the pressure. Keep it from rushing up quite so vigorously.

Could he?

Siyon let his eyes fall closed. Let his senses reach out. Let himself drift.

Maybe he was getting used to this—the way the world opened up around him, the vertiginous rush of it in all directions, the weight of every detail clamouring for his attention. Stone and wind and sea and sky and the animals that flew and crawled and swam and ran and the people, the people, the people...

It washed over him. Drew him under. Pulled him down deep.

He panicked for a moment, but the energy was still all around him. This is where it rose *from.* How deep did it go?

As Siyon sank, his breathing evened out, slow and slower, like the faint whistle of air through caverns. Stone and crystal, wrapping around him, each mote of it a speck of the Mundane, of history, of energy. No difference, really. He was the Power and the world was the power and they were all the same, if you looked the right way. There was a heartbeat, slow and steady—maybe his, maybe not, maybe both. It lulled him, rocked him, drew him deeper still.

He knew these shadowed tunnels. He'd raced through them, in his dreams, hunting. There were whispers, there were secrets, but they were always out of his reach.

Siyon didn't reach, this time. He listened as the whispers sharpened into recognisable sounds. Into a voice he knew.

"—any other way of knowing, except to go and look," Izmirlian said. A little pointed, a little laughing, a little bubbling with curiosity. Was this a dream? Had all of this been a dream? Siyon almost didn't mind, for the chance to hear that voice again. He'd chased after him, in other dreams, and never caught him. Not yet. He'd made a promise: when this was done.

It felt so far away.

"I miss you," Siyon whispered. Felt the breath on his lips. Felt the words tremble in the energy all around him.

"*Oh.*" That tone in Izmirlian's voice hooked into Siyon's heart. He could imagine how it looked on his face—that delighted surprise, that pleased smile, that bright light of possibility, of curiosity, of wonder. No one looked at the world quite like Izmirlian. No one had ever looked at *him* quite like Izmirlian.

Somewhere—very close, very far away—bells rang. This wasn't a dream. Siyon was standing in the clock tower. He was here for a purpose.

He was still in the darkness, deep in the earth, immersed in that rising energy. He was here to see if he could persuade it to settle.

Siyon stretched out—and *out*, like he was casting a net of himself over the entire city. It was impossible, and effortless. He could reach every edge.

For a moment, he held it, swelling up beneath him, like he was floating on the surface.

But he was stretched so thin, and it churned so vast and deep. So much weight behind it. So much time. So much power. He was a Flower's gossamer-thin veil laid on a storming sea.

Siyon let go before he could be torn apart. Even so, he was swept up in the rush of the energy—momentarily blocked, now released. It swirled down deep, made him sway and choke and reel—

He dragged his eyes open, desperate and in darkness, to stare up into another eye. Large as his head, burning bronze, star-pupilled and hazed over as though in sleep.

Siyon yelled and opened his eyes in truth, back in the clock tower. But he was dizzy and off-balance, tipping forward as Tower Square tilted vertiginously below him.

He was going to fall, like Zagiri had, and there was no one to catch him.

Then his face mashed against metal, like a fish hitting a net. His flailing hands scraped against it.

Someone grabbed his shoulders, hauling him back upright. Siyon rubbed at his cheek, which felt like he'd been slapped with a cheese grater, and blinked at Olenka.

"They put in the grille," she said, tipping a nod to the fine metal mesh that covered the front of the clock. "After your pal's little stunt back in the summer. Just as well, really. I'm all out of grace."

"Are you all right?" Ehann chirped, from somewhere behind her shoulder. "Did something happen?"

Not happen. Siyon had *tried*, but he didn't have the energy. Not by himself. Not to make it work.

But his heart was still racing, and his memory was snagged back in the darkness. That eye. Something buried. Something sleeping.

Had it seen him too?

It felt weird to be in the Flower district at midday. Zagiri kept wondering what was going on at Sable House, after the murder of that poor girl. She'd dropped by the Joddani townhouse this morning, but Anahid still hadn't been home. Nihath hadn't even noticed, but Nura had been noticeably agitated as she asked for news, which for anyone else would be panic.

Which showed that the outrageous news of Anahid's involvement with Sable House hadn't spread. If that had been setting tongues and ears ablaze, those belowstairs would also have been passing embers. It hadn't spread *yet*.

In the circumstances, Zagiri wasn't sure she should be in the Flower district at all—it would just be more cloth for the eventual sail of scandal. But this was where Yeva had told her to come for a chance at another path to change.

Her and Jaleh both.

"Of course I'm coming," the other woman snapped, when Zagiri suggested she attend alone. "I don't take anonymous clients and I'm not about to start for a bunch of Dockside agitators with grandiose political pretensions."

However scathing she sounded about it, she *had* agreed to Zagiri's plan. Though Zagiri thought more credit for persuasion belonged to Avarair Hisarani than to herself.

They met Yeva near the Flower district's central square, among the topiary and flower beds and strange attractions. Two workmen were scrubbing down game pieces as tall as they were. In a nearby fountain, three statue men were engaged in an anatomically improbable adventure. Zagiri craned her neck to see down a nearby arcade, wondering what strange and decadent things might be sold at the shuttered shops.

Yeva laughed at her. "And you scold me for drawing attention. Come on."

The House they ended up at was named the Twist of Fate, and its large stone entrance archway was flanked by two tall wooden carvings—one a fisherman holding a large marlin, the other a mermaid whose smile and bared knife both curved wickedly. The archway opened onto a yard filled with sunlight and tall cypress trees, trimmed and trained into elegant shapes. The tables laid out among them were empty, save one toward the back.

They'd passed another of those posters on the way down, with the crossed hammer-and-baling-hook symbol and the boldly titled MANIFESTO. The inqs were pulling it down, but it hardly mattered. There had been so many of the things put up, all over the upper city, that a lot of people seemed to already know the thing by heart. The statements about every person working for the city and having an equal place. The hardly veiled threats about how much of azatani wealth and power lay upon the actions of the lower classes. The pointed conclusion about a new day coming.

It was real. This wasn't the same old autumnal agitations. This was a revolution.

And these were the revolutionaries. Zagiri found herself measuring up the people at that table like they were the competition in a melee. Three hefty Dockside types, one older and with the darker complexion of Archipelagan descent, and another with the Shore Clan mark—crossed S and baling hook—on her bared upper arm, the third with something vaguely familiar about the frown that bunched his eyebrows. There was a middle-aged woman in the sober dress of a clerk or housekeeper, and a man about Zagiri's age with a crooked nose and the brown robes of a scholar.

All of them were watching her right back.

Yeva waved a hand at the bench on the near side of the table, so Jaleh and Zagiri slid in next to the woman clerk, with Yeva taking the end. They were hemmed in, but Zagiri appreciated that they were the newcomers here. She felt a little dizzy to be here at all. Whatever Yeva had said, about the revolution listening to everyone's ideas, she hadn't expected it to happen quite this quickly.

She glanced at Jaleh, who lifted a challenging eyebrow. So Zagiri cleared her throat and said, "Thank you for meeting us. I'm Zagiri Savani, and this is—" She stopped belatedly as Jaleh kicked at her ankles.

One of the Dockside guys snorted. "Hope you aren't expecting us to hand over our names in return, little za."

"Zin, give the girl time to catch her breath." The Shore Clan woman ran a skeptical eye over Zagiri. "You can call me the Knife, if you have to call me something, and none of the rest of them matter. Your name don't impress us much, and if this is some trick, know we'll burn your family's ships to the waterline."

Zagiri felt a moment of panic. "This isn't—" she squeaked, then stopped.

Jaleh's hand found hers beneath the table. Her fingernails dug in hard enough that Zagiri jumped. But at least it blew away the blockage in her throat. "This isn't a trick," she said firmly. "I come in good faith, to offer an opportunity. A chance to move toward fairness."

"Yeah, right," the scholar drawled. "*You* want to see the azatani brought low. Baby za and a shopkeeper's daughter. Really?" He seemed unmoved by Jaleh's glare.

Zagiri wasn't sure about *brought low*. Some, maybe—she'd *love* to see Avarair Hisarani humbled. But there were plenty of others—not just her and Anahid, but Balian, Nihath, even Azata Markani and the prefect—who wanted to see things change as well. Who wanted things to be better.

Then again, what were *they* all doing about it? *Really* doing? And if the azatani were so *naturally* at the top of the heap in Bezim, then they'd still do all right if the sea was calm and level beneath them all.

"No answer?" sneered the scholar. "Let me guess, you run the tiles and you think it means you *understand*—"

"Shut it," the clerk sitting beside Zagiri snapped. "I like that the girl's actually thinking about it."

Zagiri shot her a grateful glance, but there was little sympathy in the woman's expectant face. She wanted an answer. She wanted a good one.

All Zagiri had was: "I want to see the city made fairer. And it's become clear to me that the azatani won't make that happen unless forced at sabre-point."

She wasn't sure how well that landed. The scholar looked disgusted, and the Dockside trio mostly looked bored. The clerk nodded at Jaleh. "And you, miss?"

"I've jumped through enough azatani hoops," Jaleh stated. "But this is her idea. I'm just here to make it happen."

The Knife beckoned with one scarred hand. "Let's hear it, then. That's why we're all here."

It had seemed such an elegant and perfect idea when it had come to Zagiri, coalescing from all the pieces of a messy morning. It had seemed solid and worthwhile when she was explaining it to Jaleh, trying to get her on side. But now she was worried they'd hate it. Hate her. Send her away.

That was just the nerves. She knew how to face those down and lift her sabre anyway.

"You don't get azatani attention until you threaten azatani profits," Zagiri said. "The caper I interrupted the other night—" She tipped her head toward Yeva.

The scholar wrinkled up his nose and repeated *caper* under his breath like it was unspeakable.

Zagiri ignored that. "It was a good thought, but it's not that big, and it's a one-off thing."

"Fear of it happening again will linger," countered the big Dockside guy, the one the Knife had called Zin.

That was something Zagiri hadn't considered. Of course it would. When one trade voyage was sunk by pirates, every other trading family took note—and took precautions. Azatani were always assessing.

That might help *her* plan. "I'm suggesting a bigger strike. Something that really hits a lot of families. Because more of them than care to admit it are deeply invested in the industrial district."

Before Zagiri could get any further, the Knife shook her head. "And they employ thousands of people from Dockside and the lower city. We're not destroying the factories until most if not all of the workers are with us."

"I keep *telling* you," the scholar snapped at her. Maybe that was just how he talked to everyone. Maybe that was how he got that crooked nose. "We don't have to *destroy* anything; we can disrupt the whole enterprise by bringing the line to a halt—"

"Which we can only do with the workers on our side," the Knife argued back.

"And messing with the alchemical processes is wildly unsafe," the clerk added sensibly.

Zagiri grabbed her chance. "That's why we take out the alchemical processes instead."

That got their attention—now Zagiri was facing five varieties of a frown.

"How?" the clerk demanded.

"It doesn't matter; it still leads to loss of work," the Knife said dismissively.

"Not if it's just a process disruption," the scholar argued, like he couldn't prevent himself from making the correction. "Then they can't stand them down without risking further delay, especially if we can prepare the workers with demands—"

"None of this matters." Zin jerked his chin across the table. "Like the Ledger said, *how* you going to do that? Messing with that shit is dangerous."

"Not if you know what you're doing." Jaleh sounded cool and competent and Zagiri was extremely glad she'd insisted on coming along. "The danger comes from undirected energy. The risk is *causing* a flare. Consume a process's energy, and it simply stops."

All of them looked at the clerk woman—the one Zin had called the Ledger—who frowned. "But a flare has a very limited range. What target did you have in mind?"

Zagiri could feel the smile trying to creep onto her face; she tried to keep it tight, at least. "All of them."

That got a reaction—sharp inhales and speculative looks and the scholar spitting, "You *can't* be serious."

The Knife considered Jaleh. "*You* going to do this? How many of these flares you think you'll set before the inqs arrive?"

"*I* don't scamper about in the night." Jaleh made it sound like an uncouth habit; *how* had she and Siyon ever been involved? "But I can make devices, on a time-calculated trigger, that will cause a limited flare and can be planted to engage the energy of surrounding factories. We calculate three dozen will be sufficient if efficiently placed, so I'll make more than that."

The Archipelagan Dockside guy, silent until now, said, "Our people would have mentioned if something like this was possible."

Before the Knife could answer, Jaleh said, "Whatever mudwitch you've had doing your work is very good. I particularly liked the clogging up of the warehouse locks; that was very nice. But I'm better."

She said it simply, like a fact.

Thoughtful glances were exchanged around the table. Zin looked more suspicious than ever, but the Knife eyed her with new interest. "If this is possible, that's a level of chaos that catches my attention," she said. "I'll have to talk it out among some of the others, see if we can muster the appropriate arrangements. We'd want to plant the devices fast; that's a lot of people. How long would you need to make the devices?"

Jaleh shrugged. "A week, for preference. A few days, if I rush."

"Before Salt Night would be better," the Knife said consideringly. "We'll need them ahead of time, and one of ours checks them." She smiled, thin and sharp as her namesake. "I'll not be a part of some harebrained scheme to blow up the entire place."

"What?" Zagiri yelped. "Why would we want to do that?"

The Knife shrugged. "Why do you want to do *this*? None of my business, your reasons and feelings. I just care about what happens. So we do it my way, or we all walk out of here strangers again, get it?"

Zagiri looked sidelong at Jaleh, who sniffed. "You check one, chosen at random. I'll not have some amateur messing up my work with sticky fingers."

To be honest, the Knife's careful planning made Zagiri feel relieved about this whole business. She hadn't been sure what to expect from revolutionaries. Yeva could be strange and intense. The manifesto had been grand, but lacking hard details. But these were just people, trying to fight with whatever they could lay hands on.

Zagiri knew that feeling.

"Well, then," the Knife said. "We'll be in touch. And you lot…" She leaned forward, and the table creaked a little under the press of her knuckles. "Keep your fancy fucking mouths shut, yeah?"

CHAPTER 21

The Palace of Justice hadn't been Anahid's first preference for finding Vartan Xhanari, but though she'd waited long enough on the steps of his attic apartment for his neighbours to twitch their curtains disapprovingly, he hadn't come home.

So she had come here.

Dusk was stretching into evening, but the inquisitors' annex was brightly lit and humming like a hive with activity. A pair of runners streaked out as she approached the doors, sprinting off across the park.

Inside, the waiting area was subdued and sparsely populated, but grey-tunicked figures came and went, shouting and shaking paperwork at one another, clustering down the corridors in little knots of furious discussion.

"Who?" the front desk clerk asked, leaning forward with barely half his attention on Anahid.

"Vartan Xhanari," she repeated. "In the Special Crisis Task Force."

"Down that way." He was already turning back to the rosters in front of him.

Something complicated tangled around Anahid's ribs as she ventured down the corridor. The inquisitors' annex was no place for an azata, but she didn't know what she was anymore; she'd come to see Vartan, and the memory of their last meeting still thrummed against her skin; she'd come openly, though she'd been snatched from the street and threatened with execution the last time she'd approached him.

She was only, Anahid told herself calmly, doing as she'd promised. As she'd been bid. As far as anyone else knew, she was here to distract Xhanari from his assiduous pursuit of the barons. She was here to entice him into setting down his paperwork and engaging in other pursuits on his desk.

The thought didn't unknot her tension. Her skin felt warm; her skin crawled. She wouldn't be averse to another intimate encounter— there was still so much she was curious about—and yet the shadow of the barons soured any sweetness.

The Specials, in keeping with their standing within the greater body of inquisitorial work, were tucked away in a distant corner, in a shabby hall crammed with battered desks. It was also largely empty; two women were arguing in a corner office with the door half-open, and Vartan Xhanari stood over a desk in the middle of the room, his uniform and brow creased.

Anahid's gaze drifted from the width of his shoulders (that she had clutched as he lifted her weight) down to the narrowness of his waist (that she had hooked an ankle around) and wasn't sure if she felt more relieved or disappointed that there seemed little chance of a desk being misused.

She cleared her throat and said, "Vartan."

He looked up, and surprise, pleasure, embarrassment, worry, and sadness flitted across his face in quick succession. He glanced around, as though checking who was in earshot, before saying, "Anahid. I heard about the incident at the House. I'm so sorry."

Just like that, there was a lump in her throat, hitching her breath, as her eyes blurred over. "I don't—"

He took her hand and hustled them both into another office. It was crammed with shelves and stacks of boxes, barely large enough for the two of them. With the door safely closed, Vartan's arms folded around her, and Anahid let herself come to pieces in a storm of grief and guilt.

He weathered it, holding steady until she pulled back to wipe at her cheeks.

She'd come to distract him, Anahid had told herself, all the way here, like it might fool the watching barons.

That wasn't at all what she needed. His hands were still warm and heavy at her waist, and she marvelled at the sensation—so casual, so telling—but there was no room for desire among the fires already burning inside her.

"I want justice," Anahid said.

"Justice?" Vartan repeated. "The official report said the register was empty. That there were no suspects."

"One of those things is true." Anahid stepped back without really meaning to. She bumped against a stack of boxes; his hands fell away from her. "It was Stepan Zinedani, Vartan. He *wanted* me to know." Her teeth were grinding; through them, Anahid snarled, "He wrote on her stomach, in her own blood. He labelled her as his."

His surprise was clear; she wondered whether the official report had mentioned the writing at all. No one wanted to tangle with the barons.

No one except Vartan Xhanari.

"Look into it." She grabbed his hand, words tripping over themselves to rush off her tongue. "There were people everywhere that night. Someone will have seen something. I saw him earlier in the evening. I barred him from the House. He wasn't in his right mind; he wasn't behaving sensibly. He will have made a mistake. He will have been *seen*. And then think what leverage that will be."

"Anahid," he said gently.

She didn't want him gentle; she wanted him implacable, she wanted him righteous, she wanted him to be a bolt loosed from a crossbow. Unstoppable. "You could arrest Garabed himself on suspicion of involvement—you could, it would be sensible—and think what you could ask him then! You could search his—"

"*Anahid*," he repeated, firmer but still so unacceptably, brutally gentle.

Her vision blurred again. Anahid jerked away from him—*he* was trying to hold *her* hands now, like she could be soothed like a high-strung racehorse. "No," she snapped, though it sounded appallingly like a gurgle. "Don't say it."

He said it. "Without more evidence, I can't reopen the case. Not now, with everything that's going on. With the streets turning strange and Dockside spilling over with insurrection. Not with the demands being placed upon us. And not when—" He stopped abruptly, pressing his lips together in something that might be chagrin.

Anahid imagined that might have ended something like: not when he had already been chastised and demoted for exhibiting terrible judgment in the overzealous pursuit of a suspect.

She wished he hadn't learned his lesson.

"Will it be different," Anahid demanded, "when it's me, lying in my own blood? Because it will be. If Stepan Zinedani can get away with anything he pleases, sooner or later, it *will be me*."

It nearly had been. His uncle had asked for her death. *It will look like a natural product of poor choices*, he'd said. The news of her fate sizzling up and down the Avenues, and a sad but inevitable result of getting involved where she shouldn't.

"I won't let that happen," Vartan said fervently.

Uselessly. How could he stop it?

She would have to.

Anahid evaded his reaching hand and yanked the office door open, marching out into the open hall. The women were still arguing in the corner office, hands being waved now.

Vartan followed her. "An—Azata!"

Back to propriety. Back to following the rules. He couldn't help it. He couldn't afford not to.

Anahid didn't look back. Didn't stop until she was outside again, with the evening air cool on her face, against the fire of her anger and grief. Her breath heaving, her heart hammering.

She was alone. There was no one who would do anything—who could do anything—save her.

Not true. Siyon had come down to the District, rushing to rescue her. Zagiri had been with her—had first called for the inqs, and had been just as enraged.

Anahid still had them. But what could any of them do? What could *Anahid* do? Call the barons together and ask for Stepan's death, as his uncle had felt free to do for *her*?

She folded her arms tight, as though she could stop herself from coming apart. The motion lifted scent from her dress, sawdust and fear and pipe smoke. Faint and fleeting now, but still there. Still tangled with visceral memory.

For a moment she was back there, on that dark balcony over the beast-baiting pit. All of the barons there...

Anahid looked at the memory anew, here in the darkness, made sharp by desperation.

All of the barons there, yes, but not comfortable. There like azatas circling at the social season's first party, pressing false kisses to cheeks as they competed to be this year's most fashionable hostess.

Anahid had been thinking of them as a single trading fleet. But they were four ships under competing captains, and each would prefer to see the others sink, if it didn't risk their own hull.

The barons were balanced since the war. That was the official story. They were stable. This was better.

But a table of carrick was balanced as well. That didn't mean each player at the table wasn't watching for every weakness that they could exploit. Wasn't guarding themselves as they sought to push the others out of the game.

The other barons didn't *like* Zinedani. They particularly didn't like his nephew.

What *would* happen if Anahid asked? If she asked carefully. If she asked *right*?

She turned the thought over, like a new card in her hand. Seeing what she could make of it. What she could force from the others at the table with it.

She certainly wasn't going to start letting Stepan Zinedani win now.

"Where can I get energy from?" Siyon had asked Mayar, and he got a look like he'd instead asked where the sky came from.

Energy *was*. It had been scarce, and now suddenly the world was brimful and overflowing.

But Siyon couldn't afford to wait and see what happened next. There was so much, down there in the deep, waiting to rise. No one was going to like that.

He couldn't forget the eye, in his meditation vision. He didn't particularly want to sleep, for fear he'd see it again. When he did sleep, the burnished glow of the Mundane seeped into his dreams and tangled him in darkness. He woke with his hands lifted, fingers bronzed and tingling. He woke with the dragon figurine in his mouth, clattering against his teeth.

He languished in dreams curled tight in darkness—not just that of night, but pressed heavily by an immense burden of rock above. When he tried to reach out, it was all around him, and he pushed, and he *pushed*—

"Fuck's sake, stop!" someone shouted, jerking Siyon awake.

Someone grappling with him, gripping at his shoulders, and he was—what? He was standing at his bedroom window, wrestling with someone in leathers who shrieked, "Siyon!"

He knew that voice.

"Zagiri!" he gasped, and pulled her inside completely, away from the window.

The ironwork stairs from the workroom below clanged as one of Siyon's guardian inqs came charging up, alchemical lantern swinging in her hand. Siyon winced in the glare. "Calm down!"

From behind her own blocking hand, Zagiri squinted—at him, at the inq. "I saw the light on downstairs and assumed you were up and working, but I didn't want to deal with the inq on the gate…" She trailed off.

The inq with the lantern sighed, then stomped back down the stairs. "Fucking bravi."

Siyon found his own alchemical lantern, knocked off the stool next to his bed, and sparked it into light. A heavy bronze blanket lay over everything, with no other emanations visible. The bedclothes had been dragged halfway across the room. Did he walk in his sleep now?

"Sorry," Siyon said to Zagiri, who still had her back to the wall next to the window. "That was—" He waved a hand at the window—that she'd been coming through, that he'd nearly shoved her back out of without realising. "There's so much about what's going on that I don't understand." He scrubbed a hand over his face. He felt like he could fall straight back into sleep—and down deeper still. He didn't *want* to. "Late for visiting, isn't it? Don't you have work in the morning?"

"I don't know," Zagiri said, and what did *that* mean? "Anahid sent me a message to meet her here."

Why would—oh. "About the murder?" Siyon asked. Zagiri shrugged. Fair enough. "I'm making coffee."

It sounded like they were all going to need it.

By the time the coffee was starting to hiss, there were voices at the alley gate, and some solidity to the world around Siyon.

"Oh good, it's the angry one too." Laxmi's voice, Laxmi unpeeling from the wallpaper like some strange and unhealthy miasma, Laxmi stretching into her own, unnatural shape. She shook her wings like she'd been cramped and blinked reproachful golden eyes at Siyon. "You shoved me...somewhere."

"You and everyone else," Zagiri grumbled.

Siyon wasn't sure he'd done the shoving...or had he summoned the energy that had blanketed his room upon waking? If he could do that in his sleep, why couldn't he conjure up enough energy while awake to blanket the city?

"That coffee smells perfect," Anahid said from the top of the stairs. She looked Avenues-immaculate as ever, but there was strain on her face and shadows beneath her eyes.

"I'm sorry," Siyon said, which was the most important thing right now. "Zagiri told me what happened to Imelda. It's awful."

"It is," Anahid agreed, and her chin came up a little.

And then more, as tendrils of shadow curled around her neck, and Laxmi coalesced at her shoulder. One talon tapped at her cheek as Laxmi purred, "Mmm, revenge. Let me help you with *that*."

Anahid tilted away from Laxmi's claw. "Justice," she corrected.

"Boring," Laxmi sighed, and slunk past her, heading down the stairs.

"These inqs have the badge charms too!" Siyon called after her.

A frustrated growl rose from deepening shadows.

They sat around the workbench, and Siyon poured the coffee. It almost felt like some other time, months ago. The three of them, and no one else in the night.

"I need advice," Anahid said, with a faint smile. "From those who know and wish me best. I need to find a way out, for more than myself. I have dragged the entire House, and all its people, into trouble deeper than I can manage. The inquisitors are not interested in being involved. I have to find another way. I have to steer them to safe harbour again. I have to see this through."

The firmness of her words dragged her upright, squared her shoulders, settled her composure. Like she was talking herself into it.

"Against a baron." If anyone could, Siyon believed Anahid could. But all of his instincts, from a lifetime on the streets of Dockside and the lower city, screamed against standing and fighting.

Anahid's instincts were of the Avenues. *Demand everything*, Izmirlian had said. Anahid's lips pressed thin and firm. "He's just one baron. There are three others."

"You're going to—what?" Zagiri asked. "Get the other three on side against him? I don't think that's how they swim in those waters, Ana."

"They don't need to be on my side." Anahid was untroubled, as though discussing refreshments in her own drawing room. "They only need to *not* be on his. I isolate him and then I present him with a deal."

"You have something he wants?" Siyon wasn't doubtful so much as concerned. She looked tired, and drawn, and brittle. If she were playing carrick, he'd have told her to step away from the table. That it was time to call it a night.

But the stakes had risen beyond the point where she could walk away.

"I have the only thing that matters to him," Anahid said lightly. "My submission. The admission that I was wrong, and he was right. But he only gets it on my terms."

Siyon exchanged a look with Zagiri; he wasn't the only one worried about what Anahid was getting into. But she'd come to them.

"They do each have their own interests," Zagiri allowed. "Their own reputations. If you spoke with them separately and quietly..."

"Not too quietly," Anahid countered, taking another ladylike sip of her coffee. "The point is for Zinedani to know himself isolated. I believe they will all speak with me, though I'm not entirely sure how to approach them."

The barons didn't exactly make it easy to sidle up to them and whisper in their ears. Mama Badrosani might be easiest, if Anahid could get herself safely into the lower city. The Shore Clan kept their business locked up tight in Dockside, and as for Midnight...

Siyon lay a hand on his pocket and grimaced. "I might be able to help you get in touch with Midnight."

Anahid smiled. "That would be splendid, if it won't disturb your own plans."

Siyon wished he had anything so firm as *plans*.

"And I can perhaps help get you in with Aghut," Zagiri added casually.

Enough so that Anahid had nodded in acknowledgment, saying, "Thank you, that—wait." She frowned at her sister. "You can what? *How?* What are you—*Zagiri*."

Siyon looked from Anahid's shocked expression to Zagiri's stubborn one—stubborn, tinged with sheepish—and wondered what he was missing.

"You've taken up with the Dockside agitators," Anahid accused. "Is it that Bardha girl leading you astray?"

"She's not leading me anywhere!" Zagiri folded her arms, the sheepishness buried in a frown. "They have good points, Anahid. They're serious. Haven't you seen their posters around the city? It's not just the usual autumn troubles. It's...it's revolution."

"How is that better?" Anahid cried. "People *died* in the North, Giri. It was years of chaos."

"Then we do it better," Zagiri insisted. "We do it smarter. Because what's the alternative? Sit quietly and nod and let the Council keep grinding everyone down for a little more *profit*? I *can't*, Ana. I—" She paused, biting her lip. "I don't even know if I can go back up there tomorrow. Not with the chance on the horizon to do something *real*."

Siyon snorted. "What, you're going to just let the Council react however it likes to things?"

Zagiri blinked at him, like she was still lost in her glorious possibilities. "What?"

It seemed ridiculous she should need the reminder, but perhaps she hadn't spent as long as he had watching azatani do things that only made sense for their own self-interest. "Are you going to trust Avarair Hisarani and his cronies to react well when you shake the city under them?" Had that happened when *Siyon* shook the city?

Anahid leaned forward, eyes intent. "That's a good point. If you want to do this smarter—and honestly, Giri, I think the smartest thing would be not to be involved at all, but if you're *insisting*—" That delivered with a flat look. "Then you need to be on hand to guide it. Balance above the disruptions below. Have the answers the scared and the nervous need."

That was downright cold-blooded. Siyon gave thanks, not for the first time, that Anahid seemed to be on his side.

Zagiri's face screwed up in childish reluctance, and she whined. "But it means *more* work."

"You did decide to change the world." Anahid leaned back again. "I still don't like this."

Zagiri sniffed. "Well, *I* don't like you fronting up to a crime baron, but here we are, and I will punch Zinedani in the face myself before I tell you to sit quiet and let him win."

They smiled at each other, and Anahid finished the last of her coffee, setting down the cup before she turned to Siyon with a firm: "Now you."

"What?" Siyon gulped.

Anahid looked surprised he had to ask. "You clearly need help as well. I heard from Nihath—not very coherently, but I gathered the gist—that you have a rather firm deadline from the Council."

"The Council can fuck off," Siyon muttered, rubbing at his face.

"Exactly," Zagiri chimed in.

Which at least made him smile. It didn't matter what he said, of course. The Council were very much going to stay in his business. Until and unless he fixed all this. It was frustrating that he thought he knew what to do—or had the edges of an idea about it, at least—but had nowhere to find answers about *how*.

"Do you need another circle?" Anahid asked. "We've only just finished the parlour remodelling, but I suppose if you need to carve up a floor again, you could use the same room for tradition's sake."

He laughed; he thought he was supposed to, though the offer was genuine. Anahid would do what she could to help him find a way.

"I need..." Siyon trailed off, trying to order his thoughts. "There's something rising. Energy rising out of the deep earth. I think that's what has been driving all of this."

"Is it natural?" Zagiri asked. "Because you're the Power now? Is this the way it's going to be?"

That made Siyon hesitate and consider it. "I don't think so. Things feel...wild. Like water sloshing around. Water rushes through a breach until it levels out, right? What if I can level out the energy up here?" It was what he'd been thinking at the top of the clock tower. What he'd tried to do. "Except I can't find enough energy."

"And presumably pulling it up from below would be counterproductive." Anahid's forehead creased thoughtfully. "Where does energy come from? What generates it?"

Somewhat gratifying that she went straight to the question that Siyon had already asked. Unhelpful, but gratifying.

"Where do you see it?" Zagiri added. Because she'd been there when he'd admitted to Nihath and Jaleh and the others that he could see the planar emanations.

It was a good question. Where *did* Siyon see it? Everywhere. Coating his hands and running through the streets. Pooling around Midnight and lurking in the branches of the wishing trees in the hills. Clouding in the streets wherever a crowd was starting to gather.

What did all of that have in common?

"Belief," Siyon said. "Or maybe possibility. Or maybe just people."

"People," Anahid repeated. "Well, there are certainly plenty of those in Bezim."

"Better if they were focused," Zagiri argued. "Belief, he said. You want, like..." She snapped her fingers. "Like Auntie Geryss did in the square."

Auntie Geryss had taken over Tower Square in an amazing feat of both audacity and alchemy. She'd drummed up the crowd, and skimmed off their energy, and used the resulting power to cast out a net to pull Enkin Danelani back from where he'd disappeared to.

It hadn't worked, but that hadn't been her fault.

They were right. They were absolutely right. A public working. A public *spectacle*. A focus of belief, and of energy.

Siyon nodded slowly. "It would have to be bigger. I'd want... everybody." He pulled a face; it was unworkable. He couldn't find a space bigger than Tower Square, he couldn't find a place more central to Bezim—both geographically and in the city's idea of itself. He'd need something that somehow linked the entire city, up and down, that wasn't related specifically to what he was doing. Something to serve as a wick, carrying the flame that he struck to—

Siyon realised it the same moment Anahid said, "Salt Night."

The end of the old year, the beginning of the new, and an all-night party that turned the entire city upside down. A thing that drew them all together. That everyone in Bezim participated in *somehow*, even if they didn't parade the upper city streets, even if they didn't stop to watch the midnight fireworks on the harbour, even if they didn't exchange spicebread and cherry rakia and gifts...Everyone did something. It was Salt Night.

"It's your deadline from Avarair," Zagiri pointed out.

"Yeah," Siyon said. "If I fuck it up, I'll have no time left."

"As though he'd be appeased if you brought the stars down and made them dance," Anahid muttered.

"It means," Zagiri stressed, ignoring both of them, "that you can arrange something under the guise of it being *your job*." She smirked a little. "And I'm pretty sure that the Council's going to have plenty of other things to be thinking about than what you're doing."

Anahid sighed, far too long-suffering for the sentiment to be entirely genuine, and lifted an eyebrow at Siyon. "Workable?"

It was an idea. It was more than he'd had before the sisters had arrived. They weren't even alchemists. But they were canny and clever in their own ways.

They were his friends.

"Thanks," Siyon said.

Anahid smiled. "Likewise."

CHAPTER 22

Zagiri was annoyed that she'd let her sister and Siyon talk her into coming back to work. They were *right*, of course. She could achieve so much more, help guide the change she wanted to see.

But it meant paperwork.

Paperwork in a hurry as well, because word had come via Yeva that the Knife could muster the people they needed. As though answering a challenge, Jaleh had stepped up her productivity. She'd designed the device—she explained to Zagiri through a yawn whose duration had suggested that design had taken most of the night—and now it was just a matter of replicating the process.

Which left Zagiri only a few days to have her plan in place for the Council's reaction to a wholesale stoppage of the industrial district via massive alchemical meltdown. Anahid was right; once the pants had been scared off every azatani family in Bezim, they would leap on a reassuring solution that would make things better—for them *and* for every alchemical practitioner in the city.

After all, it wasn't going to be possible to get all those alchemical processes up and running again with only the practitioners currently registered. But fortunately, there were a lot of *other* practitioners already living and working in Bezim. They just needed a little change in the law.

Except it turned out that changing a law was a lot more complicated than Zagiri had anticipated.

Scrubbing a hand over her tired eyes, Zagiri looked over the three
committee proposals she'd pulled from the files to use as examples,
comparing them to her mess of scribbles and scratching-out. The section of definitions seemed pretty straightforward; she was going to
come back to that one, but she'd jotted down a few terms she thought
she was going to need. She'd got the sections on *Context* and *Background* around the wrong way, but she thought she had all the right
bits in the right place now. The problem was the technical listing of
proposed alterations to existing Council statutes. Zagiri didn't *know*
every place that sorcery was mentioned in the laws. If she missed one,
would it—

"What are you still doing here?" a voice asked, and Zagiri startled,
smearing ink over her pages.

From the doorway, Balian's amusement shifted into concern. "Oh,
sorry, I didn't mean to— You should get sand on that." He reached for
the jar on another clerk's desk.

A clerk who wasn't here, Zagiri noticed. In fact, the whole office
was empty and dark. In her corner of Syrah Danelani's warren of
offices, Zagiri always needed a lantern, but proper night had definitely
fallen at some point while she was concentrating.

"It's fine." She grabbed Balian's arm before he could tip half a
beach on her paperwork. "It's a mess anyway. It's the rough version." It
was her third attempt, but Zagiri could face facts.

She looked up and—oh, he was right there, leaning over her desk
and close enough that she could count his eyelashes. They were long,
and lustrous, and Zagiri knew more than a few girls who used all sorts
of alchemical charms to try to achieve what Balian seemed to have
naturally. He even *smelled* good, like he'd been in the library all day,
but also faintly of anise and something sharp and resinous.

"What are you doing here at all?" Zagiri asked.

"Looking for you," Balian said, as though it were the most natural
thing in the world. He had that little smile curving his mouth.

She could kiss him from here; she'd hardly have to lean forward at all. Zagiri could feel her weight start to shift forward, as though it were happening to someone else.

Then he glanced down at the pages again and said, "Siyon told me you've got some plan for sorcery reform. Are you drafting already?"

Zagiri flinched away, smothering the urge to cover up her messy, disorganised, awful work. Foolish, of course. She could hardly change a law without showing anyone her proposal, and she had originally intended to work with him...

"I told you I'd help," Balian said. "If you want."

She nearly blurted *yes* immediately, it was such a relief to have *someone* to help. But her work so far was *such* an embarrassing mess. "Would you *be* any help?" Zagiri asked, then realised how that sounded. "I just mean...you've been on a trade voyage for months, and then you got fired from a clerkship."

Balian laughed. "Before I escaped to the North, I had to suffer through all the usual boring education. Someone might as well benefit from it. Let me see."

Zagiri didn't know what this *usual* education was—she certainly didn't know as much about the technicalities as it turned out Balian did. He rattled off definitions for each of the standard sections in the proposal format and went rummaging in one of the nearby filing cabinets for other examples to display the various options. He shuffled the context and background material she already had—half of it still in the wrong place—and suggested better words than the ones she'd chosen.

"*Why* did you get fired?" she demanded as he fished out yet another proposal; he seemed to know exactly where everything was.

Balian pulled an expressive and thoroughly regretful face. "It's complicated. But look here, I think if you use something like this, it'll carry more weight."

And then they got down to the listing of proposed alterations and found that Balian didn't know all the places that sorcery was mentioned in Bezim's laws either.

"You can assign it to one of the general Council archivists, though, and they can chase it up for you," he suggested cheerfully. "Though it'll have to wait until tomorrow; they'll have all gone home."

Zagiri chewed on her lip. "And how long will that take?"

Balian shrugged. "Few days?"

That was tight. Zagiri didn't like it at all. If there was anything complicated in there, she'd have no time to get the proposal written before they flare-bombed the industrial district.

Maybe she didn't have to. Maybe she *shouldn't*. Despite everything Anahid had said, this session had shown Zagiri that some things were better left to those who understood them. Maybe Zagiri could let the emergency happen, and tell Syrah Danelani her proposed solution, and let more experienced clerks draw up the technical documents.

It was leaving a lot to chance. And Zagiri wasn't sure she trusted Danelani that much. She needed to present this, ready to go. Make it the easiest flotsam to grab as the ship sank. She couldn't let them have a choice.

Balian was watching her steadily. "Why the rush?" he asked softly. "Is something going to happen?"

Zagiri looked up into his face—plain, except when it was breath-takingly handsome, and not at all the usual sort of azatan. He was helping Siyon evade the Council's intrusive attention. He was friends with Yeva, had known her in the North.

She wanted to tell him. She wanted to share it with him. She wanted him to admire how audacious she was being.

She wasn't entirely sure that he would. Not enough to take the risk. They couldn't afford for word to get out about what was going to happen. This was their chance.

Zagiri shrugged. "Just in case. I want it locked down. Ready to go."

For a moment, Balian's face was steady as stone, watching her seriously. He was almost frightening like this. Almost familiar too, in some way she couldn't quite put a finger on.

Then he looked away, down to the papers in his hand, covered with her spiky scribbling and his far neater notations. "Maybe we're going about this all the wrong way. We're carefully trimming every little branch and twig. What if you cut it down at the trunk?"

Zagiri didn't follow. "What?"

Balian laid the pages on the desk and took up the pen, drawing a sharp line through everything they'd jotted down; Zagiri's stomach clenched at the casual cutting of all their work. She fumbled for the pages, like she could salvage it, as Balian strode back over to the cabinet of files.

The proposal he slapped down on the desk was positively archaic, its paper brittle with age and the binding ribbon closer to yellow than white. Zagiri tilted her head to read the old-fashioned cursive in which the title was written. "Striking from the ledger of criminal acts of the charge of—" She blinked. "*Witchcraft?* I've never even heard of that as a crime. How old is this?"

"About a hundred and sixty-five years," Balian said easily. "I actually know about this one from my research for Siyon. Midnight's organisation, though they were called the Shadow Brotherhood then, offered refuge to anyone accused of witchcraft, effectively disappearing them from the reach of the law. But eventually the city's understanding of alchemy developed and witchcraft as a crime became obsolete. Either something was unregistered alchemy—sorcery—or it was fraudulent commercial conduct. The charge of witchcraft was covered by other laws, and the redundancy was tidied away."

This was fascinating, but it took Zagiri a moment to figure out the relevance. "Oh. You're suggesting I...propose striking sorcery from the ledger of criminal acts?"

Balian nodded. "Remove all the problems. You don't have to deal with any conditional aspects, or sentencing tables, or registration regulations. Strike the fact of it entirely, and use the same reasoning established with witchcraft—that anything covered by sorcery can be prosecuted by the existing laws governing risk to person and property, and the risk to Bezim itself has been rendered null, and therefore the charge is obsolete. Neat, easy, passes the problem of finding all the instances of reference to someone else, later on."

Zagiri might use other descriptors. Sweeping. Dramatic. This wasn't just widening registration, making the gate a little wider. This was removing the obstruction altogether. Excitement bubbled up in the pit of her stomach. "Do you think it'll work?"

"Depends." He shrugged. "It's a wild idea that no one will go for in general circumstances, because why make such a drastic change if nothing is broken? Even this one—" He tapped at the witchcraft proposal's yellowed ribbon. "It was prompted because the prefect's daughter had joined the Summer Club and his political rivals were coming at her for witchcraft."

Zagiri huffed a bitter laugh. "Of course it was."

Balian smiled. "There's no motivation like self-motivation."

She shuffled the pages together and set them aside. "Let me take care of the motivation."

"Zagiri." Suddenly he was serious again. "If you're getting mixed up in anything—"

"You," Zagiri interrupted him, with a bland and blank smile, "just worry about helping me draft the proposal."

He was attractive, and easy-mannered, and very capable, and she liked him a lot. But everything needed to go smoothly. She wasn't taking the risk.

"Fine." Balian sighed and leaned back a little, and Zagiri missed him almost immediately.

But he stayed and helped her draft the proposal, and that was more important.

"Mistress," Qorja said, with unease slanting her voice, "please, won't you reconsider."

"Can you think of another way to make this work?" Anahid asked. She tried to keep her voice gentle, tried not to make it a demand. It wasn't as though she particularly wanted to do it this way. To speak with the barons. All of them. To speak with *Midnight*, who had Siyon so visibly disconcerted.

Anahid did not blame Qorja for being uncomfortable. But *comfortable* would have meant Anahid never left the Avenues in the first place. She would likely end up back there in any case, once she'd been through all this and traded her supplication—her acquiescence—for justice for Imelda. And she'd go willingly, with that justice in hand.

Willingly, if not happily. She would miss this world. She would miss this freedom. She would miss the intricate puzzle box of Sable House, being its mistress and steering its fortunes as though it were her own sort of trading vessel. She would miss all the people and their strange and wonderful and vibrant lives.

But they would *have* those lives, without fear of Stepan Zinedani. Anahid could find something else. She had that luxury.

"I am not convinced *this* way will work," Qorja admitted. "And I do not want this House to lose anything further. Any*one* further."

Nor did Anahid. "If Stepan Zinedani is allowed to get away with this, he will not be satisfied, only emboldened. We *will* lose further, at that point, and you know it. I must strike a deal that keeps us safe." She nearly said *keeps you safe*, but she had not shared that detail of her plan.

Qorja could not deny that, but still she twisted her fingers together, not quite wringing her hands. "I don't like the idea of dealing with the Zinedani at all…Mistress, he did not outlive the Bitch Queen and survive the war through honourable negotiation."

"He did not," Anahid agreed. "He did it by being a more vicious, grasping bastard than the others. Which is why I will align the only other people who give him pause behind me before I sit down with him. I trust in fear, not honour." She laid a hand on Qorja's shoulder. "It *will* work, with the support of the other barons."

"What if you can't gain that?" Qorja asked.

"I will," Anahid promised.

And set off to begin.

She thought she'd tucked the dragon figurine of Siyon's into her sash, beside the penknife that she carried everywhere by habit now, but it hadn't been there when she got home the other night, so clearly she'd forgotten to bring it.

When she went past Siyon's, he pulled it out of his pocket with a thoughtful look. "Maybe just hold it in your hand until you use it," he said, which seemed frankly unnecessary.

"I can use it right here," Anahid pointed out, "if you're so worried that I'll lose it."

"No," Siyon said with knee-jerk fervency. "I don't want to—no.

Take it away. And you *will* lose it. That's fine. I just want you to get the chance to do what you need to do first."

Anahid walked home with the sharp little points and corners of it between her fingers, as careful with her hold on it as she was with her footing. After the way Siyon had phrased it, she half wondered if she'd trip on a loose cobble and drop the thing down a drain.

But she—and the little dragon—made it home safely. Nihath was in his study, discussing something with Jaleh Kurit—who at least looked up to give Anahid a respectful nod in the middle of their discussion of *replication* and *iterative effects* and other things Anahid didn't understand.

She went upstairs, into her private sitting room, and ignored once again the overflowing correspondence Nura had piled on her desk.

Instead, she lifted the dragon for consideration. It was very cunningly carved, barely the length of her finger but rendered in fine detail, with an arched and spiked back, each foot curling with claws, the tail lashing, the little jaws open.

Anahid seated herself carefully, as though waiting to receive guests, and said: "Midnight, I call upon you."

Nothing happened. Silence fell. The clock in the corner of her desk ticked quietly.

After a moment, Anahid added: "Please?"

Still nothing. Noise came from outside—children playing kickball in the lane. Somewhere in the house, a door opened and closed again. Anahid looked toward the door; was she about to be interrupted? Was that why—?

"I did not give this token to *you*."

Anahid whirled around, half slipped off her chair. She grabbed at the arm, and the little dragon figurine fell from her fingers. She heard it bounce once on the floorboards before it landed on the rug.

A black-clad figure stood in front of the fireplace, short and slender and with hair trimmed very close to the head. He—*he*? Anahid had always heard people talk about Midnight as *he*, but it didn't seem right, looking at this figure—wore a faint frown. "Who are you?" he demanded.

Anahid cleared her throat. "We—ah. We met, at the beast-baiting pit. Though not really formally."

Those black eyes blinked, and suddenly Anahid was uncertain. *Was* this one of the two who had been on that balcony? He almost matched her memory of them, as they had almost matched each other. The same slight build, boyish face, dark eyes. Something different in the tilt of the chin, though? There was no recognition on that impassive face.

But eventually he said, "Mistress of Sable House. You are still not our concern. Goodb—"

"Wait!" Anahid leapt to her feet. As though there were any possible way she could stop Midnight leaving when he had arrived without needing the door or window or even sound. "I have the—" She looked down, on the rug, where surely the little dragon had dropped. She'd heard it bounce.

It wasn't there.

You will lose it, Siyon had warned her.

She looked up—and Midnight was still here. "You *had* the token," he corrected, blandly. "It is not for you."

"Siyon gave it to me," she blurted, and took a sharp breath of relief as Midnight hesitated, head cocked at her like a curious crow. She would play any card she could find, to hold on to this chance. "I need to speak with you. With all the barons."

Midnight tilted his chin up toward the ceiling and sighed, heavy as a frustrated parent. "This is a distraction."

"It need not be yours," another voice said, behind Anahid now, between her couch and the window.

She spun around, swallowing a shriek—there was *another Midnight*, just standing there. The window was still closed, the filmy lace curtains drawn. This Midnight looked almost exactly like the first, like the two at the beast-baiting, and yet he wasn't identical. A little leaner in the face? A little sharper in the jaw? This one watched her measuringly.

"How many of you are there?" she demanded. Possibly unwisely.

This Midnight didn't seem to take offense. "There is always one Midnight."

Anahid looked over her shoulder; there was no one there. "I've met two of you before," she snapped.

Midnight looked thoughtful. Almost wistful. "So much possible now, that was too difficult before. So much possible again, perhaps. It is difficult to remember. Not that it matters. What do you want?"

She didn't understand any of this, and every little uncertainty seemed to add a stiffness to her spine, to file her Avenue accent sharper as she said, "Justice for my murdered Flower, that is all." She looked at Midnight—this Midnight, the one for whom she was apparently relevant—and considered what she had seen. She added, "What do *you* want?"

It seemed he hadn't been expecting that. His head tilted—as if he were listening to a conversation she couldn't hear. "I have no interest in your Flower or your House—"

"Yes," Anahid interrupted, bitter as vitriol. "You mentioned."

Midnight continued, unbothered: "But I *do* have an interest in the one who gave you that token."

Anahid considered, briefly, replying with *What token?* After all, the thing had vanished. It felt like something Zagiri would say; for a moment, Anahid appreciated how much better it would make her feel to simply be blithe and obnoxious.

But she wasn't her sister. She played her cards more carefully than that. As the moment passed, she could see a way forward. "Siyon," she said. Midnight's attention focused on her—again, like it had the last time she'd said that name, to the other Midnight. Or the other... shade of Midnight. "Yes, he gave it to me. He has no interest in speaking to you." Anahid paused a moment and hedged her bet. "But perhaps I could change his mind."

Did that mouth get the faintest curve of a smile? "What is it that you propose?"

Anahid took a breath, pulling herself back together. She had prepared arguments, rehearsed her points, and they had all been knocked into disarray by the strangeness of this interview. "I have strong reason to believe that Stepan Zinedani murdered my Flower, Imelda the Dawnsong. I—"

"Yes," Midnight interrupted. "He did."

There went all her preparation again, scattered like a school of fish. "What? How do you know?"

"Wherever there are shadows, there we are." Midnight didn't even blink, as though the claim was nothing extraordinary. "I see everything that happens in darkness."

"Could you have stopped it?"

"Why would I do that?"

Anahid had to swallow hard. He wasn't dismissive, so much as genuinely perplexed. And she wasn't *here* to berate him. She was here to win him to her side. To move forward. If he *could* have saved Imelda or not didn't matter. He hadn't.

"I want," she said, through tight-gritted teeth, "him to pay for what he's done."

"You ask for his death?" Midnight didn't seem surprised; he was just clarifying.

"I would settle," Anahid noted, "for his exile. Or another significant chastisement, little as I trust the Zinedani to administer it appropriately. I wish to bargain fairly with the Zinedani. I will step out of my place and return the House to their oversight, if my request is met. If he refuses to grant this justice, and if he stands by his murderous nephew, I hope"—Anahid looked up, directly at Midnight—"that the barons will see what he thinks he can get away with and make their own plans."

Definitely the hint of a smile this time. "None of that is my concern," Midnight said. "But the others may feel differently. My support is yours for a price I am sure you can name."

Yes, she rather thought she could. "I may be able to persuade Siyon Velo to speak with you. You realise that I cannot control him, nor what he might say."

"That is not my concern," Midnight said blankly. "I speak with him, or we have no deal."

Anahid bowed her head. Well, if that was what she was going to get, she'd just have to put it to Siyon. It was only a chat. Surely he couldn't get too bothered about that. "All right. I will—"

But when she looked up, Midnight was already gone, and though she spun around entirely, there were none other in the room.

That, it seemed, was that.

The night wind was gusting from the north, adding a sour marsh tang to the sea salt freshness and sending clouds scudding over the face of the moon. The sort of night where the bravi might say the seventh runner was on the rooftops, lurking in every sudden shadow to tip an unwary runner off the tiles.

As Siyon looked over the rooftops of Bezim, he half expected to see that seventh runner in truth. Magic was awakening. Anything and everything was possible.

He reached out and hooked his fingers into bronzed energy, shimmering umber against the night sky. Pulled it close and bundled it up, tried to make a ball that he could cradle in one palm even as he reached for more—

It slipped free, sprang away, fizzing out into the wide night sky to start settling back to earth.

"Fuck," Siyon grumbled, dropping his hands. "Can you go again?"

Farther along the roof peak, Mayar rolled their shoulders. "Give me a moment."

They were up on top of Siyon's building, where there were far fewer planar emanations generated by people and objects—or stray thoughts, for all Siyon knew about anything. Siyon could concentrate on the Mundane energy that Mayar was generating for him. Eventually, Siyon would need to be able to do this in amid everything else, in the heart of the city, in the middle of a crowd. Gathering everything they made for him, while also weaving it into the blanket he needed.

Not eventually. At Salt Night. Barely a week away. But right now, he couldn't even manage this. No good leaping out of the boat and assuming he'd figure out swimming once he hit the water.

Eyes closed, balanced on the roof peak, Mayar started to glow faintly bronze.

"What are you thinking about?" Siyon asked.

"I'm not thinking," Mayar scolded quietly. "That's the point of meditating."

But Siyon wasn't going to be able to lead the people of Bezim in a meditation class, not all at once, not on Salt Night. He needed to fire their belief. He needed a spectacle. He needed to bring them together and *earn* their energy.

He'd felt it before, under Auntie Geryss's careful control. She'd shown the crowd just enough for them to push eagerly at the boundaries of what was possible. Siyon hadn't been able to *see* the emanations then, but he'd certainly felt it.

Siyon twisted a stray scrap of Mundane energy into a knot, pulling in skerricks of Aethyreal and Empyreal. He tossed the whole lot up into the air, where it exploded like a little firework, shimmering sparks into the night sky.

Like that, but more so. Big enough to capture the whole city.

"Stop that," Mayar muttered. "You have work to do."

But even as Siyon settled himself, reaching out to the energy wisping off Mayar, a window opened below them and one of Siyon's inqs called, "Someone here to see you, Velo!"

"Shit," Siyon muttered.

Mayar opened their eyes, the burnished glow dimming. They braced a hand against the roof, ready to head off into the night the way they'd come, across the tiles. Siyon supposed he couldn't blame them for being unwilling to cross paths with the inqs, even his relatively tame ones.

"Keep practicing," they ordered in farewell. "There's not much time left."

Anahid sat patiently in his living room. Siyon had been expecting her, sooner or later; he fished the little dragon out of his pocket again. "I told you not to let go of it."

But she shook her head. "It worked. Before it ran away."

Siyon had been nurturing a hope that Midnight might be so ticked off at him loaning it out that he'd take it back, but apparently no such luck. "You talked with him, then?"

Anahid frowned. She had that tilt to her chin, that purse to her lips, that said she was examining something very closely inside the intricate machinery of her mind. "More like *they*," she corrected.

"They like Mayar?" As Siyon understood it, Mayar's *they* was the closest Lyraec could come to the other options of Khanate dialects, but he supposed there was no reason Midnight couldn't use it too.

"That too, possibly," Anahid allowed. "But I believe there is more than one Midnight."

Now Siyon was very much paying attention. Thinking of Tein Geras, suggesting that very thing; thinking of Balian's research and the Cult of Midnight; thinking of the Midnight in the drunken alleyway, the one in the sober sunblasted hills. "What makes you say that?"

"I met two," Anahid said. "The first showed up to see you, I think. The other arrived to deal with me." Siyon opened his mouth to suggest it was just a performance—he didn't know *how* Midnight could step in and out of the shadows the way he did, but he certainly *could*. But Anahid continued, "When I was summoned forcibly to the barons, there were two there, representing Midnight. Not quite identical."

"That—really?"

Anahid was still thinking too hard to be bothered about him casting aspersions on her observational skills. "The one I spoke with yesterday *said* they were all one, that *he* knew everything that was done by Midnight. But he mentioned... memory. Things that are possible now. He seemed to have to reach for other information. Or perhaps consult with others." She shrugged dismissively, though Siyon had *abundant* questions. "In any case, he is extremely eager to speak with you."

"That feeling is not mutual," Siyon retorted, which from the look she gave him came as no surprise to her.

"You were saying," she said gently, "that you lacked a full understanding of the situation. Can it hurt, to find out more about what he knows?"

"What, this creepy collective of nearly identical and possibly delusional guys who can apparently walk through shadows? The one who might have *murdered* the last Power and who tried to grab me last time?" Siyon demanded.

She winced a little, like he'd scored a point. But her mouth firmed. "You don't *know* about the last Power. One of many things that aren't clear. If you choose the meeting, you can lay your own defenses. You can ask all your questions."

What was down there, in the depths of the earth? What was happening, with the power rising? Who *was* Midnight? How long had they been here? What had they seen in all that time?

Was Siyon doing the right thing?

Siyon hated that the last question clung to him like a damp sock. He was the Power. No one else's approval mattered. "And this has nothing to do with whatever deal *you* need to do with him, I'm sure."

"It has everything to do with it." Anahid's smile was faint and strained. Siyon wasn't the only one under pressure. "But if you really feel that you cannot do this, that there is nothing to be gained and no benefit to outweigh the risk, then I will find another way."

She would too. With simple calculation and rigorous planning and not looking away from any of the unpleasant options. Not for the first time, Siyon thought this would all have gone better if *she'd* become the Power.

"Fuck it," Siyon grumped. "Fine. I'll do it. Are you staying?"

Anahid slipped off her stool. "Your Midnight is not my Midnight. They made that clear. But I'd be grateful if you remind him that we had a deal." She hesitated at the doorway before adding, "Do plan those defenses. Keep Laxmi close, perhaps."

A hiss skittered around the corners of the room; Siyon smiled at the lift of Anahid's eyebrows. "She doesn't much like Midnight," Siyon explained.

"Interesting," Anahid said lightly, "when you think of who else she doesn't like. Good luck."

And she was gone, leaving Siyon considering that. The others that Laxmi preferred to avoid. Olenka. Tehroun. Fallen beings.

Midnight *wasn't* a demon, fallen or otherwise, not with that constant Mundane glow. Much like Olenka and Tehroun were still constantly wreathed in their planes of origin.

One more question. Siyon sighed and picked up the dragon,

turning it around in his fingers. Black as the tarry ooze from which the griffin had hatched. "You only have to get involved if I'm in physical danger," he said aloud, and then: "All right, Midnight. Let's talk."

"Finally."

Of *course* the dramatic asshole popped up behind Siyon.

He turned around on his stool and glowered at Midnight, standing next to Auntie Geryss's rubber fig in his all-black getup, shadowed and burnished both.

That glow was insistent. It pushed at Siyon's eyes, like a headache waiting to happen. It frayed at his patience.

"Are you some sort of fallen Mundane being?" Siyon demanded. Even as the words came out of his mouth, they seemed ridiculous. "How would that even work? Where did you fall *from*?"

"The question is irrelevant," Midnight declared. "This is not about me. We must—"

"I say different." Siyon cut off whatever portentous utterance was likely to come next. "I say I'm not listening to another word out of you until I know what your angle is. Who you are. What you want. What you want from *me*."

A frown flickered on that impassive face. "We are the one who waits in—"

"The darkest shadows," Siyon repeated along with them; that frown deepened. "Yeah, so I hear. But what does that *mean*? When did you start waiting?"

"Time doesn't matter," Midnight said, and raised his hand to forestall Siyon's angry response. His palm burned with energy, making Siyon wince. "No, this is not the important part. There are no numbers you would understand to represent how long my duty has lasted. You cannot comprehend the things I have done. I have held on as I can, as the power slipped away and took nearly all of me with it. I have become what was needed in order to survive. Until *you* have fulfilled your duty, you cannot reprimand me."

"My duty." Siyon seized on that, like a line thrown to a drowning man. "What am I supposed to do?"

Midnight's face pulled into a sneer. "That is not *my* place to know.

I have nursed my purpose for centuries of loss, and you want me to hand you yours?"

"It'd be nice, yeah," Siyon shot back, but he was floundering. Midnight really was that old. Really was that strange. Centuries spent with his myriad selves, and an eroding memory of purpose. Siyon supposed he might have come a little unhinged as well, in the circumstances.

"My duty," Midnight declared, drawing himself up, limned in bronze. "My duty is to carry you to yours."

He reached for Siyon's wrist.

"Wait!" Siyon skipped back a step, but the table was right behind him; he knocked over a stool, he pulled his arm out of the way, he—

—Was suddenly on the other side of the table, the world lurching around him, acid burning in his throat and talons pressing into his arm. Siyon retched, his vision dancing with darkness and stars.

Somewhere over his head, Laxmi snarled, "Don't get handsy."

Siyon remembered her popping out of nothing with Mayar, the night they'd fended off the griffin. Mayar emptying their guts into the bushes like the worst hangover of history. Siyon very much sympathised.

"This is not *your* concern," Midnight snapped.

"*He* is my concern," Laxmi growled, which might have made Siyon feel all warm inside if his insides weren't currently in open rebellion.

"He is *ours*." Something in Midnight's voice ground like stone, hard and unyielding. Siyon looked up, blinking away the prickle of tears, and on the other side of the workbench he seemed...bigger. A looming shadow. A thing far greater than a single man. The bright power that came off him stabbed shards of pain into Siyon's head.

"I'm not ready yet," Siyon said, his voice a croak. He coughed, and spat, and tried again. Had to try again. Panic fluttered in his veins. "I don't know what I should do, but I'm working on it. I'm *trying*. I can't leave these people defenseless. I can't abandon them."

"*People*," Midnight repeated, cold and hollow. "What do they matter? There are always more."

The tone was familiar and raised Siyon's hackles. It could have been any azatani member of the Council, dismissing any problem that didn't touch upon their own concerns. It could have been any Summer Club member, trading with Siyon when he was just another provisioner.

Siyon drew himself up as well. Made a match for Midnight, glowering on the other side of the table. Pulled power toward him—*felt* it respond to his call. "We go when I say we go," he said, gathering his will. Tried to remember what it had felt like when he'd banished Midnight in the hills. Could only try. "Now get out."

He *pushed* with all the energy he'd drawn in, and Midnight's eyes flashed wide in the moment before he vanished. Siyon was alone.

Not quite alone. "That was almost worthy of Her Majesty," Laxmi said thoughtfully, drifting over Siyon's head to peer at where Midnight had disappeared. "Except the part where you nearly threw up like an imp on his first hunt."

Siyon ignored her. He'd done it, just like he intended.

Maybe he could make this all work.

CHAPTER 23

"I don't like both of us being away from the House," Anahid said again as they neared the Swanneck Bridge. "Not right now, when things are so—"

Qorja cut her off with a sniff, beneath her broad-brimmed hat shading her from the afternoon sun. "I don't like you meeting with the barons at all."

"We've talked about this," Anahid sighed.

They had, and here they were: crossing the Swanneck, on the way down to Dockside, where a nudge through Zagiri's highly questionable contacts had secured Anahid a quick meeting with Aghut himself.

Anahid touched the sash of her dress, feeling the hard line of the little penknife. Useless, as always. But it still soothed her nerves. She wasn't entirely defenseless. She had connections. She had assistance. She had plans.

She wasn't at all sure that any of that would matter two copper knuckles where they were going.

They were pushed to the edge of the bridge by the thick traffic—ox-drawn wagons, handcarts, message-runners, workers from the industrial district. The waist-high railings were fashioned from the same alchemical not-stone as the rest of the Swanneck, still cool beneath Anahid's hand despite the autumn sun. Far below, the river churned and frothed white.

On the northern side of the river, the Kellian Way curved down into the tangles and clamour of Dockside. Anahid hadn't come this way since she'd taken ship on her unhappy trade voyage, before they all accepted that there was no cure for her shameful seasickness. On that occasion, she'd had more pressing concerns than her surroundings.

She still remembered the stink. Salt and rank, fishy rot; muck and waste; the acrid stench of tanneries and the bloody tang of butchery. Dockside reeked of people crammed together, wrestling their livelihoods out of sea and mud and blood. Even the breeze freshening off the sea couldn't push the stench away.

At the Customs House—a looming and overly grand edifice— they turned into the tangled depths of Dockside proper. The buildings down here were low and leaning, clinging together like barnacles. Many had a crossed-through circle scratched on window frames or painted on doorsteps. Like a ward against something.

The people were just as grey and hard, wrapped in salt-stained leathers with multiple amulets shifting around their necks. They stared at Anahid as she followed Qorja along narrow, twisting lanes and uneven staircases. Maybe she shouldn't have worn her headscarf, but likely that was not the only thing that marked her as azatani.

Down here, Qorja carried herself with less elegant coyness. She didn't fit in, not with her hair gleaming, her face clean, her dress plain but of excellent quality. But for the first time, Anahid wondered where Qorja had come from, before she was a Flower.

Imelda had hailed from Dockside. She wasn't alone among the Houses. For those with the inclination and a certain natural comeliness, apprenticing into Flower training could be an escape from this hardscrabble warren.

Anahid was absolutely lost, folding her hands tight so she didn't cling desperately to the back of Qorja's dress. They turned down an alleyway, ducked through a passage, crossed a stinking drainage ditch on a bridge little more than a loose board. And then came to a slightly grander stone building on a small yard—no fountain, but it was a bit of open space.

A sigil was hewn into the building's stone lintel, as though there were no chance its purpose would ever alter, and certainly no reason to be coy: an S crossed by a baling hook.

The home of the Shore Clan.

"We could still turn back, mistress," Qorja said quietly.

"When Master Aghut is expecting us?" Anahid replied, light as the flutter in her stomach. "That would be rude."

She led the way inside.

The heavy door opened directly onto a large public room, low and smoky and dim. Anahid nearly tripped up the two steps to a floor matted with rushes. The air was thick with sticky liquor and sweaty bodies and wet dog. At this hour, those few people at the tables seemed busy with their own business, whether conversation or silent brooding.

Anahid still felt eyes upon her as she crossed to the long wooden bar. The woman behind it was hefty and of indeterminate age but hard regard. Anahid said, "I'm expected."

"You came after all," the woman said with a smirk, and jerked her chin to a shadowed doorway. "Through there, all the way to the top."

There was a thug on the stairs who seemed equally amused to see her and barely tilted aside enough to let them past. The stairs were narrow and creaked beneath Anahid's tread. At the top, a thick-banded door and another hefty enforcer, his bared muscles marked for the Shore Clan. He drummed a fist on the door before he shoved it open.

The office inside could have been a shop's back room or a clerk's working quarters in the upper city. The shelves held more bundled and referenced paperwork than books, and the desk was utilitarian. Everything was tidy and ordered, with chairs for clients and curtains over the windows and a more comfortable area to one side for entertaining.

But it was Aghut himself behind the desk—his scarred face and his loud laughter and his booted feet propped up atop the blotter. Three of his people, equipped for violence, sprawled in the comfortable chairs, playing carrick on the low table. Anahid couldn't help glancing at the game as she passed—from the coins in front of each, the one-eyed man was winning, but from the cards visible on the table and in the hand of the woman with her back to Anahid, this was going to be a hard-fought round.

Aghut was just as she remembered him from the beast-baiting pit—a being entirely made of muscle, scar, tattoo, and belligerence, designed to offend azatani sensibilities from the top of his shaved head to the tips of his scuffed boots.

He grinned at her. One of his teeth was blackened, whether by nature or artifice. "An azata, come to visit me! My etiquette's rusty, za. Should I call for tea?"

One of the carrick-playing toughs snickered.

Anahid would have loved a glass of tea to wash away the mud and fear coating her throat. But that felt like a weakness she couldn't afford here. "Refreshment is not required. This is not a social call." And she took one of the chairs at the desk even though it hadn't been offered.

"I am heartbroken," Aghut drawled, stretching the words as Siyon might have. He tilted a smirk in Qorja's direction as she daintily took the other chair. "Does that mean you haven't brought me a host gift?"

Anahid's anger twisted tight at the suggestion. These barons, always *taking*. "That would be a princely gift," she snapped. "And you are merely a baron."

For a moment, she thought she'd ruined everything before they'd even begun. Then Qorja opened her pocket fan, the paper span delicately painted with feathers, and sniffed in a comically dismissive manner.

Aghut laughed—throwing his head back and tilting on his chair—and tipped his feet off the desk, sitting up straighter. "I am at that," he said. "Which I gather is why we're here. Heard you're slipping bait on your hook for Shakeh Badrosani too. Not Midnight as well?"

Anahid was no longer surprised at what the barons knew. Though she hadn't really made a secret of the message-runner she'd sent. She wanted Zinedani to worry about what she was up to. "Actually, I've already met with Midnight, through somewhat more clandestine means."

"Clandestine," Aghut repeated with some relish. "Yeah, that's those slippery fuckers down to the waterline. Give me the fucking creeps, they do. Still, can't argue with the results. Don't want to argue, given what they say happened to the last bitch who tried."

Now that Anahid had met Midnight in a closed room, she rather thought the story of the Bitch Queen's demise was likely to be entirely true. But right now, unimportant. "And, of course, I'm hardly seeking out the Zinedani."

"Hardly." Aghut stretched the word with derision. "It's downright funny, how much of a tizzy you've got Garabed in. I wonder how much he'd pay me to scoop you up and drop you in the harbour."

Chill gripped Anahid's heart. Three armed thugs just behind her. Two more on the stairs. All of Dockside between her and safety. But that safety was an illusion. She'd been kidnapped from within the Flower district.

"My experience," she said, keeping her voice steady by will alone, "is that the Zinedani are very reluctant to honour their debts. Unless forced."

"Yeah, that's about right." Aghut scratched at the stubble on his chin. "I ain't doing no forcing, though, so if this *opportunity* your message promised is something like *You save me from the Zees and I'll bat my highbred eyes at you real nice,* then frankly, za, you can go f—"

"I'm not asking you to *do* anything," Anahid interrupted. "I cannot deny that I'd be grateful if you resolved my disputes with your colleague in a satisfactory manner, but in the absence of that, I am suggesting that it would be in your interests to *not* do anything. To merely stand by."

Aghut laughed. "There's a suggestion aligned to my natural inclinations. And what will *you* be doing while I curl my hair and paint my toenails, za?"

"Negotiating justice for my murdered Flower," Anahid said, lifting her chin. This part she had no uncertainty about.

Or so she thought, before Aghut started chuckling. "Oh, I see. You're claiming Stepan killed your girl?"

"I'm quite sure he did," Anahid snapped. "And Midnight rather confirmed it."

"*Did* he rather?" Aghut said, mocking her accent. His Dockside drawl seemed all the thicker afterward. "Za, I appreciate you had other things on your mind the first time we met at the baiting pit, but did you pay attention at *all*?"

"Of course I did," Anahid replied sharply. "I could hardly fail to concentrate when Garabed Zinedani was asking for my d—" She stopped abruptly, and Aghut smirked, and Anahid couldn't blame him.

Garabed Zinedani had been asking for her death. Like asking his fellow barons was something he had to do. She'd assumed he'd had to ask because she was azatani and might cause problems, but the way the others had responded hadn't quite followed those assumptions. Because it *wasn't* just about azatani.

"It's one of our strictest rules," Aghut said, nodding slowly. Almost approvingly, like she was a student he was proud of. "A core part of the agreement we hammered out with your little prefect all those years ago." *Your*, as though Syrah Danelani wasn't in charge of Aghut's city. Maybe she wasn't, except by proxy through that agreement. "No deaths, save that we all agree it's the best option to keep the peace. So if you have proof—not inq-proof"—Aghut waved a dismissive hand, even as he leaned forward, interested in this. More interested than in any other part of this interview so far—"but *real* proof, then the Zinedani have overstepped."

Anahid's mind raced, her heart not far behind. She glanced at Qorja, who looked back with surprise-widened eyes. "Why didn't Midnight tell me about this?" Anahid wondered.

Aghut snorted. "Midnight doesn't much care about the rules."

And Anahid had pressed Siyon to meet him. She wondered—not for the first time, but with sharper curiosity—how that meeting had gone.

Not important, here and now. "There was a message," Anahid told Aghut. Hard to stay dispassionate about it. Hard not to lean forward herself, like she was begging the approval of the one person who had suggested there might be justice. "A message clearly from Stepan to me, written on the Flower's stomach. It aligned with accusations he has been heard to make, that the House should still be his. And, as I said, Midnight confirmed from his own knowledge that Stepan was responsible."

She hoped she didn't have to explain that knowledge. She couldn't.

But Aghut just nodded. "Sounds like the sort of thing that brat would do, must say. I'd certainly like to see the Zinedani brought down a little. I'd support justice, if you want it."

Anahid nearly brushed the words aside—why wouldn't she want it? But then she considered it further. "What would the consequences be?" she asked.

"Stepan's death," Aghut replied readily. Carelessly. "A fine for Garabed, if you can show he was involved, but I assume you'd have mentioned that already if you could."

What Anahid wanted anyway—Stepan brought to justice and no longer able to hurt any of hers. And she could keep Sable House.

But *Garabed* would still be here. Anahid could only imagine how angry he would be with her. For forcing this through official channels, for shaming him, for enabling the barons to look down on him and pass judgment.

Would she trade one sea snake for a shark in frenzy? Death for death might never end.

Anahid took a slow breath and folded her hands. "Thank you for bringing this to my attention. I will continue with my own negotiations, but this will be a useful point to hold in reserve."

Aghut's mouth twisted in amusement. "Have it your way, za. Hope the mud stays firm under your feet."

Zagiri crept through the night, moving swift and silent, keeping out of sight. She felt at home with this excitement rising in her. From the top of a factory yard wall, she spotted the shadow of someone in the lee of a building, so she hunkered down, teeth in her lip, ready to whistle the warning...

Then she realised it wouldn't help at all. Her fellow shadows, creeping through the night behind and around her, fanning out from a quiet warehouse, probably didn't know the bravi whistles, not even the few basic blasts that every tribe used in common. They weren't bravi.

They were revolutionaries.

The lurking shadow shifted, and there was a low flare of fire; just a worker taking a break to smoke a pipe. There were guards as well, hulking about in the industrial district tonight. They were here precisely to stop meddling from the Dockside troublemakers. They were looking in the wrong place, and for the wrong thing.

Other attempts at security abounded—warding signs painted on walls and little charms hanging from gate lintels. Trying to protect against a planar incursion, Zagiri assumed. Or against anything unexplained. Good luck with that.

Eventually, the lurking worker knocked out his pipe and slipped back into the factory. Zagiri crept along the top of the wall, with the sack shifting against her back, weighted by two of Jaleh's little tricks.

They were cunning devices, looking more like party favours than destructive alchemy. Inside each little black velvet bag, with the drawstrings knotted tight and sealed with clay, was a collection of various bits and pieces of planar material—Zagiri had asked what, and Jaleh had rattled off a bewildering list of which Zagiri only remembered *mystery silk*. The point was that the ingredients were precisely calibrated (Jaleh's words) such that when activated, the ingredients would combine, react, and spark a severe but tightly limited flare.

Tightly limited, that was, unless it picked up other alchemical energy within its radius. In that case, Jaleh promised with a smug expression, the flare would consume all of *that* and expand accordingly.

Exactly what Zagiri had in mind.

Where the factory nudged against the yard wall, Zagiri slipped a device out of her sack and twisted it sharply. Something inside started hissing, like sand running through a bell-glass, and she hurried to tuck it up under the eaves of the roof.

The higher the better, Jaleh had insisted. *It turns out that flares strike down first. I should write a paper to present to the...*

She'd trailed off. Zagiri hadn't pointed out that the Summer Club might not exist, not as it currently did, if they were successful tonight. Jaleh hadn't said anything else. Just looked thunderous and left.

Now, with her first device planted, Zagiri sprinted for her second location. Time was ticking, and the effect would be grander—more demoralising and harder to interrupt—if all the devices flared in quick succession.

The night was alive around her. The industrial district was hardly quiet at the best of times—from the factories and their yards came the grinding, whirring, clanking, grating noises of machines, and the voices of the workers who kept them fed and running. The quick patter of running feet also wasn't unusual—not with the Haruspex safe house nearby—but tonight, other parties were afoot.

The Knife had assembled two dozen, all told. They'd all lined up in a ramshackle little warehouse at the lower fringe of the industrial district. Yeva had been there, though not among the runners, and the big hulking Dockside guy called Zin had stood scowling in the corner. Each of the runners had two devices in a sack and directions on where to plant them. None of them knew where any of the others were.

If one—or more—of them was caught, the rest couldn't be rounded up.

Zagiri's second factory was a little too far from the yard wall— farther than she could easily jump and farther than she was sure the flare would reach. She could leap for *that* windowsill, grab the crossbeam, stick the device on the sill of the upper window. But she wouldn't have a hand free when she was over there.

So she twisted the device now. It was hissing as she made her jump, scrabbling at the wall one-handed for a queasy moment before she found a grip. Stretched up to the window above...

And swore aloud, because there was *already a device up there*, too shadowed to see from the wall. Had someone else been given Zagiri's spot?

Zagiri dropped into the factory yard and hauled herself awkwardly back over the wall, the primed device wedged hissing under her arm. She didn't want to waste it. How long did she have?

As she dropped into the laneway, a faint and hollow *pop* sounded farther up the hill, and then pinkish light flared up, spinning rapidly into green, firing short-lived sparks into the night. It whistled, like a kettle on the boil, almost louder than the shouting.

Even as Zagiri gaped, another *pop* sounded, and a column of intense purple light stabbed up, painting the underside of a passing cloud for a moment before collapsing in a spiral of hissing dust.

Zagiri *sprinted.* Down the laneway, with her second device hissing in her hand, and skidding out into the street. Around a corner, and there was a factory ahead, with a high window on the street. She stopped, steadied herself—even as more *pops* sounded behind her, light splashing into the night, red and blue and yellow in the corner of her vision. They were going off in twos and threes now, and Zagiri counted them without quite meaning to—thirteen, then eighteen, then a flurry to hit twenty-five.

She threw her device hard at that factory window and watched it sail true, shattering the glass and disappearing inside even as it went *pop* with a sharp white flash of light.

A moment later, every window of the factory lit up blindingly in the pale green of new apples. Doors slammed open, shouting voices in the yard, as the light twisted, whirling into yellow, streaked with red.

Someone shouted, "You! Hey, you! Stop right there!"

Like *hell.*

Zagiri didn't wait to see who was chasing her, or why. Just ran— along a lane, up a wall and down again, cutting across a block and around a factory. As she rounded the wall, a shadow moved in the corner of her eye, and Zagiri ducked by reflex, throwing herself forward into a roll.

Someone swore, above and rapidly behind her, as Zagiri rolled back to her feet and kept running. It took more than that to catch a bravi.

But that had been far too close.

"Hey!" someone called, up on a wall ahead, and Zagiri readied herself to dodge sharp around a corner.

But the shadow on the wall raised a hand to its mouth and whistled, short and sharp.

A city-wide code. *Help at hand.*

Zagiri ran *toward* the wall at full speed, bracing a boot against the rough brickwork and jumping up as high as she could...

High enough for the person atop the wall to catch her lifted hand. And then it was a two-person desperate scramble to get her up the wall, both of them breathing heavily. They both dropped flat against the top of the wall—something crunching beneath Zagiri and scratching at her skin—as a trio of factory workers ran past below, shouting recriminations at one another for whose fault was what.

Only once they were passed did Zagiri get a good look in the light of the flares at who had rescued her. "Mayar!"

They flashed a tight smile. "Slender's going to be *pissed*," they muttered. "We were supposed to be keeping our distance, not helping you out, but..."

"Thanks," Zagiri said fervently. "If anyone asks, you were never here."

"Fucking right I wasn't," they said, brushing off their leathers with a wince.

Zagiri's were covered with grit and dust as well, from what looked like... "Eggshells?" Someone had scattered them all along the top of the wall.

"Gull eggs." Mayar's nose had a wrinkle of disgust. "Alleytale says they're a charm against monsters. Utter horseshit, of course. Good luck."

And they were gone, slipping away over a factory roof.

Zagiri waited a little longer, lying flat on the top of the wall until the wildest, brightest bursts of light—in all the colours she knew and several she'd never even considered—finished splashing over the factories like spotlights.

Then she skulked her way through shadows down the hill. No one seemed to be hunting too assiduously anymore; the workers Zagiri heard were mostly clustered in their yards, swearing and shouting at one another.

She made a final dash for it, down out of the industrial district and onto the Kellian Way, the smooth surface of the Swanneck welcome beneath her boots. She only slowed her pace as she neared the other end of the bridge, glancing back up to the industrial district. The flares had died down into low, bubbling glows, like cauldrons boiling off the last traces of alchemical power.

There hadn't been as many as she'd expected. Were some tucked away and not showing? Had some of the devices failed to fire? Or had there been more confusions like Zagiri's—with a device already in her spot—and some of the flares had actually been two in one? It was frustrating that—

"Zagiri!" a voice hissed behind her.

Someone stepped out of the shadows past the end of the bridge, into the near-full moonlight that turned her usually golden hair silver. Yeva rushed out to grab Zagiri's arm, tugging at her urgently.

There was no reason to linger; the last glow of the flares was now dying back into darkness. Zagiri let Yeva pull her off the bridge and into the deep shadow of a shuttered shopfront.

"What are you *doing* here?" Yeva demanded. "You should be long gone."

Zagiri waved a hand back across the river. "Someone spotted me. I had to wait to slip away. What are *you* doing here? I thought we were meeting back at yours."

"There was something I needed to be sure of." Yeva frowned heavily across the bridge.

"I don't think anyone's chasing me now," Zagiri reassured her. "But the inqs will likely be here any moment." *She* leaned out to look up the hill; the Kellian Way seemed clear, and she couldn't hear the tramp of any approaching feet. But the wind was blowing from the north, bringing the ongoing clangs and bangs and shouts from across the river.

Time to get safe, though Zagiri wasn't ducking up the hill to the Chapel. This wasn't Bracken's business, and she wouldn't make it their problem.

"Come on." Now she was pulling at Yeva's arm and getting a confused frown for her trouble. "We need to get out of here."

"No." Yeva waved a hand toward the other side of the river. "I need to..." She trailed off.

"Claim credit when the inqs show up?" Zagiri suggested. Laughter welled up in her throat—incredulous, but also the by-product of ebbing adrenaline. She swallowed it down. "Everything that's going to happen has happened." And it worked, it worked, it *worked*.

How will I know if it works? she'd asked Jaleh.

She'd laughed, bright and wicked. *Oh, you'll know.*

The lights, the colours, the wild display. And now the shouting. Yes, it had worked.

Yeva glanced back once more, but she let Zagiri pull her away.

Into a night where suddenly change *was* possible. Zagiri was ready for it. She was waiting. And when the chance came, in the morning, she was going to seize it.

CHAPTER 24

The night was getting late, but Siyon was avoiding sleep. His dreams were getting militant—all grasping stalactites and thunder in his ears. Like something was restless. Or like Midnight had cursed him.

In any case, there was too much still to do.

Everything was coming together for Salt Night. Siyon's fumbling attempt from the top of the clock tower had shown—he thought—that the theory was sound. He just needed more, stronger, clearer. Hopefully the Salt Night crowd would be enough.

To assist with that, Anahid had brought him fresh marsh mud from the fringes of Dockside—along with a vague reassurance that her own plan was proceeding, and some interesting information about the charms and symbols she'd seen on display down there. Those might come in handy. Siyon needed some sort of display to draw the crowd into his purpose. Something they already half believed anyway.

So he'd asked Mayar to bring him news from the industrial district about what sorts of superstitions were cropping up, as well as sawdust and wastewater. He sent Nihath and his impeccable azatani-practitioner reputation up to scrape more grit off the city wall, and learned far more than necessary about which parts of the wall were allegedly haunted by the ghost of the Lyraec lion, symbol of the fallen empire. Siyon asked careful questions about the arcades and alleycanals of the lower city as he traded with the Bower's Scythe bravi for vials of salty mud from where the new mangroves tangled the sunken streets.

Siyon could draw his city boundary more clearly and precisely than ever, and he could evoke that city's newest magical worries and hopes.

And, when filing their reports, his inquisitor guards could say he was just trading for alchemical ingredients. Proper, discreet, unassuming alchemist behaviour.

Which served to support the application Balian had very carefully put together for Siyon to make use of Tower Square for really a very small amount of time at the start of Salt Night, before things got too busy, to perform a minor and subtle working in fulfillment of his commitments to the select committee and thereby the Council.

The part about subtlety was the only outright lie.

Though Siyon still had to perfect what he was actually doing.

The problem was handling the power. He thought he had a good plan for raising it, and for what to do with it once he had it gathered, but the gathering was like bailing a boat with his hands. When Siyon pulled together more than a double-handful of Mundane energy, it started twisting and wriggling, leaking out of his grip.

Siyon tried looping the energy around his thumb and finger, like he was coiling fishing line. That thought led him to start braiding the different strands of power together, like making rope. But this didn't feel like the right direction at all. A line or a rope were used to haul something *up* from the deep. Siyon wanted everything to stay down there, thanks. He wanted a soothing blanket. He wanted the energy to spread, and settle, and contain.

Like Auntie Geryss had done, trying to catch Enkin and pull him back. She'd shown him how already; she'd finger-knotted the net out of energy as they all watched.

So tonight, as the midnight bells tolled, Siyon sat cross-legged on Auntie Geryss's battered old couch with his hands full of burnished power and tried to remember everything he'd learned from his aunts about making nets.

They hadn't *taught* him, was the problem. Nets were women's work, not to be trusted to the clumsy fingers of male children, who were good only for hauling the finished product. When Siyon—too young yet to be allowed to roam the streets with his brothers and cousins—had tried to tangle himself in the work, he'd been banished to holding yarn, tugging where ordered, holding up weights ready to be looped into the emerging pattern.

But Siyon had always been good at learning by watching. At sneaking knowledge out around the edges of things that weren't for him. The flashes and twists of those gnarled fingers, the endless pattern falling from them, had been so fascinating. He'd practiced by himself, pulling threads from the ragged hem of his handed-down trousers and working them in twists and knots.

He didn't quite remember how it went, but after a few false starts, his fingers fell back into the patterns. They were slow, and clumsy, and the energy kept slipping out of his fingers.

But when it slipped, the part that he'd already knotted into pattern remained, shimmering bronze, flapping in a breeze Siyon couldn't feel. When Siyon took it up and pulled it apart again, *then* it blew away.

He was onto something here. Now he just needed more practice.

Eventually, he found a rhythm, letting the shift of his fingers, the flex of his wrists, meld into his heartbeat. All part of a deeper, wider, older beat, as the loops dripped one after another from the ends of his fingers and he wove, and knotted, and—

Something rattled, and Siyon's fingers fumbled; his head came up. Not something physical—nothing was shaking on the shelves, nothing jittering across the floor. Siyon remembered all too well what it felt like, when the earth moved. But there'd been a definite jolt in his sense of the world, and even as he blinked, faint ripples passed across the planar emanations in the room, trickling away to the south.

What was *that*?

Siyon tore apart the net he'd woven—quite a length of it, when he looked at it properly—and let the energy dissipate, shaking the last glow from his fingers. Just in time; shortly after, a slow tread came up the stairs, and Siyon hauled himself to his feet, knees creaking from being so long in the same position, in the expectation of greeting one of his guardian inqs.

Instead, Avarair Hisarani stepped into his workroom.

Siyon froze, in the panic of a cornered animal. There was nowhere to run; this *was* his bolt-hole.

Scorn sparked his heart back into beating. Had he grown so soft in barely two months of having a place of his own? There was *always* somewhere to run, there was always a fight to be had, a way to cover your retreat, a crack he could slip into where no one would follow.

Siyon had known half a hundred azatani like Avarair Hisarani—had traded most of them ingredients from the other planes—and he refused to let one rattle him.

"Here's a fucking unpleasant surprise," he growled.

Avarair's eyebrows twitched up, almost like Izmirlian's would have, in that faint and performed shock. "With such a warm welcome, how could I stay away?" Sarcasm sharpened every Avenue-crisp word.

He stepped forward, and the room seemed to grow darker. No, that wasn't a *seem*; shadow clustered in the corners, seeping down the walls, thickening under the benches and table. With it came a noxious stench of sulphur and rot, and a low and rattling growl.

Avarair arrested his own motion. "Your demon, I assume."

Laxmi was already bound to cause no injury to a human. Siyon certainly didn't mind if she wanted to try scaring the longvest off Avarair Hisarani.

"She's not mine," he said with a bright smile. "She makes her own decisions about what she does. Who she likes. That sort of thing."

"Really." Avarair set a few pages on the nearby worktable. "I can't stay, in any case. Something far more urgent has happened across the river. But I wanted to return this personally."

Siyon glanced at the pages. "What's that, then?" Even as he asked, he caught sight of a stain on a corner, where he'd spilled tea while Balian was explaining.

It was their application to use Tower Square for the Salt Night ritual.

Largely a formality anyway, Balian had said as they mopped up the tea. *I've used all the right language, made it clear this is in fulfillment of your duties, and we're outside the most high-demand times of the festival. Approval should be a matter of course.*

Something had gone belly-up.

Avarair smiled, like Siyon's sudden stomach-twisting dread was visible on his face. Maybe it was. He didn't play politics like Avarair did. Didn't play *people*. These games were beyond him.

"Things are so busy at this time of year," Avarair commented blandly. "Public Works is run off its feet with work for Salt Night. I do like to help out where I can."

"Let me guess," Siyon said. "You helped me right out of consideration."

"You're not to know how things work around here." Avarair almost dripped condescension. "It's hardly your fault, given your natural deficiencies. But this would be an unacceptable obstruction to the smooth traffic of an event that is already a nightmare of public order control. Not to mention that I believe we specified a proper alchemical working. Precisely *not* a public spectacle. If your working requires a public location, as intimated, I believe the old hippodrome is available."

Tucked away in the southeastern corner of the upper city, not far from the cliffs of the Scarp and the seacoast both. Sometimes the bravi used it for an all-blades when the matter was more honour than performance, and an audience wasn't required. On Salt Night, it'd be a haunt of those keen to avoid others—and not many of them either.

That wouldn't work. But it was quite clear that protesting would do nothing but please Avarair. "Fine," Siyon growled.

He'd find another way. Another place. Fuck Avarair Hisarani.

Who just smiled. "Don't get ideas." He even waggled a finger at Siyon. "The inquisitors are quite assiduous about matters of public order on Salt Night."

"Do you think," Siyon demanded, before he could stop himself, "that if you make it hard enough, I'll give up? Do you think that would be good for anyone? Do you think I *can*? This is who I *am*, not something you can take away."

"Anything can be taken away," Avarair disagreed. "If you try hard enough."

He didn't wait for an answer, stalking away down the stairs—past the inqs who had obviously let him in, and Siyon supposed they couldn't be blamed for that, much as he wanted to be angry at *someone*.

Siyon stepped forward to look properly at the application document. It had been stamped in red, diagonally across Balian's careful handwriting: DENIED. Rage trembled in Siyon's fingers; he crumpled the pages, screwing them up into a tight ball of fury. *Fuck* Avarair Hisarani. Fuck the whole Council. Fuck the azatani and their careful arrangements and their *rules*.

What had Siyon been thinking? Of course, even if he played by them, even if he carefully did every little contradictory thing they asked of him, he was still going to lose. That's the way the rules worked. *Their* rules.

He'd had enough. Of being their tool, of seeking their approval, of being what they'd allow him to be.

He was the Power of the Mundane—*him*, with the mud beneath his fingernails and the stone beating at his dreams, with the power flexing beneath him and bending to his will.

And he was going to do what needed to be done.

The nights leading up to Salt Night were often quiet, as preparations were made, the customary family visits were paid, and everyone caught up on their sleep before the wild celebrations.

It certainly wasn't busy enough at the newly reopened Sable House to keep Anahid from turning over—and over—in her mind what Aghut had told her.

She still wore her Lady Sable costume, as she stalked the common areas of the House, showing the face—or at least the mask—of the proprietor. Word of her true identity was spreading—Anahid knew it by the whispers that followed her progress—but until it reached the Avenues, she could pretend she was still safe.

After all, by the time the news caught ablaze in society gossip, Anahid planned to be out of the business. To have traded her involvement with Sable House for the banishment of Stepan, and the appeasement of his uncle.

It was still the best path. Regardless of what Aghut had told her—that there could be a sharper justice for Stepan, having overstepped the barons' code—it would not be wise to lean harder on Garabed Zinedani. Blood led to blood led to blood. If there was any lesson from the baron wars that echoed across the twenty years since, surely it was that without compromise, the violence might never stop.

She didn't even want Stepan Zinedani dead, Anahid told herself. That wouldn't *help*. She wanted Imelda back, and nothing could make that happen. She wanted Stepan to never hurt another Flower; that could be achieved by his banishment from Bezim, or even just his barring from the District, if actively enforced.

Anahid was prepared to be reasonable here, even if her hands still curled into helpless fists when she passed the closed door of a chamber that had been cleaned, and cleaned again, but still was not used.

Tonight became even *less* busy shortly before the bell rang Deep, when word started to trickle in that something had happened in the industrial district. Something calamitous, and alchemical, and likely to prove ruinously expensive. It was the sort of thing that turned heads away from frivolities.

"You might as well go home," Qorja said soon after, as they lingered in the entrance hall, watching the quiet square outside. "Oh, but before you do, this came in."

This was a rolled message, still carrying a lingering whiff of pipe smoke, and scrawled in a messy, sprawling hand: *See you on Salt Night, if you dare. —Mama*

"She's teasing me." Anahid tucked the message into her sash beside the little penknife. "If there's a night when it's safe for an azata to walk in the lower city, surely it's Salt Night."

"It's never entirely safe," Qorja pointed out—even as she gave a little wave and a pleased-cat smile to a departing patron. "I'll come with you again, of course."

It was reassuring to hear, but couldn't possibly happen. "One of us must be here."

"We'll go early," Qorja said firmly. "Right on sunset. Before things get too wild and while my schedule is still being followed." She lifted a hand even as Anahid opened her mouth. "Hush, mistress. It's me or Lejman, and he would prefer not to, as Shakeh Badrosani flirts *very* aggressively. But you're not going alone."

In truth, when she was in the Flower district, Anahid rarely felt alone. She was a part of something here. She had a place, be it ever so fraught. She had purpose. She had a name that was known.

She paused outside the District, amid the resinous scent of the hedge, and considered where she was going. She hadn't seen Vartan since she'd stormed out of the Palace of Justice. He hadn't approached her either, and Anahid wondered if he would. If he would leave it up to her. She wondered if she *wanted* him to.

In the end, she just went back to the Avenues.

She had a place here, as well. She could have a purpose, if she cared to take it up. She had a name that was known. All those things were true, but not in any way that gave her comfort.

The townhouse door closed behind her, into a deep and cushioned silence, broken only by the tick of the clock, endlessly marking her life into careful moments. A hush of paper from upstairs; when Anahid passed Nihath's open study door, he didn't even look up from the loose papers he was sifting through. No other movement or sound; not yet time even for the servants to be starting work. The house held its breath, as if waiting for something.

The shadows lay deep in the corridor and in the corners of Anahid's sitting room. Anahid stood in the dark with her heart racing, for no good reason. She wasn't surprised, as she'd been when Midnight had stepped out of these shadows. She wasn't in danger, as when Aghut had toyed with getting rid of her.

On Salt Night, she'd go and see Mama Badrosani. She'd have all the support she needed to confront Garabed Zinedani. And then... then it would all be over.

This—this house and its silence and its moments, this room and its desk full of invitations and notes—would be her life. All that was left. Anahid would come back here and belong nowhere else.

She turned on her heel and marched back to Nihath's study.

He blinked as she came barging in without bothering to knock. Tehroun jerked awake on the sofa, draped across it like a pale discarded scarf. For once, the sight of him didn't pinch at Anahid's heart. There were too many other things already crowding it.

"Are the inquisitors here again?" Nihath asked, as though that were the only reason she might come here.

Anahid said: "This is over. After Salt Night, I will engage a clerk for a private dissolution of our marriage."

That was all she'd come to say. She left again.

"Wait!" Nihath came rushing after her. "You can't just—why?"

The final word was almost a wail. He seemed genuinely bewildered. Anahid gaped at him. "Why? Nihath, the greater mystery is why you married me in the first place."

"But—" He needed a moment to find the next words. "But haven't we been getting on all right? We are comfortable, aren't we? We work well together? I have made astonishing advances I'd never have imagined, and you—have whatever you've been doing."

Whatever she'd been doing. He didn't care. He'd never bothered to ask. Anahid took a breath, but still when the words came, they were stiff with fury. "I have been running a Flowerhouse."

"Exactl—what?" Nihath looked startled. "But that's..."

"Scandalous?" Anahid provided, when he didn't seem capable of finishing. She took a step toward him. "Not something azatani do? Quite dangerous, actually?" The roar of the baiting pit and a bloody word daubed on Imelda's cold skin. "Yes, it's all of those things."

He blinked at her, owlish behind his spectacles. "I don't mind," he said in a small voice.

Anahid nearly laughed; she could feel it in her throat, like hysterical bile. She kept her teeth clenched tight, her breathing even, until the feeling subsided. "But I do," she said then. "I didn't know any of this was possible for me. I had never even considered looking. I don't know what else there might be. What comes next. I am stepping out to see. And I'm doing it alone."

By choice, not by default.

His confusion was obvious, but Anahid supposed that was *his* problem, not hers at all. She could walk away now, save her curiosity about one thing. "Why *did* you marry me?"

He shrugged, almost helplessly. She'd rarely seen him so flummoxed. "Isn't it what one does?"

Get married, bind families, enable trading partnerships, continue azatani lines, retain and prop up all the pillars of the society they'd built here in Bezim. *Ours.* Our city. Our certainties.

Anahid supposed it *was* what one did. Hadn't she married him for almost exactly the same reason? She'd been hunting for a husband for three years when she met him. It was what she was supposed to do.

It wasn't his fault that she hadn't realised she could step out of that trap until too late.

His frown deepened. "I don't believe my aunt will allow me to keep the townhouse if I'm not married."

His aunt, the head of the Joddani family. Anahid sighed. This wasn't her problem. She didn't have to solve or even bother with Nihath's concerns any longer. But she said, "There's no reason to bring our families and their arrangements into a private dissolution. But you're one of the foremost alchemical practitioners in the city, Nihath. I'm sure you can find a way to afford other accommodations. Possibly with a more sensible arrangement of library and workroom."

"Oh." He thought about that for a moment, then added, "*Oh.*" And then wandered back into his study, closing the door behind him.

That, Anahid supposed, was that.

She turned and found Nura the housekeeper at the head of the stairs, waiting patiently with her hands folded. She'd clearly heard all of that.

Anahid sighed. "There'll be plenty of time yet," she said, "but yes, I imagine you'll need to find a new position."

"Very good, mistress." Nura nodded.

Always entirely professional. It was part of why Anahid had hired her in the first place.

But even as Anahid turned away, Nura said, "Though, mistress, if you've a suitable role in whatever arrangements you turn to next…"

For a moment, Anahid considered the benefits of having a house-keeper of Nura's immense capability taking Sable House in hand. She didn't have the experience to take the vacant floor manager role, but with her ensuring the precision and reliability of all back-of-house arrangements, perhaps the other roles could be shuffled around and—

Anahid stopped herself. She wasn't staying at Sable House.

"I don't know what I will do next. I may be living very quietly."

One corner of Nura's mouth twitched into a smile. "Not for very long, I imagine." As she turned away down the stairs, she called back, "Breakfast will be ready directly."

Anahid smiled, alone in the corridor. Alone by choice, not default. Like her future would be.

CHAPTER 25

"Do I want to know how you knew to prepare this?" Syrah Dane-lani's voice was perfectly level but her grip on the pages of the sorcery abolition proposal crumpled the paper.

"Probably not," Zagiri replied cheerfully.

They were *meeting under sail*, which was the fancy term for *talking hurriedly while walking briskly through the corridor because they were nearly late*. Not how Zagiri wanted to have this conversation. She'd followed the appropriate procedure yesterday to schedule a meeting this morning—vital and urgent—but it turned out that when a sudden crisis erupted in the industrial district, the scheduling assistant had assumed many other problems were more vital and urgent than Zagiri's.

So under sail it was. Zagiri didn't care. The winds were blowing just the way she'd wanted them, and she didn't need her sail perfectly trimmed. And this meant Markani was also with them, skimming the proposal with a careful lack of expression on her face.

They circled the entrance hall on the third-floor gallery; something snagged Zagiri's attention in the empty space, and she had to hurry to catch up.

"There's someone *dancing in thin air* out there," Zagiri hissed, glancing back over her shoulder. The pale suggestion of a person was still there, spreading bulky white skirts in a curtsy rather than plummeting to the distant floor.

"Ghosts," Markani said absently. "Where have you been? They've been showing up all week. Relics of the Palace's past. It was the ducal residence once, you know. And the Lyraec governor's before that. I think we have more important problems." She shook the pages of Zagiri's proposal in emphasis.

Zagiri couldn't help her grin. The Palace was absolutely *buzzing*. Every second nook in the corridor had an agitated azatani argument crammed into it. Zagiri imagined she could see their words like Siyon said he could see planar emanations—words like *delay* and *forfeiture* and *catastrophic*.

The Council was ripe for a drastic solution. Zagiri had one prepared.

"We'll be lucky," Danelani muttered, "if Hisarani isn't in the bloody select committee already, whipping them up into declaring alchemy illegal in all forms and practices."

"He can't." Markani cut her gaze at Zagiri behind the prefect's back. "And I imagine Miss Savani knows it."

Zagiri did. "Converting a single factory to non-alchemical production would be expensive and time-consuming," she recited. She had planned her leap before she took it, this time. "Doing all of them at once is impossible. It certainly couldn't be done to meet the needs of all the trading ventures due to set sail in the week after Salt Night. If Avarair Hisarani tries to force it, he'll be keelhauled."

Part of Zagiri rather hoped he'd try.

She'd won. She'd *beaten* him. She was going to enjoy this.

They marched down the last corridor, Danelani's jaw clenched tight. "There's been no preparation for this. I've had no discussions. I've gauged no support."

"They'll support it." Markani sounded no more pleased about any of it than the prefect did. "They don't have a choice. Their ships have come apart in the middle of the Carmine Sea and this is the only lifeboat. You're going to be a hero, Syrah. You're going to look bold and innovative and energetic. You could run for a second term on this, if it goes well."

"*If*," Danelani growled, and paused in the corridor to turn on Zagiri, brandishing her fistful of pages—the reform, along with the notes and speaking points Zagiri had prepared for her. Everything she needed. "This is not how we do business."

That, Zagiri reflected, was probably the sound of her losing her job. It didn't matter. Not if this worked. "Maybe it should be," she answered.

Markani shoved open the door. They were met with shouting, which was nothing new, and a seething glare from Avarair Hisarani, which *was* new, and moreover glorious as the first sun after rain. Zagiri wanted to bask in it.

But there was no time. Three members on the near side of the table jumped up to grab at Danelani's white sleeve as she strode to her seat, already shouting, "The select committee will come to order!"

They didn't, not noticeably.

"This is absolutely outrageous!" one azatan bellowed. "I demand that Siyon Velo—"

"Velo had nothing to do with it," the superintendent of inquisitors snapped. "His detail reports he was at his residence for the entire night. Which, from their notes, can be confirmed by Azatan Hisarani."

Avarair looked more sour still.

"Why *wasn't* he there?" demanded an azata from farther down the table. "Why wasn't he *stopping this*?"

All eyes turned to the bottom of the table, where neither Siyon nor Nihath was present. As an emergency session for urgent and security-related matters, non-Council personnel were discouraged unless essential. Zagiri had made a point of telling Nihath that he didn't need to come. The last thing she wanted was him coming up with a clever solution to this fascinating problem.

Markani leapt into the available gap in hysteria. "The members will recall that we directed Master Velo to concentrate his attention very specifically, and in fact bound him severely to that end."

She could have added that it had been Avarair Hisarani's idea, but from the sudden shift of attention, everyone remembered who was to blame.

Avarair took his chance. "It cannot be denied, however, that the current crisis was caused by alchemy, and only alchemy can solve it."

"There aren't enough damn alchemists!" someone shouted from the far end of the table.

"Exactly!" Syrah Danelani said.

At the same time as Avarair Hisarani. In the prefect's moment of surprise, he continued with: "Which is why we must enact an emergency mandate to enlist the services of every practitioner—even those not currently formally registered—to provide immediate remedy." He waved a generous hand. "With suitable recompense for their time and the disruption of their other ventures."

Further shouting from the table—cries of *Substandard labour!* and *Who will pay for that?* and various parties insisting that certain factories should be first.

Zagiri felt a stab of panic. He was talking about press-ganging the city's alley practitioners. Forcing them to do the work. And while they would certainly be paid, this would also be a chance for a list to be made of all those practitioners who *weren't* registered.

Maybe they'd be safe for a season or two, while gratitude for their service lingered. But when that evaporated in the heat of fear, and the azatani sought to punish unlawful alchemy, that list would still exist.

This would be *worse*. Zagiri bit her lip to keep from shouting and fixed her eyes on Danelani, who had to *do something*, dammit; why wasn't she doing something?

It was Markani who spoke up: "My well-meaning colleague goes too far in his enthusiasm for a solution. Unfortunately an emergency mandate for labour can be enacted only in conditions of natural disaster or war."

"It's a disaster!" someone shouted. "Have you *seen* the industrial district?"

An azatan near the head of the table snapped, "It *was* bloody war; who set the damn things off?"

"The bloody Revarri!" an azata accused. "Always jealous of our—"

"That Northerner has met with all sorts," someone else snapped, and Zagiri's attention whipped that way, but she couldn't see who it had been.

"The Laders' Guild has claimed responsibility," the superintendent said sternly, frowning at the wild conjecture.

But that had little effect. "They *would*," one azata sneered. "Always claiming to have done more than they have. Just a lazy rabble. Where would *they* get these sorts of resources?"

Zagiri found her mouth open, and closed it again quickly.

Danelani banged her mallet on the table and dragged the meeting back to some sort of order. They seemed almost eager to calm down. As though they were hoping that *someone* might be able to solve this.

"Security questions of a prosaic nature are not the concern of this select committee," Danelani pointed out. "Though I am sure this afternoon's emergency Council session will engage the matter thoroughly. *Our* role is to consider a solution to the alchemical emergency. The junior secretary's suggestion"—and she nodded to Avarair without looking his way—"though unlawful, highlights what is necessary. We require a quick influx of *voluntary* alchemical labour." She took a breath, looking imperiously down the length of the table; Zagiri, who didn't have a meeting to control, looked at Avarair instead, and so she saw the quick flash of hastily concealed chagrin as Danelani said: "I propose we strike the crime of sorcery from the ledger of Bezim's laws."

Outrage, of course, and chaos. But not as much as there might have been; Danelani had been canny in letting them spill some wind from their sails already. Now they were shouting as much at each other as at her, this one reminding *that* one that they'd just been lamenting the lack of alchemical assistance, and two more besides berating everyone for being squeamish about technicalities and thereby risking profit.

They were already flagging when they turned their demands on Danelani.

But what about the risk to the city? Already (she replied smoothly, without even glancing at the notes Zagiri had given her) sorcery cases were regularly thrown out on the grounds that Master Velo had ensured that there *was* no risk of unbalancing the planes. Legal precedent had been established, and any genuine risk was in fact being missed by the current arrangement of laws.

But it's always been this way! No, obviously, it hasn't; that's why the Sundering occurred in the first place, but the very creation of the sorcery law was the sensible response to a set of circumstances that no longer pertain, and the Council of Bezim has always been bound not by tradition, but by sense.

But what about miscreant practitioners? Surely any crime that can be committed by alchemy can also be committed without it. Damage to property? Injury or death to a person or persons? Charlatanism or fast dealing? All could be prosecuted under existing laws for damage and injury and fraudulent activity. Indeed, this would mean the current rash of street charlatans with shoddy charms and amulets could be more quickly and efficiently prosecuted.

It went on, back and forth, again and again. Like waves battering against the shore, but the tide was inexorable. It flowed in Syrah Danelani's favour, and there was nothing Avarair Hisarani could do but fume as the water lapped at his boots.

Eventually Danelani rapped with her mallet. "Enough. The select committee will vote upon the proposal that we recommend to the Council this very afternoon the striking of sorcery from the ledger of crimes."

It carried. Not just technically, but with an overwhelming majority. Only two members voted against. Avarair Hisarani abstained.

"The recommendation will be entered in this afternoon's Council agenda as carrying the full endorsement of this select committee," Syrah Danelani declared.

It was only after the room had drained—members hurrying away to make the best use of their inside information on what was coming—that Markani turned to Zagiri and said, in a tone so dry it bordered on bitter: "It seems you've achieved your objective."

Victory fizzed inside Zagiri like a flare. "That was perfect. I hadn't even *thought* about all that business about risks being overlooked by dismissal of sorcery charges."

"You are not," Danelani said wearily, "the only person who has considered this." She rose from her chair and looked at Zagiri, flat and bleak.

Zagiri knew it should bother her. She should try to look abashed, or at least a little contrite. But she'd *won*. She'd done it! No one would be arrested for sorcery again in Bezim, and that was because *she* had overcome every silly ingrained political nonsense reason against making it happen.

She was still smiling even as she said: "I'm fired, aren't I?"

Danelani sighed. "No. Because when what you've done comes out, it will look obvious that I knew, and that I fired you but did not report it. No," she repeated, more firmly, as she drew herself up. "I know nothing about any of this. But you—" She considered Zagiri, her mouth set firm and unyielding. "You may carry on performing the functions of a clerk, you may even retain your desk in my office, but you will be no part of my strategy or planning. Do as you wish."

This was the trade Zagiri had made: her career—or at least *this* career—for this reform.

Even as Danelani swept from the room, Markani at her heels, Zagiri nodded to herself.

She considered it a good deal.

Siyon was—

He had been—

He couldn't remember. He was here, in the dark. He was here, wrapped in stone. He was here, and his eyes were closed, and something demanded his attention, something he missed, something he yearned for, and if he could just open his eyes he could—

"Siyon?" A voice. Familiar. "Are you there?"

Siyon reached for it. For Izmirlian. For the way his intonation had wrapped around Siyon's name and—

"Oh, you *are* here."

Siyon startled, wrenching his eyes open, dizzy for a moment as his awareness of the world fought sickeningly against plain sight.

He wasn't in the dark; he was in his living room. He was Siyon Velo, not—

"Whoa. Careful." Hands on his shoulders, holding him steady; a face close to his, clear brown eyes peering at him.

Balian. Not Izmirlian.

Siyon tried to say something, but the words scraped; his throat felt coated in stone, dry and dark. He coughed.

"Are you all right?" Balian's brows knit with concern.

Siyon wasn't sure of the answer to that. He didn't know how he'd got here. He didn't remember where he'd *been*. Upstairs? Waiting for Mayar for another round of practice for his Salt Night ritual? Had he fallen asleep?

His fingers were tingling. When Siyon looked down, his hands were coated in bronze energy, thick and oozing like honey. He jerked back, away from Balian's steadying grip; what might happen if he touched the azatan with *these* hands?

Balian watched as Siyon shook his hands furiously, that furrow between his eyebrows not going away. But all he said was: "Well, I brought spicebread." He reached for the bakery bag he'd clearly discarded on the worktable in his rush to get to Siyon.

"Thanks," Siyon croaked, which didn't seem to do much for Balian's worry. He cleared his throat again and almost sounded like himself when he added, "I'll make some coffee, shall I?"

Made some coffee, tidied up a little, watered the rubber fig, pulled himself together. They took the coffee and pastry out onto the little balcony where the wrought iron stairs spiralled up to the next floor. Crumbs fell onto the workmen on ladders, stringing bunting along the street from shopfront to shopfront, in the bright white of salt and new beginnings.

Balian's spicebread was fucking fancy, with not just cinnamon but nutmeg and the sharp bite of ginger and other things Siyon didn't even recognise. Nothing like the sweet-salt plain stuff of Siyon's childhood, lucky if it had a pinch of cinnamon in the whole batch. This was how the azatani did Salt Night, apparently. Izmirlian had probably eaten spicebread like this.

"I figured," Balian said, chewing thoughtfully at his slice, "it's traditional, and you *are* embarking on a new venture, of a sort."

"I won't say no to any luck I can get," Siyon agreed.

Siyon was just relaxing when Balian said, far too casually, "So what was all that, then? When I came in?"

And he tensed up all over again. "What—er. What did it look like?"

Balian opened his mouth a couple of times, so at least Siyon wasn't the only one having trouble with this. "Like you weren't even in your body," he finally said. There was something almost imploring in the look he turned on Siyon. Like he wanted Siyon to explain it all. For the first time, he looked as young as he probably was. "You were so *still*. The whole room felt...All the hair stood up on the back of my neck. And your eyes, when you opened them, they flashed bronze, like polished metal."

Siyon looked down at his hands, like they might be crawling with Mundane power again. What had happened? What *was* happening? Something was rising. Something was waiting. Something was reaching out to him, into him, through him.

"It'll all be better," he said, "after Salt Night. That will sort everything out."

Balian didn't look entirely convinced. Siyon wasn't sure he was either. One way or another, Salt Night *would* make a difference.

Siyon hoped it would be in a way that they could all live with. He worried about Midnight, and his shadowed threats. He worried about his dreams, and their stone demands. He worried that there was nothing else he could do. This was the only path that felt anything like right.

"What will sort everything out?" asked a new voice from above. Mayar came down the spiral staircase, presumably having come over the rooftops again, avoiding the inqs. "Oh, is that spicebread? I *love* this festival!"

Mayar fell greedily upon the bag of spicebread as Balian tore the paper open farther, remarking that it was light on cinnamon this year. Apparently there'd been some trouble with supply.

Siyon hadn't noticed any lack. Mayar didn't seem to mind either.

"Are you here to practice more?" Balian asked Mayar. "I don't know that it's wise. Siyon had some sort of turn earlier. He needs to rest."

Mayar shrugged, mouth dotted with well-spiced crumbs. "I keep saying he's got this."

"I just think we should—" Siyon started, then stopped. Why was he so agitated about planning this? He'd always done his best work flying from the bowsprit, making it up as he went. Every time he'd tried to pull together something serious, something staged, something formal, it had come apart in his hands.

Maybe that was why. This *couldn't* come apart. It had to work, or having failed the select committee—and the Council—was going to be the least of Siyon's worries. What might it *mean*, if the energy below kept rising to the surface? More magic filling the paths that superstition had made for it? More monsters roaming the streets?

Something that washed them all away in a tide of energy?

Siyon *needed* to succeed.

He couldn't afford to strangle this. Maybe he did need room to breathe. To make up just a little bit as he went. To leave just a little to chance. To let his instincts and the rising power guide him on the night.

Mayar clapped him on the shoulder. "That's the spirit," they said absently, reaching for more spicebread. "I'll be there with you anyway."

Siyon rubbed at his face. "That might not be wise. I still don't know where I'm doing this, and wherever I *do* end up, Avarair Hisarani is likely to be pestering me and anyone with me."

Balian shrugged. "It's not as though he can have anyone arrested for sorcery anymore," he said, then looked between Siyon's and Mayar's blank and confused expressions. "Ah, right. You haven't heard—a motion was introduced to the Council via the select committee to strike the charge of sorcery from the ledger of Bezim's laws." Balian's smile had a strange tilt to its usual easy curve that Siyon couldn't interpret.

"From Zagiri," he guessed, and that smile twitched flatter. "She did it."

Mayar made a dismissive noise. "They'll still find reasons to harass us."

Probably. Certainly Avarair would. But this would make such a difference, to so many people. And if Siyon *could* resettle the Mundane energy, who knew what might be possible in the city for all the practitioners who could now work openly?

It needed to work. Siyon needed to have everything in place.

"What if I use Tower Square anyway?" he asked aloud. "Despite having it refused?" Maybe Siyon could actually go up the tower itself again. It had been a good vantage the other day, and Zagiri had demonstrated how to capture the entire square's attention from up there.

But Balian shook his head. "They'll have orders to watch for you; he'll have made sure of that." No need to specify which *he*. "And it *will* be very crowded. Difficult to get away afterward."

Siyon wasn't sure afterward was going to matter. He would do his thing, and then the rest of the night would see whether it worked. He could sit it out in a Palace holding cell as easily as anywhere else. But he appreciated Balian's concern. "Where else is public enough? Central enough?"

"Base of the Kellian Way?" Mayar suggested. "There's a bit of open space on this side of the Swanneck. A few coffeehouses."

A bit was right; the square there was more of a squashed triangle and less a place to linger than one to pass through.

"What about out front of the Eldren Hall?" Balian asked.

Of course he would. He was azatani. The Eldren Hall was *their* fancy place, with its narrow towers and their stained glass depictions of the planes in allegory, and its murals of the grand moments of azatani history. They held their own rituals there—the Harbour Master's Ball and whatever else. Siyon didn't know. *Siyon* wasn't invited. It wasn't a place for the likes of him.

"It's not in use on Salt Night," Balian continued. "And there's that space out the front, I think it used to be where carriages pulled up, when we still kept horses before the Sundering. The crowd can spill out onto the Kellian Way itself. It's quite wide at that point. Lots of people set up there."

Siyon recalled the last time he'd passed it, there'd been a holy man shouting at a small crowd. About *him*, as it happened.

A place of ritual. It could be the place of *his* ritual.

Balian was tilting his head now, thinking through his own arguments, and their counterarguments, and onward and outward in intricacies Siyon probably couldn't even imagine. "It might work," he concluded. "If you're early, and quick, and unexpected. I'll come along too, of course. If anybody gets in your way, I can probably talk fast and official enough to make them pause long enough for you to get started."

Siyon glanced at Mayar, who was poking around in the corners of the now-empty bakery bag, picking up spicebread crumbs with a licked finger. They shrugged. But then again, Mayar still wasn't convinced about the need for the crowd. Mayar hadn't seen what Auntie Geryss had done.

Auntie Geryss had hired the bravi to spread the word, whip up the crowd, get the energy started. Siyon would just have to show up and hope; he didn't want too many people—the wrong people—knowing what he was doing, or where.

"I'll probably wind up arrested over this," Siyon admitted, glancing at Balian. "It's something you should think about. They're going to throw everything at me. Avarair Hisarani will make sure of it."

Balian swallowed and lifted his chin a little. "He can fucking try," he said.

There was Siyon's bad influence. But he couldn't help a smile. In a way, he wasn't alone.

In every other way, he was. There was no one else after all. He was the Power of the Mundane. Just him, and whatever lurked in the depths.

He would have to be enough.

CHAPTER 26

Officially, Salt Night began at sunset, but in previous years, Anahid had been to luncheons that loitered on past the Fade bell and tacked without pause into the evening's festivities.

She'd been invited to some this year as well. She'd declined.

The crowds were already swelling as Anahid crossed the bunting-decked Boulevard, one hand lifted to shield her eyes from the glare of a sun still a hand's width off the horizon. She had to thread her way between already jubilant knots of laborers and around little dancing circles, and Anahid thought she might have missed her chance to see Siyon before his ritual.

But when she reached the alleyway behind his building, he was at the gate to his apartment, arguing with his guarding inqs. One of the grey-uniformed pair was a very young man Anahid didn't know, but the other, with arms crossed over her chest and an unimpressed slant to her sharp-nosed face, was Olenka.

"Has it occurred to you," she was saying as Anahid approached, "that we're on your side?"

"Rarely," Siyon shot back. He glanced up and added, "Hello, Ana. Wait, *are* you on my side?"

Olenka shrugged one shoulder. "We're theoretically here to assist you in protecting the city."

Siyon squinted at her suspiciously; Anahid couldn't blame him. The fallen angel's motives had always been opaque.

"Not to interrupt," Anahid said, as she did, "but I wanted to wish you luck, Siyon. I can't come along. I've an appointment." Euphemistic enough for the current audience.

By the sharp cut of Siyon's eyes, he caught her meaning quite clearly. "Down the Scarp?" At her nod, he wrinkled his nose. "Better tonight than any other time. Tell me you're not going alone."

Exasperation caught like a sigh in her throat; did no one think she could look after herself? "Qorja insists on coming with me." Which was part of why they needed to go so early; Anahid glanced at the sky, where the sun slanted ever lower.

"No insult to the lady," Siyon said, "but I'd rather someone a little more intimidating."

Did he think Anahid hadn't considered her options? "Taking a legion into a lion's den won't help."

Siyon frowned grumpily, which was almost sweet.

A new voice scraped out of the shadowed stairwell behind him. "What about a hidden knife?"

Anahid *had* one of those—but from the grin that coalesced from the gloom, all teeth and gleeful menace, Laxmi was speaking metaphorically.

Golden eyes blinked, and the demon leaned one scaled elbow nonchalantly against Siyon's shoulder. "I'm not going anywhere with *that*." She flicked one talon in the general direction of Olenka, who was pointedly not looking at her. (Unlike the other inq, who couldn't seem to decide if he was fascinated by Laxmi's womanly features or terrified by her everything else.)

"And you'll just get tangled up in the ritual," Siyon agreed. He lifted an eyebrow in Anahid's direction. "Up to you."

So when Anahid swept by Sable House to pick up Qorja, on her way to the Scarp descent, it was with more hidden cargo than just the penknife snug in the sash of her dress. Laxmi's presence was a damp touch at the back of Anahid's neck, a prickle along her shoulder, a press at her waist, where the demon's tail had coiled around her in the moments before she faded into invisibility. It was strangely intimate and more than a little reassuring.

This was Anahid's first time down the Scarp. She'd seen it from a distance, sailing in the harbour during the Regatta, in the years before she'd decided the social opportunities weren't worth fighting her queasiness. From that vantage, the cliff that cut across the city was merely a dramatic piece of scenery.

On the switchback path that cut back and forth across its face, picking a careful way down, the entire thing seemed far more massive. There was no sensible place to pause amid the traffic teeming in both directions, and Anahid didn't entirely trust the steadiness of her footing, but she couldn't help sneaking glances at the view as they went. From here, the lower city was already cast into dusk by the looming bulk of the upper city. Lanterns glittered among the alleycanals, gilding the fallen arcades, tenement mazes, and crumbled old monuments. It looked romantic, with the mangroves now growing amid the ruins of mansions that had once overlooked the sea from the headland. At the farthest extent of the fallen promontory, the dome of the old observatory caught one last glint of the sun's dying light.

Romantic and beautiful, but the farther they descended, the more the decay became evident. Buildings leaned against one another, cracked and sagging. Board bridges had been laid between balconies and upper-storey windows when the former streets had disappeared beneath brackish water and silt. Paint had peeled and brick crumbled. The broken bones of the old city had been splinted with make-do, and sent back to work.

There were still some azatani circles that referred to this as *the lost districts*, as though they had fallen entirely beneath the waves. But especially on Salt Night, the lower city crawled and pulsed and heaved with life; the noise rose to Anahid's ears, on the same breeze that carried a thick stink of mud and sweaty bodies. Drums beat and voices lifted in raucous song and someone, somewhere, had a bright and brassy trumpet they were playing with more enthusiasm than skill.

As she and Qorja came down the last switchback, the Lower

Market opened up below. Even at this hour, the stalls were teeming with shoppers and raucous with touting and haggling, all of it illuminated by the smoky light of actual torches, not alchemical lanterns. The wide trading area lay atop the ruin of buildings that had been thoroughly flattened by the Sundering, and then flattened further for the easier delivery of produce hauled down from the upper city.

Beyond, precarious balconies hung off patched-up old tenements, draped with colourful flags. Anahid knew just enough about the barons' business now to know that they were advertising *other* wares—narcotics and contraband and violent services—but not enough to decode the offerings herself.

Qorja pushed her way through the crowd, Anahid following close behind. The way down into the lower city proper was wide and well-trodden, but barely any of it was actual *road*. They stepped over the packed-down rubble of fallen buildings and descended half a staircase of fractured masonry. The buildings rose up around them, once spacious apartments for comfortable artisans and middling merchants. Now walls had been knocked down and buildings shoved together—by the Sundering and by generations of alteration thereafter—and the resulting rooms packed full of people. This was prime lower city housing—with easy access to the Scarp descent, and something like fresh water. While the fountains didn't run anymore down here, some had been rigged with a hand pump and the water was still clean.

Siyon, Anahid remembered, used to live down here.

Dark was falling properly now, shrouding the worst of the neglect in ambiguous shadow. The streets—or the paths and impromptu bridges and shortcuts through buildings that passed for them—were no less crowded. Along with the white bunting of Salt Night, there were narrow red ribbons, whose importance Anahid didn't understand, fluttering everywhere in the sea breeze.

"Papa Badrosani's blood," Qorja noted quietly when Anahid asked her. "They used to say he'd died to keep the lower city safe from the Bitch Queen. Hung the ribbons in memory and protection. Honestly, I thought the cult had fallen out of fashion years ago."

Some sort of parade was going on through the old commercial district, where the marble facades of former arcades had been pried off and reused, leaving the buildings scabrous or pared back to frames.

No such depredations had touched the Old Theatre. It rose like a benevolent father over the crumbling buildings around it, topped with a verdigris-addled dome shining beneath the rising full moon.

The double wooden doors were solid, though propped open, and flanked only by layers of new handbills promising excitement, music, and ladies in sparse but feathered costumes.

It made Anahid hesitate. "I thought there'd be security."

"Mama embraces all-comers; it's getting away again that can be the tricky part." Qorja looked at Anahid. "Are you sure about this?"

Anahid touched her sash, then the sweat-damp back of her neck. She was sure there was no other way this could be done, at least.

Inside the theatre, the foyer carried memories of being fancy and fashionable, though now the mirrors were crazed with cracks, the velvet hung lank, and the gilt was peeling from chandeliers that provided barely enough light to see. In a corner of the foyer, a trio of hefty muscle had pulled a mismatched set of chairs around a table and seemed to be playing carrick. None of them looked up as Anahid and Qorja passed through, to the grimy marble stairs curving up to the mezzanine balcony and the doors to the theatre proper.

Anahid paused there, one hand on the cracked railing. "You could wait here," she suggested to Qorja.

And earned a very stern look. "Lejman will be disappointed if I allow you to come to harm."

Anahid smiled. "Are you going to protect me with a fan and a stern rhymed couplet?"

Qorja tossed her head. "Perhaps."

At least the amusement meant that Anahid didn't feel quite paralysed with nerves. She threaded her way along a row of theatre seats to where Mama Badrosani sat in a cloud of pipe smoke. Qorja waited at the end of the row, but Anahid didn't really go alone. Her skin felt reassuringly clammy.

Shakeh Badrosani gave Anahid a blatant once-over as she

approached. "You're even bolder than I was expecting, za. You'd make the sharks nervous."

The stage in front of them was set for a battle scene, with a backdrop of the sort of snow-piled winter that Bezim never saw. What looked like a genuine cannon would be more impressive without the two half-dressed chorus girls lounging against it in a drape of luridly dyed feathers, sharing a cigarette.

"You're the one who said the alternative was being a minnow," Anahid noted.

Mama laughed so hard she started to cough. "Sure sounds like me," she admitted, wiping at her streaming eyes. "Go on then, let me hear your piece same as the others."

Anahid obliged. "The Zinedanis have caused great wrong, to one of my Flowers and thus to me and my business. I intend to negotiate with them for justice."

"Negotiate." Mama snorted and parked her pipe back between her teeth. "What's the rest of what I told you, sugarplum?"

Anahid knew just what she meant. "You're all threats, in this business."

"We're *all* threats," Mama repeated, in her rough and smoky drawl. "What in the Abyss makes you think Zinedani's going to sit down and negotiate with *you*?"

"The weight of your approval," Anahid provided promptly. "Combined with that, already obtained, from Midnight and Aghut."

One eyebrow—more paint than natural—lifted. "You got Midnight in on this? Well now, that sewer rat doesn't usually come to the surface for this sort of thing." Mama leaned forward, with a creak of corsetry and a gleam in her eye that seemed almost predatory. "What *else* you got?"

Anahid cleared her throat. It was hot in here; sweat trickled down her spine. "If he refuses to negotiate, I will bring a formal complaint, to you and the other barons, that Stepan Zinedani has taken a life without due leave."

That earned her a satisfied nod. "You should just do that," Mama advised.

Part of Anahid still thought so too. But there were *reasons*. "I would prefer to end this more peacefully."

Mama laughed, loud and rough. "*Peacefully*. Oh my stars." She waved a hand. "Go, azata. Do as you like. See what *peacefully* gets you. I'll not intervene further, but don't say I didn't warn you."

"May the winds turn to your endeavours," Anahid said, like this was an azatani trade deal being concluded.

"Oh," Mama murmured, as Anahid filed away down the row of seats, "they usually do, one way or another."

Qorja kept pace with Anahid back up the aisle. "Now what?"

"Now…" Anahid had to take a breath, steady herself. "Now we make an appointment with Garabed Zinedani. As public as we can arrange—I'd prefer plenty of witnesses, but I suppose I'm the supplicant."

She ran a hand along her sash as they descended the stairs in the garish foyer. It was darker than ever in here, the shadows seeming to shift between the velvet-wrapped pillars. Pinpricks skittered along Anahid's shoulders, as though in answer.

"Or maybe," she considered aloud, "I'll simply go tonight. No sense in letting him make too many plans."

At the base of the steps, Anahid realised the shadows weren't only *seeming* to move. A figure stepped out from behind a pillar, barring the way to the door. Anahid stopped, Qorja clutching at her shoulder. Above them, a door boomed closed with echoing finality.

The figure stepped forward, into the faint light.

"So very true," Garabed Zinedani said. "But as ever, azata, you're too late, and far out of your depth."

The sun was just starting to sink behind the city wall as Zagiri shoved her way through the crowd on the Kellian Way outside the Eldren Hall. Things were growing merrier by the moment. She turned down three invitations to dance, two offered kisses, and uncountable swigs from jugs of rakia.

Well, maybe she didn't turn down *all* the rakia. She deserved a little celebration. Sure, not everything had gone the way she wanted, but sorcery was off the list of crimes in Bezim, and the azatani were feeling less unassailable, and she could claim some credit for all of that.

Plus, as she pushed her way through the thickening crowd, she heard more than one person complaining about spicebread this year— that it was expensive, or their usual baker was out, or the recipe had changed. Bakers were finding ways around the cinnamon shortage, it seemed, and Zagiri hoped they were complaining to their azatani connections and patrons.

The revolution was making itself felt, and with enough prickles, even the azatani would have to stop sitting comfortably.

Some of her smugness slipped a little when she arrived at the front steps of the Eldren Hall to find Siyon standing at the bottom, arguing with an inquisitor captain.

The passing crowds were starting to linger, like flotsam caught in a net of curiosity. Bezim liked nothing more than gawking at a bit of spectacle—especially if there was the chance of a fight, and you never knew, when people started shouting. The Eldren Hall made a dramatic backdrop, with its stained glass and towers, and there was good visibility for onlookers on the wide Kellian Way—that was presumably part of the thinking in using this for whatever Siyon was trying to do.

Except clearly the inqs—or someone giving them orders—had thought of it too.

Siyon wasn't alone—Balian was with him, along with Olenka and another inquisitor who was looking more and more worried as the argument went on.

"You know who I am," Siyon said, shaking one purple-coated arm.

The inq captain blocking the stairs winced a little. "I do, Master Velo. And I'm sorry, I really am. But the instructions from the Committee for Public Works were quite explicit. Things are very..." He hesitated but couldn't find a better word than: "weird, right now, after that business over the river and the monsters and...My chief will kick me down to the Specials if I don't follow orders exactly."

"I'm not going to be blocking anything up here, am I?" Siyon argued—wheedled might be more like it. "You can stay here and move me on if it's a problem. But I'll be really quick." He glanced over his shoulder, at the lowering sun. Things were getting tight, if he wanted to weigh anchor at sunset.

"It's not that." The captain seemed very uncomfortable about all this.

So Zagiri drew herself up, trying despite her bravi leathers to channel Anahid, and Syrah Danelani, and every other azata used to having her questions answered, and stepped up beside Siyon on the steps. "What *are* those orders, Captain? Exactly?"

Maybe, somehow, there'd be a hole in them, and they could all get what they wanted.

But the inq captain, with some relief, said: "No one allowed close to significant public buildings without the presence of the special festival security subcommittee chair or the display of his family sigil."

"Let me guess," Zagiri said, suspended between exhausted frustration and boiling rage. "That subcommittee chair would be..."

The inq captain provided readily: "Junior Undersecretary Avarair Hisarani."

The man was an octopus: many-armed, endlessly inventive, and always ending up in exactly the place she thought she'd already beaten him out of.

Siyon's face reflected a similar mix of disbelief and hopeless fury. "I'm sorry," Zagiri told him. "I hadn't realised he'd eeled his way into the festival planning as well. Can we find somewhere else?"

"Right now?" Siyon looked pointedly toward the increasingly ruddy west.

Someone cleared their throat; Balian stepped up on Siyon's other side. "My apologies, Captain, but did you mention the display of a family sigil?"

"Tower Square?" Zagiri suggested. "If we can get you up on the Last Duke, the crowd should block the inqs from getting to you before you're done?"

On Siyon's other side, Balian said, "Yes, I see. Like this one?"

He tugged a chain out from beneath the neck of his shirt, holding up a heavy ring. A family sigil, the sort used to seal trading orders and official correspondence.

The inq captain caught it, examined the face, and said, "Very good, Azatan Hisarani."

What? How had Balian managed to get hold of a Hisarani sigil? How had he *known*?

As Zagiri gaped, Balian nodded and ordered crisply, "Clear the steps. Hold the crowd at the base, if you would?"

And the inq captain nodded. Followed his orders. Just like that.

Balian turned around, face serious. His gaze skidded quickly over Zagiri, before fixing on Siyon. "I'm sorry," he said.

Siyon was staring at him too, his face frozen still. "You're the younger brother," he said.

Balian nodded sharply. "I'm sorry," he repeated. "I can explain. But I don't think we have time right now."

The younger brother. The younger *Hisarani* brother. There were three of them—Zagiri knew that. The eldest politician, the youngest trader, and the middle wastrel. Everyone knew that. She just hadn't thought...

He hadn't *wanted* them to think. He'd deceived them all. He'd flat-out *lied*.

Zagiri stared at him—at Balian *Hisarani*, not Markani. All those mentions of his brother. All those times he'd been unwilling to come up to the Palace with her. All those sly questions about what Siyon had done over the summer.

"You fucking—" she started.

But Siyon interrupted. "You're right; we don't have time. Let's get this set up." He shoved a heavy roll of cloth into Balian's arms and hefted a box into his own.

The sun was squatting low and fat on the horizon. Fortunately, there wasn't that much to set up. Just a box to make a platform, a bit of rich black cloth to drape over the top, and that was all the decoration—all the *pageantry*—required.

Siyon was his own show; he didn't need anything but that coat, and his own presence, to tell the people of Bezim there was going to be something worth paying attention to. They were already mobbing the bottom of the stairs, the crowd thickening out into the Kellian Way in both directions.

As Siyon stepped up on his box, and lifted his arms, the crowd roared its approval. Balian turned to her, but Zagiri didn't want to hear anything he had to say. She slipped down the stairs and only then spotted someone at the front of the crowd, being restrained by one of the inqs and waving furiously.

"Mayar!" Zagiri hurried over. "You're late. Let this one through; the Alchemist needs their help."

"No." Mayar caught at Zagiri's wrist, even as the inq relaxed his grip. "No—he's got this, he doesn't need me. There's something else. We have to go. You and me. Now."

Something else. Something that had delayed Mayar in getting here, something important enough to miss Siyon's show.

Something for *Zagiri* to deal with?

She glanced back up the stairs. Balian had sat down, right near the bottom, out of the way. The crowd was still cheering as Siyon waved, and laughed, and accepted their welcome on this, the wildest of Bezim's many wild nights. He *was* the Alchemist—*their* Alchemist—in his purple coat, and his slightly scruffy glory, and his anything's-possible grin.

He had this.

"What is it?" she shouted near Mayar's ear as they shoved and edged their way through the crowd, swimming against the pressing tide of curiosity.

"The other night," they called back, "in the industrial district, were your little surprises in a black velvet bag?"

Uneasiness lurched in Zagiri's stomach. How could they know that, unless... "Yes!"

Mayar glanced back, their face grim. "We have a problem."

This wasn't how Siyon had imagined starting his ritual, even once he'd shifted his thinking from Tower Square to something more makeshift. Sure, there was only so much gravitas he could bring to an impromptu performance on a monument's steps without any sort of real staging, but he'd sort of intended to *try*.

Should have known better. Scrambling to make it by the skin of his teeth was how Siyon worked. At least he had the coat. That was probably the only reason he was getting any attention. Certainly the reason that, when he lifted his arms, the crowd gave a cheerful bellow in response. They were already feeling merry, launching themselves at this night-long festival already lubricated with rakia and the joy of having made it through another, very strange year.

It was enough. It would have to be enough. He could work from this.

Siyon glanced down the stairs, where Zagiri was talking to—was that Mayar? Both of them went shoving away through the crowd. No time to miss them; no time to wonder what was going on. No time left at all.

There was Balian, waiting on the bottom step, looking up at Siyon. Balian Hisarani.

For a moment, Siyon couldn't look away from his face, hunting in its lines and angles for someone else. Perhaps, perhaps... in the knit of those eyebrows when he was concentrating. In the quirk of his smile, when something was amusing him. In his determination to see this through.

Siyon needed to concentrate. The crowd was jostling, shifting impatiently. Somewhere out on the Kellian Way, a group had started chanting a lader's song—slow for now, but it would speed up as their restlessness grew. They did that at the opera, on those rowdy matinee afternoons when the seats went cheap.

Izmirlian would have loved this. The audacity of doing this at the Eldren Hall, and tweaking his brother's nose in the process. The vibrancy and discovery of bringing together Bezim, and everything it was, everything it believed, everything it could become. The mystery of what Siyon might achieve here, and what might come next.

He'd always been so fascinated by the mysteries that lay beyond the everyday. He'd launched himself into one such mystery, with an anticipatory smile and a sense of adventure.

Siyon missed him so much that he practically *was* here. Balian probably missed him too, just as much, if differently.

He couldn't dwell on this right now.

The crowd lapped at the stairs of the Eldren Hall like a hungry sea. People climbed the trees lining the Kellian Way to get a better vantage. A festival air lay heavy over the shifting mass of people, bulked up with anticipation and a frilly edge of curiosity.

To Siyon's eye, shimmering bronze energy was already rising, like fragrant steam off fresh-baked spicebread.

He sent a brief prayer of thanks to Auntie Geryss—wherever in the world she had ended up when she fled the city—for so many of the ideas he was harnessing this evening. He wished anew that she was here; he'd love to show her what he could do. He'd love to have her help. He'd love to see what she might make in a city where magic flowed like water.

But this was Siyon's task now. His responsibility. His to achieve— or fuck up.

He was alone, and yet he wasn't *anything like* alone. There were hundreds of people crammed in front of him now, and more arriving at the fringes every moment. People jostled, craning to see Siyon. The warm brown azatani and other Bezim natives, alongside darker faces from the Archipelago and the Storm Coast, and paler faces from the New Republic or even the North. The Kellian Way was a seething, shifting crowd. People leaned out of windows in the buildings opposite and took up perches on the peaks of the roofs.

Avarair Hisarani would hear about this, if the inqs hadn't already sent a runner. He'd have his work cut out *getting* to Siyon, through this crowd. But Siyon needed to get a move on.

He plucked a scrap of Aethyr out of the air and twisted it absently into what he needed. It came as easy as ever, lifting his voice out over the crowd, far farther than he could shout on his own.

The sparks of Empyreal energy came easily to his fingers as well, when he held out his hands and snapped his fingers. So easily, in fact, that a little gout of fire burst up from each hand; the crowd hooted in delight, a ripple of applause passing over them, and the energy lifting from them pulsed a little brighter.

Look at them. Siyon had barely started. This was really going to work.

"People of Bezim," Siyon called. Named them.

And they—all of them, wherever they had been born—cheered their acceptance, their recognition, their belonging right back at him.

It washed over him, a bronzed and burnished wave, and Siyon hooked his fingers into it before he really thought about it. Not quite reaching. Not quite not. He grabbed hold and started to gather up all their eager anticipation, their curiosity, their willingness to be drawn in. On this, of all nights, they were open to something wild and strange.

Siyon could oblige. He started to twist the energy he was gathering, spinning it like twine between his fingers, even as he lifted his voice again.

"Tonight we are on the cusp. Tonight, we are at the end of one thing and the beginning of another. Tonight, we lay down who we were and turn our eyes to what we might be."

There was a bit of a cheer, some festival cries, a few unfurled flags waving—fisherclan pennants or the colours of hippodrome factions. Just celebrations, but also markers of identity. Each sent up little sprouts of energy, and Siyon reached for them, swiping them up with a finger and twisting them in with the skein of power he was collecting.

This wasn't quite what he'd had planned; he'd thought he'd need to whip them up further, to generate the energy he needed. He thought he'd have to tease it out of them, slow and steady. But now he had fistfuls already, and they were keen to see a show.

He needed to give them one. With this energy thrumming and surging, bucking at his grip like a fish on a line, he thought he could see how to do it.

Siyon gathered up the energy, tangled and twisted and barely half-knotted, and flung it up into the sky.

It flew glittering and glowing, spreading out like stars in the rapidly dimming sky...

From the gasps in the crowd, Siyon was no longer the only one who could see this.

He kept hold of the ragged edge of the energy he'd cast out, clutching at it with fingers and instinct. Siyon could feel the vast sway of it, half burning to evaporate, half yearning to be a part of something bigger.

He reached out through it and coaxed it to his will, even as his fingers started in those childhood patterns. Knotting, and weaving, turning energy into a net, even as he nudged at the vast sweep of it with his words.

"We are the sea," he said, and the sparkling energy undulated, curling up into a wave that splashed down into a shower of sparks.

The crowd murmured in wonder, sending up a new pulse of energy, and Siyon felt himself sway with it. It surged into him, buoying him up like a wave in truth.

Did he have hold of the energy, or did *it* have hold of *him*? Did it matter, when this needed to be done? When it felt so *right*, flowing through him?

"We are the sea," he repeated, "and we are the land." Now the skyborne blanket of energy shifted itself into a sparkling silhouette of Bezim from the sea, with the lighthouse and the bluff behind the city and the Scarp slashing across it. "Here at the edge of land and sea, we are the salt."

A roar of approval from the crowd, and a wash of burnished Mundane energy so strong that Siyon's vision clouded over in bronze and umber. The noise pulsed in his ears like a slow, deep heartbeat. Like the beat of the whole city.

He hung on to himself with his fingernails cutting into his palms, his breath coming harsh and rasping in his throat. He was Siyon Velo. He was the Alchemist. He was the Power of the Mundane.

Had he made a mistake? Was this going to drag him under?

But he couldn't stop it now. Didn't even mean to say the words that still pulled themselves from his throat, thrown far and wide by the Aethyr at his command. "Salt in our blood. Freedom in our lives. *Magic* in our hands!"

Siyon wasn't gathering in the energy any longer, but it didn't seem to matter. It still flowed through him, into wonder, into the twisting net spiralling from his fingers, into the sky. Like he had loosed a river, and now nothing would stop the flow of the water—from the people, through Siyon, into the city. And deeper than all of that.

In the sky, shapes formed and dissolved without any guidance from Siyon—a mermaid, an albatross, a little skink with fairy wings. There was more, and more again. A magnificent maned lion, and the stern face of Papa Badrosani, and the three-masted saviour ship of sailor lore. Others that Siyon didn't recognise: a horse galloping across the waves, a hand rising up from a deep hole, a flower melting into dripping fire. Forming and ebbing, monsters and magic, superstition and sigils.

Siyon gritted his teeth and tried to gather in the magic. The wild and furious flow of it fought against his control. But Siyon had a purpose here. He reached out, to the bounds of the city that he had drawn anew in mud and salt on the black cloth beneath him. He reached, and he felt the power yearning up beneath him as well, striving to be free. He would meet it rising, with this energy descending. The Mundane would be whole. Awake, but settled.

It felt like pulling an oar against a rushing tide, but slowly, Siyon scraped control over the power churning through him. He gathered it up, gathered himself.

"Go forth!"

It felt like a gasp in his mouth; it roared like a command across the velvet dusk, across the breathless crowd, who lifted their arms and *cheered*.

Siyon threw out his net of energy, heavier and deeper and wider than he'd anticipated. With all his senses open to the new night, he felt it rush away from him, settling heavy over the entire city, finding the boundaries that he had marked, but also the boundaries of all these people who *knew* their city, knew what it meant and where it covered.

All of that belief, that belonging, that certainty like the sinking weights at a fishing net's edge, tugging down.

The power sank onto the city. *Into* the city. Through the city and down, deeper into earth and rock and the very bones of the world.

That heartbeat was back in Siyon's ears, slow and insistent and growing louder by the moment. His body rocked with it, his vision pulsing from bronze to shadow, his own heart stuttering to match it.

He could barely hear the crowd bellowing, "Salt and magic! Salt and magic!"

The heartbeat thundered inside him...and it quickened. It stirred. It *pulled* at him.

Siyon fell to his knees, cloth bunching beneath him, the box teetering on the steps. The energy that he'd thrown out, the net that he'd laid, was caught. Was swallowed down. Was sucked away into something massive, something ancient, something in the depths and the shadows that started to glow...

You'll wake Mother Sa, Siyon thought.

In the bones of the earth, in the heart of the grounding Mundane energy, in the darkness inside Siyon's mind, a massive eye opened.

And Siyon's eyes opened as well, staring blindly out at the crowd. They were still chanting, clapping a rhythmic beat. His bones rang in perfect vibration. *Stop*, Siyon wanted to say. *Something's not right.* Or maybe it was *too* right.

It didn't matter. He couldn't speak. The energy spiralled through him, more and more of it, down into the depths. The crowd sped up. They stamped their feet; they shook the earth.

And the earth shook back.

CHAPTER 27

The foyer of Mama Badrosani's theatre had once been a place to loiter and gossip, to see and be seen, to arrange meetings and make good connections.

Too many pillars and places to hide. Too many mirrors and shadows. Too many figures lurking, and none of them here to help Anahid.

She'd been expecting Zinedani to confront her; she'd wanted him to know that she was talking with the barons, to mull over the possibilities, to work himself into uncertainty. But she'd thought she was safe on another baron's territory, at least.

It seemed that had been a miscalculation.

Garabed Zinedani watched them with an expression of resignation; Anahid backed up a step by reflex and bumped into Qorja, who clutched her furled fan. Anahid knew even before she glanced over her shoulder that there would be no escape that way; there were heavy figures descending the stairs, other shadows lurking in the depths of the foyer. Once it had been bright and glittering, now the mirrors were dark with tarnish and the chandeliers dusty and dim.

She could cry out, perhaps. But again she heard Mama Badrosani saying, words sharp and final: *I'll not intervene further.*

The Zinedani *wouldn't* try anything here, on Badrosani territory, without asking leave of the Badrosani first. Zinedani *had* known what Anahid was doing. He'd made his own counterplans.

Anahid was on her own.

The Zinedani thugs tightened their noose around her and Qorja. Two women, huddled together, defenseless. Or at least appearing so.

Anahid didn't want this to come to blood. To more blood. While that could be avoided, there was a chance it might be finished.

"Wait." She held out her hands as though keeping someone's pet at bay. "Wait."

"For what?" Garabed stepped closer, with his ring of thugs closing around her. He lifted a lazy eyebrow. "This isn't carrick, azata. We don't take turns laying down our hands and then tally up who has more points. You grab the opportunity when it's there. Or…" He shrugged. "You lose."

"Wait," Anahid repeated. Her eyes skittered across the advancing wall of threat; this was no place for gentle negotiations, but perhaps they could be held off. "I have lodged a complaint already with the barons, that your nephew took a life without leave. It reflects poorly on both of you, if something happens to me." *Happens to*—what a thing to say. What did she *think* was going to happen here? Anahid's mind skittered away from that, quick as the breath in her throat. "We can resolve this calmly, that's all I want, a chance to—"

"Fuck your chances," Zinedani sneered. "And fuck your complaint. I am *done* with humouring you, azata, and if Aghut wants to finally step up and have this fight, I'm done with him as well. That's the thing *your kind* always forget. Everything's been handed to you. You've forgotten how to grab." He waved a hand and added, lazily casual, "Careful, even she may have a hidden weapon. And don't damage the other one; she's a business asset."

"Wait—" Anahid tried, one last time, lunging after him as Garabed turned away.

But the net closed around them. Qorja yelped as she was yanked away from Anahid. Anahid's hand went by reflex to the sash of her dress, but someone grabbed her elbow and wrenched her off-balance. Another arm wrapped around her shoulder, pulling her back hard.

"Not so fancy now," Stepan Zinedani snarled against her ear.

But that was too much. Anahid *felt* the contact—his grabbing her body—break the tenuous leash she'd been holding.

Keep her from being harmed, Siyon had ordered Laxmi, back at his apartment. *Like you would me.*

Sweat sprang up at the back of Anahid's neck, entirely separate from Stepan's panting breath. It wreathed around them both, a whiff of rotting salt and the hint of a metallic rasp. "What—?" Stepan started to ask.

Hot darkness burst out from Anahid, like plunging into deep and boiling water. It shattered reality, pushing air and light and thought ahead of it. All was shadow and the dancing suggestions of movement. At the corner of Anahid's eye, shapes flashed and menace stalked; she could just make out the pulsing swipe of green-black claws and an unfurling of something like tentacles.

Somebody screamed, twisting into an awful gurgle.

This wasn't how Anahid had planned things at all. She'd wanted a chance to negotiate in good faith. To beat Garabed into reasonableness with the weight she had gathered—the support of the other barons, of how much worse things *could* be, of how little Stepan deserved sheltering. She'd wanted an end, without more violence.

Not this. Not overlapping shrieks of gleeful ironmongery and violence. Not the wet squelch of men wrung out like cleaning rags.

"Make it stop!" Stepan shouted, barely audible over the demonic ruckus. He held her firm, though; there was nothing Laxmi could do about him while he clutched Anahid so tightly, for the risk of catching her in the fringes. *(Keep her from being harmed.)* "Stop it, or I kill her!"

He shifted his arm to press across Anahid's throat.

She struggled, she heaved, but though she was a little taller, he had far more experience in this arena. He held her like a kitten he planned to drown. Anahid clawed at his arm, and he merely howled defiance into the ongoing fury around them.

Had Imelda struggle like this when he killed her?

Rage rose in Anahid like the sea rushing into a breached hull. She dug her fingers beneath her sash for the penknife. Her paltry nothing of a blade, barely three inches long. She thumbed off its ornate and decorative cap.

Enough of a blade, it turned out, when she slammed it into Stepan's inner thigh.

With a sound like wet cloth torn asunder, the circle around them flew apart, men crashing into mirrors, thudding against shabby velvet drapes, falling crumpled and bloodied on the carpet. Laughter echoed faintly in the darkness, metallic and menacing, and the air was thick with blood and fear and the sulphuric crackle of the Abyss.

Garabed Zinedani cowered against a pillar, his face blanched white in the eerie greenish light.

And Stepan collapsed like a building undermined, dragging Anahid down with him as he fell. She landed half on him, her elbow in his ribs, slipping on sodden carpeting. She pushed herself up to her knees, shoved Stepan down again, and set the bloody tip of her knife against his throat.

Rage still beat its fists against the inside of her skull. Anahid hadn't planned any of this, hadn't *wanted* any of this, but the cards were on the table now. The hands were being tallied.

Fuck these men and all their works. She could grab as well.

"Don't move," Anahid rasped, glaring up at Garabed. Stepan thrashed weakly, clutching bloody hands at his thigh. There was so much blood, and Anahid couldn't think about that, couldn't let herself flinch. She leaned more heavily upon his chest, weighing him down. "You might still save him," she gasped. She could barely hear, past the rage singing in her ears to *kill him.* (Or maybe that was Laxmi, out of the darkness.) Anahid wanted an end. She wanted an *end.* "There are alchemists who can heal this, even down here. But you leave Bezim. Tonight. You bind yourself to it. You swear on your life, and his. Both of you leave, and you *never come back.*"

Stepan lifted a limp arm, flailing sticky-fingered at her face as Anahid leaned away from him. Didn't spare any attention from his uncle, watching Garabed watch Stepan, and for a moment she thought maybe it might all work out the way she had said it would. That they would leave. That the blood could stop here.

A part of her was almost disappointed.

Then the storm clouded Garabed's face, and his lip curled. "Damn you if you think I'll run. Who are *you*, girl, to threaten me?"

"Who am *I*?" Anahid repeated. Demanded. Stepan's struggles were weakening, and the scent of blood was thick on her tongue as she dragged in a breath. It was like being back in Imelda's room, seeing her lying on the ruined mattress. She could feel the same scream clawing at the back of her throat. *Girl*. Worthless. Just a minnow who should stay in her place.

The rage inside her roared; she flung open its cage.

"Who are *you*," Anahid snarled, "that we should live in fear of you?"

She had set the tip of her knife against Stepan's throat. She had kept it there all this time.

Now she leaned forward. Pressed in. Dragged the blade across.

It was harder than she'd anticipated. The blade was sharp, but not large, and Stepan bucked and jerked and clutched at her. Anahid had to lean all her weight on him, put all her effort into it, brace her other hand over his face as new blood lapped hot over her knuckles.

She did it for Imelda. She did it for herself. She did it with anger screaming glory in her veins.

Garabed roared, and charged at her.

Anahid raised her knife—her tiny, meaningless penknife. It was dripping gore; she was bloody to the elbow, and when she tried to rise to meet her attacker she slipped and skidded. Went back down on one knee, and so his first wildly swung fist whistled over her head. Anahid slashed for his body, but his other hand caught her wrist, and his momentum bore them both over backward.

He was over her, on top of her, smothering her. Too big, too powerful, too much. One hand gripped her wrist until the small bones creaked and the knife fell from her senseless fingers. The other hand scrabbled at her chin; she bit one finger, but the others pressed at her throat. Anahid struggled, and twisted, and he pressed all the harder. He was shouting above her, and she couldn't hear a thing for the heaving of her lungs, the hammering of blood in her mind. The rage had fled, and all she had now was panic.

She was going to die.

But Stepan was dead as well. If she had to face Imelda, in whatever lay beneath the waves of mortality, Anahid could give her that, at least.

A heavy crash sounded, somewhere above her, somewhere that felt far away, and Anahid could breathe again. She could heave in air, shove the dead weight off her, blink the whirling darkness from her vision. She scuttled crabwise across squelching carpet until she fetched up against a pillar, still gasping.

Qorja stood over Garabed Zinedani's limp body with the remains of a mirror in her hands, shattered silvered glass backed by a thick chunk of wood. Her breath came as hard as Anahid's—and not at all like Garabed's, whose slumped body was entirely still. The two of them stared at each other for a long, stretched moment.

A sharp sound broke in, once and again, and again. One pair of hands clapping a broken rhythm of applause. Anahid twisted to look up the grand foyer staircase.

Mama Badrosani leaned against the mezzanine railing, laughing around her pipe and clapping as though at a command performance. "That's my girl!" she called down. "That's it exactly. We're all threats, Lady Sable! *Now* you're one of the sharks."

Still chuckling, she went back into the theatre proper.

Qorja dropped the remains of the mirror with a crunch and swayed on her feet. "Can we *go*?" she said, remarkably close to a wail.

Anahid knew how she felt. There seemed no part of her that wasn't tacky with blood. She had *killed a man*. She wanted to leave. She wanted to *run*. "Wait, where's—?"

Laxmi, she meant to ask. Even the brackish aftertaste had faded from the air. Where had the harpy ended up?

But at that moment, the world shook beneath them. The empty chandeliers rattled and tinkled, and another mirror fell from the wall with a crash. There was screaming, faintly, from outside, and a deeper rumbling. Anahid clutched at the pillar as Qorja staggered. It went on, and on, like the earth was a dog determined to shake itself clean.

She hadn't felt anything like this since summer. Since Siyon had stabilised the planes. Her fear sprang back as though it had never withered away. It was another Sundering, and Anahid was sunk, already below the Scarp and close to the waves.

The trembling stopped. For a moment, all was silent.

Until screams rose again from outside, even wilder.

As Zagiri ran down the Kellian Way with Mayar, she heard the roar of the crowd behind her. A glance over her shoulder showed the deepening purple twilight sky spangled with stars...that were moving, making shapes, rushing and bursting like fireworks.

They were running against the flow of traffic here. Everyone was hurrying up to the Eldren Hall, wanting to be a part of this.

Zagiri pulled Mayar away, into the little side streets, which weren't quite as crowded. "Where are we going?" she asked as they dodged around a knot of people spilling out of a wineshop.

"Right there," they said, tipping a nod down the hill and speeding up again—long, loping strides down the last, steeper section.

There was nothing down here, save the little bit of plaza on this side of the Swanneck. Perhaps Mayar meant across the bridge? Something in among the factories? It'd be a quick run across—the bridge was all but empty.

But Mayar slowed to a halt only halfway across, grabbing at Zagiri's arm to pull her toward the railing.

"What?" she said. "The *Swanneck*?" They'd asked about the devices that Zagiri had used to cause the flares. But those had been up in the industrial district, not down here on the bridge.

At Mayar's gesture, she looked over the railing. It was a long and dizzying drop, with the river frothing at the bottom, a suggestion of white even in evening gloom. Lanterns were coming to life along the bridge railing.

Just enough light for Zagiri to make out a clump of something stuck to the side of the bridge. A mess of pink goo, sticking together three little black velvet bags.

"Oh shit." Zagiri looked at Mayar, who had their arms folded, leaning back against the railing like they were having a casual chat. "Yeah," Zagiri admitted, "that looks like what we were using."

Three here would help explain why she'd counted fewer flares than expected on the night. Someone had made off with some of them. Perhaps the entire confusion over placement had been intentional, to cover the discrepancy. Did that mean it was the Knife? But why would she have to get tricky about it? She was *running* the show, she could just—

"One of the Haruspex guards spotted it from a crow's nest," Mayar said quietly, interrupting Zagiri's furious thoughts, "and I said I thought I knew someone who could help." They looked straight at Zagiri. "What's going on?"

"I don't know," she admitted, and then when their eyebrows twitched up disbelievingly: "I don't! This wasn't part of the plan, but on the night there was...a bit of confusion. Some of the devices might have gone missing. But I don't know why anyone would..."

Stick them to the Swanneck. Three of them, glooped together with some sort of adhesive, like someone was trying to *concentrate* their effect.

For a moment, Zagiri considered how *livid* Jaleh would be, that someone had been messing with her workings.

Mayar looked along the bridge, with barely a trickle of ambling pedestrians right now. A cheer carried faintly on the night air from the Eldren Hall; *that's* where everyone was, and Zagiri hoped it was going well for Siyon. But usually the Swanneck was packed full of delivery carts hauling food and goods coming into or going out of the city.

"Imagine," Mayar said quietly, "the impact on the city if this bridge was blown up."

"The Swanneck is indestructible," Zagiri objected. When a passing group glanced their way, she lowered her voice to add: "The Sundering didn't even crack it. And these devices only spark an alchemical flare; they don't..." She trailed off. The Swanneck's indestructibility came from its alchemical construction, a masterwork of concentrated resources, from back when alchemy was a whole area of study at the university.

She didn't think it was still an ongoing alchemical process. She didn't *think* a flare would be able to consume its energy, like had happened in the industrial district.

But when it came down to it, what did she know about any of it, really?

"I think the devices were tampered with," Mayar added, barely more than a whisper. "Look."

They both looked over the railing, but the gloaming was deep now, here in the lee of the crag. The lanterns were designed to illuminate the bridge, not over the sides, and though the moon was coming up, it was behind them.

Mayar glanced around, checking if anyone was watching them, and then snapped their silver-ringed fingers, calling up a bright spark of Empyreal fire. In two quick gestures, that spark somehow became a little knot of gentle flame, encased inside a shimmering ball. Mayar pinched a strand of glimmering *something* out of the top of the ball and then reached out to dangle the whole thing over the side of the bridge.

"How did you...?" Zagiri started, and then at their sharp look, she leaned forward to make *use* of the light they'd conjured up out of nothing.

In the flat yellow light it gave, she could see clearly that the clay seal on the drawstrings of at least two of the black velvet bags had been broken. It was also obvious that they'd been here awhile; that pink goo, whatever it was, had slipped down the side of the bridge, leaving a dark and greasy trail in its wake.

Had they been here since that night, tampered with and planted while the rest of them laid the other flares in their proper places?

"Fuck," Zagiri muttered, standing up straight again. "Why didn't they go off with the rest?"

"You're asking *me*?" Mayar demanded incredulously, but they kept their voice low.

"*I* don't know anything about alchemy!" Zagiri shot back.

"Then maybe," Mayar snarled, "you shouldn't have been fucking around with it in the first place."

Just because they were probably right wasn't going to stop Zagiri from glaring at them.

But it didn't matter. It didn't matter that Zagiri should have seen this coming, or that she should have been more careful. It didn't matter why the devices hadn't gone off with the rest, or what that pink goo was, or whether they'd go off at all, or whether they'd have any effect on the Swanneck.

They *might*. They might dissolve the whole damn thing and send every single person on the bridge—now or later, on Salt Night, the festivalgoers wandering and laughing and dancing and full of wonders—into the river chasm below.

That wasn't happening. Not if Zagiri could do something about it.

"All right," she said. "There are ways of nullifying alchemy. I've heard Siyon and Anahid talk about it. Some symbol you draw on things?"

Mayar's frown turned thoughtful. "The sigil he used for the inquisitors. Yes, I know the one. But how do we get down there?"

They leaned over the side of the bridge again. It was difficult not to be distracted by the froth and churn of the river, so very far below, glowing in the moonlight. It was a long way to fall.

So don't fall.

Zagiri made herself say firmly: "If I get up on my stomach on the railing, you can hold on to my legs. Lower me down and pull me back up."

"What?" Mayar looked like she'd suggested setting herself on fire. "No. No! We can find—look, Siyon imbued the mark into the inqs' badges. What if we put it into some liquid and *pour* it down the side?"

Zagiri felt a little dizzy with relief; she tilted back from the edge of the bridge. "Would that work? What sort of liquid?"

Mayar hesitated, which wasn't a good sign. "Something that evokes cleanliness and certainty. Seawater, maybe?"

They both turned seaward; the breeze was fresh in their faces, like the sea was breathing on them directly, but it really *wasn't* that close. They'd have to go all the way down into Dockside—either the long way around down the Kellian Way or through the warren of the slums. Was there time? Zagiri didn't know why the devices had held this long. She didn't know if they'd hold a bell longer.

Then she staggered—everyone on the bridge staggered—as a tremor rocked the city. The bridge itself didn't so much as creak or crack, steady as ever, but the people all fell about, clutching at one another and the railings.

A passing party of university students collapsed into Zagiri and Mayar, one of them shrieking, another trying to run and tripping over his own feet. The world shook, and all through the upper city, buildings swayed alarmingly. A flock of birds took flight from somewhere, shrieking in the darkness. A dull *clang* sounded from the bell tower.

And then it subsided.

In a moment, the Swanneck was mayhem, people shoving and rushing in every direction. Zagiri drew back against the railing, pulling Mayar after her; they were clutching something and grinning from ear to ear.

"Or," they said, as cheerfully as though the city hadn't just lurched like a ship in a storm, "rakia might work." They held up a flagon, bound in cheap raffia twine, left behind by the students. "Sunshine and alcohol, bitter bite. I say we give it a try."

Zagiri stared at them for a moment, utterly speechless. How could they *carry on*?

But they had a point. Whatever had happened, this problem remained.

"Right," Zagiri said, pulling herself together. "Do the thing. Draw the mark."

Mayar wet a fingertip with a little of the rakia and drew on the side of the glass—a circle with a slash through the centre. It flashed for a moment, like some last lost beam of sunlight had caught the wet lines, and then was gone.

"Give it here," Zagiri said, grabbing at the flask and setting her other hand against the railing. She couldn't quite bring herself to lean out. What if the earth shook like that again? "Can you—hold me steady?"

With Mayar's hands tight at her waist, Zagiri leaned out, ignoring the part of her mind shrieking about how far down the river was. (It was the bravi part, and she wasn't sure if it was terrified or exhilarated.) A kiss of spray rose faintly from the chasm. Zagiri tipped the bottle a little, but that breeze blew the dribble of rakia away. Damn. She'd need to tip it against the side of the bridge, but there was an overhang here and she couldn't quite reach.

"Zagiri," Mayar said above her, with a faint note of panic. Maybe it had only now occurred to them that this thing might go off at any moment.

"I need to be a little lower," she called back. "Can you tip me up a bit?"

Just a bit. She *wasn't* being lowered over.

They shifted their grip, tight enough to leave bruises on her hips, and hefted Zagiri up a little so she could hinge more fully over the top of the railing. "Hurry," Mayar grunted.

"But I'm having so much fun," Zagiri muttered as she carefully reached down, tilting the mouth of the flagon gently against the white not-stone side of the bridge to let the nullified rakia spill over the surface, dribbling down.

When it reached the bundle, the pink goo started to hiss with a thick orangish smoke. Zagiri coughed and twisted away, and she heard Mayar spit a curse word.

The devices came away from the side of the bridge, tumbling down into the chasm, leaving a spiral of smoke in the air.

"Haul me up!" Zagiri croaked.

Mayar did, heaving as the railing clipped her in the ribs, knocking all the air out of her.

Zagiri had never been so glad to be gasping for breath and seeing stars. She lay on the bridge for a long moment, fingers pressed to the cool not-stone, breath fogging the surface.

"Zagiri," Mayar said urgently, down on one knee next to her. "Something's happening."

"Something's *not* happening," she contradicted happily, then blinked, pushing up onto her hands. "Oh fuck, that earthquake."

Mayar frowned again, edged with uneasy fear as they looked up toward the upper city. "Something's *happening*," they repeated.

Oh. Oh shit. "With Siyon's ritual?" Zagiri scrambled to her feet.

"Maybe." Mayar reached out tentatively, fingers grasping at air. "There's something…shifting. A lot. We have to find Siyon. Right now."

Zagiri didn't need to be told twice.

CHAPTER 28

The earth under Siyon shook.

The stairs juddered beneath his feet; behind him, every magnificent stained glass window of the Eldren Hall rattled and chimed, but the noise sounded far away. As far as the crowd's chant now turning to shrieks, as far as the thrashing of shaking trees, as far as the smearing sky.

Siyon staggered, and the step clipped his heels, and then he was falling, tipping backward, the deepening indigo of the new evening sky closing overhead like a cavern, netted in a fine filigree of shimmering bronze energy, arching delicately over the city. Through it, the rising moon looked just like a giant golden eye, and Siyon was sure for a moment that he would fall deep, and deeper still, and forever.

He didn't. His back hit the steps, jolting the breath from his lungs and smashing pain into his hip. He lay there, clutching at the cloth they'd spread out, as the world kept shaking.

Until, blessedly, it stopped.

Someone appeared above Siyon—and now Siyon saw Izmirlian in his brother's face. The ferocious burn of his eyes, the steadfast set of a differently shaped jaw. A swift glimpse of how Izmirlian might have been, had he been focused on the matters of this plane, instead of far beyond.

Siyon ached all over. His bones were still shaking. *Something* was still moving. All that energy, that Siyon had coaxed out of the crowd, that had flowed through him...

It was still moving, down in the depths of the world. It was churning, and coiling tight, and everything Siyon had thought—about tamping down, about reassuring, about binding into somnolence— was wrong. Terribly, awfully wrong.

Didn't they understand, all those people he could now hear shouting in relief and ebbing fear and rising anger? It wasn't over yet.

"Come *on*," Balian bellowed, hauling Siyon's arm over his shoulders, all but dragging him up. Siyon couldn't see his mouth anymore; somehow, it made his words fainter. All Siyon caught of the rest was: "—out of here."

He clambered up to his feet, half climbing Balian to get there. Balian Hisarani, brother to Siyon's lover, brother to Siyon's enemy, kept him steady even as they turned around and started up the stairs.

"Wait," Siyon mumbled. *Up* was wrong. Down. He needed down. Didn't he?

But he couldn't manage to turn himself around. Could barely put one foot unevenly in front of the other. Let Balian steer him up the stairs, to the columned portico that ran along the front of the Eldren Hall.

"—before the crowd turns," Balian was saying, or something like it. "Then maybe we can—oh *fuck*."

Siyon wasn't sure he'd ever heard Balian swear before. He looked up blearily to see what had caused it.

Midnight stepped out of the deep shadow of the portico, dragging it behind him like a thick, plush cloak, defying the moonlight. Every line of him gleamed with burnished bronze energy—he looked like some metal-cast statue walking out into the night.

He looked down on Siyon with deep-shadowed eyes and said, "*Now* will you listen to me?"

"Who *are* you?" Balian breathed, with an edge of fear shaking his words.

Siyon expected Midnight to ignore the question completely, to lunge forward, to lay hands on Siyon and drag him—where?

Siyon couldn't resist. More than that, he wasn't sure he *would*.

But Midnight tilted his head, as though thinking about the question surprised even him. "So much power," he said, almost wonderingly. "It makes so many things clear. It washes away the years. I am... I am a memory. I am a duty. I am the last thread trailing through the centuries. I am the wick on a candle that *must* be lit."

Now he did reach forward, but it was almost tender, like an elder reaching for a newborn child. His fingers were gentle beneath Siyon's chin, tilting his face up. Gentle, but cold and hard as stone.

"You must come now," Midnight said softly. "Or she will come to you. You claimed this. It has become yours. And it is almost too late."

Another tremour spasmed beneath Siyon's feet. Or perhaps—as Balian's grip tightened around Siyon's ribs, and nothing else seemed to shift...Perhaps it only shook *inside* Siyon.

She, Midnight said.

Be careful, you'll wake Mother Sa, Mayar had said.

But if you did...then what?

"Take me there," Siyon croaked, and grabbed at Midnight's wrist. He was smoke and shadow; Siyon's fingers closed too tight, around something far too narrow, and yet hard as diamond.

"I am merely the path." Midnight laid his other hand over Siyon's. "You must take yourself."

"Wait," Balian objected, but he was far away.

Not far enough. "Step back," Siyon warned, but Balian's grip tightened stubbornly on him. Siyon dragged his eyes—bronze afterimages dancing across his vision—to look at Balian. "Let me go."

For a moment, he thought Balian wouldn't. Then his mouth pressed tight, and he ducked out from beneath Siyon's arm. His legs nearly buckled against the sudden insistence of gravity—down, yes, *down*—but he locked them straight.

Balian's eyes burned, like a demand all their own, but he took another step back. Committed to this course.

Stubborn, thorough, but not afraid of what might be out there...

Siyon was thinking of another Hisarani altogether—perhaps

inevitably; wasn't he always?—as he stepped forward. Reached forward. Toward Midnight. *Into* the shadow.

And he fell properly, this time. Deep, and deeper still, and forever—

"Wait," said a voice. A known voice, a loved voice, and Siyon reached out by instinct. He jolted to a stop.

Not in the void, but somewhere else. There was a low roar, like the ocean, in his ears. He blinked, and the shadow was so dark it was blinding bright; he blinked again, and moon dazzle bled from his vision.

A crowd teemed around him, beneath a low and massive moon. Not a crowd of people, or rather not *only* people—there were the pale outlines of djinn padding on cat feet, and the feathered-and-flamed bulk of angels, and the scaled-and-furred monstrosities of the demons of the Abyss.

All of them, mingling together, shifting between market stalls, browsing the wares, shopping and chatting and eating and drinking and laughing.

Siyon turned, and turned again, and stopped as a figure stepped out of the press. Burnished dark curls just a little too long, warm brown eyes clear and curious, a mouth twitching from haughty fashion into a smile of pure delight.

"Wait," Izmirlian Hisarani said again, wonder in his face. "You're really here, this time."

Siyon's heart ached to see him. He wanted to grab him, hold him, *kiss* him, but—"This is impossible. You're—" Not dead. He had to hope, most fervently, that where he'd sent Izmirlian wasn't death. But...

"Gone," Izmirlian agreed, with a slow nod and a wistful glint in his eye. "Yes. I am. Probably this isn't real. It couldn't possibly be. But we know about you and the impossible, don't we?"

He held out a hand, with a little challenging quirk to his eyebrow.

This wasn't where Siyon was supposed to be. Something was tugging at him. A memory, a duty, a candle that must be lit.

But he was only human.

He took Izmirlian's hand, pulled him close, and closer still. He still smelled the same, orange blossom and sandalwood lifting from his soft curls. He still tasted the same, keen and eager against Siyon's mouth. He still made the same little noise when Siyon dug clutching fingers into his spine.

"I miss you," Siyon whispered against his mouth. Again; he'd said this to Izmirlian in dreams, or something like that.

"And I miss you, so much," Izmirlian whispered back, but then he was easing away, out to arm's length. He kept their fingers tangled together, though, tugging at Siyon with a blooming smile. "Come on, I have so much to show you."

Siyon's turn to say: "Wait."

He wanted to. The desire to stay was so strong it felt braided through his rib cage, dragging him forward. Behind Izmirlian he could see that strange and mingled crowd, moving through a market, the stalls full of wonders offered by the beings of all the planes. There were strings of seaweed and shimmering chainmail mesh, the pelts of unknown creatures, and jars filled with loose scales in every eye-watering colour, twisted pieces of coral and jade, chimes and horns and drums…

There was Izmirlian, waiting for Siyon, wanting to share this all with him.

He'd promised. *See you soon.*

But he wasn't done. He *couldn't* stay. Not yet.

"Oh." Izmirlian's face cleared like the eye of a storm. He stepped closer again. "Oh, I see. I hadn't realised—you're not whole. You should take this."

And he pressed something into Siyon's hand, folding fingers over an object small and hard, that pricked at Siyon's skin with familiar sharp points.

Siyon opened his hand.

The little obsidian dragon sat on his palm.

The market clamoured in his ears. The scent of sandalwood and orange blossom engulfed him. Siyon closed his eyes against the burn of tears.

—and opened them again in darkness.

He was alone. No Izmirlian, no market.

No Midnight.

Siyon dragged in a breath, and it was cold and dusty in his throat, smelling of age and neglect, tasting of stone and depth, making his ribs ache. He'd been here before—he'd chased answers through these tunnels in his dreams, again and again. Like reflex, he closed his eyes and opened them again.

He was still here.

Siyon lifted a hand—an empty hand, the dragon figurine gone as though it had never really existed—to call a spark of light into being, but he stopped with his fingers and thumb still pressed together.

He didn't need to. He could—not quite see. There *was* a bronzed sheen creeping across his vision, limning curved stone walls and a ragged ceiling, trickling away into tunnels and crannies. But more than that, he could *feel*.

Feel, not just see. Like Mayar had said.

Stone around him, pressing from all sides, stretching down into the heart of the world. Somewhere high above were the flickering traces of people, bright sparks like the twitterings of birds on a distant rooftop. The power that had seemed so immense when it flowed from the crowd through Siyon was now shown to be paltry. A mere libation, poured into thirsty earth, compared to the rising tide.

Siyon hadn't understood. The Mundane had lost so *much*, in the centuries it had been without a Power. None of them had any idea what slept. What waited to wake.

Now something deep and ancient and powerful licked around him like water lapping at a raft. When Siyon took a few steps in the darkness, he felt the resistance and the yield. It was like wading through chest-high water.

The current tugged at him. It would be so easy to give in. Let it sweep him away.

Siyon resisted it, fear tickling in his chest. So much power. So much stone. It might swallow him up, chewing like he was dinner, and that would be that. He'd be buried down here as well, alongside so many other mysteries and truths. Did you hear about the Power of the Mundane, who disappeared without a trace?

Well, at least he'd never have to sit through another committee meeting.

Laughing helped. It pushed back the looming enormity of the Mundane all around him and reminded Siyon of who he was. The Power of the Mundane, yes, but also Siyon Velo. Let him feel more around him than just the unrelenting press of stone and power and demand.

Let him feel a breeze on his face, slow and tickling first one cheek, then the other. There and gone and back again. Out, and in.

Like breathing.

I am merely the path, Midnight said. *You must take yourself.*

Siyon held up a hand. Let the breeze, and the energy around him, play through his fingers. Oriented himself; it was coming from *that* way.

He straightened the collar of his purple coat and walked into the darkness.

Being able to sense his surroundings didn't make them any easier to navigate. Siyon caught his toe on the uneven floor, banged his hand against a roughened wall, had to scrape through narrow gaps with his coat snagging and skin scraping. He left blood on the edge of the rock as he hauled himself through, and he could *feel* it in the dark, like an offering, like a binding, like another layer of the power in this place.

Frankly, he didn't really appreciate having to work for it like this. Hadn't he done enough?

Or maybe he hadn't. Maybe this was the rebuke for having waited so long to walk these tunnels properly, and not merely in dream.

Siyon struggled forward, and the burnished glow grew brighter all around him.

He didn't know how long he'd been down here. It could have been moments, or a bell or more; if it turned out to be days, he'd not be surprised. He breathed in dust. He tilted his body to the dictates of the stone around him. His heart beat, slow and steady, pressure against his eardrums and in the tips of his fingers.

Wait. That wasn't *his* heart.

Siyon couldn't quite hear it, but he could feel it, through his palm on the rock wall, and echoing low in his stomach. He *knew* it. Had heard it before, in the depths of his dreams.

Now it was all around him, drumming at Siyon's skin. It didn't caress so much as it wrapped him up. Didn't lull so much as *demand*. Siyon closed his eyes, swaying with it.

Almost without thinking, he *reached*.

Not across the planes, but as Mayar had taught him—across the Mundane, reaching for the energy—the essences—that were all around. Reached out and found the bones of the earth, deeper than memory and cold with the weight of eternity.

And tucked within, like a hidden truth, were the bones of something else entirely.

The lives above and the power buried, Imelda had reminded him.

What is buried remains, Midnight had said.

Siyon opened his eyes, and there was a figure standing in front of him in the tunnel. Not human, but a being of shadow and bronze power. Like the memory of a man; a memory that had shaped everyone who came afterward, folded into its purpose as well.

"Yes," Midnight said, a breath of a word, fading into the breeze in Siyon's face. "Come."

He—or the memory of him—stepped aside, holding out an arm as though inviting Siyon into his parlour for tea.

Siyon walked past him, felt him fall in behind even as Siyon kept going, walking heedless now, with his fingertips barely brushing the stone around him. He could hear the heartbeat. He could *see* it, thrumming in the darkness, shimmering before his eyes. It drew him around the final corner, Midnight in his wake.

The cavern was massive—it had to be, for so was the body within it, coiled around itself like a cat before a fire. It was covered in a thin layer of crystalline rock grown one stalactite drip at a time over hundreds, or even thousands, of years. The enormous ribs, bigger than the hold of a cargo ship, made the stony skin creak as they rose and fell.

The heartbeat was deafening. The hot gust of breath seared Siyon's face. The bronzed glow of the Mundane energy was a halo, dazzling as it picked out the spiked spine, the folded wings, the long tail curled around an elongated snout. The mouth, gently parted in sleep, was full of swordblade teeth.

A halo around the dragon.

The dragon who huffed, and shifted, making the whole chamber gently sway. It turned its neck, just a little, until Siyon could see its face.

"Mother," Midnight whispered, behind him. "Mother, it is done, as you asked."

An eye opened in that sharp and pointed face. It was large as a coracle and had the clear pale-parchment colour of a newly risen full moon.

Siyon tried to pull back, but Midnight was behind him. He was caught fast—like *he* was the one encased in rock. He put out a hand, flailing for balance, and steadied himself against the dragon's curled-up front foot.

Something in him rang like a struck gong. A deafening, shattering peal of victory, of perfect harmony, of *rightness*.

The pressure evaporated behind him. *Midnight* evaporated behind him; Siyon could feel him simply dissolve into mist. Gone.

His long years of duty now over.

Siyon snatched back his hand, but it was too late. The dragon started to stir, muscles shifting beneath scale and stone. The thing was massive—bigger than the Eldren Hall—and every part of it sharp and deadly. The teeth that overhung its jaw seemed as large as Siyon, and serrated like a sailor's knife. The claws that curled from a lazily stretched talon looked as sharp as a well-tended sabre.

It had been buried here, and maybe it *should* have been. Maybe they were all far safer with it locked away forever.

Siyon tore himself away, pulling every sense he had back into

himself and shoving them into his mental pockets. He scrambled
backward, back into the tunnel, and just in time too.

The dragon stretched, tearing up the accumulated stone skin of
centuries, sending stalagmites crashing as its tail swept across the cavern and its claws carved gouges into the stone floor. The tunnel convulsed around Siyon, shaking him like dice in a cup.

Ink and ashes, what must it be doing to the city above?

As the dust cleared, Siyon got a good look at the dragon, now
scraped clean of its rocky case. There was something still wrapped
around it, something that pulsed with a bronze energy.

Something that tied it down.

Chains of Mundane power looped around and around the dragon's vast, scaled bulk. They sank down into the stone floor before rising again on the other side—Siyon could *feel* them now, could trace
them with his eyes over the dragon's flanks that heaved as she tested
her bonds.

A low, disgruntled rumble in her massive throat, and she thrashed.

The bonds held, cutting into her hide, rubbing against her muscles, but the cavern shook again, so hard that Siyon staggered back
against the wall.

Much more of this, and she might collapse the ceiling on both of
them. She couldn't, she *mustn't*; Siyon didn't want to die down here.

As though his desperation were audible, the dragon's head swiv-
elled around, and one moon-pale eye fixed upon him.

Siyon froze. The dragon's eye narrowed. She shifted again, but
more gently this time, a bare nudge of her shoulders against the
restraints.

She blinked, slow as a cat.

Siyon eased forward, watching carefully for that massive and
barbed tail, free of restraint. The chains were just power—just Mundane energy. His fingers twitched at his side. He could reach out; he
could touch them. He knew it, like he knew the world around him.

He could break them.

But should he?

Even as he dithered, the dragon grew impatient. Legs bunched beneath that massive scaly bulk and *heaved*. The cavern lurched around Siyon; he landed on hands and knees, dizzy and winded.

Maybe she *should* be tied down, but if she kept up like this, she was going to shake the city down regardless. If he'd come earlier, the first time Midnight asked, might he have woken her more gently? Had time to explain? Had a chance to come up with some other alternative?

Useless to ask now.

Siyon eased himself up into a crouch, hands out and low and empty. "Easy," he said. "Stay calm. I'll get you out and then..."

And then what?

One problem at a time.

He sidled crabwise a little closer. Close enough that he could *reach*, tangle his mental fingers in the burnished chains that bound her.

They came apart with the barest tug. The energy surged and flowed back down into the earth, and Siyon *felt* it settle. Calm. Easy. Grounded.

Oh. *This* was what Siyon had wanted. This was the way the Power should feel.

This was the Mundane plane made whole.

In the moment of stillness, of *rightness*, the dragon stood to her full height, stretching up, wings flaring the little they could in the confined space. Another rumble came from the chest over Siyon's head, this one contented and eager.

She was, he had to admit, magnificent.

Then she crouched again, like a cat about to pounce.

"Wait!" Siyon shouted. "No!"

She launched at the ceiling, smashing into it with massive shoulders and rending claws. Crashing, scrabbling, tearing through the stone.

Up. Toward the city above.

Siyon, in a fit of stupidity that left part of him shrieking in the back of his own skull, lunged forward to grab hold of the massive tail, just below the final brutal barb. He leaned back, dug his heels into the rough cavern floor, and heaved. Above him, the dragon scrabbled, sending rock crashing down, and *screamed*. It was a sound like stone tearing, like a storm wind, like destruction and ruin.

"Wait!" Siyon shouted back.

What was he *doing*? But he couldn't let it climb out into the city.

The dragon's tail twitched in Siyon's grip—he couldn't even get both hands around it—and then she kept climbing, pulling Siyon off his feet, sweeping him wildly through the air as chunks of stone rained down around him, one clipping his thigh with a glancing blow that left him feeling nothing but djinn-prickles.

He held on tight, though. He didn't know what else to do. He couldn't just let her out. No. *No.*

A voice came back, thick and golden, slamming into Siyon's head: *Yes.*

In his shock, he let go and tumbled down to land—winded— on the cavern floor. With a final earthshaking crunch of stone, the tail slithered away through the wound in the cavern ceiling and into darkness.

It took a moment—of dust clearing, and of Siyon blinking the sparks from his vision—for him to realise that not all the stars *were* in his head. It was night, up there. There was a pale dusting of moonlight dancing down among the lingering Mundane glow.

There were screams, faint as seagulls on the breeze.

Siyon dragged himself—battered and bleeding and breathing hard—back to his feet. He had to get up there. He had to...do something.

A dragon. Fuck. He'd released a fucking *dragon*. He could *feel* her out there, brighter by the moment.

His fault. His to fix.

Siyon hauled himself up, and kept hauling. Pulled himself up the tumbled rockfall and into the jagged rent through the stone above left behind by the dragon's explosive escape—scrambled, clambered, slipped, and skinned his palms and swore and hoisted himself up again in desperation.

And the Power bubbled up with him.

CHAPTER 29

Zagiri raced with Mayar back across the Swanneck Bridge, the span empty as though everyone feared more earth tremours. There was a knot of people up the hill on the Kellian Way, though, and as they came off the bridge, Zagiri realised why.

The road had been barricaded, just up from the square, where the buildings pinched in tight on either side.

Zagiri skidded to a halt, grabbing at Mayar's sleeve. "What?" they gasped, pulling a face at the blockage. "Is this some festival thing?"

No, it certainly wasn't. Two wagons had been hauled out and wedged together, end on end, then buttressed with what looked like teahouse furniture—a table, a dozen chairs, even a length of counter. Both sides were teeming with people—on this near side, there were a double handful of Dockside toughs and others in rough clothing; on the far side, an increasing crowd clamouring to get through. Under the street lanterns and the festive alchemical lights strung along the Kellian Way, things were starting to get rowdy.

Off to one side, the teahouse had a symbol painted over its window in dripping black paint. A crossed baling hook and hammer.

"No," Zagiri said. "This is some revolutionary thing."

"Fine." Mayar gestured to the narrow side street they'd come down in the first place. "Let's go around."

But Zagiri didn't think it was any coincidence they were here, when she'd just pried some sort of improvised explosive device off the side of the bridge. A device made from resources *she'd* arranged to provide, and not for any such purpose as that.

She marched forward, to the edge of the square—though still well back from the barricade—and shouted, "Hey! What the fuck is all this?"

A few of the toughs on the barricade glanced her way. One hefted a length of wood and started in her direction—which gave Zagiri a brief moment of panicked reconsideration—but another grabbed his arm and said something. The guy changed direction, heading over to the teahouse to call in through the open door.

Zagiri definitely recognised the person who stepped into the doorway. A big guy—tall as Siyon, and twice as broad across the shoulders and around the arms, and wearing the same scowl he'd had on his face every time Zagiri had met him before now, both at the Flowerhouse meeting and in the warehouse before they planted the flares.

"Zagiri," Mayar said quietly, behind her shoulder, "we need to get moving."

"Just a moment," she said, without looking away.

The guy called Zin waved the others back to the barricade and came sauntering down the hill to where Zagiri waited in the square. He wasn't carrying anything; then again, with arms like that, he didn't really need a weapon. He squinted at her consideringly. "You. You're the za came with Yeva. The one with the bright ideas." He stopped, a couple of paces up the hill. "That you, on the bridge, fucking up our surprises?"

Zagiri's rage flared again. "That *you*, on the bridge, nearly getting a whole bunch of innocent people killed?"

"What people?" Zin waved a plate-sized hand over his shoulder. "Why do you think we've got the barricade up?"

She had to admit, the bridge was still empty. Had they set up on the other side as well? "This *wasn't* the plan!" Zagiri shouted. "I didn't bring you those things for whatever you wanted! You can't just fuck around with alchemy like that! What if they'd gone off some other time, when the bridge *was* full of people?"

Or when Zagiri had been crossing it herself, after setting her flares. When she'd met Yeva, distracted and dragging her off the bridge, surprised to see her there. *Something I needed to be sure of,* she'd said.

Yeva was involved in this. And she hadn't said a word to Zagiri about it.

Balian, the revolution, Yeva—no one was telling Zagiri the *truth*.

"And what if it had worked?" she shouted at Zin, riding on a new wave of anger. "What if you blew out the *only bridge* across the damn river?"

Zin shrugged. "What if the azatani couldn't get to their trade goods, their factories, their ships, their *everything*. All of it on *our* side of the river, running on *our* work, and yet what do we get? *Scraps*, if we're lucky."

"What about everyone else?" Zagiri demanded. "What about the people who live down there, and work up here? What about *food*? What about everyone who isn't azatani?"

"Like you care," Zin sneered. "Little za, patting yourself on the back for fixing one paltry law." He lifted his voice back at her, the raw bellow of a working man: *"You want change, or not?"*

But Zagiri refused to be cowed. She stood her ground and glared up at him. "You want to kill people or help them?" she challenged right back.

He fumed, but he looked over her, to the bridge, and something shifted in his face. "The bridge wasn't my idea," he said grudgingly. "I just put together the barricades. We've got people all over the city tonight; I didn't think we needed..." He trailed off.

"Then who—?" But Zagiri could guess. Who was in charge? Who had insisted on taking the devices, dispensing them herself?

Who was openly marked as following the agenda of the Shore Clan, and of Aghut, first and foremost?

"The Knife," she said.

Zin's gaze flicked back to her, grumpy and measuring. There was something very familiar about that expression on his face.

But before Zagiri could pin it down, the earth twitched beneath her feet.

For a moment, she thought she'd imagined it—only the rumble of a heavy cart on a nearby street, blown out of proportion by her jangling nerves. But then it happened again, a little shudder, and she saw concern crease Zin's heavy brow. It wasn't just her.

"Maybe we should—" he started.

The world heaved.

Zagiri fell to her knees on cobblestones that danced beneath her hands. The barricade clattered and rattled; the people on it shouted; someone in the crowd beyond screamed, and then everyone was doing it. Tiles rattled down from roofs—one, then two, and then a rain of them. From Tower Square, farther up the hill, the clock bell gave a dull clack, like it had split asunder.

Something smashed onto the cobblestones bare metres away from Zagiri; grains of shattered brick peppered her hastily closed eyes. She could feel blood oozing from a gash in her forehead as she blinked, looked up. A whole chimney had slid off a roof.

Hands gripped at her shoulder, pulling her up into a staggering crouch; Mayar kept hold of her as the pair of them shifted back, into the middle of the square, away from the groaning and swaying buildings.

Any moment now, one of them would fall entirely.

But the shaking quietened.

Zagiri looked along the Kellian Way, sweeping up the hill toward the Eldren Hall, the parklands, the Palace itself.

The darkness shifted, like a building climbing to its feet. Moonlight caught in glints on the sharp edges of its vast bulk. A long, serpentine neck unfurled into the sky, and massive bat wings stretched out to block the stars.

Zagiri remembered dizzily that moment back in the summer, when she'd been waiting outside the Palace for word of Siyon, and he'd come smashing out a window in the arms of something that had turned out to be Laxmi. Not, as she'd originally thought in her panic, a dragon.

But this...

The dragon flapped its massive wings once, experimentally, and Zagiri could hear the whistling noise of them even this far away. It launched itself into the air, wings clawing at the night sky, bricks falling away from its body, moonlight shattering off every scaled curve of it.

The ground had stopped shaking. No one was screaming. All of them stunned, staring skyward, at the monster dragging itself into the air.

Behind Zagiri, Mayar said, "Oh *fuck*."

What could they possibly do in the face of *this*?

What they could.

Zagiri grabbed at Mayar's arms. "Get the Haruspex. If they aren't already on the move. We need—like with the griffin. We need to get the bravi on the rooftops, spotting where there's danger, and where there's safety, and who needs to go where."

"What's *left* of the rooftops," they muttered, and they had a point, but they were also nodding. "I'll fetch them. But I can't stay. Siyon needs us more."

Siyon had been the one to deal with the griffin after all. "Where is he?" Zagiri demanded.

"Up there." Mayar looked to where the dragon had appeared. "That's all I know."

"I'll meet you there," Zagiri said. "After I get Bracken moving."

Mayar took off, back across the Swanneck, already whistling a short, sharp code.

Zagiri turned back up the hill, where Zin was striding toward the barricade that had half toppled. There was a lot of shouting going on, and someone crying. Zagiri ran to join Zin; one of the wagons had come off a wheel, and she helped lift it. Little enough help, next to the laders and other Dockside bruisers around her, but it earned her a bit of a nod from Zin, and that was all she needed.

"You said you have people all over the city tonight," she said.

He frowned at her, suspicious and unwilling to give her any more than he already had.

But a shadow swooped over them, blotting out the moonlight, plunging them into a darkness deep and cold as fear.

In the wake of the dragon, Zin nodded shortly. "What do you have in mind?"

"Get people safe," Zagiri said. "Get them out, where it's damaged. Get them patched up, where they're hurt. If you and yours can work at ground level…" She hesitated; where *was* going to be safe? This wasn't some newborn griffin, still trying to figure out how its own limbs worked. This was a *dragon*.

Nowhere was safe. But they'd do what they could.

"Get people into the Flower district, if you can," she said. "They'll be setting up there for the emergency. They know what they're doing. And look to the rooftops. The bravi will be out; they can tell you what they see, where the roads are blocked, where they need opening."

Zin looked disgruntled, though whether that was about taking orders from her—a prissy little za in training—or something else, Zagiri neither knew nor cared. All that mattered was that he nodded.

"This is our city," Zagiri said. "No dragon gets to trash it."

He jerked his chin. "Get going, then."

She got going, running up the hill, into the narrow twisting streets, heading for the Bracken safe house. To raise her tribe to defend their city.

And then…then she needed to find Siyon and find out what the *hell* was going on.

Occasionally, as Anahid raced back up the Scarp, she thought she should feel worse about having just murdered a man.

Panicked people streamed in both directions, rushing her along as they pushed up the Scarp and shoving against her in their desire to get *down* the Scarp, some of them bleeding and all of them desperate. Anahid's dress was soaked in blood and her hands were stained with it, and no one cared at all.

She and Qorja steadied each other on the frantic journey up. Neither of them were talking about what had happened. Neither of them had the breath.

As they pushed through the milling crowd in the garden at the top of the switchback ascent, the ground started to shake again.

Screams rose around them, and the entire crowd dropped as one, into careful crouches or throwing themselves down flat. Screams from down the cliff-face suggested not everyone had been in a position to find any steadiness.

It got worse. The bushes all around them rustled as the ground heaved and lurched; Anahid fell against the side of the fountain, grabbing at its bowl with her blood-grimed hands, and yelped as the bowl cracked in front of her eyes, water spurting out to soak her.

When it subsided again, Anahid could barely believe it. She stayed clinging to the edge of the fountain, as the water flow ebbed, trickling down the cracked granite. Some panicked primal part of her mind insisted that if she moved, so would the world.

Qorja leaned over her shoulder, dark fingers prying at Anahid's paler ones, as she whispered, "Mistress, we must get moving, this is no place to—"

The screaming started anew, from farther up the hill; Anahid flinched and grabbed at Qorja. The pair of them staggered to their feet.

Not far, from here to the Flower district. They were nearing the gate in the hedge when a wide-winged shadow passed overhead, blocking out the sky with its bulk. Anahid looked up and nearly lost her breath to it—the glittering expanse of its paler belly scales, the bright moonlit sparkle of its talons, the near-silent press of its passage.

Something that large couldn't possibly fly, and yet there it was, swooping down over the river and turning out to sea in a wide, lazy circle.

She'd seen a tiny version of it. Had held it in her hand. Had dropped it on her floor.

Dragon.

Anahid caught at Qorja's hand and dragged the gaping woman after her, into the District.

All was chaos. People were running every which way: patrons fleeing in various states of undress, Flowers shouting from balconies and windows, serving staff racing through the streets. There was a low glow of fire clawing at the windows of one of the Houses as Anahid raced up the hill. The night was a clamour of screams and shouts and cries for help.

But nothing else. Anahid stopped, still holding on to Qorja's arm. "The emergency bell."

When the griffin had hatched, the Flower district had leapt into action, gathering itself into work teams and arranging a place for the injured to be assessed and treated. There had been no disorder. Trading had even continued.

The emergency bell wasn't ringing.

"That's the baron's business," Qorja said, and then her mouth dropped open.

"The baron we left lying dead beneath the shattered remains of a mirror?" Anahid demanded.

She regretted it when Qorja flinched. She wasn't the only person who'd killed a man down in the lower city. But delicacy would have to wait. There was no one left to wrestle composure from this chaos—thanks to them.

It fell to them to do the wrestling.

"Show me where it is," Anahid ordered.

They turned away from the road up to Sable House, along a topiary-lined avenue that was ordinarily quite stately, when one of the trees wasn't sagging under the half-fallen weight of a House frontage. People were running out of the House, carrying belongings and screaming for help. Anahid and Qorja shoved through the chaos. A Flower with her hair falling down ran into Anahid, then looked at her bloody dress and screamed.

Anahid kept going, out into the central square of the District. The pleasure gardens lay in disarray, the carved stone figures of their giant game sets toppled and one of the fountains spraying water up into the air.

In the cupola of the central gazebo, a gleaming brass bell was housed. Anahid hauled at the trailing rope. The bell clanged, then clacked, and then Qorja elbowed her out of the way and set to ringing with a steady rhythm.

"Someone," she shouted over the gonging noise, "will need to tell people what to do."

Oh, ink and ashes.

Anahid stepped out of the gazebo. Already people were hurrying into the garden, forming up on the lawn in what was presumably their designated places. They had done this so many more times than Anahid. Some looked relieved, now that someone might tell them what to do.

That relief faltered a little at the sight of Anahid.

"Where's Zinedani?" someone called.

"Not here," Anahid called back. She wasn't getting into the why of that, not now, not here. "I am Lady Sable." That got a rippling murmur and a few welcoming nods. Even if she wasn't wearing the right clothes, or the thick lace mask, enough had heard the story of the azata causing trouble at Sable House, it seemed. "We have been shaken badly. The whole city has been shaken! And we cannot wait for the Zinedani. We must bring ourselves into order as best we can. You all know, better than I do, what can and should be done, and how to arrange our resources to achieve it. I ask a representative of each House to step forward, and we will make our arrangements."

And for a wonder, they nodded and gathered in a circle with Anahid.

They didn't need her input at all, of course—thankfully. The Joyous Bounty, which had been turned into the makeshift hospital on the night of the griffin, was reported as being on fire—a squad was quickly dispatched to assist with fighting it. Other Houses volunteered as useful sites for hosting the injured or serving as a rallying point for rescue squads.

As tasks were assigned, individual Houses turned away to get started. The purpose carved through the chaos the night had been. People were still running, but they were running *to*, and with a goal, and in organised groups.

As the last of them turned away, Anahid staggered over to the central fountain and dipped in her hands to drink. It was only as she noticed the dried blood spiralling away in the water that she realised the state she was still in—blood-caked and smeared with grime, dress still sodden and hair bedraggled. No one had mentioned it.

She supposed she was hardly the worst off this evening. If nothing else, they'd left two men dead in the lower city.

Anahid dipped handfuls of water, scrubbing at her face, at her neck, at her palms and knuckles and wrists. She hardly seemed to have any effect.

"Mistress?" Qorja said at her elbow. The bell had fallen silent. No one needed the ongoing reminder that the emergency persisted.

Something swooped in the night, like a giant bat passing overhead. Anahid looked up as the dragon went winging over the city again, heading back up toward the Palace and university hill.

It didn't seem to be *attacking*. Only flying. As though it was enjoying the freedom.

But what was it doing here? Where had it come from?

Anahid had a terrible certainty that all of those answers boiled down to one common element: Siyon.

"I'm going out there," she said, grabbing Qorja's hand before the other woman could do more than open her mouth. "No. You get up to Sable House. Make sure everything is all right, every*one* is all right. Send them to help with the rescue and healing teams. Someone needs to. But my sister is out there somewhere, probably right in the middle of it all, and I'm not coming back until I've found her."

Qorja looked at her for a long moment and then nodded. "Come back to us, mistress. Sable House needs you."

Anahid had been going to give them back. To trade herself for Stepan Zinedani's censure. Things had not at all worked out the way she'd planned.

She hurried out of the District. If only she still had Laxmi with her. Perhaps the demon had gone back to Siyon, who might well have greater need of her. But Anahid didn't have to go alone; groups were setting out to find and bring back those in need of aid, and Anahid trailed in the wake of one of them.

The city wasn't mired in as much chaos as Anahid had been expecting. The District group swiftly met up with a pair of street patrol inqs, escorting a knot of people grey with dust and staggering with fatigue; the inqs turned back out into the city, and the District group gathered up the people and ushered them onward.

Anahid turned up the hill.

Where a building had fallen, blocking the street, there was a crew of labourers already working to clear a path through the rubble and shoring up tilting walls with lengths of timber. A whistle from overhead made Anahid look up—a pair of bravi perched on a more stable roof.

One called down, "There's another on the next street over; neighbours say someone's still inside."

The work gang split, half of them heading back down the street, following the bravi's directions.

Anahid hurried on, working her way uphill as best as she could. "Hey!" someone shouted at one point. "Get back here!"

Anahid ignored them.

She finally made it out onto the Kellian Way not far downhill from the Eldren Hall—which looked untouched by all the mayhem, serene and stately as ever.

The same could not be said of the parkland just across the Boulevard. Trees had toppled, and the lanterns had all gone out, but there was still enough moonlight for Anahid to see the mess in the heart of the parkland.

Anahid had seen a shipwreck once, on her brief voyage up the coast to Revarr. A great swath of broken wood and strewn goods along a beach, barely recognisable as a ship until she started to pick out the awful skeletal remains of hull ribbing and one forlorn length of spar-crossed mast.

The Palace of Justice was gone. There was a mound of crumpled masonry, twisted beams, and shattered glass in its place. The entire mass of it seemed to have burst outward, scattering chunks of itself halfway to the Boulevard. Smoke rose thickly from the ruin of the western wing, catching at Anahid's throat with her shocked gasp. The bronze dome lay to one side, dented and tipped up to the sky.

As she gaped at the destruction, a heavy hand landed on her shoulder. Anahid screamed and whirled about, grabbing at the sash of her dress. Nothing there now; she'd dropped the penknife.

But it was Lejman, holding up his hands with a startled and apologetic look. "You shouldn't be out here alone, mistress." She opened her mouth, but he added: "We are well, at Sable House. But we need you well also."

Anahid felt so much better for having him with her that it almost made her laugh.

Instead, she startled again as a deep roar tore across the night; the shadow of the dragon launched itself from the top of the crag, swooping out over the western hills to swing back around, bearing down on the city.

Over the parkland, Anahid saw people running—not *away* from the dragon, but *toward* it. She'd have known one of them anywhere.

"Come on," she said to Lejman, and started after her sister.

CHAPTER 30

Ink and fucking ashes, he'd really done it this time.

Siyon scrambled up the ragged tunnel the dragon had carved out of the rock and tried to think over his own mental screaming.

The power buried. An actual *dragon.* Was *this* Mother Sa, the essence of solidity, the mother of monsters, the harbinger of a new age of heroes? Shit, what had he *done*?

What else could he have done? If he'd gone along with Midnight— a *baron*, a mystery, a lurking strangeness—and found the dragon earlier, would things have happened differently, or just sooner? If he hadn't released her bonds, would she have settled down, or shaken the whole city into the sea? If the committee hadn't been demanding all his attention, might he have figured out a way to calm the Mundane energy before it even woke her?

Too late now to pour the rakia back in the bottle.

The rubble shifted and slid, the air thick with dust. This was nothing like climbing a building in the dead of night, but Siyon pushed onward—upward. Every moment that he climbed, the dragon was already up there doing...who knew what? Siyon reached and pulled and hauled himself up the jagged rocks, but he was too deep, this was too far, *he* wasn't a dragon who could—

He reached the top, surprising himself as he reached for the next hold and grabbed not raw stone, but a chunk of masonry with a face of mosaic.

He knew that mosaic. It covered the floor of the entry hall of the Palace of Justice, a piece of Lyraec grandeur preserved for hundreds of years, standing through all the shifts of Bezim's history since.

Siyon blinked against dust and moonlight, dancing specks of Mundane power and the hellish glow of fire. He could barely make out the ragged edges of torn walls. He could see, over to one side, the curve of the fallen bronze dome.

The Palace wasn't standing anymore.

Above it all, passing like a cloud over the stars, soared a shadow with widespread wings. The dragon screamed from on high, like a chain twisted to breaking. She stretched and rolled in the sky, like a dog let off a leash.

All Siyon's wonderings about keeping her underground—if he'd moved faster, been smarter, done something different—vanished. She would never have remained chained and buried. She was made for this: soaring majestic and free, burning bronze.

Siyon hauled himself over a jagged edge of broken floor and into the hallway that had once led to the courtrooms. Now the ceilings were caved in, the corridors thick with rubble and dazed clerks, smeared with dust and blood. Some other part of the building was on fire; the air pushed warm against Siyon's back as he staggered through the damage.

His fault. He had to fix it. He had no idea how. The dragon wasn't going back to sleep, not even if he made it a nice glass of warm milk and sang it a song. It was *awake*—like the plane, like magic. *Look cold upon the world as it really exists.*

It existed now with a dragon in it.

Siyon stumbled—over fallen masonry, and something softer that he was horrifically certain was a dead body—as he clambered his way out of the ruins of the Palace. There were chunks of it scattered all over the parkland; a nearby tree leaned half-fallen. The nearest people were running figures on the distant lantern-lit Boulevard, and over there, just visible marching up the Kellian Way, came a squad of grey-clad inquisitors.

Bless their stubborn duty, but what the fuck did they think they were going to do with a *dragon*? Arrest it for public nuisance? Smack it on the nose with a dowsing rod? Did they think the paltry charms Siyon had laid into their badges of office would protect them against *this*?

Siyon tugged his coat straight—that stupid purple coat—and sneezed in the resulting cloud of stone dust.

The dragon, soaring out over the ocean beyond the lower city, tilted massive wings to turn north, in a wide circuit.

Siyon knew it without looking. He could *feel* the dragon. Night had fallen properly while he was underground, but he could look up unerringly at where she—*she*? How did he know *that*?—was gliding like some giant seabird over Dockside.

No sign of the actual seabirds that usually hung hopefully over the city in festival, feasting on discarded bounty. Gulls were too smart for this.

The moon glinted off her scales, striking sparks from the spikes down her back. And there was something else in the sky as well. Faint and delicate, a barely there shimmer of burnished power arching over the city, like a massive net.

Siyon's net. Siyon's intention. The barrier over the city that he'd woken with his ritual.

It didn't seem to bother the dragon; Siyon *felt* her wing tip brush at the dome of power, and it only warmed her. *She* was of the Mundane as well.

Siyon wondered what it was like, to soar on the wind like that, to see the city from way up there—and for a moment he was dizzy, clutched by gravity like he had been in Laxmi's claws, looking down at the bobbing ships of the harbour far below.

Siyon shook his head, blinked his vision clear.

And saw two people running *toward* him, across the park. Or one running, half pulling the other as they kept turning to look at the dragon.

Mayar seemed absolutely fascinated. But Zagiri was keeping them on track.

Siyon had never been so pleased to see anything, even as he wished they were anywhere else. "Trust you pair to run *toward* the trouble." His voice rasped in a throat that felt lined in stone and razorblades.

"What the *fuck*," Zagiri gasped, hauling at Mayar's elbow.

Mayar grinned at the sky, tilting to track the dragon in moonlight. "Mother Sa!" they said, all breath and wonder. "The stories never said she was so beautiful!"

She *was* beautiful. Like cliffs in a storm, like an oiled and serrated knife, like Laxmi or Olenka in natural form. A violent, burning beauty of pure planar power.

Zagiri stared horrified at the mess of the Palace. "Did it come up through there? Was it *buried*?"

"Sleeping," Mayar corrected. "For hundreds of years, at least. *She* is the reason Bezim retained the spark of power that made your alchemy work all this time."

They were probably right. The power buried, awaiting a Power to return the Mundane to a place where she could fly once more.

Had *that* been what caused the Sundering? Had that university committee of the Department of Alchemy, attempting to perform the Great Work and become the Power, come just close enough—raised just enough power—to make her stir?

Maybe. But it took Siyon to really trash the place.

"What's she going to do *now*?" Zagiri asked. Definitely the more important question.

Siyon knew his own luck better than to hope the answer was *go away somewhere else*. She couldn't stay—what would they feed her? But he wasn't going to be able to knock her into the river, like he had with the griffin.

He looked up—to the patch of sky that he knew contained the dragon—as she skewed back inland. Her wings flared black across the stars as she came into a perch atop the crag over the city. Rocks broke away from the grasp of her talons, crashing down toward University Hill. She stretched her wings in the moonlight, lifted her snakelike neck, and *shrieked*.

It was the roar of lions and the screech of smashing rock. Even at this distance, it echoed off the buildings and rang inside Siyon's skull. It was full of pain, but with a sharp, bright edge of new joy. She ached, stiff and sore from an age of forced sleep, alone in the dark. But now she was *awake*, and the sky was wide and clean and—

Siyon blinked hard, dragging his awareness back to here and now. To *himself*. "What?"

"I *said*," Zagiri said, crouching a little, "here she comes."

Not straight at them, but into a shallow swoop over the hills, lit from beneath by a faint bronzed glow that must have come from the city wall, marked out and empowered anew by Siyon's ritual.

Could he use that? Could he use this domed defense he'd raised over the city after all? If he hardened it somehow, while she was on the outer side, could he keep her out?

Too late; the dragon tilted her wings, veering back toward the city, and—

Something shot up from the wall, spearing past the dragon's head as a deep *thunk* reached Siyon's ears. It spiralled away in the wind, lost in darkness.

"Ballista bolt," Zagiri gasped. "I heard they still have them up on the wall."

"Them?" Siyon echoed.

As the second bolt speared into the dragon's side.

She screamed; Siyon slapped his hands over his ears and couldn't stop the piercing sound. Neither Mayar nor Zagiri moved at all. The dragon jerked in flight, rolling over, wings flailing.

And tumbled from the sky, in a spiralling arc, to slam into the houses between the wall and the parkland.

Siyon was already running—*toward* her. The ground trembled as the dragon crashed down. He saw again that bolt punching into her side (the crossbow bolt lodging in Izmirlian's throat). The awful arrest of her flight (the jolt of him against Siyon's side). The pained twist to her neck (the way his weight had slid, as his knees gave way, as Siyon caught him).

Siyon ran. He had to reach her. He had to help her. He *ran*, and his every step kicked up bronze sparks from the grass.

"Wait!" Mayar shouted, surprisingly far behind him.

Zagiri was back there as well—why were they so *slow*? "What are you *doing*?"

Siyon's heart hammered, his breath rough in his throat, a clamour of pain and panic and desperation in his mind.

No, something insisted, inside him. Something outraged, something angry, something that hurt. The sky was his, this plane was his. It had been so long and now to be torn from the wing, how dare they, how *dare anything*—

No, wait.

Angry, so *angry*—

This wasn't him.

Siyon skidded to a halt, near the edge of the parkland. Burnished lights danced in the corner of his vision; when he glanced back, he'd outpaced Mayar and Zagiri by far. In the grass, faint footsteps glowed bronze for a moment, fading into shadow.

Had he—used Mundane energy to somehow run faster?

There were screams all around him—the people who'd been in these houses fleeing for their lives, down to the Boulevard, out across the parkland. Amid the ruined buildings, the dragon flailed, neck thrashing, wings buffeting, smashing walls and spreading rubble in her anger and pain.

Her anger. *Her* pain. *Her* feelings.

In *his* mind.

They washed at him like waves at the shore, constant and inexorable. If Siyon let them, they would swamp him.

He couldn't let them. He had a city to save. This was *his fault*. He had to fix it.

She was injured; Siyon could feel it like a pain in his side from running so fast. Injured, but not badly enough to ground her. If he let her get up again, how much more destruction would there be? But he couldn't push her out from here, not inside the city. What other option was there?

She'd been bound with chains of Mundane power below. Who had done that? Had it been the last Power, however many hundreds of years ago?

Could Siyon bind her again?

As the dragon got her feet beneath her, neck lashing and tail sweeping through another row of houses—as all that happened, Siyon closed his eyes and reached out all around him.

In front of him, the dragon *pulsed* with energy, bright and burning bronze, but he tried to reach past her, for the low and measured glow of the city instead. For the thing that had been drawn through his ritual, as all the city said: *Us.*

It was there, low and simmering but leaping to his fingers eager to be used. It was awake, joyously alive, as enthusiastic about its freedom as the dragon had been.

Siyon gathered it up, its power and its essence, this energy of the city that he loved.

What was a city, but an agreement to live together in relative harmony?

What was this dragon, but the ruination of harmony?

Siyon coiled energy around his fist, twisting it into rope. He spun it out farther and farther, even as wind buffeted him, and somewhere nearby a fire crackled, and a broken building groaned. Siyon stayed focused on the energy growing in his hands, on what he needed to do.

Make a bond of power long enough, strong enough, to chain the dragon down again.

"Siyon!" Zagiri cried, sharp with panic and close behind his shoulder.

Siyon looked up and saw the dragon, rearing up over the houses, her neck snaking skyward as she stretched out her wings. Her belly was pale, and blood streamed darkly down her side from where the broken-off tip of the ballista bolt still jutted out.

Sympathy twinged at Siyon's side, but he pressed it gently down. She couldn't stay free. Look at the damage she'd already caused.

He drew back his arms and tried to remember how to do this, the lessons of his childhood, before he'd fled his fisherclan destiny.

He threw his rope, to hook it around her. To pull her down. To bind her again.

It sizzled out from his hands, rippling through the air, and swung around the dragon—once, twice, thrice. Energy flared, sizzling along her skin; the dragon convulsed. She twisted and snapped at the air, then scrabbled in the ruins, trying to pull away. But Siyon held on, setting his feet in the earth of the city that was *his.*

The dragon screamed and then toppled forward, falling full length along the ground. For a moment, the night was silent and shocked around them.

Siyon had done it. He'd bound her. He'd stopped this.

So why did he feel so awful?

Scaled ribs heaved with the dragon's laboured breath; she twisted her neck, tilted her head and looked straight at Siyon.

Her eye was massive, bright as moonlight and deep as the ocean. The pupil was star-shaped, black and silver-spiked, skewering him with her regard. She saw him. She knew him.

She was blisteringly, beautifully angry, her rage as brilliant and sharp as a diamond.

No, she said.

Siyon didn't hear it; he felt it. Not words, but emotion and truth and demand.

No.

That simple. That profound. She refused. She denied Siyon's restraint. She would not be bound again.

How dare he even try it.

He felt her shift. Felt her enormous muscles flex. Felt her gather herself within the bond he had cast around her. She pressed at it, every muscle bunching, pushing at his temerity. Testing his grip.

Siyon held on grimly. He didn't know what else to do. He had no other answers. She *had* been bound, once.

But the Mundane had been in decline then. Its Power had been dead, its energy dying.

Now...now it was awake.

The dragon got her feet under her again and lurched upward. The Mundane rope he had forged shattered at the pressure, exploding away from her in shards and fragments.

It blasted through Siyon, scalding his vision into bronze and darkness and nothing else.

Faintly, he sensed her shaking off the lingering energy like so much wet sand.

Distantly, he felt her wings stretch, her claws dig in to the ruined houses beneath her.

In the instant before she launched herself into flight, she *roared*.

And it slammed through Siyon like one wave too many. The hull of his consciousness, already ravaged by the blast of power, came apart completely.

He fell into darkness again.

The dragon roared—an awful sound, one that rattled Zagiri's bones and set her ears to ringing—and launched into the air with a heave that seemed to shake the earth anew. It scrambled and dragged at the air, no grace at all to its clawing flight.

But Zagiri was distracted. Siyon, who'd frozen stiff a moment ago, collapsed.

She grabbed at his shoulders, but the fucker was so damn tall that he skewed in her grip. "Help!" she gasped, and then Mayar was there, getting under Siyon's sagging body on the other side, both of them staggering to lay him gently on the grass.

Siyon's head lolled, tipping back on his neck. His eyelids were half-open; beneath them, his eyes glowed a dull and fading bronze.

"Oh shit," Zagiri muttered, barely hearing her own voice over the ongoing whistle in her ears from the dragon's cry. The buffeting wind of its wings lessened; Zagiri looked up as it twisted around in the air and started flying in earnest.

Straight west, back over the wall in two ferocious wingbeats, and disappearing into the night. Zagiri thought maybe she heard one last, almost forlorn cry.

No, wait, that was someone calling her name.

Through the smoke and the dust and the night, she could see two figures running across the park toward them. One was large and hefty and dark, but the other—

"Anahid!" Zagiri leapt to her feet and into her sister's hug. "Are you all right? Are you hurt?"

Her questions overlapped with Anahid's; her sister laughed and scrubbed at her face with a hand that just smeared more grime—and blood?—across the track of her tears. "When I saw that thing rear up over you…" She trailed off, eyes tracking away to the west. "Is it going to come back?"

Good question. A *vital* question. "I don't know," Zagiri admitted. "Siyon might."

Except Siyon was still out cold, Mayar checking his pulse, his breathing, his eyes. At least those were now back to their usual colour, though Siyon didn't even stir when Mayar brushed the lid fully open and then closed it again.

The large Archipelagan man with Anahid—who Zagiri recognised as someone from Sable House—said, "Inqs on their way, mistress."

Three pairs of them, hurrying across the parkland, cutting against the tide of people fleeing the dragon's destruction. But one lone figure was well in front, and Zagiri recognised that stride, as purposeful as justice.

"What a fucking mess," Olenka snapped in greeting. "Where's—?" She stopped as she caught sight of Siyon lying on the ground and looked back over her shoulder.

At the Palace, Zagiri realised. The fire had been brought under control, and some sort of cordon around the building had been set up, people being brought out of the rubble to have their injuries treated. There were knots of grey-tunicked inquisitors and other people striding around giving orders.

"Who's in charge?" Anahid asked.

Olenka's mouth twisted grimly. "That's still under debate. The prefect was entertaining at home for the start of Salt Night." All three of them knew where the prefectural apartment was, high up in the Palace building that was now little more than a mess of rubble.

Zagiri swallowed hard and looked down at Siyon. Syrah Danelani dead, and the city a mess, and there would definitely be those who blamed it all on the irresponsible Alchemist. Who wasn't even awake to defend himself.

"We can't let them get hold of him," Anahid said, as though having the same thoughts.

Zagiri nodded. "The Pragmatics could squirrel him away and

make all sorts of problems. We need him safe, at least until the dust settles a little and we can figure out what happens next. But they'll come looking in Bracken—Mayar, is there any chance Haruspex could take him in?"

"We'll handle it." Anahid nodded to her man from Sable House. "Lejman, will you be able to carry him to the District by yourself?"

Lejman went down on one knee and gently lifted Siyon's prone body in his arms, as easy as carrying a child.

As he rose, Anahid said, "There are search parties all over the city, gathering up the injured and homeless and otherwise needy and bringing them to the Flower district. We'll be merely one more rescue. And from there...well, we'll figure something out."

"Move fast and move now," Olenka ordered. "They're starting to get organised, over there."

"I'll come with you." Mayar hurried after Lejman and Anahid.

Zagiri didn't blame them. The people gathered around the ruins of the Palace were boiling like a hive of frantic bees. Nothing good was going to come of confronting it.

But that's still the way she went. If they were going to figure out what to do next, someone needed the answer to that other important question: Who's in charge?

An answer started to come into horrible focus even as Zagiri hobbled closer across the parkland. One of the figures standing at a makeshift table near the base of the Palace steps, pointing and shouting and generally being obeyed, looked awfully familiar.

As Zagiri loitered in the lee of a battered plane tree, Avarair Hisarani dismissed one squad of inquisitors—who took off at a fast march across the parkland—and turned back to a stack of paperwork. How had he managed to find *paper* in all this mess, let alone a pen?

His attention jerked up, to something Zagiri couldn't see behind the broken bulk of a fallen wall. He pointed, then quite clearly said: "You."

Balian stepped into view. Balian Hisarani, his *brother*.

Despite all her better instincts, Zagiri left the shelter of her tree to drift closer. She was desperate to hear what they had to say to each other. To know just what was going on.

A whole mess of people were sitting—sometimes lying—on the grass between her and them. People covered in dust and weariness, in some cases clutching bandages to bleeding heads or other wounds, but none of them injured enough to be taken away for further treatment. Zagiri snatched up a pitcher of water and a cup from a table and moved into the mass of them, stepping carefully over and around people who were too dazed or drained to move. When a hand lifted, she paused and poured, then waited while the water was drunk.

All the while, she kept glancing at the brothers Hisarani. The two of them who remained. They were speaking too quietly for her to hear, at first—Avarair looking stormy and pompous as ever, and Balian unusually serious.

But then Balian said, interrupting, and a little louder: "No, I don't see that at all!"

Avarair responded more quietly; Zagiri edged a few steps closer.

"Don't get ahead of yourself," Balian snapped. "Our father still lives; you aren't head of the family yet."

"Our position in Bezim is *my* responsibility," Avarair snarled. "How does it look, that you countermand my orders in public and allow *this*!" He threw out his hands, encompassing the Palace, the park around them, the state of the entire city.

"How does it *look*?" Balian repeated, with more vitriol than Zagiri had ever heard in his voice. "Of course *that's* what you care about."

"I care about this city!" Avarair shouted.

"No," Balian said coldly. "You don't. And you don't care about Izmir and what happened to him. And you don't care whether Siyon Velo really is what he says he is; you just hate what he was."

"Where is he?" Avarair demanded. "Tell me, or—"

Balian smiled, and Zagiri had never seen that on his face either, that cold line to his mouth. He looked a lot like Avarair. "Or what? You'll have me arrested? You and the rest of your friends now seizing the loose lines of this city to haul the sails into trim? How would *that* look?"

Avarair slammed his pen down on the table. "Are you fucking him too? Is that it? Remember what happened to the last Hisarani he ensnared!"

He marched off, into the rush of people, already shouting at someone else now.

Balian turned away, then stopped as his gaze snagged on Zagiri. She was close enough to hear. Close enough to be recognised.

For a moment, she thought Balian would come over to her. That he might try to explain. Might even ask for forgiveness for his deception. For fooling her.

She thought she might want him to.

But then he just tipped her a little nod—the perfect angle, actually, for the younger son of a first-tier family to the younger daughter of another. As though they were standing in a drawing room, rather than amid the shattered remains of their city's government.

Balian walked away, and Zagiri stood there.

Until someone gasped, "Water!" and she turned to help.

Powers knew, there was help and more help needed.

And if the Pragmatics were the ones making sure they gave it, then the trouble was only beginning. For all of them.

EPILOGUE

Barely a week after Salt Night—after the earthquake, and the dragon—the city was already starting to get back to normal.

Starting, but with a long way to go. As Anahid walked down to the Flower district, she had to wait on the Kellian Way while new-cut stone was hauled aloft in patching the opera house's facade. She had to cut through the commercial district because a row of fallen houses still blocked her preferred path. She passed teahouses operating in the shell of their buildings, tables sprawling out into the street through the now-missing front wall. On corners where the rubble still awaited clearing, purple-coated criers hawked petty charms, though they still tended to fade away into the alleyways when the inqs came by.

Bezim had renewed and rebuilt and remade itself many times. This was only one more hitch.

Anahid's final detour was past the office of a private clerk, who handed her a sheaf of papers wrapped in purple ribbon and lifted his voice over the hammering from repairs next door to tell her that if these orders suited her purpose, they could be considered final and delivered.

With the papers tucked through the sash of her dress, Anahid finished her stroll into the District, past the gate where someone had painted a mural of a naga, arms spread in welcome.

The bustle was greater than ever. Deliveries were nearly back to normal, and a House that had sustained significant damage during the earthquake was hurriedly refitting. On the new banners that billowed from upper windows, a black-sequined shape flew across a glittering night sky. It looked like the newly renamed Dragon's Lair would be open for business tonight.

Let it never be said the Flower district was short on audacity.

Sable House had suffered little—what the building lacked in grace it made up for in solidity. Anahid nodded to Lejman in the yard and met Qorja just inside. "How is the new floor manager doing?" she asked.

Qorja wrinkled up her nose. "He calls me *Miss Raven*," she complained, but then allowed, "He is very thorough. Oh, mistress. You have a visitor."

Anahid's turn to pull a face. She lay her hand against the sash of her dress; she wanted to review these papers. She wanted them delivered.

She wanted her marriage over and done with.

"Is the visitor important?" she asked.

The visitor was Mama Badrosani.

She waited in one of the private dining nooks, and when Anahid gave her greetings, Mama poured a glass of tea and offered her new-year salt crackers and olives, as though *she* were the hostess. Her fulsome curves were wrapped in purple satin, her hair dressed with yellow diamonds, her laughter as loud as it had been in the foyer of her theatre, in the wake of ambush and murder.

"Mistress Badrosani," Anahid began.

Interrupted by a snort. "After everything," Badrosani said, "I think you've earned the right to call me Shakeh. We're colleagues now after all."

"Hardly that," Anahid said firmly. "I would not aspire to such heights."

"Wouldn't you?" Mama Badrosani slurped at her glass of tea. "You oust the old order, rally the District like the reigning baron would, and now you're going to slide back into the obscurity of being just another House mistress? Not going to step up and challenge the Zinedani daughter for a share in things?"

Anahid wondered, fleetingly, which daughter it was. She remembered Vartan Xhanari (she remembered all sorts of things, and refused to dwell on them) telling her about Garabed Zinedani's daughters. One married out of Bezim, and one into a lower-tier azatani family. If she was already taking charge, this was surely the azata. If the other daughter came back from wherever she'd married to, would that confuse matters? Would there be opportunities?

"No," Anahid said firmly. "All I ever wanted was my House."

It was more than she'd planned to have, when she was planning, and she was...not happy with it. Not given how she had come to be here. She flexed fingers that still sometimes felt tacky with drying blood.

She had swum in the depths with the sharks. She was content with her little rock pool.

"Huh." Mama Badrosani chewed skeptically, as though she couldn't conceive of anyone wanting so little. Perhaps that was why she was a baron. "Well, it's all going to be *very* interesting. That's not the only barony in dispute, you know. Turns out Midnight disappeared on Salt Night and all. Hah!" She barked a laugh and spat an olive pit into her palm. "I didn't think anything could dislodge that old shadow. There's been someone of that name running things since I was a girl slitting purses in the street. Just goes to show. Nothing's forever."

Mama Badrosani watched Anahid for a moment, her eyes glittering with amusement and something else. Something far sharper.

Nothing was forever. The prefect had also not survived Salt Night. Would the agreement she had hammered into existence, holding the remaining barons to their own sort of account for the last twenty years, outlast her death?

Perhaps that depended on who came next, at the head of the Council. And that, even after a week, was far from clear.

After Badrosani had gone, Anahid finally climbed the stairs to her office.

Where she found someone already waiting.

The woman was tall—taller than Anahid, perhaps even taller than Siyon—and broad across the shoulders, standing at the window with well-muscled arms braced on either side of the opening. Her hair fell black as ink down her back, but the skin bared by the loose cowl of her robe was almost Northern pale. Her figure curved like a Khanate sword—generous and deadly.

What was she *doing* here? Why hadn't Qorja mentioned her? Had she just *let herself in*?

"Can I help you?" Anahid demanded.

"Always," the woman purred, and she turned with a grin that sliced like a knife, dizzyingly familiar. "Cousin," she added.

Anahid had never seen her in her life. Not like *this*. Not with skin instead of scales, and no horns among her hair. *"Laxmi?"*

It was—it *obviously* was. The same sensual arrogance in the casual shrug of her shoulder, the same glint of her strangely human teeth, the same knowing tilt to her smirk as she considered Anahid. "More or less. Turns out we had a little too much fun down there."

"You've...fallen?" Anahid couldn't stop gaping. Kept looking for her horns, her tail, her hooves, and finding nothing but smooth forehead, a dangerously curved hip, and very dirty bare feet. Her eyes were still yellow, though a paler shade; arresting but not quite so strange.

"Seems so." Laxmi propped herself against one corner of the big black desk. "Took me a little while to get my bearings."

And now here she was. "Siyon will be so pleased to see you well," Anahid assured her.

"Will he?" Laxmi lifted a skeptical eyebrow. "I heard he'd disappeared entirely. Do you know something the alley gossips don't?" Her mouth slid into a sneer. "Anyway, I didn't do it for *him*."

Her stare was still bold, still challenging, still skewered straight through Anahid.

"I'm sorry," Anahid said. "For this. But thank you so much for your help."

Laxmi's smirk curled. "It was fun. And you did pretty good yourself, baby." That hung between them for a moment, as Anahid's horror at the memory of blood on her hands—blood *everywhere*—twisted around a flaring coal of satisfaction.

She'd done unspeakable things. But she'd *beaten them*. They'd come for her, and she'd won.

After a moment, Laxmi looked down. Almost as though she was taking pity on Anahid, which seemed unlikely of a harpy.

Ex-harpy.

The ex-harpy said, "So it seems I find myself at a loose end, and I figured…" She shrugged. "This seems like a place where there's sure to be *something* I can do."

She was six feet of muscle and menace, for all she was now human, with her robe slipping open to bare one leg to mid-thigh.

There were no end of somethings she could do, in the Flower district.

Anahid started to laugh. "Yes," she managed, "I think something can be arranged."

Yeva Bardha looked remarkably unsurprised to find someone tapping at her bedroom window. Perhaps she'd been expecting Zagiri to come looking for her, and since the Northern ambassador had been keeping herself—and her family—to herself since the ruckus on Salt Night, of course sooner or later it was going to come to this.

"Yes, what?" she demanded as she opened the window. She was dressed simply, in the white shift she and her mother wore under their heavier Northern bodices and overskirts. Her blonde hair was braided down over one shoulder.

Fine, if she wanted to be belligerent, Zagiri could play that game too. "Not inviting me in?" she demanded right back.

"If you wanted tea, you should have come by the front door," Yeva said, which was probably a fair point.

All things considered, Zagiri didn't want this visit to be any more official—any more noticed—than it had to be. Everyone was watching everyone else at the moment, even more than usual, and every step was being carefully calculated.

Syrah Danelani wasn't the only Council member dead after Salt Night. In keeping with tradition, the Council had gone into abeyance while families chose new representatives, where necessary. They had to find somewhere new to meet as well; it had taken four days and a working group of Summer Club alchemists just to get the ruins of the Palace stable enough to start being cleared. Rebuilding would be a long time coming, if it was even possible.

None of this had inhibited the maneuvering for the prefectural election. More like a feeding frenzy. Syrah Danelani had looked likely to win a second term in office; now she was gone, and everything had changed.

Zagiri wasn't the only one seeing opportunities in the upheaval. But she wouldn't be helped by gossip about her visiting the Northern ambassador. Not when rumours persisted that *foreign elements* had somehow been involved in all the recent chaos.

So here she was, crouched on the lower-storey roof beneath Yeva's window, clinging at the sill. Hardly a position of strength from which to accuse: "You planted the devices on the Swanneck."

There'd been time for Zagiri to think about it, since Salt Night. Since she'd dangled over the side of the bridge making sure no one died from some misguided attempt at bringing the city to a standstill. She'd had time to think about seeing Yeva on the bridge, the night of the industrial district flares.

Her sharp and pale chin came up, and Yeva said imperiously, "And if I did?"

"It was foolish," Zagiri stated. "People could have been hurt. Or killed."

Yeva's shoulders twitched in the barest shrug. "Maybe people need to be hurt to realise they should be paying attention."

"What?" Zagiri gaped at her. "Are you serious? People who've done nothing wrong—"

"They prop up the system," Yeva snapped. She leaned against the windowsill now, eyes blazing. "They go along with it, because it's *easy*, because it's *safe*, because they *can*, and thank goodness they aren't worse off. They are *weak*."

"They're *people!*" Zagiri cried. "They're just trying to live."

Too loud; light stabbed out of a neighbouring house as someone pulled open the curtains at the window. A charm swung from its cord, casting a shadow out into the night. Everyone was getting them now. They really worked, Zagiri had been told, more than once.

She flattened herself against the wall next to Yeva's window and waited until the curtains were closed again, the light gone.

Yeva's window was still open. "What do you want from me?" she asked, cold as a Northern winter.

"What I've always wanted," Zagiri countered quietly. "I don't want you getting in trouble. And I don't want anyone else getting hurt."

Yeva looked unconvinced and unimpressed. "What do you want *from me?*" she repeated.

Zagiri didn't see this going well, but she'd come to ask, so she might as well. "I want you to talk to me before you do anything else."

"Do what?" Yeva demanded, snide and haughty. "With whom? Autumn is done, the Dockside troubles are over; at least four different people have assured my mother of this."

Zagiri had heard it too, repeated again and again, as though it might become the truth if the azatani said it often enough. None of them had met the revolutionaries. None of them had seen Yeva insisting that this year would be different.

She didn't bother disagreeing. "Do what you want; I know you will anyway, just...talk to me first."

"So you can undermine it?" Yeva demanded. "Turn me in? Stop me?"

"Have I turned you in so far?" Zagiri demanded right back.

Yeva tilted her head sidelong, not quite admitting the truth of that, but having no counterargument either. It was true after all. Zagiri had known who she was involved with. What she was up to. And told no one. She'd even *helped*.

Look how that had turned out. She'd gotten what she wanted. But the cost had nearly been too great.

"Where is the Sorcerer?" Yeva asked suddenly.

"I'm not telling you that," Zagiri said, knee-jerk and defiant, almost shocked. How could Yeva think that she would?

"But you do know." Yeva considered her. "Gossip from Dockside says he fell into the earth, was swallowed up, taken in when the dragon came out. That's not true, is it?"

Zagiri had heard wilder stories, and from far more educated people than whoever was gossiping in Dockside. That Siyon had ridden away on the dragon; that Siyon had been taken by the Pragmatics, or one of the other factions, and was now being held against his will, possibly in some sort of alchemical durance; that he'd vanished into thin air and was now a spirit, haunting the city; that he actually *was* every single one of the two-knuckle purple-coated alley magicians.

"It's none of your business," she stated.

"It is," Yeva countered. "It's the business of everyone in Bezim."

Zagiri had an uncomfortable feeling that she might be right. But right now, there was little she could do about it. "Why do you want to know anyway?"

"I'm curious." Yeva shrugged. "He is still a strong figure, for the whole city. One of your lowest sons, risen to such heights. Having achieved so much. Having *destroyed* so much. He could do a lot, with the reputation he's built."

Zagiri wondered how horrified Siyon would be about that suggestion. She hoped he'd have the chance to be.

Yeva's tone softened even further toward curiosity. "What are *you* going to do?"

Zagiri shifted her boots on the tiles. She didn't owe Yeva any honesty, not in the circumstances, but...there were few people who might understand what she had in mind, and fewer still she was currently speaking to.

"I'm going to become the Savani councillor," she declared.

Yeva blinked. "You? But...we haven't had the Ball yet. Aren't you still a child?"

Impressive; Zagiri hadn't thought she'd been paying that much attention to azatani traditions. "It doesn't matter. I'm going to do it anyway."

She waited for Yeva to scoff—the way almost anyone else would, if Zagiri said that to them.

But Yeva tilted her head again. Not quite yes, not quite no. "All right," she said.

Just like that. All right. As though anything could be achieved— or perhaps, as though nothing *could* be achieved if it wasn't attempted. It made Zagiri feel weirdly better about her own wild ambition. About all the fights she would need to have to make it happen.

"All right," she echoed, and leaned back from the wall. "Well. Good night then, I guess."

"Hey," Yeva said, leaning out a little. "Next time, bring me some rakia? Mother won't let it in the house, and I'm missing it."

With a bright grin, she closed her window again.

Siyon woke gently, which was weird all by itself. He'd grown accustomed to lurching out of dreams of desperate searches and claustrophobic caverns that he now realised must have been to do with—

The dragon.

The dragon, the caverns, the earthquake, the ritual. Salt Night.

Now Siyon was *very* awake, staring at a strange ceiling (watermarked and cracked) and clutching a strange blanket (thin, faintly musty, frayed under his chin).

Where *was* he?

Siyon dragged in a chestful of air, and he knew that smell, he knew the way it caught at the back of his tongue with mud and salt and too-damp-for-too-long. He'd breathed it for years, young and scrabbling and desperate.

He was in the lower city.

"Oh shit, I think he's awake," someone said.

He knew that voice too. It belonged here, the same sort of old, nostalgic familiar.

When Siyon turned his head—and it took a ridiculous amount of effort, his neck stiff as a salt-warped board—there was Daruj. Same wicked grin, same braided hair, same insouciant slump in a rickety chair, pushing it back on two legs in defiance of all common sense, with his feet up on the end of Siyon's pathetic excuse for a bed.

They could have still been sixteen; they weren't. "I assume all that wasn't a dream." Siyon's voice was a scratched and rusty thing. He coughed and screwed up his face at the awful taste in the back of his mouth.

"Water?" Daruj pulled his feet down, stretching across to an upturned barrel that was serving as a table for a patched pail and a battered tin cup.

Siyon remembered this taste as well, sharp and metallic and just on the edge of brackish. Lower city water, not the cleaner stuff that ran through the upper city's fountains. But he still drank, and drank, and held the cup out for a refill. He was parched as though he'd walked for a week.

The last thing he remembered was trying to bind the dragon again.

Trying, and failing. Shards of his twisted rope of Mundane energy blasting through him. The dragon's scream.

Then blackness.

"How long was I out?" Siyon asked after the third cup of water. He was expecting a day, maybe two. He'd need to get moving soon— when just sitting up in bed to lean against the rough brick wall didn't leave him feeling mildly exhausted. But the city wouldn't wait. There would be questions asked, about what had happened on Salt Night, about what it meant. He needed to be out there, answering them, making sure that—

"Brother," Daruj said gently, with a tired smile. "It's been a week."

All of Siyon's barely built plans collapsed again. "What?"

The word scraped at his throat, catching and hauling a cough out of him, and then another, each leading to the next, like his throat was too rough to calm itself.

Siyon reached for the water cup, desperate even for that awful lower city water, and Daruj stretched to grab it for him again.

Before he could, the cup lifted from the barrel by itself, floated straight across the room and into Siyon's hand.

Both of them stared.

And then Siyon choked anew, coughing even worse now. He downed the water, letting it soothe his throat at least.

Daruj stared at him. "What—and I don't wish to overstate my alarm here but I feel it needs to be noted—the fuck."

Siyon lifted the cup; it was trailing the faintest threads of the burnished bronze power that had carried it to his hands. Even as he watched, those threads—barely there to begin with—dissolved into nothing.

It reminded him of something on Salt Night—not the more obvious parts that stuck in his memory, like the close regard of the dragon, or the way she'd casually shattered his attempt at binding her, but earlier. Running across the parkland to reach her, outpacing Mayar and Zagiri—both of them bravi—and the sizzle of energy in his footsteps. The fleeting idea that he'd somehow used that power in his speed.

Siyon held the cup on his flat palm and willed it to go back to the barrel. When it stayed resolutely still, he imagined those faint threads of bronze energy carrying it across. When it still didn't move, he tipped his palm a little, just enough to get it moving.

It fell off his palm and clattered to the floor.

Daruj considered it. "Perhaps you need more practice. Keep at it. Mayar'll want to see it too."

Siyon blinked. "Mayar's here?"

"Popped out for food." Daruj jerked a thumb over his shoulder, to the warped and empty doorframe behind him, through which Siyon could see a staircase leading down, and a void in the ceiling that might have been intentional in construction, but more likely had fallen in. "One of us has been here the whole time."

"Are they looking for me?" Siyon asked. Not really a question that needed an answer, given that they were down here; both he and Daruj had spent some heady, ridiculous years in the lower city, and neither of them had ever been eager to return. But there were perks that came along with the decrepitude and the awful water.

Daruj smiled. "Looking isn't finding."

Neither azatani nor inquisitors were very welcome below the Scarp. And Siyon was just one more fish in a hostile sea, down here. He had breathing room. He could figure out...a lot of things. Starting with how much he needed to figure out.

He glanced at his hands, turning them over like his fingers might have stray bronze streaks on them. Anything seemed possible, right now.

"Oh," Daruj said, like he'd only just remembered, leaning down to snag a parcel from under Siyon's bed. "And Anahid sent this down. Said it had been left at her house with a note that it was for you."

The parcel was wrapped in plain brown paper, tied up with twine, but when Siyon managed to get it open, the notebooks inside were clearly of very fine make. A whole stack of them—six, seven, eight. Someone was gifting Siyon fancy notebooks?

A single page fluttered free onto Siyon's threadbare blanket. It wasn't signed; it didn't need to be. He recognised the hand—it had filled out a lot of paperwork on his behalf.

I'm sorry, Balian had written. *I needed to find out for myself, if you'd truly granted Izmir's greatest, wildest wish, or if you were the dangerous charlatan others suggested. When I heard Tebol Markani complaining that his aunt was sending him to you, it seemed like a gift from fate.*

I came under false pretenses. I stayed because I wanted to.

Avair's having me watched. Don't approach me. But I wanted to apologise. And to give you these. I can't say that Izmirlian would have wanted you to have them, because he just about took off at the wrist any hand that dared touch one. But I think you deserve to have them.

Siyon didn't breathe as he opened the topmost notebook.

He knew this hand too, whiplash and angular, sharp as its author's tongue and quick as his mind. Siyon had read it scribbled in hurried pencil when the owner had lost his voice to Siyon's impossible alchemy.

On the page that Siyon had opened, Izmirlian had written about seabirds seen over cliffs somewhere; Siyon's vision blurred over before he could read more, and he closed the notebook before he dripped tears on its pages.

The leather cover had complex tooling, intricate swirls and spirals twisting into leaves and knotted rope. Expensive and fine, like their owner.

Eight notebooks of Izmirlian Hisarani. So much more than Siyon ever thought he'd have.

He remembered then the dream—or whatever it had been—when Midnight had dragged him down to the caverns. The strange market, and who had been there.

You're really here, this time, Izmirlian had said. As though all those other dreams, when Siyon had thought he heard Izmirlian, when he thought maybe Izmirlian had heard *him*...

Probably just Siyon's imagination. His memory given scope by his wandering mind.

But Siyon traced his fingers along lines in leather, and thought of burnished power limning his running footsteps, of things moving by themselves, of impossibility after impossibility.

Siyon had always assumed, even as the promise left his lips, that the only way he'd see Izmirlian Hisarani again would be when he, one day, with everything else he needed to achieve done, found a way to step outside the planes himself.

He was probably right. It probably *had* been his imagination and his wandering mind.

But maybe.

Maybe.

Siyon lifted the notebook to his face and breathed in. It was still there, the faintest scent of sandalwood and orange blossom.

He smiled.

The story continues in . . .

Book THREE of The Burnished City

ACKNOWLEDGMENTS

This book was written on the traditional and unceded lands of the Wurundjeri Woi Wurrung of the Kulin nation.

Shadow Baron owes itself to Nivia Evans, whose keen editorial insight took it from the best I thought I could manage to something amazingly better. (And who at least appeared to remain calm as I pulled the whole thing apart and put it back together again. Twice.) Huge thanks as well to the whole wondrous, dedicated Orbit team, in both the US and UK.

This book also owes itself to everyone who enjoyed *Notorious Sorcerer*. From the authors who blurbed and raved about the book to the readers who tweeted and reviewed, it's been a wild boost every time to know my words resonated for you. Hearts and flowers to you, and *especially* to the booksellers and librarians I've encountered along the way, enthusiastic and professional champions all.

A virtual toast and big hugs again to Jennifer and Ginger, whose encouragement and consideration have carried me through a lot of wild ideas, annoying hiccups, and rejuvenating distractions.

Thanks to Sam for not just the glorious map but also the wild glee, the Siyon doll, the swords, and the kumquat tea. To Peat for endless interesting discussions, and for encouraging me to drink the beer. To the Fantasy Faction forum crew for the cheering and chats. To Marissa for the reading and reassurance. And to the entire Armada for the perspective, the understanding, and the camaraderie.

And finally, all my love to my husband, who keeps me well-fed and liberally punned, who sold my book to everyone who'd stand still to hear about it, and who staggered along with me when life was nothing but work. We made it! Cheers!

extras

orbit

meet the author

Gray Tham

DAVINIA EVANS was born in the tropics and raised on British comedy. With a lifelong fantasy-reading habit and an honors thesis in political strategy, it was perhaps inevitable that she turn to a life of crafting stories full of sneaky ratbags tangling with magic. She lives in Melbourne, Australia, with two humans (one large and one small), a neurotic cat, and a cellar full of craft beer. Dee talks more about all of that on Twitter as @cupiscent.

Find out more about Davinia Evans and other Orbit authors by registering for the free monthly newsletter at orbitbooks.net.

if you enjoyed
SHADOW BARON

look out for

THE HEXOLOGISTS
A Hexologists Novel

by

Josiah Bancroft

The Hexologists, Isolde and Warren Wilby, are quite accustomed to helping desperate clients with the bugbears of city life. Aided by hexes and a bag of charmed relics, the Wilbies have recovered children abducted by chimney-wraiths, removed infestations of barb-nosed incubi, and ventured into the Gray Plains of the Unmade to soothe a troubled ghost. Well acquainted with the weird, they never shy away from a challenging case.

But when they are approached by the royal secretary and told the king pleads to be baked into a cake—going so far as to wedge

*himself inside a lit oven—the Wilbies soon find themselves
embroiled in a mystery that could very well see the nation turned
on its head. Their effort to expose a royal secret buried under forty
years of lies brings them nose-to-nose with a violent anti-royalist
gang, avaricious ghouls, alchemists who draw their power from a
hell-like dimension, and a bookish dragon who only occasionally
eats people.*

*Armed with a love toughened by adversity and a stick of chalk
that can conjure light from the darkness, hope from the hopeless,
Iz and Warren Wilby are ready for whatever springs from the
alleys, graves, and shadows next.*

1

THE KING IN THE CAKE

"The king wishes to be cooked alive," the royal secretary said,
accepting the proffered saucer and cup and immediately setting
both aside. At his back, the freshly stoked fire added a touch
of theater to his announcement, though neither seemed to suit
what, until recently, had been a pleasant Sunday morning.

"Does he?" Isolde Wilby gazed at the royal secretary with all
the warmth of a hypnotist.

"Um, yes. He's quite insistent." The questionable impression
of the royal secretary's negligible chin and cumbersome nose
was considerably improved by his well-tailored suit, fastidi-
ously combed hair, and blond mustache, waxed into upturned
barbs. Those modest whiskers struck Isolde as a dubious effort

to impart gravity to a youthful face. Though Mr. Horace Alman seemed a man of perfect manners, he sat with his hat capping his knee. "More precisely, the king wishes to be baked into a cake."

Looming at the tea cart like a bear over a blackberry bush, Mr. Warren Wilby quietly swapped the plate of cakes with a dish of watercress sandwiches. "Care for a nibble, sir?"

"No. No, thank you," Mr. Alman murmured, flummoxed by the offer. The secretary watched as Mr. Wilby positioned a triangle of white bread under his copious mustache, then vanished it like a letter into a mail slot.

The Wilbies' parlor was unabashedly old-fashioned. While their neighbors pursued the bare walls, voluptuous lines, and skeletal furniture that defined contemporary tastes, the Wilbies' townhouse decor fell somewhere between a gallery of oddities and a country bed-and-breakfast. Every rug was ancient, ever doily yellow, every table surface adorned by some curio or relic. The picture frames that crowded the walls were full of adventuresome scenes of tall ships, dogsleds, and eroded pyramids. The style of their furniture was as motley as a rummage sale and similarly haggard. But as antiquated as the room's contents were, the environment was remarkably clean. Warren Wilby could abide clutter, but never filth.

Isolde recrossed her legs and bounced the topmost with a metronome's precision. She hadn't had time to comb her hair since rising, or rather, she had had the time but not the will during her morning reading hours, which the king's secretary had so brazenly interrupted, necessitating the swapping of her silk robe for breeches and a blouse. Wearing a belt and shoes seemed an absolute waste of a Sunday morning.

Isolde Wilby was often described as *imposing*, not because she possessed a looming stature or a ringing voice, but because

439

she had a way of imposing her will upon others. Physically, she was a slight woman in the plateau of her thirties with striking, almost vulpine features. She parted her short hair on the side, though her dark curls resisted any further intervention. Her long-suffering stylist had once described her hair as resembling a porcupine with a perm, a characterization Isolde had not minded in the slightest. She was almost entirely insensible to pleasantries, especially the parentheses of polite conversation, preferring to let the drumroll of her heels convey her hellos and her coattails say her goodbyes.

Her husband, Warren, was a big, squarish man with a tree stump of a neck and a lion's mane of receded tawny hair. He wore unfashionable tweed suits that he hoped had a softening effect on his bearing, but which in fact made him look like a garden wall. Though he was a year younger than Isolde, Warren did not look it, and had been, since adolescence, mistaken for a man laboring toward the promise of retirement. He had a mustache like a boot brush and limpid hazel eyes whose beauty was squandered on a beetled and bushy brow, an obstruction that often rendered his expressions unfathomable, leading some strangers to assume he was gruffer than he was. In fact, Warren was a man of tender conscience and emotional depth, traits that came in handy when Isolde's brusque manner necessitated a measure of diplomacy. He was considerably better groomed that morning only because he had risen early to greet the veg man, who unfailingly delivered the freshest greens and gossip in all of Berbiton at the unholy hour of six.

Seeming to wither in the silence, Mr. Alman repeated, "I said, the king wishes to be baked into a ca—"

"Intriguing," Isolde interrupted in a tone that plainly suggested it was not.

Iz did not particularly care for the nobility. She had accepted Mr. Horace Alman into her home purely because War had insisted one could not refuse a royal visitor, nor indeed, turn off the lights and pretend to be abroad.

While War had made tea, Iz had endured the secretary's boorish attempts at small talk, made worse by an unprompted confession that he was something of a fan, a Hexologist enthusiast. He followed the Wilbies' exploits as frequently documented in the *Berbiton Times*. Mr. Horace Alman was interested to know how she felt about the recent court proceedings. Iz had rejoined she was curious how he felt about his conspicuous case of piles.

The royal secretary had gone on to irk her further by asking whether her name really was "Iz Ann Always Wilby" or if it were some sort of theatrical appellation, a stage name. Iz patiently explained that her father, the famous Professor Silas Wilby, had had many weaknesses—including an insatiable wanderlust and an allergy to obligations—but none worse than his fondness for puns, which she personally reviled as charmless linguistic coincidences that could only be conflated with humor by a gormless twit. Only the sort of vacuous cretin who went around asking people if their names were made-up could possibly enjoy the lumbering comedy that was the godless pun.

Though, in all fairness, she was not the only one to be badgered over her name. Her husband had taken the rather unusual step of adopting her last name upon the occasion of their marriage. He'd changed his name not because he was estranged from his family, but rather because he'd never liked the name Offalman.

Iz had been about to throw the royal secretary out on his inflamed fundament when War had emerged from the kitchen pushing a tea cart loaded with chattering porcelain and

Mr. Horace Alman had announced that King Elbert III harbored aspirations of becoming a gâteau.

His gaunt cheeks blushing with the ever-expanding quiet, Mr. Alman pressed on: "His Majesty has gone so far as to crawl into a lit oven when no one was looking." The secretary paused to make room for their astonishment, giving Warren sufficient time to post another sandwich. "And while he escaped with minor burns, the experience does not appear to have dissuaded him of the ambition. He wants to be roasted on the bone."

"So, it's madness, then." Iz shook her head at War when he inquired whether she would like some of either the lemon sponge or the spice cake, an inquiry that was conducted with a delicate rounding of his plentiful brows.

"I don't believe so." Mr. Alman touched his teacup as if he might raise it, then the fire behind him snapped like a whip, and his fingers bid a fluttering retreat. "He has long moments of lucidity, almost perfect coherence. But he also suffers from fugues of profound confusion. He's been discovered in the middle of the night roaming the royal grounds without any sense of himself or his surroundings. The king's sister, Princess Constance, has had to take the rather extreme precaution of confining him to his suite. And I must say, you both seem to be taking all of this rather in stride! I tell you the king believes he's a waste of cake batter, you stifle a yawn!"

Iz tightened the knot of her crossed arms. "I didn't realize you were looking for a performance. I could have the neighbor's children pop by if you'd like a little more shrieking."

War hurried to intervene: "Mr. Alman, please forgive us. We do not mean to appear apathetic. We are just a bit more accustomed to unusual interviews and extraordinary confessions than most. But, rest assured, we are not indifferent to horror; we are merely better acquainted."

"Indeed," Iz said with a muted smile. "How have the staff taken the king's altered state of mind?"

Appearing somewhat appeased, the secretary twisted and shaped the points of his mustache. "They're discreet, of course, but there are limits. Princess Constance knows it's a secret she cannot keep forever, devoted as she is to her brother."

"Surely, you want physicians, psychologists. We are neither," Iz said.

The secretary absorbed her comments with an expression of pinched indulgence. "We've consulted with the nation's greatest medical minds. They were all stumped, or rather, they were perfectly confident in their varying diagnoses and prescriptions, and none of them were at all capable of producing any results. His condition only worsens."

"Even so, I'm not sure what help we can be." Iz picked at a thread that protruded, wormlike, from the armrest of the sofa.

The secretary turned the brim of his hat upon his knee, ducking her gaze when he said, "There's more, Ms. Wilby. There was a letter."

"A letter?"

"In retrospect, it seems to have touched off His Majesty's malaise." The royal secretary reached into his jacket breast pocket. The stiff envelope trembled when he withdrew it. The broken wax seal was as sanguine as a wound. "It is not signed, but the sender asserts that he is the king's unrecognized son."

Warren moved to stand behind his wife's chair. He clutched the back of it as if it were the rail of a sleigh poised atop a great hill. Iz reached back and, without looking, patted the tops of his knuckles. "I imagine the Crown receives numerous such claims. No doubt there are scores of charlatans who're foolish enough to hazard the gallows for a chance to shake down the king."

"Indeed, but there are two things that distinguish this particular instance of blackmail. First, the seal." Mr. Alman stroked the edge of the wax medallion, indicating each element as he described it: "An *S* emblazoned over a turret; note the five merlons, one for each of Luthland's counties. Beneath the *S*, a banner bearing the name Yeardley. This is the seal of Sebastian, Prince of Yeardley. This is the stamp of the king's adolescent ring."

"He identified it as such?" Iz asked.

"I did, at least initially. Of course, I like to believe I'm familiar with all the royal seals, but I admit I had to check the records on this occasion. Naturally, there is much of his correspondence that His Majesty leaves me to open and deal with, but when something like this comes through, I deliver it to him unbroken."

"The signet was no longer in the king's possession, then?"

"No, the royal record identified the ring as lost about twenty-five years ago, around the conclusion of his military service, I believe."

"That's quite a length of time to sit on such a claim." Iz reached for the letter, but the secretary pulled it back. She looked into his eyes; they glistened with uncertainty as sweat dripped from his nose like rain from a grotesque. "What is the second thing that distinguishes the letter?"

"The king's response to the correspondence was...pronounced. He has thus far refused to discuss his impressions of the contents with myself, his sister, or any of his advisors. He insists that it is a hoax, that we should destroy it, though Princess Constance won't hear of it. She maintains that one doesn't destroy the evidence of extortion: One saves it for the inquiry. But of course, there hasn't been an inquiry. How could there be, given the nature of the claim? To say nothing of the fact that the primary witness to the events in question is currently raving in the royal tower."

"The princess wishes for us to investigate?" she asked. Though Isolde held little affection for the gentry, she liked the princess well enough. Constance had established herself as one of very few public figures who continued to promote the study of hexegy, touting the utility of the practice, even amid the blossoming of scientific discovery and electrical convenience. Still, Isolde's vague respect for the princess was hardly sufficient to make her leap to her brother's aid.

Mr. Alman coughed—a brittle, aborted laugh. "Strictly speaking, Her Royal Highness does not know I am here. I have taken it upon myself to investigate the identity of the bastard, or rather, to engage more capable persons in that pursuit."

"I'm sorry, Mr. Alman, but what I said when we first sat down still holds. I am a private citizen. I serve the public, some of whom come to me with complaints about royal overreach, the criminal exploitations of the nobility, or the courts' bungling of one case or another. I don't work for the police—not anymore. Surely you have enough resources at your disposal to forgo the interference of one unaffiliated investigator."

"I do understand your preference, ma'am." The royal secretary rucked his soft features into an authoritative scowl. "But these are extraordinary circumstances, and not without consequence. The uncertainty of rule only emboldens the antiroyalists, the populists, and our enemies overseas. You must—"

Isolde pounced like a tutor upon a mistake: "I *must* pay my taxes. I *may* help you. Show me the letter."

Mr. Alman tightened like a twisted rag. "I cannot share such sensitive information until you have agreed to assist in the case."

"There is another way to look at this, Iz," Warren said, returning to the tea cart. He poured water from a sweating pitcher into a juice glass and presented it to the dampened secretary, who readily accepted it. "You wouldn't just be working for the Crown; you would be serving the interests of the private citizen who has come forward with the claim...perhaps a *legitimate* one." The final phrase made Mr. Alman nearly choke upon his thimble swallow of water. "If the writer of this letter shares the king's blood, and we were to prove it, I don't think anyone would accuse you of being too friendly with the royals."

Isolde bobbed her head in consideration, an easy rhythm that quickly broke. "But if I help to prove that he is a prince, I'd just be serving at the pleasure of a different sovereign."

"True." Warren moved to the mantel to stir the coals, not to invigorate them, but to shuffle the loose embers toward the corners of the firebox. "But if you don't intervene, our possible prince will remain a fugitive."

"You think we should take the case?"

"You know how I feel about lords and lawmen. But it seems to me Mr. Alman is right: If there's a vacuum in the palace and a scramble for the throne, there will be strife in the streets. We know who suffers when heaven squabbles—the vulnerable. Someone up on high only has to whisper the word 'unrest' and the prisons fill up, the workhouses shake out, the missions bar their doors, and the orphanages repopulate. And when the dust settles, perhaps there'll be a new face printed on the gallet bill or a fresh set of bullies on the bench, but the only thing of real consequence that will have changed is the number of bones in the potter's field. Revolution may chasten the rich, but uncertainty torments the poor."

Isolde patted the air, signaling her surrender. "All right, War. All right. You've made your point. Mr. Alman, I—"

A heavy, arrhythmic knock brought the couple's heads around. The Wilbies stared at the unremarkable paneled door as if it were aflame.

Alman snuffled a little laugh. "Do knocking guests always cause such astonishment?"

"They do when they come by my cellar," Warren said.

The door shattered, casting splinters and hinge pins into the room, making all its inhabitants cry out in alarm. It seemed a fitting greeting for the seven-foot-tall forest golem who ducked beneath the riven lintel.

Its skin, rough as bark and scabbed with lichen, bunched about fat ankles and feet that were arrayed from toe to heel by a hundred gripping roots. Its swollen arms were heavy enough to bend its broad back and bow its head, ribbed and featureless as a grub. The golem lurched forward, swaying and creaking upon the shore of a gold-and-amethyst rug whose patterns had been worn down by the passage of centuries.

"A mandrake," Iz said, tugging a half stick of chalk from her khaki breeches. "I've never seen one so large. But don't worry. They're quite docile. He probably just got lost during his migration. Let's try to herd him back down."

With hands raised, Warren advanced upon the mandrake, nattering pleasantly as he inched toward the heaving golem that resembled an ambling yam. "There's a sport. Thank you for keeping off my rug. It's an antique, you know. I have to be honest—it's impossible to match and hard to clean. I haven't got one of those newfangled carpet renovators. The salesman, wonderful chap, wanted three hundred and twenty gallets for it. Can you imagine? And those suck-boxes are as big as a bureau. I have no idea where I'd park such a—"

The moment War inched into range, the mandrake swatted him with a slow, unyielding stroke of its limb, catching him on the shoulder and throwing him back across the room and violently through his tea cart. Macarons and petits fours leapt into the air and rained down upon the smashed porcelain that surrounded the splayed host.

The mandrake raised the fingerless knob of one hand, identifying his quarry, then charged at the royal secretary, who sat bleating like a calf.

Follow us:

/orbitbooksUS

/orbitbooks

/orbitbooks

Join our mailing list
to receive alerts on our
latest releases and deals.

orbitbooks.net

Enter our monthly
giveaway for the chance
to win some epic prizes.

orbitloot.com